KIPLING PLASS

ALSO BY BERKLEY WENDELL SEMPLE

Poetry

Lamplight Teller
The Solo Flyer
The Central Station
Flight and Other Poems

BERKLEY WENDELL SEMPLE

KIPLING PLASS

PEEPAL TREE

First published in Great Britain in 2024
Peepal Tree Press Ltd
17 King's Avenue
Leeds LS6 1QS
England

ISBN13: 9781845235925

Supported using public funding by
ARTS COUNCIL
ENGLAND

CONTENTS

PRELUDE

Someone calls my name and I come back from my reverie. People are leaving, a mourning throng in funereal black, lined like ants on the narrow track that leads away from the graveyard to the road. Someone urges me out of the cemetery yard with a hand between my shoulders. I go, dry leaves crunching under my feet. I should have said something, mentioned some small kindness, made some pithy pronouncement – no long speech to tempt the listeners' patience, no tearful tribute, no theatrical flourish of showy grief. The thing had to be simple and plain.

Even in the church, we shied from the mic when called to the rostrum. The silence became unbearably taut. Finally, an old man rose and wobbled forward to mumble something indecipherable. Then another and another stepped forward. Their brevity elicited applause. In all, perhaps ten minutes passed. Even the preacher, sweating hard, made quick work of his sermon. It was about divine love, about loving the loveless. I was drawn to the scar on the preacher's otherwise handsome face.

Outside the church, four pallbearers lifted the coffin onto the bier, and wheeled it out, feet first, to the hearse, for the short, slow ride to the graveyard. We on foot processed to the cemetery, singing old hymns I remembered from childhood: "Shall We Gather at the River", "Rock of Ages", "Blessed Assurance", and, most plangent, "In the Sweet By and By", where we sang of our hopes to meet on that beautiful shore.

In the cemetery, no one called on me to say anything and I stood apart and watched. What could I have said? That I knew the boy who became the dead man, that he was so, and he was so. Perhaps no one remembered who I was. For an earlier generation, my name and face would have meant something. There were no faces I recognised among those who were clumped thick around the hole in the ground, peering down at the burnished, old-fashioned coffin, at the little window in the top through which the tenant would not see the last ritual of his passing. The earth reclaimed its lump of clay. There was no crying, no show of grief or sadness. This seemed fitting.

I knew the boy but not the man. That I was there at all was an accident – as, too, was his reason for being here. A week earlier, on a misty foreday morning, driving east on the Rupert Craig out of the capital, he had fallen asleep at the wheel of his brand-new RAV 4 near Non Pariel, swerved right, crossed into westbound traffic and was broadsided by a speeding padi truck. That was it. He was fifty-nine, three years older than me. I might have said to the people here that the dead man was a childhood friend – but just an acquaintance when we were men. But they knew his age and they knew more about the man than could be said at such a moment. Little was said and most of it was lies. I said nothing. I did not want to lie.

Out on the road, I stood on newly mown grass plunging down to a trench reeking of new spawn and pollywogs among the hyacinths and regia. It was the season when, as boys, we would have waded in and, with our arms plunged up to the elbows in mud, culled wriggling hoori, hassa, sunfish, even alligators and snakes from the murk. Most of us had fled the country, some like me to the snow countries up north, others to the islands. In ten years, the country had been emptied of its bright and beautiful, drained of our talents and brains. Now, some were returning home to visit. Things were changing.

There were bright streetlights along the road, once a two-lane blacktop where the tar bubbled in high sun. Open cowpasture of tawny sawgrass had made way for houses; jhandees flailed behind whitewashed palings and there was a car in every yard. As if by magic, some witch's wand was turning spiffy and new all that had been old and decayed.

I had imagined the place different, but not as different as it was. It was twenty-five years since my last visit, and I saw the results of the recent economic boom. New buildings were going up everywhere; skeletal frames and scaffolding towered in the sky. In the street near my hotel, a thousand foreign tongues were raised in the cadence of commerce. Those of us returning, coming in from the cold, saw that, with oil, everything Guyanese was in vogue. They had even resurrected me from the dustbin of history, so that I might say wise and foolish things on their television shows. I was now a guest speaker and lecturer, invited into the private homes of important people who remembered that once, a long time ago, I had run marathons and won medals in important races. And here I was, a guest in my own country. I had changed, too, but though glad to see all this new prosperity, I did not feel renewed.

Standing in the road I felt dazed and vague. Images of men and women slid across my retinas without being fully apprehended. A riot of words struck my ears. They signified nothing. I hear an insistent chorus of waves from the sea, and a small voice, sounding like my own, with a child's lilting timbre, soft and adolescent. It spoke the Creole of courtesy and good manners; it said, *Open your eyes.* I did and recalled myself to the present. Somewhere nearby a televised cricket game blared. The wind, reeking of crab and kelp, rode into Abary. A flock of ibises, brilliantly pink, passed overhead in a chevron, making for the marshes. I stood with my hands folded across my chest and waited for Audibey to come with the car that would take us back to Central.

I watched the departing crowd, strangers to me, studying the faces, trying to link a new generation to my own. They were heading for the rumshop and I imagined the ready banter of reminiscence once the rum was on the table, the drumming, the music, the mean talk, then, near false dawn, the descent of drunken joviality into fisticuffs and sometimes knife play.

I could not remember what the new buildings had replaced, except the church had once doubled as a dance hall. In its stead was a bond warehouse, square with a curved roof, on which a rooster weathervane half-turned in the wind. It seemed incongruous. I began to doubt what I knew.

The cemetery itself was larger, more populous. Where once the proliferating green had been left to grow riotous and wayward, meticulous order now reigned. The neem and samans had been delimbed or made to canopy over the path that divided the plot. The narrow tracks between the tombs were kept weeded and the closely mown lawn had been edged with a fierce accuracy. Its green was so green it seemed artificial, like astroturf. The tombs, lined up just so on a grid, were newly whitened, save where lichen grew at their bases. The vanity of the living impinged upon the careless dead.

Coming into the village earlier that day, riding shotgun while Audibey drove, I'd asked her to stop so I could walk into it. She walked alongside me, tall, thin, and pretty. Her face was more our father's than my own, with an Indian hint of her mother in the long straight nose and the luxuriant, anthracite-dark hair harnessed behind with a little girl's red ribbon. She was thirty, twenty-six years my junior, the late late child of our father, who had been thought long past his seeding time. She'd been a surprise for him and me, but not her mother, who was young enough to be my father's daughter and my sister. Perhaps there is hope for me, yet.

The lights through the trees dappled the tombs below. I tried to remember who was buried where, but time had weathered away epitaph and date on the shale and concrete. Once, long ago, I had slept on the tombs in the mora's shade and shied down mangoes from a tree that was no longer there, eating the fruit nourished by my ancestors and slurping its juice from my fingers.

As we walked on, I recognised names on the newer tombs. Here was Mary Abna, a childhood sweetheart who died of leukaemia while I was at the university, and there, Dado Narine, and next to him, his wife, Two Panty, whose real name, blurred on the basalt headstone, I could not recall. Over there in the bamboo shade was Ma Tussette, the obeah woman, and her beloved brother, Uncle Percy, the old sluice watchman. There were many many more.

So much death. I felt weary and turned back to the road.

"Which one is he, the dead man?" Audibey asked.

I was puzzled and looked at her uncomprehending.

"What do you mean?"

"In your book," she said. "The one you wrote in the exercise books in Dad's library. Which boy is the dead man?"

"You read the book?"

"Yes. It is good. I like it. Dad read it too."

"Really?"

"We talked about it. He said you could have been a novelist."

"Really?"

"Yes! So, who was the man?"

I told her.

She nodded calmly. "Are the rest of them alive, your friends in the book?"

"Some are. Where are the books now? I haven't seen them in thirty years."

"They're where they always were, on a shelf in Dad's library. He put them in plastic covering."

"He did?"

"You can read it over now that you are here. When did you write it?"

"I was sixteen when I finished the first draft. Then I worked on it when I was twenty or so. I was at the university then."

"Here?"

"Yes, at UG. I was twenty-two when I went to the States."

"I wasn't even born then," she said, smiling. "You are old enough to be my father instead of my brother. You are an old man, you know that?"

"I know," I said.

"Why didn't you ever have children?"

"I don't know." This was an honest enough answer. I had taken no precautions not to have them.

"Don't you want any?"

"I am not sure."

"When we came to visit you when I was little, you lived with a beautiful white girl in that snowy place."

"Iowa."

"Yes, Iowa, and the white girl's name was Hildred. What happened to her?"

"She went away and never came back."

"You were teaching at that little college. Are you still there?"

"No, I moved to a bigger college in New York."

"The big bad city?"

"It can be called that."

"Why are you always sad? I mean you look sad."

"I don't feel sad."

"Your face tells it, though."

I said nothing. It was not how I saw myself. Lonely but not sad, fatigued maybe.

"It's your eyes," she went on; "they seem far away. They look like they are begging for something – pleading."

"A girl I once dated called it the orphan's gaze. It's the look that allows you to be adopted and given some tenderness. Women will always be there to take care of you." They did, mostly, and I was never in want. But it was never the cure for all that ails me.

We had driven on in silence to the church to await the arrival of the dead. She left me there and went to Berbice to visit friends. I suspected there was a lover somewhere further up the coast.

Now, waiting on the road, I was anxious for Audibey's return. There were still stragglers going to the rumshop. A lifetime teetotaller, I did not want to be invited to join them. I could refuse, of course, but that would only encourage further insistence that I down my fires like a man.

It was getting dark. The trees turned silhouettes, and flocks of egrets homed for the marshes and the stacks of the old brick kiln. The evening litanies of village life began. Thin boys wielding switches lashed and yipped the cows out of the backdam to their pastures behind the houses. Girls, dark and pretty in their summer frocks, came out onto the road, strutting past like models, their faces shiny with health, boys in small groups trailing after them. Lights came on in the houses. Children were being shouted at. One was being beaten, the bawling loud and theatrical. Mosquitoes made halos around our heads, whining for lifespans longer than they are allowed. Tractors coming from the ricefields passed in trains, leaving clumps of mud on the road from the plough blades hanging behind.

The crowd had thinned out, leaving only a clique of four young men passing a spliff between them, laughing with too much mirth. One said very loudly, "The fucker was a gay, but nobody could tell he that to he face." They laughed and shuffled and smoked their spliff. One of them with spiky dreadlocks looked at me and turned back to his companion. Then he looked at me again, crossed the street and stood very close to me, peering at me, his head slanted to one side. I looked at him. He smiled. He had white, feral teeth.

"What the fuck," he said. "You mean is youself standing here like a stranger among we and don't say a word."

I said nothing. He called to the others excitedly. "Come and see who we have here."

They shuffled across the road, their pants low on narrow hips.

"Look at he," the boy said. "Take a good look and tell me who is he."

They walked around me. One touched me lightly on the upper arm.

"He favour somebody I see on TV."

"Is he," said the first boy, "the big run man, Kitting Pass, the marathon man from big marathon race and school textbook."

"Yes," said another. "Is the bad skunt runner. He won big Olympic medal and all kind of skunt. Shake the man hand, nuh."

Two of them grabbed my hand and began to pump it vigorously, all the while talking to each other in that vulgar, amiable way they have.

"Kipling Plass," I said.

"Yes man," one of them said, "come and drink with we nuh."

"Yes, man," said another, "you must fire one and two and three with we."

Audibey came just then, pulling her car very close and pressing on the horn. I walked towards her. The boys followed.

"Another day," I said. "I will be back. We can have a few beers then. But look, have a few on me."

I reached into my pocket and held out a twenty US dollar bill to get their attention. They looked at me and I gave the money to the nearest of them and got into the car. Audibey pulled away, leaving the boys behind.

"Yes, they recognise me from their textbook."

She smiled. "So they know who you are?"

"They called me Kitting Pass."

"Close enough," she said.

We drove on. At the turn in Airy Hall going into Huntley, the light went out in all the houses.

"A blackout," Audibey said, "but they're rare these days."

"Yes," I said, "that is another difference. When I was growing up, we had them almost every night, sometimes for many days in a row."

"So Mommy said. She called and said I must take care of you. Were you in love with her?"

"Why do you ask?"

"It's the way she always talks about you, with such fondness."

"I'm her stepson," I said. "Of course she loves me. But to answer your question – no, I was not in love with her, but I cared for her very much. We have history. What did she tell you?"

"She told me everything – about the pandit and about the baby she lost. Why do they call her Peep?"

"I don't know. Did she tell how she came to be with our father?"

"She said she was sick after she lost the baby and ran away and lived with you and Daddy while she recovered. Then, when you won the athletic scholarship to America, she stayed on with Daddy until they had me. Is that it?"

"That is it," I said. "That is how my friend became my stepmother, so my sister could be my daughter."

"Don't forget that Daddy could be my grandfather."

I did not eat with Audibey that night. I went to the library and found the exercise books still there. The covers were faded and the face of the long-dead prime minister was blurred in sepia on the blue. My name was written there in careful cursive, and the number of the book. I picked up the book that said #1. The pages had gone yellow. I was tender with the turning of the leaves. I opened the first page. Chapter One was written on the top and the number of the page was below. I sat close to the open window that gave onto the rice field, and, by tallow candle and the silver moon, read my history.

1. MORNING COMES

Sun comes up like a big egg yolk over the sea, over the wide canal and the river, over the high treetops. Curlews and kecks raise up from the basmati in a big flock what darkens the sun, wings beating like rain on a rooftop, cawing loud and long. The village wakes up with somebody hollering, a baby crying, a cow lowing on the savannah, a fowl-cock crowing or music turn on loud in a house. Then the rookootooks of all the sounds together: people screaming, car horn beeping, birds cawing, tides running with a splashing sound, water gushing from the standpipe's throat, dogs barking, donkeys braying. Morning come to Mahaicony.

I run along Main Road, my barefoot slapping on the macadam, through Catherine, through Bary, pass the houses lining both sides of the road, pass trees what hide the face of the houses, pass a plough-blade cake-up with mud on the road corner and an old brukup car by the koker and the splash of fish in the trench. I run and feel lithe like a spore-flower in the wind. I run toward the sea and the sea calling, *Come and drown your black body in the deep-deep abyss of my skuntian darkness*, or mayhap it just saying, *I am the big sea, hear me holler and roar.*

The sea going out until it so far out that you can't see it. Is a gone sea, leaving starfish and four-eye fish in the tide pools, and strange kreketeh snail on the beach. Then egrets, sandpipers, curri-curri, hoatzins and harpies with owl-like faces, plovers and noisy black rook bird come for breakfast. I run through the crowd of them and they fly up and circle back in midair and land again.

I run pass driftwood white like cloud, and long ropes of kelp and pieces of broken trawls, and the bruk-up skeleton of the trawler *Hans Bahlin* with barnacle and green moss clamp on its wood like cracra sore. I run and the morning is bright and shiny and new; the air fresh with smells of cedarwood and crab and dead leaf and spawn of fish and salt on leaf. I run and run where the beach sand is hard and my foot doesn't sink in mud. I run fast until I too tired to run and realise I reach Novar, because Coolie people on the beach doing puja and chanting to Krishna, their god of many hands, to their god of elephant face and to Hanuman, their monkey-face god of mischief and fun. They burning agarbathis and sagebrush and sandalwood and lighting banga fires and setting them on the sea with food offerings and bunches of bright flowers, to float away on the waves.

I sit down with Rag, who really name Ragubir Rampartab under a corrida tree. Rag is an old fisherman and he tells me that his wife Nandrani sick bad with sugar disease and going dead soon cause she don't want to eat or drink. Rag cry, saying he use to beat she up good and proper when he was a drunken skunt and live in the liquor bottle and how he sorry bad, sorry more than bad because she was a good wife and don't cause he no trouble – like take a sweet man to do secret nastiness. Is he self was a terrible husband to treat she so bad when he suck down daru in his youthful days, and spend time in whore house with bush whore and with bad woman in this village and that village. He cries like a woman with plenty eye-water falling. It makes me want to cry, too, so I leave Rag and run back up the beach.

Rain start fall when I reach Goodfaith Beach; is devil rain self, coming down hard slantways, rain-claws tearing and ripping away fistfuls of sand. The sky turn sodden and dark, and the sun is just a yellow glare behind grey curtains of cloud. I take shelter under a benab what a fisherman put up inland of the beach under the cedar trees. I feeling tired like rass, like I going faint away. I sit with my head between my knees and close my eyes. Then I run like the wind self all the way home to Mamai house.

Mamai in the kitchen blowing the red eye of fire in a coal pot so the kindling catch and flame up high around the kettle. I come up the back step ready to set foot in the house, but Mamai closes the half-door quick so I just stand there looking at her, and she looking at me. We say nothing. Mamai too fine I think, too magga, like a starvation child. She face hard and fine like she doesn't eat properly, but she eyes big and round and clear like nighttime gingimanan manicou. She head tie-up African style with a cloth round and round. She still has on her pink nightie what thin and worn-out and showing her small bubbies. I feel so guilty looking at her bubbies that I look away. She smiles.

"Boy, go wash your foot," she says in a soft voice.

I look at my foot and it cake-up with mud and small pieces of wood and leaf, with cow dung between my toes. I go downstairs in the yard and wash my foot at the standpipe and go back up. Mamai change into a house frock. She leaning out the front window with she fine beetee in the air, looking over at Mr. Ramsammy house where Anita milking a cow near the back step. Mr. Ramsammy up on the back landing, scratching his seed and brushing his teeth and spitting down on the septic tank below in the yard. When Mamai hears me, she comes inside and sits down at the table so we can eat – roti make from real flour and corn beef stew chased down with special Ovaltine tea.

We don't talk while we eat because is bad manners to talk with mouth full of food. Pure nastiness. And Mamai doesn't have much to say ever. She too quiet. The woman born so. This makes people mistrust her and think her secretive and cunning. But Mamai never care about such things. She doesn't know how to be anything but she own-own strange self. She's the kind of woman who doesn't like to deal with other people. Maybe that is why people say she is mad-cuirass woman. All I know is Mamai not regular in the regular way of a woman. Today, she more regular than usual. She talking to me at least, not just sitting in a chair staring out into space. She not crying and crying the way she does sometimes, with sadness of the heart and depression of the soul; she not hearing voices of jumbie skunt what sometimes provoke her nerve with secret whispering inside she skull, making her holler and scream and carry on. This happens two times before when Mamai run-out she mad head and neighbours have to come to help me put her to bed.

After we eat, I go downstairs and heat the mud oven what we use to bake pastries and bread, while Mamai rolls pastry dough. I fire the banga to a blaze until the fire burns down properly so there is no tall tongue of fire, just red banga burn down black with secret fire inside. I put on the door, so the oven stays hot, and go upstairs. Mamai finishes rolling pastries and puts them on a baking pan ready for baking.

She has made pine tarts, patties, cheese rolls and salara; we bake butterflap, cheese straw, tennis rolls and shingle too. It takes us almost all afternoon to done bake. After that, Mamai goes upstairs to take a nap while the pastries cool down. I sit on the veranda and read *When He Was Free and Young and He Used to Wear Silks*, a funny book of stories by this man, Austin Clarke, a Bajan, and howl big laugh until my belly nearly bust.

Near sunset, I help Mamai take the pastries out to the road to wait for Sookuru car to Central. Mamai leaves me in the road waiting because she says she having nara in her small belly what hurting her. I sit down in the road-corner grass reading my book when Carl rides up on Bhoje bike, towing Hari on the crossbar. Carl gets off with his long, tall self and push he nasty hand in Mamai basket and grab two cheese roll and start stuffing them in his dutty mouth like a hungry-belly dog.

"That is for customers, man," I say.

"I is customer," Carl says.

"Please for a salara, man Kippy man," Hari says.

I give him one and the two of them get back on the bike and ride away laughing.

"We going hunting tomorrow," Hari holler.

Sookuru pick me up late, and all the way to Central he picking up and dropping off this and that body. In Central, I drop off the pastries at three different shops and go back home. Is getting dark. Mamai laying down in the big chair reading *The Scholar Man* by O.R. Dathorne. The radio on and the death news coming through. A man what sound like Wordsworth McAndrew saying that Winston Saul, a resident of Cove & John, depart this world on August 17th. He was the father of Naomi, Cyril, Shanti, Simone, Selma, Rudolph, Ralph, Desmond of the United States, Joyce, John, Joan, Kaye of Trinidad, Carlos, Kate, Clive, Derek, Desiree, Winston Junior and Frank of England. The body will leave Likins Funeral Home at...

"Sookuru come late?" Mamai say.

"Yes, Mamai."

"But you get there before shop close?"

"Yes, Mamai."

"You going to film show with Anita tonight?"

"She don't like cowboy film show. She say is too much shooting in it. They showing a movie name *Last Train from Gun Hill* starring Kirk Douglas and co-starring Anthony Quinn. I going with Derek."

"Alright, but I going to sleep after *Let the Lion Loose*. I have to go to Berbice and buy flour tomorrow. Bathe and eat your tea before you go."

"Aright," I say and go into the bedroom. I hear the theme song for *Let the Lion Loose* startup. Mamai like this radio show too bad. Is pure big people lovey-dovey stuff, with killing and lying and plenty other big people fuckery.

That night, after I come home from film show and lay down under the mosquito net, I dream bout Anita. In the dream, she standing by a riverside in a nice frock what make of white lace looking whiter in the moonlight. She calls me in her nice voice, what like a song of the sweet Guyana singer, Ms. Pamela Maynard. Anita's mouth not making sound at all, but I read her lips them to see that she saying, *Come to me*. When I get in front of her, she pulls up her frock and tells me, "Kiss it." In the dream, something sweet goes out of me and leaves a nice lithe feeling. Come dayclean, I wake all sticky and clammy.

2. RUNNER, RUNNER

Plenty days Mamai silent, sitting by the window, looking out at nothing at all. She there and not there – away from sheself. I go to school and come back; she still there in the same position. When she's like that, I go to the backdam for firewood and come home with wood heavier than my weight, balance on my head; I go swim in the wide canal and feel for tilapia in the roadside trenches and ride stray donkey across the low pasture; I climb high limb of the tallest mango tree to pick ripe mango and eat them sitting in the tree; I play soccer, cricket, rounders in the schoolyard. I come home late in the night when stars out plenty, and the moon big and silver and shiny like coin. I travel far from home.

One time, I hear that the great runner, Clement Fields, live in Wismar and I decide to go there to see the man and to talk to him good and proper about running. Is a man I admire. Is he what make me start run. One time, he run a marathon what pass through the villages. Me and Carl stand on road corner and watch the runners come up from Berbice, Clement Fields leading a big crowd of runner. He ahead of the closest man by three minutes. He just a small man with fine leg and a white patch in the front of his head. I remember how he run smooth and soft, not breathing hard, hand and leg moving with a rhythm like dancer. Since then, I read about him in newspapers plenty time. I start run like him.

I go and see Clement Fields one-time Mamai run-off out her head. I leave her sitting by the window staring into the distance. I thief money from she purse for fare to Wismar. I take an early bus to Georgetown and take another bus to Mackenzie. I cross the Demerara, brown, vast, running silent between banks of stalls and rum shops and other small buildings. I climb a high hill of white sand and watch where the Pullman train with a thousand-thousand car rumble down the line, full with bauxite, wheels screeching and scraping and sparking. It was long in passing over the trestle, long in going by where I standup looking, the noise painful to listen to. The din from the bauxite mine across the river loud too, and smoke, black, white and red, pour out the big pipe over the low buildings. From the hill, I look back and see boats on the brown water and people waiting on the landing. Everything look far from where I was. The sound of music playing, people shouting and cursing, roar of engines and beeping cars was raw in my ears. The rookootooks of town life lashing me right left and centre. I miss the sound of wind in the trees and birds in the sky.

Mr. Clement Fields live in a quiet place name One Mile, a little town with houses facing one another across a narrow laterite road. His house on the right, concrete with a flat roof and paint green like all the houses on the street. The houses here different from houses in Mahaicony. They not on stilts. I don't see any rice field at all, not even coconut tree. I see pear tree and cashew tree and fat-pork tree what grow everywhere. I think this is poor people place and lack plenty thing. I think maybe this Wismar place have lazy people because I don't see no garden and no arbour of vine and no cow and no sheep. Is a place of dust and dry sand, not green like the village.

When I knock on Mr. Clement Fields's door, a woman come and ask in a nice voice who I am. I tell her that I is Kipling Plass from Mahaicony and come to see Mr. Clement Fields, the greatest runner of all time. Is a short, clear-skin woman, neither fine nor fat; she look like a mother. She tell me come in and I go into the house and see Mr. Clement Fields sitting down in a big chair in the dining room. He listening to the radio on top a glass case thing, and I see all kind of trophy and ribbon and medal in it. He have four glass cases full up like that. My heart full up with love and I want Clement Fields to be my father. I want to hug up with the great man. I want he wife to be my mother and not a mad woman sitting by the window looking out morning till night.

I sit down near Mr. Fields and Mrs. Fields go in the kitchen and come back with cake and drink.

I tell Mr. Clement Field that he run real good. That I see he one time in Mahaicony.

He laugh a nice laugh and slap he fine leg and clap he hand and rub them together.

"So you come all the way from Mahaicony?"

"I think about running all the way here, but it too far."

"That is far," he say. "Where your mother and father?"

"I don't have no father," I say. "I have a mother but she mad."

Mrs. Fields asked me to explain. I did.

Mr. Fields look at me and shake his head slow and sad. Mrs. Fields get up and hug me up tight to her soft bubbies. She have a nice flower smell and I just stay where she holding me close. I want suck she bubbie but I don't say so. I just let her hug me up and say in she soft nice voice, "Oh dear, oh dear, oh dear," sweet and lovely like real-real mother to a child.

After I hug up with the woman, I drink cool five-finger carambola juice and eat cake. Mr. Clement Fields show me all the trophy and ribbon and medal in the glass case and tell me in what race he win them. He have four children and he call them and tell them to take me out and play. Three boy and one girl. We go in the back yard and they show me Guinea pig and rabbit in little cages. He have a big tent thing in the back what look like the Umana Yana where he hold party and thing. We go out on a big sand pasture where they have a cricket pitch and a rounders circle and play. Mr. Clement Fields have a club call Clem-O-Shine. I play with his children and eat some more food. One of the children name Claire and is she I like most.

In the late afternoon, Mr. Clement Fields walk me down to the river and we cross the river. He put me on a bus and pay for my ticket and wait till the bus leave. As we sit in the terminal, he tell me all about running technique. He say I must relax and get comfortable when I run; I must be at ease with myself; he tell me what food to eat and drink to drink.

I tired too bad when bus come and sleep good and proper all the way to Georgetown. Conductor have to wake me up. I get in the Georgetown bus back to Mahaicony.

When I get back home is almost eleven in the night. The village quiet-quiet. A big moon in the sky and plenty star twinkling. Mamai still sitting by the window, looking out on the darkness. She pee-up herself. I can smell it. I just go and sleep because I tired bad. But next morning, when I wake up, she making tea in the kitchen and singing, *Good news, the chariot is coming, good news the chariot is coming, good news and I don't want it to leave me behind*. I stand there looking at Mamai and she turn and look at me and smile a nice smile and say, "But is where you go all day yesterday."

"I went to see Mr. Clement Fields in Wismar," I say.

She don't say nothing to that. She just crack an egg in the frying pan and start sing she church song again: *I have a long white robe in Heaven, I have a long white robe up there. Good news the chariot is coming* – and other skuntian words. That is when I learn that madness come and go. Is like tide on the river, going out and coming in, but not so regular. Mad people don't have no way of helping theyself when they run off in the head. They don't have any power. Is like something inside them tell them what to do, like demon what take over the small girl in *Exorcist* film starring Linda Blair. Mad people like Kangalang Harry Arnold, though, have demon in them all the time. He have madness that is always around. It don't come and go like Mamai madness. I frighten bad that Mamai going catch madness what don't go away. I know if she have stay-around madness, they going put she in mad house or maybe, like Kangalang, she go start walking street with she bubbie and patacake showing to everybody, without shame or care for sheself. I frighten bad.

3. ANITA IN THE SCHOOLYARD

First time I see Anita, she was sitting by herself on the schoolyard fence, holding a flower up to the sun and pulling off petals one by one and singing a song so soft I can hardly hear. The place is noisy with girls playing rounders and talking in little circles. Anita by herself. She not wearing school uniform neither. She has on a frock what tear up by the hem and she doesn't have on shoes, not even push-toe rubber slipper. She hair comb nice, though, with a part in the middle of her small head and plait in two long rows on both sides of her fine face. Her hair oily and dark like coal. From then on, I want to be near her. I don't understand it. Is like she is for me and me is for her. But I don't like the feeling. I don't like that every time I see her, I want to hug her and say nice things to her. Sometimes I see her and feel like crying because of the strange tender feeling I have for this Coolie girl. I should feel so for Simone, who is the nicest looking girl in school, but I don't. Is Anita I have the tender feeling for.

I don't like how I feel, so try not to go near her. But I can't stay away from the Coolie thing. I like how she quiet, and hardly say a word all day, not even to answer teacher question. She eyes them is the first thing I notice. She has big round eyes shining in her small face. I like how she smell – like coconut oil and fruit. But I uncomfortable around her. Something not right with the girl. She not regular. She too brazen the way she looks me straight in my face. It make me nervous, make me clumsy, make me not regular. I get vex and pinch she or mash her foot when nobody looking. She always alone in the same spot. She too strange.

Them schoolgirls say Anita comes from Creek in the backward part where poor Coolie people live. They say her father does beat up her mother bad, even on the public road, and how her mother takes other men and leave he skunt high and dry. They say Anita people so poor that her mother have to sell her patacake so she can eat daal and rice. *Coolie wata rice pork and spice, wash yuh beetee with daal and rice* they sing. They say if it wasn't for Blackman minister, Anita would never come to school at-all, at-all. They say how this Anita, with her one-grain dress and she barefoot Coolie rass, does stink up the whole classroom. Look she nuh, them say, look how she always smiling with her teeth skin-up like roast dog self.

One girl say, "One time, when we shying star-apple near Madoo place by Waterside Canal, we see she mother hug-up with a man behind coconut tree. He had he hand up she skirt and rubbing up she patacake. If you see them run when we holler at them. Was a man we call Shetland Pony, who real name is Dorcus Ramlattan, a dougla man from near Bath. I see them with me own-own eye." Another add, "My mother say women like Anita's mother going dead early cause god watching them dutty ways and this Anita is like she mother self. See how she sit on fence with she leg wide open. See how she does look at Kip strong-strong with she brazen self; see how she playing with flower, like a lil girl in fairytale book. One of these days I going give she one slap cross she nice face." And another say, "The girl have lice; I see nit in she hair, and she have cracra and junjah and cheera corner mouth. My mother says cheera is sign she don't eat proper. But is why Kip always looking at she so strong? Is like Kippy like Coolie meat."

"Hear this now! Me mother say Anita real-real father is a man name Ramsammy from Abary," says Dorothy Smith. "He used to have plenty cow and sheep and thing, but now he like we. Me mother tell me a true story bout he – well that is not quite true, girl, is lie I telling. Mami never tell me. What take place is I listen with me brazen self when Mami talking to Bacharan daughter, Sita, the Coolie lady what sell bara and polori. She say how Anita grow up with her grandmother in Creek cause was pure violence and skunt between her whoring mother and drunk father."

"But what wrong with Kippy, though?" says Eve Kalicharan. "What between him and the Coolie thing with she one-panty self? Is like she have plenty power over him; he only have eye for she. Maybe she work obeah and make he fall in love with she dutty rass."

Them schoolgirl always talking loud enough so I hear them. I just stand there and look away but my ears always open. Is from them I learn all I know bout Anita. I sieve truth from gossip but is a hard thing to know truth from true lies. Anita strange, though. Even other Coolie girl don't like her. They talk about her the same way Black girl talk about her.

Anita doesn't talk back; she acts like she doesn't hear them. I don't know what happening to me. I dream plenty dreams about her. Two times I dream me and she holding hand on Main Road; me and she kissing up behind school under the back step in home economic building – the kissing place, where last year, Manish Wata get catch with Tar Baby, a black-black Coolie Madras girl, doing nastiness. The headmaster expel them from school.

Why does she look at me like she waiting for me? It makes me pagla and soft inside. She has lip what turn up like duck and shows her white teeth them and her pink tongue. I feel upset and vex. I pinch her neck real hard. But she doesn't holler or nothing. She look at me with her round eye and her white teeth. Then she kisses me. Is the first time I kiss a girl. I just shock. She holds me around my neck and kisses me hard. Anita's lips soft and sweet. I kiss her back. I just standing in the schoolyard kissing Anita. I don't even hear people laughing and carrying on. But when I come to myself and look round, I see people laughing and pointing and talking. Anita still kissing me while I looking round like frighten boy.

"Oh lord, look – Kip kissing up the nasty-skin girl," says Arlene Simmons.

"I never see such thing in me born days," says Bina Patel.

"She going give he junjuh," says Joy Carla Forde.

"She going give he plenty lice in he hair," says Desiree Gomes.

"Is like Kippy like she. He kissing she back," says Sabita Cowsilla.

"Kippy is a dutty boy. My mother says them Plass has mad people in the family. Kippy cousin, the English Black man, is mad like cuirass."

"Is what happening here today-today, in the pure light of day, girl Orita girl? Kippy come out arts and craft room and walk toward the Coolie bitch like bad John. This boy too mad; next thing you know is big pashway. What mad-skunt Kippy go and do? Let we go closer and see if Kippy using he tongue on her in the French style. Boys always want put tongue in girl mouth. Is a nasty business, though sometimes it feel nice. One time, behind Marcel them cake shop, I let Carl suck up my tongue. He like it, but when he try and touch me patacake, I give he one slap cross he blackface. That is when he cuffed me in my head. Carl have a bad heart, but that is another story."

"I hear my mother say that Kippy's mother make him with her cousin, the Black English man, in the big house where Aunt Esther with her fat self talk name all day. The Englishman is Kippy's mother uncle son. Kip is an incest child and that means he ain't regular. Is probably why he kisses up the Coolie stink girl. Them Plass use to own plenty land in Creekside during riot time, so the story goes, but Coolie people kill out the whole family and leave only the English Blackman and Kippy mother. The two of them commit skunt and make Kippy, so we can't blame he, and is also because the Coolie work obeah on Kip and make he basodee. Kippy go have to go see Ma Tussette so she can take away Coolie spell and bacoo jumbie demon from out he brains what the Coolie girl put there with her kalimaipuja business, so Kip go like Blackman negro girl in the regular style," says Marva Gill.

"Kippy not mad," Simone say.

"Kippy read too much book. He always talking book book book and running in the morning by heself all the time. Is pure madness in Kippy's head since he small."

"I feel up he tolo one time when me and he share a desk in Teacher Desmond class."

"I like Kippy."

"Everybody like Kippy, but he mad like cuirass."

"Yes, he make Coolie girl take away he mind. Is cause he is incest child and don't have a regular father."

"Kippy never should born so he don't turn mad like Kangalang Harry Arnold and walk around smelling like latrine with he big tolo hanging out he pants like black mamba snake."

"O God! Run girl, run. Here come Teacher Clive; he has a vex look on he face. Run nuh. You so slow, girl. I don't want any licks today. Teacher Clive too stern with he fine self. I hear he does fuck the buck girl English teacher even though he have wife. Teacher Clive does frighten me too bad... Stop now, stop, let we stop right here, Orita girl, and see what happen. Teacher Clive have Kippy by he ear and taking he upstairs. Headmaster go bust Kippy beetee today with licks from the big cane. I sorry for he rass," says Simone Peters.

"Bell ringing. Run you slow rass and get in line before Teacher Clive gets vex and beat the whole class."

"Here come the Coolie girl walking slow and soft, strolling like she on catwalk with she lice-hair self. Why she smiling up so? Look she pretty self; this girl madder than Kippy."

"Is true. Look how she laughing up with she own self like she hearing a joke in she own head. Is so whore does smile to theyself when they remember things."

"Say something to she."

"Teacher Clive looking."

"But where Kippy skunt? He probably in headmaster office now, waiting for he licks. Kippy beetee go bust today-today."

4. A MURDERER DREAMS OF RICHES

Mr. Ramphal, the richest man in the village, tell a man to go see another man who live in Tain, and he went. The man take Madhoo taxi and go up there and stand in the man yard waiting. This man come down and give him a paper bag and go back upstairs without saying a word. The man stand in the yard, holding the bag, not sure if he should move or not move. He wait there like he waiting for something. Then he go out the yard to Main Road to wait for bus. Is a hot day. Tar bubbling in the road. He see a dog, fatigue with heat, moving slow and staggering, and a Coolie woman, skin shiny with sweat, hiding under her umbrella. The air thick and hot. In the distance, heat shimmering like a wall of liquid glass. It hard to breathe. The man with the paper bag sit down in the bus shed with it on his lap. What's in the bag? It soft like paper but have some weight. He lift it up and put it down and weigh it in his hand like scale weighing fish or coal or provision at market. He average the bag weigh ten pounds, the most twelve. How Ramphal go know if he open the thing and take a peek? He can't know.

The only instruction Mr. Ramphal give he is: "Don't look at what you bringing." Why Ramphal say this? That is something people say about bacoo in bottle. *Don't open the cork*. It don't feel like bacoo in the bag. And who is Ramphal to tell him what to do and what not to do? He is big man, not child or woman. Who is Ramphal to say where he can look and not look?

What Ramphal is, he not sure. The man own rice field and tractor, and plenty cow. The man own couple fishing trawler. How the man come to get all these things he don't know. People say the man have bacoo what make him rich. People say Ramphal sell he soul to the devil. They don't understand how this man, who five year ago own just one rice field, turn sudden rich like oilman of Arab country. Mr. Ramphal don't reveal he secret but the man with the package know two things about how Ramphal get some of his money. Is not fishing. He know that Ramphal trawler *Amassagana* not for fishing. Is for bringing ban goods from Suriname. Fishing is only play-play.

When he work on *The Amassagana*, the man didn't do any fishing. He just load ban goods in Paramaribo and take off ban thing when they reach Bary sluice in the night. Was he and five man he didn't know good. He mostly stay by heself when he work with them men; they drink too much rum and was sometimes too drunk to drive the trawler properly. Then Mr. Ramphal take him off the boat and have him spraying pesticide poison in rice field what make him sick. After that, he weed trench for the man and drive tractor for the man and beat-up other men for the man. The man was big lender of money to small farmer up and down the coast, and when they don't pay, he and the man son-in-law, Mohun, and sometimes the other one, Tit, go see the farmer and give he some lash to hurry up the payment. One time, he went with the man grandson, a fellow people call Stepping Razor, but who really name JagMohan. This JagMohan like cutting people with cutlass and knife. In Dundee, one time, he went with Stepping Razor to collect some dollars from a man name Mohabir who owe Mr. Ramphal, and this Stepping Razor don't even ask question, just start with the cutlass business and chop Mohabir five-six time cross he head and back, saying all the while, "Pay the man, pay the man, pay the man." He never went to collect with Stepping Razor again. The man serious, body thin like twine, face hard and sharp like razor self. Instead, Mr. Ramphal tell him to pick up package for him. This is his first trip.

What inside the bag? He want know and how can he know except by looking? Is curiosity what kill kitten, he think. Play with fire and fire go burn you. Fuck with Ramphal and Ramphal go fuck with you. But then he think, *Fuck it. Wah cum suh duh wha tuh much guh ova.*

When he open the bag and look inside it, right away he start sweat and feel like fever burning in his belly. He look at the money, plenty big roll wrap round with rubber band, same size, same thickness. He close the bag and stand up and go outside the bus shed and look up the road and down the road. Then he go back in the shed and take out a roll and count the money. Is ten thousand dollars in a roll. He count the rolls and see is twenty-five roll. He do a bit of primary school mathematics and come up with a total of two hundred and fifty thousand dollars. He whistle and do the math again. Then he close the bag and sit in the bus shed for a long time, quiet, his mind racing like horse round Rising Sun race track. Three bus pass but he don't get up to flag one down. He just sit there and think and he think for a long long time. Then he get up and flag the next bus.

The first thing Ramphal ask him when he bring the money is, "You open the bag?" He think of saying no but he don't.

"Yeah," he tell Ramphal.

Ramphal look at him strong with his red-red eye and smile. The man frightening for so. He can't say what it is about the man that make his skin crawl. Maybe is the way Mr. Ramphal laugh, inside heself, so nothing showing outside. This Ramphal not regular.

"Why?" Ramphal say. "Why you open the bag when I say not to open the bag."

"Cause is me eye," he say. "I responsible for what I see in there. But nobody own me eye."

Ramphal laugh he funny laugh behind his eye. All this time he staring at the collecting man very hard, as if he is surprised, but he face saying something soft.

"You take any of the money?"

"Not a cent."

"Why not?"

"I is not a thief."

Ramphal look like he disappointed. His head move forward a little from his long fine neck and the inside smile come again.

"You is a thief man," Ramphal say.

"No," he say.

"I see you," Ramphal say, but this time he not smiling. "If I find you was a thief, you would not be walking in this world."

Mr. Ramphal take a roll out the bag and peel off some bill and give it to the man. When he reach out and take the money, he finger touch with Ramphal finger, and a shock went through his body like electric. This time Ramphal looking at him and laughing his secret laugh.

"I can't trust you to do this anymore," Ramphal say. "Is too risky. I told you not to look in the package."

That night in his little logie near Canal Dam, the man torture himself with thinking too much. All night long, while mosquito whine and beetle crash on the naked bulb hanging from a wire above his head, he keep asking himself over and over again why he didn't take the money and run. He keep finding reason not to run and saying to himself that he do the right thing. But when he think again, he tell heself he is a stupid skunt, a fucking jackass. He could be in Mabaruma or Lethem by now. Why he didn't take the money and run? This fighting with himself go on until morning comes. What disturb he most is Mr. Ramphal, how the man talk like he know what's in his head, how the man laugh like jumbie, mocking and jeering. Why didn't he take the money and run? But it too late now. He lay on the bed top under the mosquito net, sweating and thinking, *Stupid, stupid man*. Then he think about the way the man laugh behind he eye without showing laugh on his face, the way the man talk with his voice rough like sandpaper scratching on metal. He think, "Next time is boat." He think about that a long time and then he smile and smile and go to sleep, because a new butterfly of a plan just flutter into his head.

That night, he dream a dream, but is not a dream, is a reality that turn into a dream. In this dream, he's holding a big rockstone over his head and below is a sleeping man. They are in a jungle place he knows is Eteringbang and the man sleeping is he brother, Raj, who smiling in he sleep and dreaming a nice dream, because two days before Raj find big gold, but he didn't find none. In the dream is plenty noise of insect and jungle animal, and sound of big river water running, and bat winging in the sky, and big black nightbird what eat bat. He can hear squeal of big-eye manicou what live in high treetop and only come out in the nighttime. And there's a loud noise when he bring down the rock and crush Raj head.

In the dream, Raj body trembling like he have fit, so he have to give Raj two more knocks, *bladam blam*. Then he thief Raj gold and dream a dream of riches.

5. THE TRIP

Mamai already wake-up, dress, and ready to go to Berbice to buy ban flour. Cocks crowing, cricket singing, dew falling like rain. Crappo in the dasheen leaf near the back gutter making a loud noise. Mamai wearing a pink frock with a small belt tie around her fine waist. She head tie-up African style, and she wearing leather sandals what she cousin, Mr. Plass, bring from England. She carrying a small bag over her shoulder. We go out the yard along Mr. Ramsammy cowpen fence; cow laying down on their side, chewing cud and lashing mosquito with their tail. People still asleep.

We go out to Main Road to wait in the dark for the Rosignol TATA bus. Mamai quiet and still. Too quiet and still. Something in the way she stands, like a monument, makes me tremble. She does get like this sometimes, just before she runs off her head with madness. I go close and touch her hand. She looks at me for a long time like she doesn't recognise me. Then she smiles only with her lips them, which makes me lonely and sad. Something wrong I think. But just then we hear the bus come up the road, bright light blazing and blinding. I put out my hand and wave it down.

Mamai gets on quick like she scorn to stay with me another minute. I stand in the road looking after the bus until it goes around San Souci turn and disappear. I go back to bed and try to dream Anita so I can have the nice warm feeling again. But sleep doesn't come. I get up and do what I always do. I run.

It still cool and the sky full of dark clouds. The east glowing with the fire of sunrise. I run north toward the sea. I imagine frothy wave lashing against rockstone and drifting out and coming in again. In the pastures, I see firelights and the silhouettes of milkmen leading cows to milking posts. I run pass a mile of sugarcane bowing in the wind; I run pass the coconut estate where coconut branch eat away by worms, with blight on the fronds. The macadam under my bare foot turn gravel what cut at my soles. I run on the red laterite and reach the canal and cross it on a two-plank bridge. I run on soft mud sucking at my foot in the shadow of tall jamoon trees and reach the sea at early ebb, and run on the sand and shell for two miles, racing the longshore current. I sit down in the water and cool my beetee and my toes. In the distance, a trawler moves along the horizon with a flock of egrets flapping behind and the sun half-in and half-out the sea, rising into the morning of the world.

I sit for a long time and the sound of the sea makes me think how there is too much sea in the world and that mean no good. The sea is a murderer what drown plenty slave man. I think of white bones of slaves moving with the currents deep down in skuntian darkness. Then I think that if there was no sea, I could walk to America. But, no, without sea there would be no river and no fish and a great thirstiness in the land.

A long, slant-way shadow falls on me. When I look up, Paloo, who really name Pedro Phillips, standing above me with his bend-back self. This man too old to be alive, I think, with his rough face black like tar and his red-red eyes like ole higue eye. Maybe Paloo just come from sucking out the blood of some new babychild, like Christopher Lee in *Horror of Dracula*? He has a cutlass in his hand and a big bunch of bananas on his head. He looks at me and looks at the sky.

"Boy, you not Paulette one-grain son?" he say in his ole higue voice, what coming from deep inside his fine-body self, like from hollering in a drum.

"Yes, Mr. Phillips."

"Big rain coming. Hustle you tail home now," he say, and broadsides the cutlass against his leg.

I get up and run. Behind me, he laughing big laugh like a villain in cowboy film show. When I look back, he not on the beach. Is like he disappeared and gone. Most like he turn into a big bat and fly away like Dracula.

6. THE WORK OF HUNTERS

Me, Carl, Derek, and Hari liming near Poopaloops' shop, sitting with our backs brace-up against the paling fence watching Mr. Ramsammy, Anita father, beat his wife, Ms. Sabita, with a white shoe. It takes plenty time. Sabita crying boohoohoo tears saying, "Done nuh, man, done nuh." Mr. Ramsammy don't stop. He keeps giving she licks like peas, saying, "Take that and that and that, you whoring skunt you," every time he knocks her with the white shoe. It gets boring after a time, so we take a stroll near the burial ground to shy mango. Then we go kill birds in backdam rice field. Carl good with a slingshot and bring down ten kiskadees quick-quick. I shoot four birds. Derek don't shoot any. He don't believe in killing innocent bird. Derek too soft with his auntie-man self. Hari gets five, two kiskadees, and three kecks, what are just cage birds and not good to eat.

We decide to roast the birds, but nobody wants to clean them so Carl pitches them in the trench. On the way home, we see Coolie Bai Ramlotar taking food in shiny tinin to his father what works in the rice mill in Burma. Coolie Bai Ramlotar hobbling down the road with his pagla self. He is not a regular boy. He mad like skunt and he catch fits. Something wrong with his body too. He is twist-up like a cedar tree trunk. One leg long and one short so he walks hop-and-drop and can't talk properly with his tie-tongue self. Carl picks a fight and he beat up Coolie Bai good and proper, and eat out his father's food. It was curry fish and rice, cook coolie style with plenty of geera masala. Carl wants to bugger-rape Coolie Bai but Hari says no. Carl is a wutliss skunt who practising to be a dangerous bad man. Carl going die soon, like his father who get hang in Mazaruni Jail a long time ago, when Carl still in crib pissing and shitting on his baby self. Ma Tussette tells us the whole story one time. Carl's father, a man name Malik, rape and kill a woman in Corentyne side. He chop up the lady and throw the body in a waterside canal. She washed up, though. People say the dead can talk, and this dead woman points her dead finger at Malik who confesses when police burn his balls and tolo with electric wire. Carl cruel same like his father. He takes things too far. We don't let him bugger-rape Coolie Bai. We leave Coolie Bai in the road, spitting out blood and making wee-wee-wee pig sounds of suffering.

Is a hot day. Sun is a blazing ball of heat burning into your brain, making you hot inside like when you get a bad-bad fever. We go to Dado rum shop where drunk men are playing draughts. An old man we call Bredda, who really name Dunstan Laveau, a palawala from St. Lucia, playing draughts with Hak Deonandan, who is also from somewhere else, another village. Hak doesn't say anything about himself, and we don't ask him. He is one of them secret Coolie what always looking very closely at things with his penetrating bright-bright eyes. He looks at you like he knows something about you he is about to tell. He makes people uneasy. In the bar, too, is Kangalang Harry Arnold with his mad-skunt-self, sitting in one corner talking to himself, saying Ekereko, Ekereko, Ekereko, over and over again.

We take turns playing draughts and get beat by Bredda who clever and bright and see we moves long before we make them. Soon we hungry, wind twisting we stomach like nara skunt. We go out on the road, listening to the houses. When we hear plate scrape, we know where to go. Is Ma Tussette's house, a logie what lean to one side like old bruk-up man. Ma Tussette sitting on the veranda gumming fry-fish and cow-pen bhagee and rice cause she don't have proper teeth.

We call out, "Good afternoon, Ma Tussette. Ma Tussette, good afternoon. You have any food for we, Ma, sweetheart?"

"Come in, chiles," she says, "come in."

We go in and sit down like nice boys while Ma dish out food, humming old people hymn from the bible, one of the psalms of David. We eat with mouth close cause Ma real proper and tolerate no bad manners, no animal behaviour. Ma is around a hundred years old. She lives alone. She used to deliver all the village baby, but now she just works obeah and put spell on people so they turn into snake or dog or creature of terrible ugliness. But she is also a true bush doctor who knows cures for everything. Is she them girls go to when they want throw-away belly. She does still deliver babies, too, though.

When we finished eating, Ma says to us, "Kip, you go sweep the yard. Derek, you go wash the plates." Then she says to Carl, "Carl, that bitch drop again, see who want them puppies." That is all she says. When we leave an hour later, Carl carrying a bag of new puppy dog over his shoulder. The puppy squirming round in the bag, shitting and pissing, and making sad puppy noise. When we reach Bary, Carl throw the bag of puppies into the river. Carl too cruel. We walk on but Carl stands there, smiling up with himself, looking at how them dogs drowning.

We pass the coconut estate. The pickers are up and about, using tall bamboo poles with a sickle grassknife tie at the end to cut coconut from the dwarf trees. On the other side of the canal is empty cowpasture with parch-up grass; the watering holes them dry-up and crack. We go to the sluice on the canal near Danraj Dam.

We have a pissing contest. Carl pee the farthest. Some boats tied up to the stelling shillyshally on the water. Carl unhooks a boat and goes out on the canal. Is a tree-bark corial without main mast or mizzen, a paddleboat what Amerindian people invent. Carl stands up in the corial. It cant from one side to the other and throw Carl overboard into the dutty water. We laugh. Carl get vex and bend Derek finger so far back it almost breaks. Derek cries out with a scream. So, Carl kicks up Derek good and proper until he stops *meh-mehing* like little girlchild.

We sit on the sluice-house step next to Uncle Percy, Ma Tussette brother. He tell me he's reading *The Kingdom of This World* by Alejo Carpentier, a Cuban. Uncle Percy turned ninety last year, but he is a strong old man. Ma Tussette calls him Small Bai because she is bigger than he. This small bai not small, though he tall and thin. Uncle Percy never get married; he lives bachelor style. The two of them close. Ma always worrying her old head about Uncle Percy and he always worries about her. They live in separate houses in the village. Ma always saying, "Boy, look see how my small brother doing." And he always giving me fish or fruit or money to take to her. "Boy, tell me big sister I aright; the woman worries too much."

We sit on the sluice-house rickety step and wait for the fishermen. Is low tide. We can see the roots of the mangroves sticking through the mud and a bunch of small buck crabs moving back and forth. We can see the Bary River that swallows up the canal in a gulp. Water drink up water until the Bary River, too, get lost in the Atlantic a mile upstream.

Of the fishermen, Deodat Singh comes in first, siding the trawler *Son*, along the mooring planks. His son, Prakash the Small, is sitting on the thwart, mending a seine. This Prakash is a dwarf boy who stopped growing when he turned ten. Now he fifteen and barely four feet.

Not far behind, we can see Bhojedat big trawler, *The Mengelde*, coming in. Bhoje manning the outboard motor what quiet, purring like a cat. We help Deodat unload baskets of butterfish, bangamary, and mullet, a few cuirass and catfish. Then we unload the dead man.

"Daddy catch he like fish in we seine," Prakash the Small say. "Anybody know he?"

We put the dead man down in the grass and stand around and look down at him. He a dead man alright, but not stink or fat with bloating yet, with rotten guts. He is small and black but not a Blackman. He the type of Coolie what blacker than Blackman, maybe one of them Madras fellows from Corentyne. His eyes wide open but cloudy and unblinking. He has boney legs and a fine face with a grey moustache.

"He look like Balram," Deodat say.

"Balram dead," I say. "He drink poison last year."

We stand there looking at the dead man. He wearing fishing clothes, and have an earring in one ear like a pirate in *Sinbad the Sailor* film starring Douglas Fairbanks Jr. I think how the man not involved in his own life anymore. He has little black creatures in his ears and nose-hole, what moving round in there like lice on dog or polliwog in rain pool.

Carl sucks his teeth. "He not from we village," he says. "Let we throw he skunt back in the sea."

Deodat gets vex, looking at Carl with a severe face. He says, "Carl, is man this, man, you understand. Respect due."

"What me care 'bout dead man," Carl say.

Deodat gets plenty vex and kick Carl in his head like Jimmy Wang Yu in *Master of the Flying Guillotine* film. Carl falls down *bradap brap* next to the dead man in the grass. Deodat picks up a piece of tree branch and starts to beat Carl good and proper, saying, "Is man this, is man this, is man this," raining down lash on Carl skunt. Carl hollering murder, crying like a soft child. When he tries to get up, Deodat lick he down with another swift kick *bladam blam* like star boy Chia-Hui Liu in *The 36th Chamber of Shaolin* co-starring Lieh Lo. Deodat starts to massacre Carl again, with whip lash, leaving plenty marks all over Carl's back and leg. Carl bawling like small girl getting her hard-hair comb, going "Oooooohhhhhhh, aaaaaaaaaaaaah, howwwww." Deodat too cruel to beat Carl so like snake. He sweating now, but he doesn't stop until he hears Bhojedat.

"What now, Deodat," Bhoje holler. "You go kill he?"

Deodat turn round fast like he going swing the branch at Bhoje. Deodat has this lostway look in his eyes, like if he in a trance or something. But Bhoje not the kind of man you play with. Bhoje is a giant man with a big muscle and dark hair on his body like porcupine quill. He is the best fisherman in the village. Bhoje looks at Deodat real strong in his eye and Deodat drops the tree branch in the grass. Carl on the ground fold-up like boa constrictor in a coconut tree. He making a soft sound like a man straining to coonsie over latrine seat.

"I only teaching he a lesson," Deodat says in a soft way.

"How he going learn lesson if you kill he?"

Bhoje walks over to Carl who curled up in the grass. He nuzzles Carl's stomach with his big bare foot what has hair on the toes.

"Carl, you get up from there now," Bhoje says. "Is no time to play-play."

Carl get up quick. "I didn't do nothing wrong, Bhoje," he says, dusting heself off. "Make Deodat stop take advantage on me."

Bhoje sucks his teeth. "What the rass going on here?"

"They find a dead man," I say.

"Daddy catch he like fish in the seine," Prakash the Small say.

"What dead man?" Bhoje says.

"The man lay down in the grass over there," Deodat says. "We bring he up this morning in reef seine."

Bhoje walks over to the dead man. He looks down at him for a long time, saying nothing. He shakes his head sad-sad. He looks at each of us in the face.

"Is Nurse's man, I mean Ms. Alice," Bhoje say, shaking his big broad head sad sad, like pitty-po-boy.

"The lady, who work at the clinic in Dundee?" Hari ask.

"The same," Bhoje say.

"Ms. Alice have husband," Carl say. "He tall and black like tar. This man not a Black man."

"Yes, I know the man," Deodat say, "He is a fixer-upper of things, fridge and stove and whatnot, a tall man, quiet like. His name on the tip of my tongue. It go come to me."

"This must be she other man," Prakash say, "the Coolie one. Them boys say he wife left he and gone to Foreign and Away plenty years now. He from Novar or Goodfaith and use to work in the rice before he start fishing not long ago. But he not a friendly man. Quiet. I never hear he talk a word."

"Husain," Bhoje say; "that is his name. He's a Muslim man."

Derek get closer and stoop down in the grass looking at the dead man like doctor ready to inspect a patient. He wearing his cry-baby face like he getting ready to bust big girly cry right in front we. Chupidness. This boy never going learn the hard and regular ways of man. He looks up at me then, and I shake my head, pleading with him not to cry. He man-up then good and proper. He pick up a piece of stick from the grass next to his foot and start digging out the sea lice what clump thick in the dead man's ears and nose-holes, moving around in there like latrine worm. Derek doctoring the dead, I think. But he not making any progress. The sea lice them hold on firm to flesh. The little piece of stick snap and break in Derek's hand.

"What the rass you doing?" Deodat say.

"They eating he," Derek say. "I don't like this."

"That is what they do," Hari say. "They eat dead things, like we do."

"True," Carl say, "you never see me eating alive chicken or fish."

He laugh his kehkehkeh laugh, but nobody laughs with him. I close my eyes and try to imagine myself dead. I try to absent myself from my senses, feel nothing and see nothing, and think nothing. But it don't do no good. I am thinking; I am doing, I am feeling. I am alive.

Carl stop laughing quick when he see nobody laughing along with him. He look across at Bhoje who looking at him with serious disregard. Derek gently put down his piece of broken stick next to the dead man's head and he get up and walk away toward the canal. His shoulders shaking like leaf, but he don't turn round and show us his tears. I am glad about this.

"You want me to ride and tell Nurse that she man dead, Bhoje," Carl say.

Bhoje shakes his head. I can see that he thinking hard. Three furrows in his forehead crinkle up close; his eyes them half-closed. He shakes his head twice like if he dismissing something. He rub his temples with his hairy hands and let them drop down by his side.

"You know where Ms. Alice live?"

"Is that little white house under the big a mango tree near craspah. I see she sweeping she front yard couple of times before"

"Kelly," Deodat shout suddenly. We look across at him.

"What is this Kelly?" Bhoje say.

"Kelly Lynch," Deodat say, "that is the name of Ms. Alice husband, but he don't live with she. He come and go two-three times a month. He live with another woman in Cove & John, have couple children with she. He don't have any with Ms. Alice, though. Is like he sharing she. Is big people story not for the ears of small-boy."

"You know Ms. Alice good?" Bhoje ask.

"Me and she get along well. She always buy fish from me. We talk couple of time. She is a quiet-type woman, like Kip mother. She alright though, a nice soft lady. She is the kind of nurse what delivers baby. What they call them, Kip boy?"

"Midwife," I say.

"Yes that," Deodat say. "I wonder how she feel delivering baby everyday and it seem she can't make she own child?"

"I go ask she when I see she next time," Carl say.

"You not going do that," Bhoje say. "What she feel is not for we to know. Is a private matter."

"She don't have to answer if she don't want to."

"And you don't have to ask because it's not your rass business," Bhoje say.

Carl suck he teeth, but don't say anything else. Bhoje looking at he strong, until he looks away.

On the canal, more fishing boats coming in and roping off on the planks. Rain start fall, slowly at first and then hard, but it only last a minute or so. The sun still out, bright like brass. More fishermen come and stand around the body.

"Get on you bike and ride, Deodat," Bhoje say. "Go tell Ms. Alice she man dead; she need to know. But don't bring her back. Then go tell the police. Them will come quick. No need for them to talk with her."

Deodat get on his bike and gone. Bhoje looking at we strong. Then he give we our marching orders.

That day we did not take the short way home. Me, Hari, and Derek walk south toward Main Road along Bary Dam. But halfway there I convince Hari and Derek we should get on Crasspah Dam, which mean we had to swim over Cross Trench if we didn't find a plank bridge. We did, and cross over on warped rotten planks that hardly hold our weight.

"We doing all this so you can watch a woman cry?" Hari say.

"So we can comfort her if she cry," I say. "She sweet man dead. Is a hard thing."

"You going comfort her?"

"Yes," I say.

"You going hug her round she neck like American movie star and say *there, there, there* while you rub she back."

Derek giggled into his hands.

"How you going comfort the woman?" Hari say.

"I will say sorry she sweetheart dead. I will ask if she want me to fetch water or clean chicken coop or run to the shop and get whatever she want."

"We will do what she want us to do," Derek say.

"Yes."

When we close to the woman's house we see Deodat leaving on his bike. He already tell the woman. She leaning up against the fence with her hands on a paling staves. She trembling. Then she let out one long cry of pure hurt and pain what go on and on and come back like a echo, repeating the sadness over and over. We stop on the dam looking at her. The woman look at us and then she turned and walked away slowly into her house. We went home.

7. FISHERMAN 1

Husain wakes up with the dream still inside his head. In the dream, he is on Mr. Ramphal's boat when big monster-man bite off his head with teeth like shark. The dream was so real yet so impossible. He sits up in bed under the mosquito net and sees the moon in the open window, like wolf moon. He closes the window and sits down on the bed. Alice laying down there snoring loud like man, sweating through her nightie so he can see the hard nipple of she bubbie up against the damp cloth. She face turn down in the pillow, like a drown man floating in the sea. How she breathing, though? He reaches over and turns her head so she doesn't stifle. She opens one eye and close it quick and start snoring louder, like a donkey braying.

Husain goes into the kitchen and dip some water and wash his face over a basin. The morning noisy with animal sound and sound of the sea and river; sounds of trees quarrelling and sound of Alice snoring. Four-thirty in the morning.

Husain sits at the kitchen table and recalls the dream. But now he not so frighten because dream is dream and this is morning. He has had plenty dreams before, falling dream and drowning dream, and dream in which Alice giving he top-stick and dream where she down below on her back in the regular way and him on top doing nastiness good and proper.

But what so frightening about the dream is the detail. The dream like real-life self and he can see Mr. Ramphal boat and he standing on the boat. And he feels when the wolfman bites him hard in his neck and then tear away he belly with sharp teeth, and sink he hook nose and hairy jaw inside and rip way his stomach to shreds. The thing so real.

He goes out to the veranda and hears the sound of mosquito whining and cricket and beetles banging against the naked lamp bulb. Lights come on in Vishnu's veranda across the road and

Vishnu standing there doing jumping-jacks with his hands going up and down like the wings of a hummingbird.

Inside the house, Alice stirring. She in the kitchen preparing tea. What is it going to be this morning? Rice pap, bread made of rice flour, rice-mar tea, leftover cook-up rice with a boiled egg? Rice flour bake, fucking cassava bread skunt; fucking rice flour float with fry egg? Fucking rice flour bread with nut-butter skunt? – stink rice what have weevil, dutty rice what not mill properly so it full of dust and stick together and smell bad. Because the good rice gone out the country with all good things. The good people gone and leave riffraff like himself. They call it brain drain; whose brain gets drained he doesn't know.

His wife gone to foreign two years now and last year she send a letter saying he is not her husband anymore. Since when, he ask himself. He read the letter over and over again. How he can just stop being her husband all of a sudden? Then Mala sends another letter saying she divorce him. Divorce. He has to think about this word. He never hear this word before. Is a foreign word. The letter says she getting married to another man. This bothers Husain bad, cause now he picturing Mala and the man in bed, doing nastiness in all kinds of ways. Mala moaning and saying how it feels good, saying, *Deeper, more*, or *Pull my hair* – like she used to do with him. It takes a long time to get over this. But he can't blame her for never coming back. All the good people gone or going, so what left back is the dregs, dreg-people and dreg-goods in a dreg-country. What he has to do is leave like the rest of the bright people. Take a trip to Suriname on Mr. Ramphal's boat and never come back. Start a new life somewhere else.

The muezzin hollering down the dawn. Husain kneels and faces east and mouths the words he always mouth, but without conviction. In the prayer is no expectation, no belief. Is like his life; just doing and saying without hope or meaning. When he finish, he sits back down on the chair and forgets what he just prayed.

Alice comes in the veranda carrying a plate of something hot and steaming and put it on his lap. Metagee with duff and cassava and eddoe and yam with salt beef and a big piece of fry anafolk fish on top, everything swimming in a white coconut sauce, smelling like a new day and a new life. Alice smiling down at him.

"Happy birthday," she says. "I know is your favourite."

Husain thinks to himself, *What the skunt? You mean is forget I forget my own birthday?*

But what he says to her is, "Thanks, girl. Thanks for remembering."

"I get something more to give you later," Alice says, and she give him a wink and shake she high Black woman bamzee and go back in the house.

Husain looks at the plate of food on his lap and start cry.

He eats the metagee and goes in to get ready to go out to sea. Alice standing in the bedroom with her head tie-up and water beading on her shoulder. She using another towel to wipe her back and the backs of her thick legs them. Husain never see anything so beautiful. To France with the sea just now. Is pure thoughts of patacake and bubbie touching and rubbing-up take over; and his tolo standup and says yeah man, it looks like we ready for pokie.

"Come and get your birthday present," she says.

And Husain did so until she begs him to break and leggo his seed because he giving her sweetness what so lovely and hurting. And he does. Then he lay down content with her head still on his shoulder and he wide awake, thinking.

The first time he put eyes her was at Dado shop when she comes inside to buy some rice or something. He sitting there drinking with Curry Cuirass and Hak Deonandan. Hak telling them a story about a man who drowned. Telling it like it is a funny joke.

"The man fall in a hole full of water near the river," Hak says. "The hole deep-deep and we can't get him out because we don't have rope and the tree branch them too short. All this time the man paddling with his leg and hands them, trying to stay afloat. Me and a man name Eddie watching. Then the man drown. He stop scream and go under and we never see he again."

Then Hak laugh like the story is a big-big joke and Curry Cuirass takes a big drink of rum.

The woman, who is a handsome Black woman, comes out of the shop and goes out to the road and Husain follows her and stands near her as she waits for the bus. He tries out some nice words on her, saying how she nice and thing. The woman only smiling like a small girl child with her hand covering her mouth, which makes Husain think she has rotten teeth. But no. She has good teeth. He sees them when she busts a big laugh when he cracks a nice joke.

She is from Belladrum and at the start Husain have to jump a fence at night to see her, coming up from canal-side where nobody can see him. She have a husband who lives with another woman up the coast. That is four years ago now.

She still lives by herself in Belladrum but she coming and spend two-three days in his house. He doing the same in her house. He sharing her with the husband, and that is alright. These days he going in the yard from Main Road where everybody can see his Coolie skunt, cause he doesn't care a rass by then. Sometimes he passes the husband coming out the yard while he going in, and sometimes he coming out while the husband going in. They don't say anything to one another except goodnight, because is bad manners to do otherwise.

He doesn't wake Alice when he leaves; he dresses quick and quiet in his fishing clothes and goes down the stairs easy like thief man to Main Road. He takes Long Dam to Canal Dam what takes him to the sluice and *The Amassagana* shillyshallying on the river.

8. WAITING FOR MAMAI

Mamai doesn't come home that night. Two times I think I hear her voice but is only the ghost of her voice. Outside dark, and rain falling hard, beating a rhythm on the zinc roof. The moon bright-bright. I listen to a cricket game on GBC Action Radio. The West Indies team in Australia. Viv Richards lashing six and four like he always does. I drink tea, sitting on the veranda looking out to Main Road for my mother. She doesn't come. I go to lie down under the mosquito net and read by candle *The Year in San Fernando* by this man, Michael Anthony, a Trinidadian. The book is about a stupid boy what name Francis and some funny rich Black people. This Francis character is not regular. He acts like a child smaller than his age.

Then I drop asleep and dream a long dream of Paloo chasing me through sugar cane and bizzi-bizzi. I run and fall and Paloo lean over me with his big rotten teeth to swallow my head whole, like a monster crocodile in a film show. I wake up in a cold sweat, cuffing the air.

Mamai still not home. I go out to the road and stand in the rain watching bus after bus come and go. Rain falling harder still and make rivulets what run over my bare foot. I still waiting for Mamai when they come with the second dead man. Uncle Percy leading an old horse by hackamore. Two men dress up in yellow rain-cloak walking behind him, with heads bowed down low like a preacher at prayer time. The horse is very old with a bald shiny black back where the saddle used to sit, its ears tear-up in a couple places and rib bones them showing under its thin skin. The horse moves slow with the weight it carrying on the cart, where the dead man lay down lalaff and silent. He is bigger than the other man Deodat catch in his seine. Only this man smells stink and blood has seeped through the crocus bag covering him, around where his belly should be.

The horse stops when Uncle Percy pulls the hackamore, its big head too heavy for its neck. A black tick big with blood fasten inside one ear.

"Boy, what you doing in the rain?" Uncle Percy say.

"Mamai didn't come home last night."

"Well, you can see I don't have she here. This is a killing rain," he says. "Go back home before you get sick."

I go up close to look at the dead man.

"He is the second one this week," Uncle Percy say.

"Is Teach, isn't it?" I ask.

"Yes. The man used to be a teacher, but he give it up to raise chicken and say he want to be a writer. He was a good cricketer and footballer."

"The man wife leave him, I hear," one of the men with the cart say. "You know, the woman what have a funny hand."

Teach covered up to the neck with a rice bag. Only his face showing. Is a face that looks full of pain and surprise. Water from my face drip down onto his face. I feel sad. This man what use to be alive and talking about writing a book about fishing, who hit big six when he play cricket, now not able to wipe rainwater from his face. I wonder who will care for Teach now he dead.

Uncle Percy pulls the hackamore and the horse move on and they go down the road. I stay in the rain.

I think maybe police arrest Mamai and take her to the police station and rape her with their badness and wicked heart. And when they done with her, because she's the only witness to this terrible skunt, they take her out to the pasture behind the police station and boom bye-bye in Mamai head-back with big magnum gun like in *Dirty Harry* film show. Then they throw she in a septic tank with coonsie and worm and dung beetle to stay forever in skuntian darkness – all because Mamai go to Berbice to buy ban flour so she can make pastries and cake.

Mamai wasn't always a criminal, not until Prime Minister ban food from Foreign and Away. People were honest and this honesty made them righteous. The ban shames them good and proper because they turn thief and lawbreaker and start deal in contraband. Mamai call it a tragedy. She say thieving is survival, but she doesn't say this with seriousness. She only half-believe what she say. She can't justify thieving, so the ban to blame and people what make the ban. Who was I to judge her? She had me to feed and house to take care. I was fatherless, but fatherless different from other boys. My mother didn't have a sweet man who visit her room and stay the night to do nastiness. Yet I born.

Mamai bake pastries for three cakeshop in Central. She sells cake and soft drink, polori, mitai, tarts and pattie. She successful in a small way because she didn't sell cakes with rice flour. So, every two weeks she has to travel and buy wheat flour and other ingredients which ban.

Is not the first time she doesn't come home. One time she left and go away and don't come home like regular. I was younger then. Now my heart sick with waiting. My mind full-up with dreadful scenes of thing what happen. I thinking Mamai run-off she head, and wander away from the road, from people there. She gets lost in a vast field of cane, the tall stalk roaring like a storm when a fire set on the dry leaf and it burn-up Mamai in a big skuntian blaze. O love, O love, O Mamai, O mad-mother, lost and gone.

Carl says maybe big truck knock she down and pitch she bruk-up skunt off the road into the tall road-corner grass and that right now, this minute self, she lying there dead or hurt so bad she can't move. She just waiting for rescue. This frighten me bad. But Carl says this in a jokey way to make me laugh. Carl says plenty of things this way.

9. MR. PLASS AND AUNT ESTHER

The first time Mamai leave me and go away I was nine. When she doesn't come back for five days, a strange man name Mr. Plass come and get me and bring me to live in a big house in Zekendren. I learn later that the man is Mamai cousin, her only other relative next to me. Mr. Plass is a tall fine man who doesn't like talking.

The big house is next to Estate Dam, near Main Road. From the back veranda, all you see is rice field that goes out far pass where the eye can see. It starts just behind the house. Is a new house and shiny with new things inside. Across the street is a burial ground and tombs paint all kinds of colour under the green leaf of mango and coconut tree.

I sleep on a square piece of sponge on the floor in the backroom of the house. Mr. Plass doesn't seem to sleep at all; he works rice field in the day and reads books at night. One room is a library with books all over the floor and stack up high in a crazy-man way, some tear up and scatter round the place. None on the bookshelf them, which are naked and waiting to be filled with the books on the floor.

Mr. Plass is serious read-man, but it's like he doesn't take any pleasure in reading; is like he searching for something in the books, and when he doesn't find what he looking for, he get vex and tear out a page and rip off cover like a small destructive child. Four times, I see he do this terrible thing. One time, I see he tear up a poem book by John Figueroa what has a poem name "Blue Agave" – a poem that I like – inside it. The next time, I see he tear out plenty page from a book name *Interpretation of Dreams* by a nice-looking white man call Sigmund Freud. This gets me so vex that I want to cuff Mr. Plass hard in his face. When he see me standing in the hallway watching he tear-up the white man book, he *slamblam* the library door in my face. Mr. Plass not regular. Possibly Mr. Plass has a demon inside he like that small girl in

Exorcist film and he searching for a cure in all the books he read. Mr. Plass mad like Mamai. Sometimes he stays silent for days, walking up and down in the house; other time he just start big crying like woman self; still other time, he soft with tenderness and talk to me in a regular way.

One time, he takes me to Gonsalves' shop and buys a soft drink and salara cake. That's the time I like the most when he is calm and collect. Then, he even talks a couple of sentences. He doesn't sound like people in the village, though; he sounds like foreigner Englishman, with his soft voice what sweet to the ear. His words are different. Mamai says Mr. Plass has a big degree from a college in England where he born and live plenty years. To me he just a crazy skunt who likes to tear up precious books.

He looks different too, tall and thin and frail, like congo pump tree, but softer, like flower or auntie-man. He walks slowly with a rhythm like he dancing, deliberate and sure and neat. Everything about him is neat, except he library what look confuse and where he spends the most time when he in his rickaticks, talking to himself and waving he hand over his fine head like mad skunt.

Three times a week Aunt Esther come and do the housework and cook the food. She's a fat woman who laughs easily and gossip all day. She's not an old woman but she have old woman ways. When work is done, she plants her fat beetee on the veranda chair and watches people pass on the road. She knows people's secrets and likes to talk them. She is pure entertainer. Even sad story makes her laugh. If you tell her a man get hit by a big truck and dead on Main Road, she busts big laugh what shake-up her fat *chin-chin*. I notice she is most happy when people sad. Most of the time I don't like her too much, but sometimes I do. She can cook good.

"I know about the whole world," Aunt Esther like say.

I didn't doubt her because the village is a small world, but I think some of the stories Aunt Esther tells about other people is pure lie, makeup to entertain her friends. These stories make me feel bad for people, shamed of what I know about their secrets and bad behaviour, so that when I see them on the road, I can't look them in the eye. So, I try not to stay around her too much.

I, too, know this whole world. But I don't understand it the way Aunt Esther does. Is a puzzlement to me.

10. LIMERS

Carl says the best thing to do in the village is nothing at all. So, we do a lot of nothing since school close for the holiday. We sit on the koker morning until night. Watch the tide fall on the *Burma*, carrying the rice chaff out to sea. We there still when the tide turn and the river come back the other way. When sun hot, we take a shade by the rum shop and gaff. Carl tell a story about what girl he fucks or want fuck. We know it is pure lie he telling. Girls don't like Carl because they know how he cruel; how he like to hurt people and thing. Maybe is because girls see that Carl don't like them, that he only pretending he like them.

Time goes by slow. We watch the traffic, one car every fifteen minutes on Main Road. The sun burn up we skin and turn we black like tar. Days go by like this. We doing nothing because nothing is the best thing to do.

Sometimes the nothing we do is go out to Arka cakeshop close to Main Road and play draught and watch Arka dutty-skin children run around in the yard, and Arka wife, with she bubbies hanging down like bunya bird nest, digging copra with she legs wide open so we catch fat-eye up she skirt. Is a careless woman this. Arka's big daughter, Clarita, serves the buns and mauby and is careless like her mother. She doesn't wear panties. Arka is a tight-fist man. All the children dress up in rags and look dirty even when they clean. Arka's big daughter is destined to get plenty children with plenty man. People know this and she can't stop it. She wants to escape Arka's two-room logie as soon as she can and too much man knows this too, and planning for it. Carl says he going to be first to give she what she wants; he going reach right up into her tree and quick pick she ripe cherry. Only Adventist church can save she from what coming for her.

But is Derek Clarita like. She always bringing he fry fish wrapped up in old newspapers and sending he little note with bad spelling and bad grammar. Clarita left school early so that she can help dig copra and sell cake in the cake shop. But long before this, she was dunce like goat backfoot. Teacher Cora tried plenty hard, but Clarita have hard-head and hard-ears. She doesn't listen well, and she can't keep anything in her head. She brain full up with surviving. She have to learn the hard way. Carl says Clarita destined to be a bush whore, but only after he has her plenty of time. Clarita not paying no mind to Carl, though. She watching Derek like chicken-hawk. She always giving him a wink of love. But Derek doesn't notice them things unless it coming from boys. I ask him how he stays so; he says he born so. He's a sad boy in this place. Derek's father and mother spoil him too much with nice things and make him soft like rice pap. Derek in love with Carl. People strange so.

Doing nothing is hard for an entire day. The hours crawl slowly like a sloth. The heat of the sun saps your energy and leaves you weak and limp like a wet rag. You run out of things to say and story to tell. You fall asleep on your hand over the draughts table and dribble up all over the pieces, or you go to the cemetery yard and sleep on the tombs in the shade of the big Buxton spice mango tree. But God help you if you wake up when it dark, in bacoo and jumbie hour, then you own-own shadow can kill you. Mostly I take a book and read. The cemetery yard not a place for me.

Some days we get lucky and get entertain good and proper when we not hunting or fishing or thieving coconut from the estate. One time we sleeping in Arka cake shop when Hari come and tell us to follow him. Hari Doolam is a wutliss Coolie. He destined to end up in Mazaruni Jail for cow-thieving or choke and robbery. Hari already chop a Black man from Belledrum for insulting his mother. He is quick with cutlass and knife. Another time Hari beat up his father in public. This great sin Pandit Prajapathi preach against in the mandir and the Right Reverent James sermonise on it in the chapel, saying, *Children respect your mother and father so that your days can be long upon the earth.* Is a Bible verse. Yeah. But Hari's father, Godee Blue, who is also name Hari, knock daru too bad.

Hari not no drunk. Not yet. He is seventeen and tall and thin and serious. He doesn't skin teeth and laugh-laugh. No – and he always clean. But he wutliss still and bound to end up in Mazaruni prison because he has a criminal mind. He bright for so, but his brightness suited only for criminal behaviour. Hari is the kind of boy who thinks that locks not meant to lock things up but be broke into.

We follow Hari, Carl walking close and asking every two minutes, "So what we go see, Hari, where you taking us?" We go down School Dam, pass the primary school on the right. The schoolyard empty, except for cow grazing on the low grass. We pass the pasture behind the school. When we meet backdam, Hari give us a sign that say stop and we stop and he put his hand to his lip for silence, like Gregory Peck in *The Guns of Navarone* when they getting ready to kill German Nazi skunt.

Carl goes first and look over the black sage bush and quick he put his hand over his mouth and laugh quiet. The rest of us excited now.

"What you see?" we say. "What in the bush?"

"He fucking her," Carl says. "He giving she hard."

When we hear a low moan we rush forward and peep over altogether and see Satbama with her leg spread and her eyes close, and the bare beetee of a man going up and down, up and down, between her legs. And right there, Carl pulls his pants down, his big tolo spring out his brief, and he starts beat meat, going aaaah and ooooh till he seed shoot out like bullet on the black sage leaf. Then we all pull out we own tolo and start beat meat, too, and we mess up the bush around with seed slime. Not Derek though, he just staring at Carl with wide eye and touching he self lightly and groaning and moaning softly. Then Satbama starts hollering, "Oh laaaaaaaaaawd, oh gaaaaaaad" and the man between her legs them stop sudden and start to tremble like fish outa water. Hari rush in on the couple, screaming and laughing, and Satie and she man untangle quick and rush for their clothes, but Hari grabs them and runs off hollering into the bush. Pandit Prajapathi runs after him with his long-long tolo slapping his legs them like a bullwhip. Satie stands there naked as the day she born, trying to cover herself with her hands them. But she bubbie too big and she belly soft and flab over she triangle of dark-dark patacake hair.

We looking at Satie and she looking at us. Derek's mouth is wide open like small bird getting feed and he trembling like leaf self in a breeze. I smile at Satie and she smiles back and licks she lips like a sexy movie actress in a film show. I go forward brazen and say, "Let me touch you bubbie, man Satie man."

She says, "You the big man, eh Kippy, you the brave boy?"

"Nah," I say, walking forward.

I tell myself if I don't get a touch, I can get close enough to see big round nipple on she bubbie them. Already I see she patacake hair close-up. This hair darker than hair what on she head and a little sweaty. She has a strong smell that draws me in. I moving forward and not able to stop myself. Is like Satie is a strong magnet and I am just iron filing skunt.

"What you go give if I let you?" Satie says.

This is a big question that talk of a fair exchange. You give me this, I give you that. I understand this rigmarole. Is like giving over money for a piece of cheese in Poopaloops shop.

"What you want, man Satie man?" I say.

"You get a bob?"

"Right in my pocket," I say. "I get four."

"Gimme," she says.

"For what?"

"So you can kiss it," she tells me.

This Satbama is a real bad woman, I thinking. She bound to become a bush whore in interior goldfield. I don't tell her this though. I am not a stupidy skunt boy.

"Alright," I say and hand over two bobs. "A kiss for each bubbie."

"Alright," she says, "is a bargain."

Her nipple rubbery and have a memory in it. I don't feel any pleasure, but it makes me comfortable having it in my mouth. I want to stay with Satie for many days. I suck on one bubbie, then the other. I feel like little pickney and miss my mother. So, I start crying right there. I crying and sucking and crying and sucking like small pickney and Satie says, "There, there, there", like she is me mother or some old woman when in truth she no more than seventeen. Carl pull me off after two minutes and plant he self on Satie bubby, slurping and sucking and making nasty noise. I get fed up with the sound he making. I lonely all of a sudden and want to be by myself. I want my mother. Where is Mamai?

11. TRUE LIES

I go to visit Aunt Esther and ask her to tell me about my family. Is something I've always wanted to know. Mamai is always silent about this. Is like she give birth to her ownself, or stork bird just drop she out of the sky rather than she comes in the world the regular way, through patacake hole. She never talks about her mother or father. She never talks about the past. She gets vex and sad when I ask her. Sometimes I hear people, like the girls at school, say something about her family and come home and ask her if it is true. She never answers the question. She just says people can say what they want to say. So, I ask Aunt Esther, knowing she can't resist telling. I didn't care if the story was true or false. I wanted a past and this past could be true lies.

Aunt Esther don't hesitate to fly her mouth. She never does. So right away, as we sit on the veranda, looking out on Main Road at sunset, with the moon suddenly bubbling up like balloon over the heads of trees, and bats start to fly, Aunt Esther laughs she big fat woman *ahahahaha* laugh, and start telling the story of Mamai family. I bring my chair nearer and suck up her words like them is pepper pot stew and rice.

"Your grandfather was a man named Kurt Plass, a farmer," she tells me. "Them Coolie people chop up him and his two daughters and his wife during riot time. It was a sad sad thing. Your mother and Edgar see the whole thing because they were hiding in a secret place. Since that time, Edgar not the same, and your mother not the same. Madness come and mash-up them good and proper. Is just them two left in the world and they come too close, and thing lead to thing and so you come into the world from cousin loving up cousin. You is an incest child abomination and suffering go come on you."

Aunt Esther say how in 1962 big riot takes place between Coolie people and Blackman people. She calls it Black Friday but was not just one day was black; plenty-days was black because dark matters take place. All because of a Coolie dentist, she say. This dentist was only good for pulling teeth, but like most Coolie people he want everything for heself. He want to own the whole country. This coolie was into big obeah and black arts magic what gives him the power to control people mind and make them do what he says. Plenty politicians have this black magic power. Yeah, man! He only want to take and take and take from the poor Blackman and the Amerindian man them. His wife was a white skunt that he bring back from America. Nothing good can come from marrying white people. They are the devil self. So, this Coolie Hindu devil marries a devil wife. He form a party to run the world after the backra gone back to England. It was a big party with all the colours of the people in the country. They fight the backra white man with talk and long-water words and get freedom from the skunt whiteman government, from the white governor man and the white people who still owning everything and telling Blackman and Coolie people what to do. It was not like a real fight with cuffing and kicking and biting and blood flowing, and raping and shooting and looting. It was, Aunt Esther say, a fight with plenty words, with big people standing-up and quarrelling back and forth in parliament. With the white people saying, "No no no no," for a long time, then saying "Yes, yes, sure, maybe, perhaps, possibly, let us think about it, let us consider it, let us sleep on it." This takes plenty years. Then the white people pack up and go with all the money.

The Coolie dentist man becomes Prime Minister and his wife becomes powerful secretary of obeah and spell-casting. The second in command was a devil niggerman skunt lawyer with a white smile and plenty of big words in his mouth. People know he as a big talk man, standing up before microphone and talking like a book of pure skunt. But he was also jokey, like a regular Black man, and sometimes he sit down in village rum shops to take toops of rum with the common man. But he was still the same devil and know the black art obeah the same way as the Coolie dentist.

And as is the way of devils not to be content with their position, soon the Coolie man and the Niggerman fighting one another for control of the party. The first party gave birth to a second party. The Coolie people stay with the dentist and the Black people go with the niggerman skunt lawyer. And things bruk-up bad *bladam blam*, and the real devil come to the villages in 1962, bringing plenty woe and fire and fury to fuck up Coolie-Blackman togetherness forever.

Then *bladam blam* in the street, and *pow pow pow* gunfire skunt. People in the street flinging rockstone; people in the fields firing the young cane; people in the city shying Molotov through panes of glass to explode *boom, badang brang* and blow up a big building. A boatload of Black men get bomb-up on a river, killing all aboard, legs, arms and heads everywhere. Little Coolie girls get rape, patacake bust-up, bubbie tear off, beetee-hole penetrate; head bust-open so brain and blood leak out on the floor. Blackman get hang on a coconut tree; Coolie man get chop and burn in the cane fields; choke and robbers and thief man rage in the city; tall fires blaze and burn everywhere; Blackman poison Coolie cow and run from villages where plenty coolie people live, and Coolie run from Blackman villages, and the blood flow between them.

"I was twenty then," Aunt Esther say. "I know your grandfather. The man was stupidy; he trusts them Coolie. He did think because they work for him and he does business with them, he is safe. So, when all the Black man running from the village, he says he not going nowhere, says he knows the people and the people know he. He say Danram is he friend and Sookraj Sookdeo is he pal; and Baldeosingh and Bachu Bhagwandin used to shy padi in his rice fields; how he and his longtime friend Garbati Raidu thick like fingers upon a hand. Yes. And all this was true, yes, all this was regular, before the riot, when people were sane, before the devil and his minions land down in Mahaicony and bring big skuntian race war. But land not flesh and family. Land is a thing never done. Deadman don't own land; dead man owns quiet grave and worm. Your grandfather never understand this and he put his whole family in danger of death. I hear that when them Coolie come for he that night, he go down the step of his great house without big bazooka gun, not even cutlass, laughing a little laugh, showing a little skin-teeth to all them Coolie man standing around with cutlass and axe and mattock, serious-serious. He only stops laugh when the first chop take off his hand and the second chop, *slash lash*, cross he stupidy head. He died not knowing he wife and pickney would die just so like he, screaming and hollering from chop and cut and jook till deathself close their mouth. Except for your mother and this mad one whose house I does clean." And Aunt Esther laughed in that mirthless way that makes everything she says sadder.

"Yes," she continued, "this same Mister Plass and your own-own mother witness the thing and live to tell tale. The two of them send plenty man to jail and to the noose on the derrick, to swing sweet and low in the wind. The two of them were witnesses for the prosecution and tell the bloody tale to court and judge. Them not the same since, your mother nor Edgar, who was a nice small boy, bright-bright and smart. How Edgar come to be at the house to witness murder, you might well ask. Well, is a long story, but let me tell it true. Edgar was at Queens College that time, living with his mommy and daddy in Georgetown. His father was a big Government man and his mother was a big headmistress of a girls' school. He was a bright boy and he was not even born here. He born in white man England, though he parents from here.

What happened was the government offer the father, Edgar Senior, a big job and he come back home with little Edgar and his wife from England. His wife was a clear-skin girl, named Darla, with nice green eyes. We use to call her Dollie Eye. Edgar about five then, an only, lonely boy child. I think it is Kitty they live. Edgar uses to spend the holiday with his father's brother, which land Edgar owns now. Is so Edgar come to be in the village when the Coolies attack and slaughter the Plass family. Your mother's great aunt, her name was Tantie Pinkie, a tall woman with long-long white hair, come and take your mother because she was the only living relative. Is so your mother grow up in Abary with Tantie Pinkie, a spinster without chick nor child.

After that, is years before Edgar come back here. His mother and father go back to England and take Edgar with them. Edgar study in big whiteman university. He was twenty-something when he comes back and straight away start to go round your mother. Tantie Pinkie dead by then. Your mother and Edgar come close again. Is the violent death what brings them together.

Murder. That is why the two of them so close. That is why the two of them not regular in the head, why they didn't see wrong as wrong when they come together and make you in the incest way. You might come mad just like them and not be regular in this world. It is known. Incest children run-off and end up in Berbice Mad House. But never mind, child, never mind, don't mind me at all, at all. Watch yourself, though; watch close."

One time, when I small, when I staying that time in Mr. Plass's house for two weeks, one morning early, I hear voices and wake up and go in the living room. Mamai and Mr. Plass sitting in one chair talking softly. He holding her hand and smoothing back her hair and saying something soft over and over again. I go closer and listen. It was her name he saying, soft like if is a precious thing, with respect and feeling, and something else: sadness. I feel I was doing something wrong listening to them, so I go back to my room and lay down. In the morning, Mamai takes me back to the village. She never say where she'd been.

When I get back from seeing Aunt Esther, I ask Ma Tussette if it is true-true story she tells about my family and riot business before I was born. Ma says it is mostly true, but Black men and Coolie live together peaceful before political business. She says plenty of people died because of the riot times. She says my grandfather and his daughters and wife did get murder, true, and my mother and Mr. Plass see the big rigmarole, true.

I ask her if it is true that I am an incest child, and my father is my own cousin. She says that is rumour business and I shouldn't hurt my head with bad-mind talk. She asks if I hate Coolie people and I tell her no. She says that is the right thing, cause Coolie and Blackman poor together and is only rich Coolie and rich Black politicians what always make we fight one another in big pashway of blood and fire. Devil is devil, she says, Coolie or Black.

12. SKYLAB AND THE HOLE IN THE GROUND

The story goes round that Skylab could fall from high in the blue-blue sky. So much bad thing happen here that people think if it fall anywhere, it go smash in the face of Guyana good and proper and wipe the whole country from the earth. Is a big satellite what could come down in flame on us like *fire rass.* We have nothing to do with building the monster machine with wings of pure steel and iron eye that see in the skuntian dark of pure space. That doesn't matter. Skylab falling and we can't get out the way.

Anita thinks she has a way to save me and she alone. She digs a big hole in the ground near the cow pen. We go inside one day but it's too small. We have to stand up close together, face to face. We can't move. It is dark down there. What if rain falls? She says rain not going fall. What if a snake crawls inside the hole? She going to chop it with a cutlass. What if jumbie comes inside with us? She going to kill it with the magic of her Coolie mind. Alright then. In the hole, she holds my hand tight. She smells of soap and coconut oil. She says I must be hers forever and ever, her own-own true love, like in fairytale book. I do not know how to be unkind. Forever is a long time; how can I last so long? I cannot. I know this. I don't tell her we both going to die long before forever come. Maybe we going to die soon, this very year, when Skylab falls from the sky.

I imagine big flames sky-high over the pasture of Abary. I see burning birds ignite by Skylab fire falling in flocks from the sky. When it lands, the whole village catch fire and the houses blow up like skyscraper in *The Towering Inferno* picture. I see people running and burning with cow and donkey in the dry fields, and black smoke bring night to the day. Then is nothing but ash and burn black stumps of courida in the pasture.

I hold Anita's hand tight in the hole. "Let we make this hole a little bigger," I say, "big enough so we can move around and lay down at night." She agrees. I leave all the work to her and go hunting with Carl.

Sunshine bright and breeze blowing. The road empty. Carl pulling a long bamboo pole with a noose at the end to catch iguana. His three bad bitches yap at his heel. Them dogs mangy and magga but are good hunters of labba and accouri. We walking up the road to Bary. When we get near the mandir, we see Pandit Prajapathi on the road corner talking to Bhojedath. The pandit talking and Bhoje nodding his head, yes man, yes man, like stupidy skunt. Pandit P wearing a white kurta and his coal-black hair slick back with coconut oil and his beard trim just so. He looks like Samuel Selvon on the cover of *Turn Again Tiger*. But Pandit P not no Samuel Selvon. Pandit P is a skunt, and rapist of girl children. When we see he last, between Satie's leg, he was naked as the day he born.

Carl says good afternoon and busts out a big laugh as we walk pass. Pandit P get vex and start cuss Carl.

"What I do to you?" Carl says, "I didn't do you nothing, Pandit P; why you get it in for me?"

"Carl, I warning you," Bhoje say; "is big man you talking to."

"What I do, Bhoje?" Carl say.

"Nobody saying you do anything, but one day marabunta go bite and persons go get hurt."

"I didn't hurt nobody," Carl say. "I not the one running around naked in cowpasture. I not the one interfering with small girl."

"Lies," Pandit P holler, "rotten stinking dutty lies."

Bhoje looks at me hard and says, "Kippy, is three times now I tell you not to lime round Carl. Where you mother?"

"She gone away, Bhoje," I say.

"So where you get permission to go hunting?"

"Is me who give myself permission," I say.

"So now little pickney giving theyself permission. That is how things is now? Lil pickney ruling the world of big people? Is that what you saying to me, boy?"

"The children gone wild," Pandit P say; "the world turn upside down."

"Carl, you go on your way," Bhoje say. "Kip, pass you rass home and pick-up book before I maltreat you rass right here and now."

Carl moves off with his long pole dragging on the road, his dogs trailing behind. I go home the way I came.

Anita near the cowpen fence feeding chicken. I stand there with a foot up on the fence. She looks up and smiles. A tender feeling flood inside me and I want hug-up she fine self, right there and then. I want to do anything she tells me. I want to please her.

I duck under the fence wire and grab her and hold her hard against me. She tries to push me away, without trying too hard, and I hold on and she lets me. She puts her hands them around my waist and rests her head on my chest and stays still. We stand like that for a long time, hug-up close. Her breath touches my bare skin like a feather, and I think, yes, is nice to have this lovey-dovey feeling for a girl and the girl have lovey-dovey feeling for you.

When we pull apart, she stands there looking at me.

"But is what get into you though?" she says.

I look down and see my foot in a big pile of cow shit.

"Boy, you mind somewhere else," and she drags me up to the standpipe so I could wash my foot.

I follow her to the bench under the house, brace up against the kitchen. She sits there silently, holding my hand in her lap.

I sit there thinking about Mamai gone so long and not coming home. I used to like it when Mamai leave me alone. Used to imagine the nice things to do by myself in the house. But now I miss her. I don't get enough sleep cause I waiting up for Mamai night after night.

Upstairs in the house, the board creak as Anita's father, Mr. Ramsammy, moves around.

"Daddy not feeling good," Anita says. "He have nara paining his stomach. Go up and talk to him nuh, Kippy."

"Alright," I say.

"Tell he you like me bad. Talk to he respectful. He vex because he think you hiding-hiding round the place like thief; like you going thief me away. Tell he you want permission to come round sometime, nuh."

Mr. Ramsammy sitting in the veranda with just his bukta on, tolo hair showing above the waistband. He legs them fine and black from sun. He tall and skinny and he chest cave-in, with grey hair what coarse like coconut fibre. He taking toops of rum from the neck of a long bottle of highwine. He is the kind of man who don't care if Monday falls on Friday, a don't-care kind of man Mamai says wants to die, but don't know how to pull the trigger, a man with plenty worries in his head what he doesn't talk about.

"Blackman," Mr. Ramsammy says, "come *siddunk* hey." He has a rough voice full of smoke.

"Kip," I tell him.

"Blackman," he says again.

"Kippy," I tell him. "My name is Kippy."

"Blackman."

"Kipling Plass."

"You is black, not true?"

"But is not me name," I say.

He drink another gulp of rum and wipe he mouth with the back of one hand.

"Why you always sniffing round me daughter? Is what intention you have toward the girl?"

"I like she bad," I tell he, the way Anita tells me to say it.

"So what," he says. "Plenty boy like she, but she is me own. I is the owner. What you go do with the girl? You going touch she patacake?"

"I don't know, Mr. Ramsammy," I tell him.

He look at me fierce and then cuff me hard across the side of my head with his bony hand. Eye-water comes and my nose start burn right away. Something in my head pops like a bladder. A voice in my head say *kill kill kill*. I know the voice. Is a voice my mother tells me to mind. "Think before you act," she says. I do that. I get up and go down the stair.

Anita in the yard feeding the chicken them and singing a Coolie song from an Amitabh Bachchan film show name *Zanjeer* that me and she watch at Mr. Ramphal cinema. I don't say anything to her. I take the craspah home, tasting blood in my mouth. I want to cry, but I don't and think up two-three ways to kill Mr. Ramsammy. My face hurting bad where he cuff me. I try and sleep but sleep not coming and all. I have cutlass in my hand chopping dutty drunk skunt Ramsammy into plenty of small pieces. Then I think about the dead man who float up in the canal name Teach and how he wanted to be a writer.

13. FISHERMAN 2

When he wakes up alone in the big bed made for two or three, the silence press down heavy on his chest and he has to fight to get up, heave himself up from the no-noise heaviness in the house. She's gone away, and this is a relief and a pain.

He should not think about her, with her strange ways that made her a poor imitation of his idea of a wife, a thing of word and attitude, not regular though, a thing of flesh and bone and biology, but lacking, to his mind, something essentially human. She is not no robot, no – not a machine looking human like Yul Brynner in *Westworld*, but when she hear a thing and like it, she'd repeat it over and over again until the thing lose all meaning and substance and sense. Bible verse from her mouth was like this, and had he not known the pleasure of love as well as raw pain and strife, as the son of a skuntian father and a bush-whore mother, he would have thought the world a terrible, empty place, without love and fucking, a place where people only praise God and die and go to Heaven or Hell.

He gets up and prays a short prayer and, by the wavering wick of tallow light, reads a page or two of *The Star-Apple Kingdom.* He marvels at the book's profundity. The poet looks close into things, so close he makes the thing he's seeing different, turns it into a thing never seen before. This is a kind of magic. He likes this Derek Walcott book. He would have liked to teach poems from this book to his school class, but they would only laugh and make joke and he would feel hurt. Was that why he didn't teach anymore, because the children threatened his love of books with their stupidity and incomprehension? He puts the book down and writes another memory of his marriage in his journal and signs the date and puts it away and gets up.

Teach opens the window and looks out. He sees the veranda light and the moon behind dark clouds. Four-thirty in the morning. She would have been up by now, rattling pots and pans in the kitchen, making breakfast, ready to start a quarrel if he say "Good morning" in the wrong tone. The day would be ruined. Is just silence in the kitchen now. Silence and memory, and him sitting there instead of putting on his clothes and going out to meet *The Amassagana*.

He used to like her food, though; he used to enjoy that and, when she felt sorry for him, a bit of she nice patacake and big bubbie. But he'd grown to hate coming home from work to see her sour face, listening to her quote bible like a preacher or hear the insults that greet him or follow him out of the door. He was a deputy headmaster and he supervise plenty people because he had college certificate and read plenty books. He didn't like the way she treat him as some kind of low life.

He gets his journal and starts writing again, adding a sentence and erasing a sentence, writing down the thing quick as if he would soon forget. Then he stop and read.

> I'd come home from playing soccer with the boys, and funny-hand Charmayne – whom I'd married that year out of love or pity or the pity of love – I cannot tell – would lay into me good and proper with her insults. It was your skunt this and your rass that. Sweaty and mud-splattered, I'd unhook my shoes on the sidedoor of the upstairs landing and walk in past her to the kitchen. I'd get me a cold Banks from the fridge and coconut buns from the tinin and hurry out to the back veranda to watch the sunset.
>
> I would imagine Quamina and Cuffee, hero slave rebels, in the shapes the clouds made, striding in a ruckus band across the plantations, murdering the white masters and raping their daughters, leaving waste in their wake. I would see decapitated heads and arms piled up and rivulets of blood in the dust. Such were my sunset reveries at that time: violent and bloody.
>
> After a while, Charmayne would calm down. She'd move into her crying phase. There'd be copious tears and sniffled sentences, muffled words accusing me of being

ashamed of her on account of her funny hand. I'd have to go over and comfort her. We'd end up making rough love on the kitchen floor. Her funny hand, thin with short, stubby, dactyly fingers would be forgotten. This deformity had something to do with an inherited disease. I'd take that withered half-hand and kiss each deformed finger lingeringly. This bought her great pleasure and she'd squeal and wiggle and ask for more in a voice that was not like her own.

Two days later it would be back to the same old shit, with the bitch laying into me good and proper. The soccer season bled seamlessly into the cricket season. I'd put down one set of kit for another. I'd join up with Bhojedath and Lickamore Chops and the rest and play for the Abary team. I fielded silly mid-on and when I batted I looked pretty when I hooked fours across the boundary line. The girls would cheer and blow kisses.

Sometimes Charmayne would come to the games. She was there that time I made a double century against Novar on that nice pitch in Calcutta. It was the height of my cricket career. I can feel the pleasure of that day even now, a sweet excitement. Charmayne didn't like cricket. It was too long; the rules puzzled her. She'd sit in the bleachers and knit me a new hat or socks. She sat apart from the cheering women like some thesis against joy.

When Saturday morning came, she'd slink away to the Adventist Church down the dam, wearing one of those hats that obscured the pastor from the pew-sitter behind her. No doubt she repented her nagging ways, going up to the altar when the roll was called, to stand in front of the preacher in her white-white dress and big hat, head bowed, mouthing her repentance and praying, I imagine not unjustly, that I would die. I stayed home in bed and kept backsliding.

She'd come home from church with her mouth full of accusations, saying how I didn't love God; how I didn't love her; I was the spawn of the devil. She would go on like that for hours, like a spouting basilisk through the penitential morning. She'd call me chuntari, wassooka, weakling – brimstone words which hit hard.

I'd give her silence in response.

We'd sleep apart silently that night and others following.

I was a teaching High School in Central then. After work, we'd get teams together, two sides of seven, and go out to the savanna pitch. I'd go home only when I gauged that she was asleep. Some nights, when there were no mosquitoes, I stayed downstairs and slept in the hammock beneath the house. Charmayne would wake me for tea and the bread of nagging. She'd accuse me of having a sweet woman, some whore on the side.

There were whole days when we had no words to say. I waited for her to leave me. We slithered like eels away from each other, tried not to touch. I slept on the outer twelve inches of the bed, like a grown man would with another man. I controlled my cravings.

"It's my hand," she said one morning; "you hate my hand. You only pretending to love me."

I never pretended any such thing I wanted to tell her. I just could not remember why I'd married the virago. I confess that troubled me no end, not remembering why I had willingly fettered myself to a ball and chain.

"You selfish," she'd say; "you only care about cricket and football and book book book."

There was some truth in this. But I did not let on. I'd continue to fork pepper-pot and rice into the hole in my face.

But she slapped the fork away, knocking it to the floor, but not before a tine cut me across one cheek. I dabbed my cheek with a paper napkin.

She ran to the bedroom, crying.

I fought an urge to be cruel, to hurt and destroy her. I wanted to see her cry, see her in pain, in some form of discomfort and terror, which I saw as some surcease for my own discomfort. Other times I felt the tenderest feelings. This, too, was suppressed as we moved like dancers around one another.

Finally, she left. I came home from work one day and she was gone. There was no note. She had cooked enough to last four weeks. Pots were piled in the fridge. She had removed my beers, put them in a box under the kitchen table.

The sky that night was empty; there were no wars or slave revolts. Rain began to fall. I felt the first twinge of loss.

He shakes his head. Three years. So long ago it seems. He stopped teaching to write poetry and raise chickens to sell. He made some money on the chickens but not on the writing, though a few of his poems get published in a magazine. Twice a month he went out to sea on *The Amassagana*; he liked being with the men, working the seine, and when the business with the ban goods start, he like that too, and the money from Mr. Ramphal, and doing a dangerous thing, subverting a government he hate.

He was on the road by five, lighting the darkness with a torchlight, down the dam to the sluice where *The Amassagana* waited.

14. BLUE GANESH

We in the yard of the mandir shying Buxton spice mango from the tree. The sun hot, no wind blowing. We all half-naked in short pants. We sweating like canefield chamar when we take a rest. The heat thick around us and we move slowly because we don't have too much energy. Carl lay down on his back stroking he big tolo through his pants with his eyes closed tight and lip moving without making word. Derek watching Carl and biting off big juicy mango flesh from the seed and licking his fingers them with plenty slurping-sucking sound. Lamuta Dave under the guinep tree stirring up ant nest with a piece of stick and singing in his big man voice:

> If you see me, little brown girl,
> Call her fuh me, call her fuh me.
> If you see me, little brown girl,
> Call her fuh me.
> Baby want she tolo.

Lamuta Dave going end up in Berbice madhouse in a white room with padded walls from nervous breakdown; he worrying all the time about his sick mother. I think that one day he going hang himself like a mad character in film show what screen in the primary school building one weekend.

Another time we see a film show name *My Lover, My Son*. Is about a mother what sex up her son. That is a serious film show and have plenty of sex scene and thing. That is the first time I see that woman patacake have hair, and the white actress lady has small breasts with a pointy red nipple. We ask for *My Lover, My Son* to be shown again because we love this picture. The white woman naked as the day she born. White people wutliss bad.

Lamuta Dave singing and stirring up ants' nest. Hari out by the front yard fence walking round and round the blue Ganesh statue that has an elephant face and breasts of a young girl but is a man-god. Hari stopping sometimes to push it or try to lift it, like he testing how much it weigh. Is a big statue and Hari straining against its weight. Then he stop and puts his hand to his lip like a scholar man and shake his head, yes, then shake his head, no. I see Hari do this before and know is pure mischief that he planning.

"What Hari doing to the blue Ganesh?" Carl say, taking he hand out his pants and daubing it on dried leaves.

"I don't know," Derek say. "It look like he trying to lift the thing."

"Yeah, buddy," Lamuta Dave agree.

Hari leaves the blue Ganesh and comes back under the tree.

He looks at Carl and me and says, "That thing don't have no proper weight. It make of something soft and light like cordwood. Bet you and me can lift it up, Carl. We can float it."

"I ain't giving meself godee," Carl say.

"Godee, buddy," Lamuta Dave say, busting big kekkekek laugh.

But Hari smiles to himself, stroking his face softly. Then he busts out a big laugh and claps his hand like a small child.

"Me and you, Carl," he says, "me and you, buddy."

Now Carl smiling his big white smile, rubbing his hands together like villain Silver Fox in them Chinese filmshow.

"You is a dangerous Coolie," Carl says and throws his hand across Hari's shoulder. The two of them walk to the blue Ganesh. Now they walking around the god and pushing and pulling.

"It not so heavy," Carl say.

"It going float," Hari reply.

"Nah, buddy, nah," Lamuta Dave say.

Derek not listening. He looking out on the road with a smile on his face.

"Look who coming," he says, and we all look toward the road.

Satie there with she bad woman self, walking into the mandir yard. She wearing an old frock that doesn't have any sleeve and she hair clean and oil up with coconut oil good and proper. She rolling her hips like a big woman. I feel my tolo raise up and my inside turn hot like fire. Satie has a big broad smile on her face so I can see her clean teeth and her red-red lips. She walks past Carl and Hari and Lamuta Dave and pull my hand and take me behind the big mango tree and pull out she bubbie.

"Suck," she says. "I giving you for free."

And I fasten my lips on her brown berry nipple and suck suck suck, deep and hard. Satie just trembling like palsy person skunt and going oooohh ahhhhhh whooooooooo. It never occur to me that the girl enjoy this suck-bubbie thing till then. Then she start to tremble and push me off and tuck them in and leave without a word. When I come back to the boys, they looking at me and laughing.

"Here comes the bubbie-sucker," Hari says. "This boy like suck bubbie bad."

"From now on we calling you Bubbie," Carl says.

"Yeah," Lamuta Dave says. "Yeah, buddy, yeah!"

We go to the canal for a swim and cool down. We in the water a long time, diving and swimming and jumping off the koker. I diving with my eye open under the water when I see my mother lying deep down, drown, she eyes wide open and dead. But when I reach out to touch her, she disappears like watamumma or fair maid self. I come out of the water, get dress and go home.

15. KILLER OF DOGS

We sitting on Lamuta Dave's back step gaffing about this and that, and he tells me the sad story about how he turn dog-killer. Since he gets retrench from the rice mill is the only job he can find other than thiefing coconut from the estate. Bhoje get him a job as a fisherman but the trawler rocking on the sea too much and makes Lamuta sick bad. He get a temporary thing weeding trench, but that job is done. He has to work to buy pills for his mother. The blue pill run out last week and now the red and black tablet low, with only four pill left. When them gone, what? Maybe his mother gone too. Ms. Minette getting worse from the wasting away disease. She doesn't have the strength to move her own weight. Lamuta Dave has to lift her everywhere, to the latrine, to the veranda; he has to bathe her and dress her, and wipe she beetee when she coonsie. Lamuta Dave turns father of his own mother. Is a strange thing this, he tells me, confusing.

Sometimes I go to the house to help him, but the woman has a smell that bother me bad, a sick smell that doesn't go away, a smell of pee, and something rotten that makes me want to vomit up. So, when I go there now, I don't try and help Dave clean the lady, I just help feed her food like a baby or give her the three four five six tablets she takes. One and two times, mostly after she just bathe, I comb she long grey hair and tie it behind her head in a rough style. Mostly, though, I sweep the yard and wash out the wares and pull razor grass out from bed in the kitchen garden or train chichira and carilla vine on the arbour.

After that, I sit down under the old house and drink cool limeade swank with Lamuta and gaff man to man about woman and patacake and bubbie and bust big laugh. Mostly is Lamuta talking about this thing and that thing and going on boohoohoo about the troubles of poor people – and how he turn puppy dog killer.

One morning, Lamuta goes to see Uncle Charlie about the work he hear the man have. This Uncle Charlie is a cantankerous man who live by himself and do his own thing. He doesn't take a woman to live with, though he has a son named Junior who plays in the masquerade band. Uncle Charlie is a hunt man who sell wild meat and sometimes burn charcoal. He has plenty of cows and sheep and thing and plant big farm. Is a man people call self-made because is heself that get what he has. Nobody give him anything. Most people are like that here.

After some chitchat, Uncle Charlie says, "Let me show you how it work." He takes Dave to the kennel where he keeps plenty dogs. The place smells bad like dog coonsie and piss. Uncle Charlie brings out a tray with a litter of puppy dog.

"Here's what I want you to do," Uncle Charlie tells Lamuta Dave. "Take them by the neck like so and put them in the bag." Lamuta Dave watch as the old man grab them puppy rough by the neck and drop them into a sisal sack.

"Put three of four of them at a time," the old man says.

Lamuta Dave watch close so he don't forget. All them puppy black and white with wet black noses. They making puppy-dog noise in the dark bag, their bodies worming around in there like wind in a hungry belly.

"Use this," Uncle Charlie says, producing a big cricket bat. Was a Clive Lloyd special make by Gunn & Moore with the great West Indian cricketer's silhouette on the flat side near the handle with a rubber grip. To Lamuta Dave the bat looks too big to beat small puppy with.

"It only takes two or three licks," the old man say, and bring down the bat two time on the bag real quick. Lamuta Dave hears bone break. Puppy noise stop and worming stop. The bag starts to bleed.

"I get fifteen more left," the old man say. "Them bitches breed like flies. If you still want the job, is you own. I going to give you twenty dollars. When you done, take the bag them and dump it in the river."

Lamuta Dave say he tell the man he has to think the job over.

"That man cruel for so," I say as we sit on the step eating boil egg and rice. "Did you take the job?"

"The job don't suit me, at-all, at-all, Kip," Lamuta Dave say, "but I is a desperate man."

"Why he don't kill the bitch them if he don't want puppies?"

"I ask him that."

"What he say?"

"He say them she-dogs is good hunting dogs. He say he can't count on no bull-dog to do the work proper like a bitch, but they useless to him once they get puppies; they hard to manners."

"So, he just keep killing the puppy them?"

"He or the boy he gets to do it. Is a hard thing to do all the time."

"Try the rice mill."

"I go there today, all the way to Burma. The foreman tell me things bad right now."

"Is truth he talking," I say. "Maybe you going have to go thief coconuts like Balram and them in the Letter T Estate."

"I hear the estate watchman shooting people there. A man from Belledrum get kill last month. The watchman shoot he while he high in the tree. One bullet in he beetee. The man get stick-up in the tree and he bleed to death. Was a man named Pennywaller."

"For coconut?"

"Yeah, that is the kind of country we living in."

We get silent for a long time. The mango tree in the yard whispering like market woman. Sound of the sea riding into the village on the back of the wind; hightide breakers crashing and back-lashing on rock at Bary Beach. Inside the house, Ms. Minette cough a cough what sound like liquid shake up in a cover-down bucket.

"Is you turn," Lamuta say. "Give she the medicine in the purple bottle, in the small spoon. Give she the brown tablet in the blue envelope. Let she sit up while you feeding she."

"I know what to do," I say,

"But she is me mother; that count for something."

I get up and go upstairs to Ms. Minette's smelly room.

The woman at the window looking out on the waning light, weighing no more than eighty pounds. Veins in her hand like fine snake crawling under her skin. Ms. Minette turns and looks at me and suffers a smile to paint her face. The smile falters, goes sideways and disappears into a grimace. She reaches with a bony hand for her stomach, bending over so low her forehead hit her knees. I look away like it is a shameful thing I seeing.

I look at everything else except Ms. Minette. I look at the little bed in one corner, at the wall cover-up with old newspaper turn yellow. Frames with fading photographs hang lopsided on the walls. I look at Lamuta Dave's own bedding, fold-up in one corner to be used at night where he sleeps at her footside in case of emergency. The room smell faint of pee and something else I can't place, something I don't know.

"Come close," the woman whisper. Her voice tremble. I kneel down by her side, like a supplicant at the church altar when the roll is called.

"I sick bad today," Ms. Minette say. "The thing cutting me up inside."

"You want the medicine?" I say.

"Yes, the pain licking me up bad."

I bring the medicine, the liquid in the purple bottle and the pills in the little envelope. I put the pills on Ms. Minette's tongue and spoon her the liquid painkiller as a chaser. She swallows painfully.

"What would Mammy do without her good son?" she says, like if me is Lamuta Dave, so I get close to the woman and wave my hand across her eyes them. She just looking straight ahead like a blind person.

"Is me, Kippy, Ms. Minette," I say.

"Kippy boy, Ms. Minette done done done," she says. "I gone for channa."

I think about the dead puppy Uncle Charlie kill. What did the mother do when she finds out she puppies gone from the litter? Panic like any mother when she calls them and they don't come? What if Mamai calling me and I not coming? What if in the thick of her madness, she calling me to rescue her? I start to cry like a skuntian girl with eye-water running down because I forget about Mamai who may be in a madhouse because I is a bad son and abandon her. I look at Ms. Minette and see my own mother in her, with her hair wild on top she head and body thin-thin like pinta.

"I should brush your hair," I say to Ms. Minette.

"Not today," she says.

I remember when Ms. Minette weighed twice as much and tie she head in African style with bright colour cloth what form a tall cone. How long ago that seems now, when I was nine or ten and living in Croft house with Mamai.

When I go back downstairs, Lamuta Dave leaning on the gate looking out on Main Road. I wipe tear stain from my face and come up and lean on the gate beside him.

"I was thinking, Kippy," he says, "that if Mamee dead, I go have no other relative on this earth. None. Not one. I don't even know what village Mamee from; she never tells when I ask. Is like she had no life before I come along."

"I is an incest child, Dave," I say.

He doesn't say anything for a long time. He just shakes his head and looks out on the road, as if wishing for something there.

"I was telling you the story," he says sudden, "bout the puppy dog and Uncle Charlie."

He has to work himself up to kill the first set of puppies. They ready and waiting, worming their little bodies in the sisal sack. The puppy them crying and crying. They sound like small children. He sits with the cricket bat balance across his legs. He looks down at the sack. They just dogs, he tells himself. A puppy bark a small bark. He couldn't use the bat. He picks up the sack and sling it over his shoulder and go down to the river. The morning tide in V-shape wave swift-running north to the sea, water swirling and whirling in quick eddies. The mud of the banks on the other side of the river exposed. Small crab with big pincers dart in and out of holes in the mud.

Lamuta Dave lift the bag with both hands and swing it twice around, like hammer thrower in Olympic, and let it fly. It arc over the river and dive down and sink immediately. The waves rush over it. Lamuta Dave stands watching the water, half-expecting the bag to surface. It didn't. Something in him rears up what makes him want to cry, but he swallows it. Is just survival, he tells himself, medicine for his mother.

Uncle Charlie pays him twenty dollars.

Lamuta Dave walks four miles through three villages to the pharmacy and buy the blue pills for his mother. On his way back he stops at a roadside snackshop in Airy Hall and plays draughts with some Coolie fishermen. He usually good at draughts but not that day. He misses moves, forgets to capture kings, lets his kings get captured.

"You do good," Uncle Percy tells Lamuta Dave. "You is a boy with plenty of heart, strong-strong like a bull cow."

But Lamuta Dave look at heself in he dirty khaki pants and tear-up shirt. He feels shame to see himself so. He stop going to school a long time now – to work in the rice field and weed trench and lift cement block and mind cow and slaughter pig, and wonders if this is all life will be.

16. A VISIT TO CENTRAL

Is morning. Sky dark in the east with big black clouds about to burst, thunder rolling far away. I waiting for Sookuru car to take me to Central when Lamuta Dave stop and tell me another drowned man found in Novar this time. He see the dead man heself when he was walking home from Dundee.

"You can't tell whether he a Black man or not. Animals tear away the man face and suck out he eyes. A little buck crab in his mouth and he bloat up with wind and stink like dead dog. Yeah, buddy, yeah, I see him with me own-own eye. I have to go now, buddy, my mother waiting for her milk."

"Might be Yankee Bai, or Crabfoot, the man who used to live in Boo Leggae bottom house or Big Willie Soto," I say. "Uncle Percy say they leave on *The Amassagana.*"

"Might be, Kip boy," he says, "might be one of them for true. But I gone, man. I have to feed Mamee."

He goes up the road toward Poopaloops shop. Sookuru drives past me and gives me a sign to say he going up the road and coming back. I watch a Coolie girl with long shiny black hair get out of the car. Is Ramdat daughter, Bina, a thing Hari use to play with until he big she belly. She goes away and comes back after five-six months without a baby. Hari tell how he go to Bina people's house in Champlain, how he holler out, "Where is my boy child?" and Bina mother, Hemwattie, comes out and cuss Hari good and proper and throw night soil from her chamber pot over him. Hari don't go see Bina anymore. He calls her a bitch. Bina doesn't talk to Hari. She tells everybody he is a no-good skunt.

Sookuru drives up in his 1954 Saloon II Morris Oxford. The car old bad and have bald tires. I get in and Sookuru driving slow like kreketeh snail, the car coughing and spitting out black smoke. Sookuru always saying he going to buy a new car. He never does. After one old car dies, he gets another old car and another and another. I can see the road right through the car flooring. Sookuru asks about my mother. I tell him maybe my mother dead. I tell him she gone way five days and don't come back.

Sookuru says, "Your mother pretty, boy. When me and she been in school, I use to try a thing with she, but she didn't like Coolie man."

In Airy Hall we stop and pick up Pokey Lotan, who really named Clive Luncheon, who going to Central. Nobody calls him Pokey Lotan to his face because he is a big ignorant man who likes to chop people with his cutlass. We call him Mr. Luncheon. Pokey marry to a fat woman we call Fat Girl though she really name Dulcinea Gray, a dougla who likes to share out the beef and give away the pork to Tom, Dick, and Harry.

Sookuru gets out of the car and helps Mr. Luncheon put about five bags of copra in the trunk. Now the car riding low, close-close to the road, making the bumper scrape and spark on the macadam. Pokey riding shotgun with Sookuru; he smelling like rancid coconut oil.

"Is where all them drown man coming from?" he asks Sookuru, as the car crawl slow into Huntley.

"Nobody know," says Sookuru. "Is three drown man come up already. The police looking for a missing trawler name *Amassagana*. Big investigation start."

"I hear two of them man belly was cut open and pack with stone. You know why that is, Sook?" I say.

"I ain't know that, boy," Sookuru says.

"Well, is so the body get weigh down in the sea and never come up," says Mr. Luncheon.

"So, you telling me some man kill them fisherman?" Sookuru say.

"So I hear, boy, so I hear."

In Central, I get off by the bridge and go into the police station to make a complaint about my missing mother.

A big Black constable says, "Where you father, boy?"

"I don't have father," I tell him.

"Well, you mother probably went and see she man friend. She have man friend?"

"No," I tell the ass.

He laughs and whispers to another constable what standing close by. "Well, maybe she works sodomite," he says.

The two of them laugh *kehkehkeh*. He tells me to take a seat. I sit down next to a drunk man who dribbling on himself and smell like pure pee. After two hours just sitting and smelling pee, I slip out into the sun. I buy a salt-fish float and an ICEE Cola and go down by the wharf on the Mahaicony River to eat and watch fisherman unload fish from the trawlers. Rain starts to fall. I run up the road to see Aunt Esther.

Aunt Esther too fat to get up. She sees me out on the road and hears me calling, "Let me in!" like a child what afraid of a rice-eater dog. She leans out and bust big laugh and say, "But eh eh, is who man-child come see Aunt Esther? Is Kipling Plass. Come out the rain, boy. You is not a stranger here."

I go in and up the stairs. Aunt Esther lalaff in the big Berbice chair on the veranda what full of plants. She like a fat whale with her arms big like lantern post. She has on a frock that doesn't have a sleeve but she smell nice, like Limacol and Ammons talc.

I say good afternoon and sit down in a chair near her. She grabs me real rough and hugs me tight and presses my face into her big flabby bubbies. When I try to get up, she squeezes me tighter, till I nearly stifle and then she lets me go. She laughs out a big laugh and the flesh of her arms jiggle and sway like walrus blubber. Aunt Esther is a real beast of a woman. But she kind and can cook and keep the house good and proper.

"How the fatherless boy doing?"

"I alright," I tell her.

"You not alright," she tells me, and pinches my hand hard with two fat finger. "You fine like trench reed. What your mother feeding you? Never mind. I never see fatherless boys fat."

"Mamai gone," I tell her.

17. THE DEATH OF MS. MINETTE

Lamuta Dave bathing his mother in a half barrel cut long-way and resting on concrete blocks in the back yard under the mango tree. He bring she down the back stairs in his arms like a baby and put she careful in the tub of water, cradling she head high with one hand. The woman naked like the day she born. But when I look at she, I don't think nastiness like I do when I see naked woman; I don't think of sucking she bubbies. I thinking that this woman too thin to live more long. I thinking that Ms. Minette going die soon. Lamuta Dave put a plastic bag over her hair so it don't get wet. The woman eye kick back deep in the head, which like pure bone. She have little strength left, just to wink she eye and move she lips over bare black gum. She making umh umh sound like cuirass what just come out the trench.

"Mamee getting worse and worse," Lamuta Dave say.

He washing under Ms. Minette neck with a soapy nenwah, then under she small, dry-up bubbie, then reaching down in soapy water to wash she patacake and beetee crease. I standing there thinking this is a wrong thing for a son to do. But Lamuta Dave just humming a Sparrow calypso and washing way dirt from his mother skin, she back and now behind she ears them and between she bony shoulder.

Lamuta Dave mother use to be a bush whore in Eteringbang before she take up with a man name Hanson Goveia – who we know as Moron – what use to have a nice size house near the canal in Waterside. He use to mind plenty cow and sheep and had about a hundred head of brindle he pay village boys to mind in backdam. Moron was born bushman. For years he just go in bush and dig gold. When he get old and bruk-up, he take Lamuta Dave mother from the whore house and bring she to live in the waterside house. Moron did have sugar and high blood pressure and need woman hand to take care of his old skunt. Lamuta Dave mother was strong for the job until she get sick with the disease that shrink up she big body good and proper. Not long after, Moron fall down in rice field and dead. Vladimir Goveia, who we soon name Curry Cuirass, come and say he is Moron big son from up the coast and he throw Lamuta Dave and he mother out the house.

In my mind, I still see Curry on that day. He tall, strapping, with a face like a shoe and peeling redman skin what burn easily. I remember him standing on the veranda of the house throwing clothes out the window: panty, brassiere and frocks what flutter in the air before they land in the mud below and Lamuta Dave running to catch then clothes in midair and his mother sitting down in the grass with she head in her hand propping sorrow and moaning soft. It was plenty people standing round, watching the show and whispering, and some protesting. Curry was cussing and carrying on, calling Lamuta Dave mother bad name, whore and prostitute and worse. Is only when somebody run fetch Bhoje that things stop. He talk to Curry Cuirass calmly, the two of them sitting in the veranda, whispering out of earshot. After that, Lamuta Dave go upstairs and take him and his mother things out the house and go live in Sulieman bruk-down house near the burial ground. We never like Curry Cuirass after that. People shun him. His only friend was Hak Deonandan.

Lamuta Dave school days done since then. But wasn't no big loss; he is real big dunce, like Arka big daughter, Clarita. He head not good for sums or reading book. He leave school and straightway start work: shying padi, thiefing coconut, weeding trench for ricefield Coolie man, Mr. Madoo, what own the dry goods store in Novar, and burning coal to sell. But is mostly Bhoje who help keep Lamuta Dave and he mother soul and body seam together with a little freck.

The wasting way disease Ms. Minette have is a thing name leukaemia, a blood disease. Is Dr. Macharan self who say so. Is a monster disease what eating up the woman from inside. Carl say Ms. Minette catch this disease from whoring plenty in Eteringbang. No, the thing don't have nothing to do with nastiness, Bhoje tell us. Is a thing you inherit.

We look at Lamuta Dave to see if we can see sign of the wasting away disease on him. No. He big like ogre giant in fairytale book. He over six feet tall with big-big head on broad shoulder and muscle for so. Already he have hair on his face and chest like big man.

Lamuta Dave take his mother out the barrel of water and fold her in a towel over his shoulder, carrying her like he carry padi bag in rice mill. The woman making cuirass sound like before, only now it sound like she in pain or something.

"Is alright, Mamee," Lamuta Dave say, "is alright, girl; I only taking you back upstairs now."

I standing there looking, when Lamuta Dave look down from top of the step.

"Is alright," he say; "turn over the barrel and come upstairs. I going dress Mamee and put she in the veranda to sun. You want food, buddy? I have food."

He go into the house and I stand there a moment thinking about my mother. Then I start crying like baby again. What if my mother dead like them drown man?

I turn over the barrel of bath water and go up into the house which old but clean like whistle. Wood ants already eat through one wall. You can see sky through the roof over the kitchen. The floorboard worn out from plenty walking back and forth. Sulieman was a Muslim and worship Allah. He never marry nor even have woman friend and he dead without chick nor child. He was a hermit-type man. He dead two days before people find out. We have to put money together to bury him. The house left just so and start rottening cause nobody want live in the place near Sulieman jumbie.

Lamuta Dave in the veranda feeding his mother daal and rice with a baby spoon. He crushing up the rice before he feed Ms. Minette, who just spitting it out like baby. She dress up clean now with talcum powder on her neck and she black face shiny with coconut oil. She smell of Limacol.

"She don't hear nothing," Lamuta Dave say when I sit down with my half calabash of food. "She don't see and she don't talk. But she alive. But is what it mean to be dead not the same as the way she alive? Mamee less than human now. She can't walk or talk or hear. What is she now? Is she alive or dead? I don't know."

"She breathing," I tell Lamuta Dave. "That mean she alive, but it don't mean she want be alive. If she can talk, maybe she say is better she dead. I don't know. Look like she suffering bad."

"What you want, Mamee? You want dead or alive?"

Ms. Minette just sitting there staring, blinking sad and slow.

"What the police going say if I kill Mamee?" Lamuta Dave ask. "She suffering too bad, buddy."

"We shoot horse when they suffering too bad," I say. "Meself see a man named Kundok shoot he horse when it break two leg."

"Alright then," Lamuta Dave say, and go in the house.

I look on the road, which clear. Sun burning down to make the space shimmer with heat. Silence in the village like in library.

Lamuta Dave come back with two pillow and press it down on his mother face and hold it there a long time. I ain't say nothing. I just eat my *daal* and rice and think of my own mother. Ms. Minnette don't fight or say anything. She just make long sigh like wind force through bladder, then she fart a big fart like donkey fart.

"She dead yet?" I ask.

He take away the pillow from Ms. Minnette face. The woman staring back at us with wide-wide eye and mouth open to catch fly. She have on an ugly dead face like if she straining to coonsie over latrine seat. But she not making the cuirass sound anymore. She quiet and gone from everywhere. Lamuta Dave put an ear to her chest and listen. He put two finger by she nose hole to test if she breathing.

"She dead," Lamuta Dave say. "Let we put she on the bed."

We take Ms. Minnette inside and put her on the rickety bed. She weigh much more than she look. We stretch her out and close she eye and mouth. Lamuta Dave crying and carrying on all the time. I tell he to go back to the veranda and sit down while I find coin to put on Ms. Minnette eye.

Lamuta Dave in a state when I leave. He holler down from the veranda for me to toll bell when I get to the church. I do that. I climb up the steeple and pull the rope on the bell and hear it bang bang bang bang until people run out their house saying, *Who dead? Who dead? Who dead*?

I tell them Lamuta Dave mother, Ms. Minnette, dead from wasting-away blood disease name leukaemia.

18. BLACK MARIA

No manjack see who thief the blue Ganesh from the yard of the mandir. People asking how you can thief such a big statue, what heavy like lead. We sitting on the corner of the road looking at the scene. The police them in the yard with Pandit P and Bhoje, walking around and pointing at the ground, at footprints, at the place where the blue Ganesh use to be. Hari drawing circle in the sand with a piece of stick. Carl touching he big tolo through the pocket of his pants. Derek looking at Carl with lustful eyes. A Black Maria pull up and more policeman come out. A couple have gun like filmshow villain or soldier in *The Dirty Dozen*. They go into the yard of the mandir. Satie at the standpipe across the street in front of Bachoo shop letting water gush over she bucket. She looking at me strong-strong like she willing me to come and suck she bubbie. Satie too brazen with her sexy self. I don't feel like sucking bubbie today. I sit between Hari and Carl and feel protected. Anybody that can thief a god from he own house is plenty powerful. Is true that Hari and Carl go end up in Mazaruni prison, but right now they powerful like King Kong self or Prime Minister Burnham. When time ripe, I going ask them how they manage to thief the blue Ganesh. Is not a small thing to my mind. How come nobody see them?

Pandit P look like he arguing with them policeman. They just shaking they head sad-sad like pagla persons and saying nothing at all. The space where the blue Ganesh used to be don't look right – an absence, like Mamai house since she been gone. I miss the sounds she use to make – sound of pot rattling and spoon rubbing up against each other; sound she make when she cooking or humming Methodist hymn over the squeak squeak squeak of washing clothes; even the sound when she piss in a chamber pot before she go to sleep.

Pandit P come out the yard with the police and start point

finger at we, saying in his fine-tune voice, "Is them do it; is them hooligans do it."

Carl say, "I didn't do nothing, Pandit P. Why you always accusing me?"

Bhoje say, "Carl, nobody accusing you of doing anything."

The police look at us strong but don't say nothing.

"How we going thief big heavy god," Hari say. "Maybe this god went back to his house in India."

"You talking pure shit," Pandit P say.

"You mean this blue Ganesh god don't have power like Christian Jesus, son of the most high?"

"Hari," Bhoje say, "have respect. Is big man you talking to."

Hari steups he teeth and get up and walk up the road.

The police drive away in the Black Maria toward town.

Pandit P turn away and go back in the yard of the mandir, holding he head like is mad he mad.

Bhoje standing in the road, looking at us close, as if he can see into we head and read we mind. He ain't saying a word.

"If I find out is one of you did this thing, heads go roll. Since school out, is pure mischief going on. Take you rass out me eyesight before I let you taste my hand."

We get up to leave but he call we back. "I change me mind," he say, "I get work for all-you."

"What the job paying, Bhoje," Carl say.

"The job ain't paying one red cent. We going to burial ground and dig grave for Lamuta Dave mother. Carl, you run quick an tell Rass Mouth send the spade and the pickaxe he borrow from me."

When we get to the burial ground, Bhoje don't know where to weed so we can start digging. Lamuta Dave mother not from the village, so we can't bury her just anywhere. Bhoje standing there with cutlass in his hand, scratching he head. We sitting in the shadow of a neem tree, cooling out among the tombs. The trees them tall and big and block out the sun. It cool there. Some of the tombs green with moss and some cover over with nutgrass. Some paint and some not. Some have writing telling you who born when and what year them bury. Lamuta Dave reading out the name of a man name Jacob McKenzie, loving father of Wendy, Rex, Joy, Paul, Maple, Jonathan, Denise, Bernice, Patrick, Willard – sunrise to sunset.

"I don't know this man, buddy," Lamuta Dave say.

"You too young," Bhoje say. "That is a man named Chung Lap what used to sell clothes and thing on a bicycle."

"It says here the man name Jacob McKenzie," Lamuta Dave say.

"That is he real-real name, but plenty people call he Chung Lap or Long Boots or Uncle Jake," Bhoje say.

We make it a game and start reading off dead people name what already rotten inside tomb and turn jumbie and ghost many years now. Some of them tombs have no name. The rain and wind and sun done wash off the names from concrete.

"Alright," Bhoje say. "We going dig down in the back where they don't get tomb."

We dig under a big calabash tree six feet deep and three feet wide. Bhoje hollering every time we try to take a break.

"What's the hurry?" Hari say. "Ms. Minnette not going anywhere."

Ms. Minnette in Sulieman old house in the same barrel Lamuta Dave use to bathe her. She cover with rice bag sisal and big pieces of slow-melting ice so she don't get spoil before we put she in the mud and root of the ground. Lamuta Dave don't have money to put her in Lyken Funeral Home in big dead people fridge. Two days since the woman dead and gone. Everyday, Lamuta Dave take Sookuru car to Central to buy ice to keep Ms. Minette from spoiling.

Bhoje making a coffin for free. It going take another day he tell Lamuta Dave. He have we planing wood and sanding the coffin top which have a little window in it so that Ms. Minnette can look out on the goings-on of the world. I wonder if the dead know they dead. Is better to be alive, I think, though living not always fun and games. Pain in this life come along with pleasure and sometimes there is more pain that pleasure. Too much pain make man drink poison.

After we done dig grave, Bhoje take we to Dharma rum shop on Main Road. Dharma daughter, Savitri, sweeping the yard. Hari go up to her and say, "Savitri, is long time I want fuck you, you know."

Bhoje slap Hari hard on the back of his head. "Boy, watch your mouth," he say.

Savitri giving Hari a wide smile.

"The girl like me bad, Bhoje," Hari say. "You don't see how she smiling at me with teeth like roast dog?"

Bhoje just push Hari into the shop. Carl at the counter, talking to old man Dharma.

"Give we a half bottle of rum and a Pepsi for chaser."

"Soft drinks for all-you rass," Bhoje say.

"I is big man," Carl say.

"Soft drink," Bhoje say.

"A cold beer then," Hari say. "I can use a cold one."

"Soft drink too soft," I say.

"The only one old enough to drink is Lamuta Dave. How much years you have, Lamuta?" Bhoje say.

"I is eighteen, Bhoje."

"Me too," Hari say.

"You think me born yesterday?" Bhoje say. "You born one year after Dave. I was there when you mother take-in. That mean you is seventeen, like Carl, which mean Kippy is no more than fourteen."

"Fifteen," I say quickly. "Me father give me a little taste of rum plenty time."

"Boy, close your mouth," Bhoje say. "Everybody know you don't have father. Soft drink for everyone."

Bhoje buy a quarter of high wine rum for he and Lamuta Dave, but Carl and Hari begging for a taste all the time so Bhoje pour a cork full into our I-Cee Cola soft drink.

19. THE SEA

I like the sea in the mornings when the water get suck back from the land, leaving starfish and tall sea plant with leaf like flesh stranded there among firewood and seashell, conch and kreketeh, and birds come swooping down from the sky to feast on small fish left in pools of water. Sometimes, the sound of the sea comes into my head and make me forget things and soothe my worry mind. After a time, what the sea saying, I saying too and we become one thing, talking to one another in the same voice. Then I have peace.

Is two miles to Goodfaith Village and I run all the way and back. I don't think about the distance, I just stretch out my leg and run. Before I know it, the distance done.

This morning bright, so I can see far out to sea. A trawler there and white cranes flapping behind it. Then a big ship what fetch cargo moving slow down the horizon line. Is a ship of iron and steel. I imagine it full of white people doing ship work, cleaning and scrubbing down things, like Bhoje and other fisherman do on their boats. The ship so far out it might be in another country.

A woman digging up shell when I get back to Bary. I see her from far away. She sitting near the wreck skeleton of the *Hans Bahlin*. It cant over during a hurricane and drown eight people. That was long time now, when I was six years old, nine years ago. The *Hans Bahlin* still on the beach like the bone of a dead donkey in a pasture. Is a haunted thing, and even little pickney know not to play in it. It was own by a man name Ramdass, a big man with plenty money and thing. Ramdass dead now. He get into a row with his big son Patrick, who chop him up good and proper.

The woman bent over, digging at the sand with a piece of stick. She head tie-up African style with wrap-around cloth, the same as her dress. She have a bucket near her, and she putting in it shell she dig up. When I get closer, I see is Ma Tussette. She don't look up when my shadow fall on her. She continue to dig and put shell in bucket. Is the nasty shell that look like triangle she alone eat.

"Good morning, Ma," I say.

Then she look up at me, with her cloudy milk-eye what frighten small children.

"I did ask meself when manners going come out you mouth. You generation slow to good manners."

"I sorry, Ma."

She get up and dust sand from her tall frock what go all the way down to her foot. She not a smiling person. Everything that come out she mouth is discipline. Is a hard woman to like for long and she don't get better with time. What she do that make we vex is telling truth truth truth, even when she see we hurting from it. The woman don't have sympathy. So when you ask her something, you must prepare yourself for plenty talk what hurt and clarify. The woman mouth don't have cover. That's why I don't like ask she nothing.

"Pick up the bucket and come," she say.

I hungry for so and want to go home and eat but can't say no. I pick up the heavy bucket and follow Ma Tussette to another spot where she sit down again and start digging up more dutty stink shell.

"Get a stick and help Ma, nuh," she say.

I do that. She and me sitting in one place digging up shell. It take about an hour to full her bucket. I know what coming and don't even wait for the witch to ask. I pick up the bucket and start walking back to the village behind she old rass, she clothes making a dry sound like tree branch rubbing up against a house.

At the sluice, she cuss out some boys what passing a rum bottle around and gambling. This woman too much. Them boys just bow down their heads, silent. Them what speak only say, "Yes, Ma," like small children. She call them by name, saying you, Balram; you, Larrick; you, Oswin. Ma have good memory for names and faces. The witch. She send Oswin, a rotten-teeth boy, to fetch water so she can wash mud off her foot. He get up quick and run come fetch the water.

Ma and me sit in the grass in the shadow of the sluice house. Uncle Percy leave his book name *Where the Hummingbird Flies* by this man, Frank Hercules, a Trini, and run come hug up Ma like long lost child. She take his face in her hand and kiss his nose and eyes them.

"But is where you go so early when I pass this morning, Small Bai," Ma say.

"Me sister," says Uncle Percy, "I been out to Central at the police station to answer more questions about them dead man what washing up on the beach. Is a bad thing."

"It bothering me you out here alone when night come," Ma say.

"Never mind that," Uncle Percy say. "I bring something for you from the market."

Uncle Percy turn and go towards the sluice house. Ma sit down on the grass.

Boat tie-up on cleat on the canal bank, rocking back and forth. Cuirass bubbling up and eating fly in the hyacinth bloom. Little fishes what stripe like tiger skating on the water. It brown with leaf-stain, and where a propeller turn it churns muddy. A whole lot of plastic bottle floating round, Jarvex bottle and cooking oil bottle and old seine twine up in the tall grass near the banks. People dump old fridge in there, too. This is the sea side of the canal. Plenty dirty thing come in from the sea. The canal separate in two by a big sluice gate. The village side of the canal clean. We swim there plenty and, when tilapia in season, we use castnet to catch them or feel for them with bare hand when tide low.

Ma Tussette eye corner have spider-web wrinkle. She have a smell like Limacol and sweat and naphthalene ball in trunk of old clothes. She sitting on she bony bamzee humming a song I use to sing in the Methodist Sunday school, a hymn people always sing at funeral. *In the sweet by and by we shall meet on that beautiful shore*. Which means that when we dead, we will meet as jumbie skunt in the afterlife. Mamai say believing in afterlife is for people what don't think. She says the only life man have is this one on earth and the only God is the God of sufferation and death. Mamai say she know this since she small, that God is really a God of hurt and pain. She don't explain, but since I small I know that Mamai god is not the god of the sky. I don't even know if she have a god. I don't think so. I never hear she talk about it. But she talk about church couple time. She like the singing, but the preaching and the teaching is nothing to her – pure skunt. Mamai beetee never touch church pew; she don't believe in no beautiful shore in the sweet by and by.

"All the beauty you ever go see is in this world," she tell me, "and all the life you go ever live is here on this earth and in this time. Afterlife and heaven and the other place is pure Anansi story."

But Mamai don't mind when I go to Methodist Sunday school. She used to ask me what I learn. I tell she how Jonah get swallow in the belly of a whale; how Samson slew the Philistines with donkey jawbone; how Delilah fuck Samson and cut off he hair when he sleeping and make he lose he strength and turn koonoomoonoo skunt, so them bad people can blind he and bind he with big rope and make he into their slave. Is a good story with plenty nastiness and death – like the film show starring Victor Mature.

Ma Tussette, though, is a Jordanite and she sing on road corner with some other sisters dress-up in long white dress. They talk in tongues, saying, "Lacra, malacca, sabacra, tabraca," something, something, "the lord is spirit of love." And she sing, "Oh carry the tiding hohohoh…home," and she knock tambourine on she old leg and stamp she long shepherd crook on the ground in a rhythm. Sometimes, she does dance cumfa in trance and turn up her eyeball so you only see white. Sometimes, she preach a short sermon saying, "See, hear, and feel, children, the work of the spirit who move within and through we, in the dance, in the trance of the drum and the drumbeat, in the tambourine. Feel him, praise him and feel him in you soul. *Malafala, balawala, tafaldamala*, the spirit of the Lord is kind."

I find these Jordanites worship Christ God but they also worship the African spirits of the ancestors. What I like about them is what they call "service". This is a nice fete with plenty food, a freeness what involve dancing cumfa, eating food and knocking drum. Sometimes, when a girl catch cumfa and fall down on the ground, twisting up she hand and leg like a person what having a fit, you get chance to see nakedness. But is the food I like most; it don't have meat in it, but it plenty.

Ma catch me looking at the side of she wrinkle-up face and put she cold eye on me real hard and steups she teeth like she see something there what not regular, something she disapprove of.

People say Ma Tussette can see into the future with her bright eye. I ain't know about that. Is a serious god-power thing. Human beings don't have such power. But Ma know plenty thing other human don't know. Maybe she know where my mother is; maybe Ma see Mamai in she obeah eye. I want to ask her, but I don't know how to ask. Ma don't do nothing for free.

Rotten-teeth Oswin come back with water and start wash Ma foot with his hand. Ma sitting back in the grass looking down at Oswin head with his big Afro. When he done, he stand there waiting, like he want to ask she something.

"No," she say to him. "The girl don't like you. Find another one."

Oswin turn and walk away slow with the empty bucket beating against his leg. Uncle Percy come with big parcel of dry fish and give it to Ma and hurry back to the sluice house.

"The boy need to see dentist before all he teeth rotten away in he stink mouth," she say.

Ma stand up and I follow with the heavy bucket of dutty shell, which I put on my head to balance it.

"Ma," I say, but before I can say more word, she answering my question.

"Boy, you mother in Berbice Mad House in Fort Canje."

She don't say nothing more and I don't say nothing. The walk home longer than it ever been and the bucket heavy like blacksmith anvil on my head. I want to cry but can't. I just walking and looking but not seeing. I want to scream but I don't have strength in me. We turn away from the waterside, down the dam that lead to Main Road. Walking in front of me, using her stick, Ma look older today. She body slightly twist to one side and she have a hop and drop limp. I never notice that before.

When we get to Ma house, she go up and sit on the veranda to rest she old legs. I sit down on the back stairs shucking shells, crying and crying and crying for Mamai.

20. STRANGE LOVE BUSINESS

Derek crying and carrying on, saying how Carl doesn't love him. We in Tantie Lane cake shop on the road corner eating buns and drinking mauby. Sun bright and shining hot. Derek trying to beat me at draughts for an hour. I don't understand this man with his girlie ways. But I don't say so because me and he is friends. But he is a puzzle to me. How can a man want kiss-up man and get buggered? I don't know. We don't know any man like Derek around here. Derek destined to get beat up everywhere he goes because this place doesn't tolerate slackness.

"He don't love me back," Derek saying.

"How he going love you," I say. "Carl is man what love girl."

"I love he bad."

"Maybe what you want is to try out a girl," I tell him. "Maybe you going like it plenty, touching girl patacake and kissing up she mouth and bubbies them."

He doesn't say anything to that. He just pushes his piece across the draught board so I can eat his king.

"I don't know, Kippy," he says.

"I going take you and see Satie," I tell him. "She going to change the way you think. Once you suck girl bubbie, you not going prefer no nastiness with man."

"Alright," he says, "alright."

Satie in the pigpen downwind of her father's house. There is no house behind hers. Is open pasture of crabgrass and black sage and bellyache bush where sheriga live plenty all year. If you want sheriga, come out here with a bag and a grass knife and get all you want for a curry. The place is always muddy, though, and full of mosquito and sandfly. Is not a place to build a house. It too low and when the trench overflow, it drown the whole place. But is a good place for a pig pen, not for cow though. When cows eat crabgrass they get sick and dead.

We cross a little trench to the pasture. We can see Satie leaning over the pigpen fence, bamzee in the air, shaking out a bucket of slop into the trough. Pig making piggy noise, going weeeeee, weeeeee, weeeeeee. The place smelling high to rass. We come up behind Satie and look in the pigpen. Four big sows in there. One lay down with eight piglets sucking her bubbies. The pig pen separated into four parts. One part for each sow.

"That one over there eat all she babies," Satie say. "She had ten. She just eats them. I ain't know why, but this thing bothering me too bad, man Kippy man. I feel like poisoning that pig. Why she do that, Kip boy?"

"I ain't know," I tell her.

"Maybe she hungry bad," Derek says.

Satie gets down from the pigpen and looks at us.

"If is bubbie you come to suck, Kip boy, is not a good day. A man suck up me bubbie proper last night. He bite me too. He is a dutty man." She bust big laugh.

"Satie, you does like too much man," Derek says.

"I hear you like man too," Satie says, "you with you funny ways."

"That is what people think," I say. "Derek girly-girly, but he like plenty girl. He like you and want suck up you bubbie. Is why I bring he."

"Where the money?"

I give Satie a dollar.

"This for you or the auntie-man?"

"I tell you Derek not no auntie-man," I say. "He likes you."

Satie doesn't say anything. She just *steups* her teeth, pull out she hand them from the frock sleeve and roll down her dress to her waist so she bubbie free in the air. She have nice bubbies that feel like another tongue in you mouth when you kiss them. Satie sits down and braces her back against the pigpen wall.

"Come then," she says. Derek moves closer and starts to suck Satie bubbie. Satie looking down at him all this time and rolling she eyes them like don't-care pickney. Derek making slurping sound, then coughing sound. Then Derek raise up he big head and vomit up all over Satie bubbie them. Vomit look like pumpkin stew and fish and particles of green grass. Satie let go a loud scream and knee Derek in he face and run quick and jump in Cross Trench water *boodung bup splash.* Derek still on his knee coughing up pieces of vomit.

"You don't like it?" I say.

"She smells like pig," he says.

"She smell like she self," I tell him. "She smell like Satie. She just not who and what you want smell. You is a real skunt."

"I try, Kippy," he says, "I try."

Satie still washing off in the trench when we leave. She cussing and carrying on as we walk past, calling Derek lowdown dirty skunt names. We ain't say nothing. Was nothing to say.

We walk to Canal Dam down to the sluice to watch fishing trawler come in. I vex with Derek too bad. Now I have to think of another way to cure his girly behaviour. Maybe he needs obeah potion from Ma Tussette or prayer from the most high God of Adventist and Methodist church. Maybe he needs Jesus Christ as his saviour, to save him from working sodomite buggery. Maybe Pandit P has poultice for the business.

Uncle Percy on the sluice house landing reading a book name *To Sir, with Love* by E.R. Braithwaite. He doesn't even look away from the page when we say, "Good afternoon, Uncle. Uncle Percy, good afternoon." So we just go up the dam and leave him licking his finger and turning page like a man in a trance. I think Uncle Percy marry book; he have no wife nor children, just book all over his house. And now that he almost ninety, no chance he going get wife or child. Is he and book, until death do part them. As far as I know, he never interested in woman or in man for nastiness. Maybe, long before I born, he come to the end of a woman or two or three. It looks to me like a stupidy and strange choice to choose a book over bubbie and nice patacake, strange and not regular. It is almost as strange as Derek choosing man over woman, tolo over patacake, nasty hairy man chest over soft sweet bubbie with lollipop nice nipple of sweetness. How come?

I am thinking maybe I have to get a nice clean girl like Simone, who full of loveliness, to let Derek kiss up she bubbie so it changes him good and proper into boy what like patacake instead of tolo. I have to try to see how this business work.

Derek walking behind me crying like the biggest baby in the

whole world. Chupidness. I stop and wait for the stupidy skunt. When he catch-up, I put my hand round his shoulder and kiss his big head and say, "Is alright, is alright." And he stops crying, the skunt. I take my shirttail and wipe his eyes them and slimy snot what coming out his nose. Nastiness and stupidness skunt. Derek not prepare for the regular world.

I walk on home, imagining that when I get home Mamai will be in the kitchen cooking some nice thing, or rolling out cheese roll dough on the kitchen table. Even if she just sitting in the window and staring out at nothing at all, I still go be pleased because she is home where she belong. But when I get home, the house, as I know it will be, still quiet the same, an absence you can't full with anything else. I sit down on a chair in the veranda and look out into the pasture.

I see Anita near the cowpen, pulling a heifer to the back fence post. She straining with the cow what stubborn and don't want to move. She stops in the middle of pulling and stand still like she is weary. Then she goes behind the cow and lashes it with the rope that's tied around its neck. The cow start to run and pull Anita forward till she stumbles and falls. The cow pulls her through the tall grass. I run downstairs after her. When I get there, the cow has stop and Anita tying up the rope on a courida tree stump. She knee bruise up and bleeding. We go and sit down under another courida tree nearby so I can tend to her knee. She sits down with her back brace against the tree and I kneel in front of her, cleaning she knee with my handkerchief.

"Mamai in the madhouse," I say.

"I know," she says. "Is Simone what tell me when I see she at Dado shop this morning."

"You knee hurting?"

"No, just burning a little. Sit down, man Kippy man."

I sit down by her and she leans she head sideways on my shoulder and close her eyes. She takes my hand and puts it on her lap.

"You love me, Kippy boy?" she says in a soft voice.

"I love you," I say, "I always love you."

"Not when you first see me, though. You proper use to pinch me up when you see me in schoolyard. Is like you wanted to make me cry."

"I wanted you to see me," I say.

"I see you. I like you all the time."

"Is you what make headmaster clap licks on me. Remember?"

"Yes. And since then, is just me and you, boy, me and you."

"Me and you," I say.

And for no reason at all Anita starts to cry. She doesn't cry hard. She cry soft like Mamai. I feel eye water running down into my shirt collar where she head resting and I feel her body trembling next to me. I hold her close and we silent sitting under the courida tree for a long long time.

21. SUNDAY MORNING

Naked Jesus wink at me. He's on the cross, hanging up on the church wall, behind the rostrum. I look again but nothing happens. Is just a carved-wood white man nail on a tree, pain on his face, wearing a crown of thorns. The preacher, a tall dark man in spectacles, wearing a suit and tie, though the temperature is a hundred degrees in the shade, has sweat dripping down his face. His sermon is about the goodness of good men and the badness of bad men, and how the Lord in his wisdom condescend to spare the righteous and punish the wicked. "I say to you, my brothers and sisters, if you do unto the least of my brethren, you do it unto me, because the least is most in want of more, and the more we have is the least most of us give away, so that our more is never done, but the man with least has less, and then nothing at all. If them that have most will share, and them in less want will share, then none of us will need. Let us share," he says.

He confuses me good and proper. Just as soon as I hear the sermon, I forget it. I just listen to Sister Melba sing and feel alright. She's fat and broad like a fridge. Her face is dark and round like a full moon. She sings a nice church song my mother always sing, a song Jim Reeves perform on a record, saying how, *Across the bridge there's no more sorrow, across the bridge there's no more pain, the sun will shine across the river and you'll never be unhappy again.* Sister Melba put her blackness into the song and make it sad and mournful. Is nice to know there is something better somewhere else.

Sun shining hard when I come out of the church. I stand in the yard under the belltower looking up at marabunta building nest in the belfry. Carl standing nearby, trying to hold Simone's hand, pulling her hard against him, saying, "Girl, I dream about you two times this week; we was doing nastiness. Come let me touch you nice bubbie, let we run behind the courida tree."

Simone says, "Boy, stop nuh, boy." Simone too beautiful.

Every boy in the village except me in love with her. She knows it too and makes us compete to carry her book when schooltime come. But if you only look at Simone, her father, a man we call Lickamore Chops, who really name Layton Edmonds, ready to chop you with a cutlass. He too protective. Simone is the kind of girl who suffers from too much love. Girls like her bound to rebel and start to choose wrong. Is then her mother and father will learn a hard lesson. Children not like dogs on a lead or cow tie-up on a pasture tree trunk.

"I want taste you tongue," Carl says, and tries to grab Simone's hand again. But she bruk-way and runs out the churchyard to Main Road and gone.

I agree to meet Carl later to play drafts at Tantie Lane shop. First, I want to see Bhoje to talk to him about Mamai. I walk to Bary to the big house paint pink near the dam. Is the biggest house in Bary and use to belong to Mr. Haynes what dead plenty years gone. Is Bhoje wife house now. Bhoje have plenty cow and sheep, and a combine what cut rice and a tractor what plough the field. He has land and a big shop in front of his yard which sells all kinds of things, and he has three fishing trawlers. Before he turn rich, he was just a poor coolie skunt, son of Rass Mouth, a man what fixes leaks in pots and mend shoes. Bhoje mother, Sweet Baby, was a little dry-up woman who sick bad with sugar and blood disease. I hear she talk only one time. The woman quiet bad. She so small I ain't know how she give birth to a big giant man like Bhoje.

Rass Mouth, who really name Gangaram, is a small doukouna man. We call him Rass Mouth because every sentence he speak has rass in it; like "bring that rass bucket over here," or "boy move you rass," or "this sun hot like rass." Rass Mouth doesn't get vex when you call his false name. Sweet Baby dead when car knock her down on Main Road and run over her head. Rass Mouth take another lady quick-time name Nora Darlin, whose real name is Indrani Ramgoolam, from somewhere in Corentyne, and he start to make babies with her quick, like a man running out of time.

Bhoje wife, Jenny Haynes, is a Black woman who not so black; she light-skin with long coppery hair and a white white smile and eyes what look green. We call her Ms. Haynes or Bhoje wife; she doesn't have a false name. This woman is a doctor, but not a doctor of human body or cow body – a vet. The way Bhoje explain it, Ms. Haynes is like a doctor of stars and things of sky and cloud, something call astronomy, and is true this woman always peeping-up at the sky through a big glass-eye engine and writing what she sees in a little book. I see she plenty of time doing this chupidness. The glass-eye machine is on the front veranda all the time. She is a lecturer at UG. We see her only on weekends. Sometimes she stays away for many months and this make Bhoje have to take plenty sweet woman in a secret style.

Is she I see first when I come in the yard. She sitting on the back step reading a book name *Wide Sargasso Sea* by a white woman name Jean Rhys. Bhoje wife is pretty, bad. She gives me her white, white smile and I fumble to get out "Good morning" from my tie-tongue mouth.

"I come see Bhoje to help get Mamai out of Berbice Mad House," I tell the Haynes woman.

She ain't saying nothing. She just looking at me like I am something to inspect closely, like stars through her glass-eye machine. Then she gets up and closes the book and smile.

"He went to sea," she says in proper English, like an actor in *My Lover, My Son*. "Come in," she says; "let's have tea."

We don't have tea. We have orange juice and a nice biscuit from a tin in what say Nestlé on it I never see before. I know them thing ban from Guyana. But I eat and drink and Ms. Haynes tells me to take more. So I do, and when she not looking, I slip two biscuits into my pants pocket. The woman looking out at the road like she lost away.

"What's your name?" she says.

"Kipling," I say, "but people call me Kippy."

"Kip," she says like she trying to taste my name on her tongue. "Kipling, like the writer?"

"Yes," I say.

"Kip, what happened to your mother? You said she is in the Berbice Mental Hospital."

"I don't know, Miss," I say.

"Jenny," she say.

"I don't know, Miss Jenny. My mother went to get ban flour at Springlands and she hasn't come back. Is Ma Tussette what tell me she is in the madhouse. So, I go see Aunt Esther and she tells me a story. She says my mother was carrying ban flour when police stop her. But when they search her body and feel she up, she gets vex and run-off; so, they put she in the madhouse."

"You don't believe this Aunt Esther?"

"I ain't know. She just like talk and tell stories. The way thing happen is not how she tell it. She add thing and subtract thing and divide and multiply thing, so what you end up with is lie and truth mix up – like true lies."

"Where are your siblings?"

"Sibling?" I say. "What you mean, Miss Jenny?"

"Where are your brothers and sisters?"

"Is only myself, Miss Jenny."

"You are an only child?"

"Yes."

"Where is your father?"

"I don't have father, Ms. Jenny," I say. "I is my mother son."

Ms. Jenny just watch me and smile. I just drinking up her free orange juice and eating up her biscuit good and proper.

"So, your name is Kipling?"

"Yes Miss, my mother get it from a book she use to read."

"Plass is your surname?"

"Yes. Is my mother's name."

"You know a man name Edgar Plass?"

"No Miss, the only Plass I know is me and me mother, and Mr. Plass what stay in Zekendren."

"I am talking about the same man," she says. "We went to school in England. What is he like now?"

"Like, Miss?"

"How does he get on?"

"Get on, Miss?"

"Behave."

"He quiet-quiet. He works in the rice field and read plenty of books. But he doesn't read, I think. He just searching in them book for something. He have a way."

"A way?"

"He not regular; he doesn't talk regular and walk regular; he not like people around here. He more like you."

"You look like him when he was young. He was very bright and very kind, and quiet, tall like you and thin, a runner too. I see you running past in the morning."

"Aunt Esther says he is me father. She says I is a incest child."

"It's an old story," Bhoje wife says. "I did not know your mother well. I knew Edgar. A long time ago something terrible happened to him and your mother. They have a bond. Terrible things happen to people all the time, Kip."

She looks out over the banister toward the road and starts one big crying. I don't say anything or do anything. I don't know what to do. I just eat a biscuit and watch eye-water come out her eye. She doesn't even say anything when I get up and leave her on the veranda crying big *boohoohoo* long-water tears.

My mother, when she cries, cry silent as if she doesn't want people to hear. Sometimes she makes no sound. Sometimes she just sitting and eye-water flow small rivers down her fine face. This can last days. Them times I have to fend for myself and stay out she mad way. Them times she doesn't eat any food. Them times just tears flowing plenty in a silent way.

Ms. Jenny, though, cry with noise. She have a hiccup cry as if she trying to get something out that doesn't want to leave her body, something like a fish-bone stick-up in her throat. Ms. Jenny shakes and starts and stops; her whole body shake like leaf on a tree. She goes, "How, how, how, how," in a short sad moaning way that makes me sad, too, like when I listen to a sad love song by lovely and sweet Pamela Maynard. Mayhap something bad happened to Miss Jenny. I going to ask Bhoje about this.

Up the road I see Kangalang Harry Arnold sitting under the big calabash tree near Cross Dam, digging he seed. He stinks like pee and the rags he wearing don't cover he big black tolo what hanging out he tear-up pants like donkey tolo, and he tolo hair dirty with mud and piece of grass and thing. He has a dirty beard too and dirty Rasta hair, but he is not any dread. He is a mad skunt.

Kangalang Harry Arnold mad since before I born. What made him mad, though, nobody knows for sure. Bhoje says Kangalang turn mad after he comes back from being dead. Bhoje says Kangalang was a big-time bushman long time ago and get drown in a deep hole in Ekereko. When he crew mati find he floating in the water, they put he down for dead and had he on ice waiting for a plane to take he dead self out the forest. But Kangalang comes back from being dead. That was twenty years ago. He doesn't talk after he wakes up, not much. All he says is, "Ekereko." Is an answer to any question and a question for any answer. When he's hungry and want food, he points to his mouth and says "Ekereko." He sleeps where he wants to sleep and eats mostly fruit from trees, like sakiwinki monkey. Sometimes people who cook for him have to look hard to find him. Kangalang can sleep in coconut trees and chicken coop. Mostly, he likes to sleep in boats by the sluice or on burial ground tomb.

When I come near, he stops dig he nasty seed and smell he hand and wipe it on his raggy-raggy pants.

"Ekereko," he says, and points to his mouth.

"Ekereko," I say. "You hungry?"

"Ekereko," he says. I take out the biscuit I thief and hand them to Kangalang. He smiles his rotten teeth smile and stuffs them in his big dutty mouth.

As arranged, I meet with Carl to go to Tantie Lane shop for a mauby and draughts. When we go in, Tantie Lane daughter, Marcel, behind the counter.

Carl says, "Marcel, is long time me and you don't kiss up, girl. Remember that time behind latrine in Dado yard? Me and you girl, me and you."

Marcel doesn't answer him. She just put the soft drink and buns we order on the counter and run in the back room.

"Why you have to hurt her?" I say.

"I ain't hurt her," Carl say. "I only tell the truth. Me and she nearly do wickedness one time. We come close. She have nice bubbies."

Carl beat me the first two games.

"My mother in Berbice Mad House," I tell him.

He doesn't look up from the draught board. He looking at how to catch my king, though he hears me.

"Who says so?"

I tell him.

"That obeah witch know plenty things. So how we going get her out this madhouse place?"

"I don't know, Carl man."

"Well, I going put me mind to it and see what come up."

I make a move on the board. Carl makes a move and huffs my king.

Is then Lamuta Dave comes in and says the police identify the next drown man as Willie Soto, the captain of the *Amassagana*, though they can only tell from the clothes he wear.

"This the third one," Carl say. "Dead man washing up all over the place."

Willie, I don't know well; is a man who keep himself to himself, but he have a wife who we know as Mi Amor, a pretty woman who one time would buy the cakes Mamai make and I sell on my bicycle from a wicker basket, who always use to talk to me and treat me nice.

22. A BURIAL AND A VISIT

Willie Soto dead and gone, buried quick in his straight house. The coffin was closed, rightly so. What was inside didn't favour Willie at all. The man spoil from floating around dead in sun and rain and salt water. Nothing was strong enough to ward off the stink coming from the coffin. We burn sage and spray perfume, but stink overcome nice scent and reign like king in the place. At the funeral, we standing around holding hankerchiefs over our noses and covering our mouths with our hands. We anxious to get the body down inside the hole, throw in the dirt, and done. I was standing next to Bhoje and Hari and a couple other people from nearby villages, but not too many. Is a small funeral. Nobody crying, shedding long-water tears. Nobody singing hymns in the old style. I only go there to see Mi Amor again and pay my respects to her. She standing by she self under the calabash tree near the grave, alone and sad. She left the scene quick when the thing was done.

Willie wasn't like Mi Amor. He was a stranger even after living plenty years in the village. We know nothing about the man before he come to Mahaicony. Mi Amor was what Willie call his wife, so we called her that, too. Big Willie was what she called he, and we did the same. He was a brown man with more of a whiteman look. Story go that he was from one of the Spanish-speaking islands or the Caribbean side of Columbia or Belize. We know he as driver of plenty kinds of vehicles: cars, combines, tractors, trawlers, and he could fix them, too, so they work. People like this about he, the skill he had with machines, but nobody got close enough to the man to say that he was so and he was such; to we he was just a mystery. He did not laugh or smile or talk much. He was a big man, tall and strapping, older than Mi Amor. They had no children.

Two days after we bury Big Willie, I borrowed Bhoje's bike to ride out to see Mi Amor. But rain fell overnight, leaving the dam clumped up with mud so I had to leave the bike in bushes near roadside and walk, slipping and sliding along the way. I worried bad about Mi Amor. She had no family around, and she and Willie lived in Recess, which was remote, south along the Danraj Dam, far inland from Main Road, beyond where there was electric light and lantern posts, and running water from a standpipe. It was half a mile from the nearest neighbours.

The place had been total bush when they moved into a house and yard belonging to an old couple called Means, abandoned when they died and their son left for Foreign. Creepers climbing up from cracks in the concrete yard tore boards from the side of the house and went on to grow inside. Lichen greened up the side of the house and animals moved in. We never knew whether the son had sold the house or whether Big Willie and Mi Amor just squatted. We never asked. But one month after they moved in, they'd cleared the land, replaced the rotten boards and put new galvanise on the roof. Not long after, we notice animals in the yard – chickens, ducks, sheep, a cow and her calf, geese, guinea hens – and a new fence around it to keep them in and keep goats out, or they ate everything. Mi Amor plant a kitchen garden behind the house and when I visited with the cakes, I saw guava and genep and gooseberries, sapodilla, stinking toe, mango and mamey, and tall suckers of bananas, cherries, and soursop.

They keep the place spick and span, and if you walk near, you bound to see them in the yard at some hard, back-breaking labour. But it was not regular for people to come so far from the road, except when they hunt for accouri and labba or raid the spice and turpentine mango trees when they in season. Mi Amor and Willie come to Main Street only to buy food and other things from the shops, or to sell greens and ground provision at the market. They were strangers mostly and stayed so, never inside our circle. Willie, especially, seemed to like it that way. He was stand-offish and quiet – speaking English like a Cuban or not speaking at all. He was never seen guzzling daru in the rum shops with the men.

It was Mi Amor we like. She was funny and light, a laughy-laughy girl who like crack joke to put you at ease. Is she I talk to when in the early days I went around selling cakes on my bicycle. This was before Mamai baked just for the shops. Mi Amor always buy from me, so riding down the dam to their place was a guarantee of a sale and I did it all the time, even though it was far. Me and she use to sit on the steps and gaff while Willie did things in the yard. Sometimes Mi Amor talk to he in Spanish – which impressed me – and she tell me it was he who teach she Spanish, and she teach him English. They were a real lovey-dovey pair, always touching one another and saying kind, gentle words, holding hands and what not, and smacking lips in front of everybody. Such public niceness was not regular. But the two of them secretive too, holding themselves apart from us, living in a different world while still part of the village. She doing the talking while he silent by she side like bodyguard. Sometimes I think she was the big boss man in the house, the way he let her take charge of things when dealing with other people.

Mi Amor was standing in the yard when I get there, hanging frocks upside down on polythene string tied up between two carambola trees. A mangy mongrel got up wearily from its spot under the genep tree and barked at me. Mi Amor shush the bitch and walk over to the gate. She was smiling. I did not expect this. I expected her to be sad, in tears, unable to rouse herself from her bed of grief. But she look regular to me, even a little happy.

"You come and see if I alright, nuh?"

"Yes," I say.

"I alright, man Kip man. Come in and close the gate behind you. Never mind Rosy; that bitch can only bark; she don't have teeth to bite. But you whole foot cake up with mud; go and wash yourself off by the gutter cistern."

I did, then sit on her veranda while she go into the house. Hummingbirds darting about the place, dipping their long beaks into bells of flowers along her fence. The air was ripe with the smells of fruit and dried cow dung. Mi Amor come back with a little tray with glasses of soursop juice and coconut biscuits and put it on the little table between us. She sit in a Berbice chair with her long legs stretched out. She sigh, pick up her soursop juice, sip it, put it back down, and sigh again. There was a smell to her, of sweat yes, but something sweet too, something fruity, like passion fruit or semitu. I liked her smell. I liked her face too, which was shaped like a heart, small with smooth dark skin and a wide mouth, eyes big and bright like moongazer eye.

"Kip boy," she say, "I don't know how long I can stay in this place since Rafael gone. It get too lonely. I never been afraid before. But now is like I lose my nerve. And the work too much. I can't keep up with it."

"Big Willie name is Rafael?"

"Yes, Rafael Sotomayor. You is the only person except me that know he real name now in this place."

"What is *your* real-real name?"

"Myra George. That is not a secret."

"Is to me," I say. "Everybody think you name Mi Amor."

She laugh her nice laugh, covering her mouth with her small hand.

"Mi Amor is Spanish. It means my love."

I look at her close. She was maybe twenty-seven or so, small and tight, with nice breasts and long thick hair she tied behind with a piece of cloth. There was hair in her armpits, dark and shiny, and I found this very sexy, pleasing to me, and I trembled inside. Suddenly, I was aware that me and she were alone, far from other eyes.

"The man didn't speak good English when I meet he," she said, "just the Español and the French Haitian talk, because before he touched down here in Guyana, he live in Haiti and get to learn their palawala, but when I first know him he couldn't string together five sentences of English. But I like he, big as he was and clumsy. Though he was good with machines, he was always bumping into things and falling off heights of ladders and rooftops. People laugh at him and say the red man stupid, the red man dunce. That is what they call he, red man, though some call he Big Willie because he so strong and strapping. He tell them he called Soto, but it was really Sotomayor. He would laugh about things and I never get what was the laughing matter. I see this big man trying as hard as he could to avoid trouble, trying hard not to bring attention to himself. They laugh and he laugh and so it go. When I first knew him, he was with Margaret – Margaret George, my uncle's daughter on my mother's side, my first cousin. She get tired of them laughing at she man and she get vex at he for it, and take it onto she self to insult he as well, cursing and carrying on in the rum shop and calling he names. He just smile. He hardly understand what Margaret saying and she couldn't understand why a man of his size and power allow Tom, Dick and Harry to disrespect he without lifting he big hands and cuff them down left and right. She become ashamed of he. She see he not as man but as manatee.

"Margaret tell me he from the Dominican Republic. 'Dominica?' I ask her. 'No,' she says, 'Dominican Republic.' I never hear about this Caribbean nation. True I didn't get far in school, but I am not no dunce. Is just that geography was never my best subject.

"Is through Rafael that I get to know about the place and how he couldn't go back there because of the political situation he get involve in, where people get shoot with guns and chopped with machete. He had to fly far from that rigmarole. By the time he tells me this, he was my man and Margaret was out of the picture – gone from Grove with the soldier man she meets in Tempe at a blues dance. I don't want you to think that I thief the man from my own-own cousin, Kip boy. Is true that the first time me and he eyes make four, I get trembly inside and soft and open like flower petals. It was not like me to feel so soft about a man, because they mostly cheap to get and easy to dashway like dutty water. I did have three before Big Willie. Two weren't more than boys, fumbling to feel my breasts and touch me up, good to practice sucking tongue with and walk around with, holding hands on the village road. The other one, Clemsford Morgan, did use his hand on me once in a not-loving way and make my face black and blue. I go to Hope and tell my brother and he make Clemford what people call he today: One Hand Clem. He still lives in Grove with a hook for a hand. My brother did that for me. Is so I was dear to him, God rest he, bless he soul. Them policeman should never have shoot him up so and leave me brotherless in this big world. He was as big as Big Willie and just so sweet. People frightened bad of him, and he would say, 'My sister, them woman so frighten of me I can't even get close before they start scream murder.' He was lonely and wanted to dead so them policeman killed him.

"Is true that I covet Big Willie in a secret way, but I never thief the man from Margaret. I did covet he in the Bible way, like David covet Batsheba, but I didn't send Uriah upfront to die in any war. No, never, never. Ask Margaret if you think I lying. I never do anything to her. I only covet. Is a small sin. You is a bright boy and you know what covet means? It means to desire what belongs to another person. Is a sin. I guilty. What more I must say? I did love he without knowing he, and I did feel, though he never say the words, that I was already his darling girl. Knowing this make it hard to be in the same place as the man, because the feeling between we two was strong-strong. The thing gets so that every time we meet, we drawn to each other, wanting to touch, to feel, to hear, and be near one another. It was like torture self. But we resist the force of nastiness, which is a big force. Then he falls off the rooftop of a high house and almost break his neck. This was in Danzig up the coast. They take him to the hospital and two days later news come saying the man kick the bucket and dead. I bawl like a banshee to hear this, knowing how all I needed to say was not said and how all I wanted to do was not done; how all the fantasy I make in my heart would never be fulfil. But the news was rumour, a fart of wind. By this time, Margaret gone with she soldier man to the city, to live with him in Ayanganna. I go and tell she what happen to Big Willie. She says, 'He not me man anymore; take he if you want he. Me did see how the two of you always lusting after one another; you the bitch in heat and he the dog following and sniffing you backside for the opportunity. Goweh, you rass! You is a dutty girl and thief of man.' She cursed me, Kip, lashed me good with she hot tongue. I didn't say anything to the bitch. I just leave the yard and go. I hear her laughing behind me. Love is never secret, Kip; it bound to show itself in some way.

"They tell me that he in the general hospital and I make my way there quick to get he out that place before the hospital kill he. He in the hospital ward looking very much alive. When he see me come in, a smile blaze up he face. He say, 'Mi amor' – like me and he together for years. I go over there and sit in the bed beside him. He takes my hand and kiss it one two three four five times and says, 'Mi amor, mi amor, mi amor.' And I say, 'Tell me your name' and he say, 'Beeeeg Willie.' 'No,' I say, "Tell me your real name.'

"Is then he tell me is Rafael Sotomayor and I could see that he frightened to say his own secret real name. Then I ask him how he came to be here, but he wouldn't tell me. I press him and he say, 'No, mi corazón, por favor no preguntes.' Tell me, I say again and again, and he only speak to me in Spanish. He say, 'Mi amor, es un secreto… Mi amor, no me amarás después… Mi amor, acreage para poder susurrarte solo a ti.' Tell, me, I say again, and I pull the blind around us in that ward where there was no privacy and I lie down next to him and he whisper his story in his bad English. I can't tell you because I promise never to tell. Is a sad sad story and now that he dead and gone is the thing we share, like his name. Is the story that make me cry sometimes, Kip, not the death."

"You don't feel sad?" I say.

"I not sad, Kip. Death don't make me sad. It make me want to live. I just planning how to live. I can't plan how to die. That is not up to me. I want a baby and Rafael didn't have it in him to give me a baby. His seed wasn't strong. We quarrel before he went out and dead. It was over money and wanting baby in my womb and wanting ring on my finger so I can say I is he wife and he is my husband. The marriage thing was vanity. I could have live without that. It was a small thing. But how do you know that your conversation with someone going be the last? What we must do is make every conversation good and kind."

I pick up my soursop juice and take a big gulp. It cold and sweet.

"What will you do now?"

"I don't know," she say. "I don't know. I must find a father for the baby I must get. That is the thing to do. You want to be the father of my baby, Kip? I see the way you looking at me with your young wutliss self."

"I don't know," I say.

She laughed. Her laugh was pleasant with sadness in it.

"You won't know," she say. "You yourself is baby."

She was silent for a while, then she cried. It was a soft cry, but it lasted for a long time. I sat with her and did not say a word until she told me she was okay and thanked me for coming to see how she was. I thanked her for the juice and left.

23. FISHERMAN 3

Big Willie Soto wake up foreday morning next to Myra who snoring loud. The place tar dark. Sun still sleeping in the sea. Mosquito whining in his ear, mango tree limb rubbing up against the side of the house like ghost trying to get inside. He crawl out from under the mosquito net and stand looking down at Myra, one of she nice bubbie coming out the nightie with nipple sticking up. He think maybe he should wake her rass and do a little nastiness before daylight come. But no, not this morning. Last night, he and she had big row over money. She didn't have none and he didn't have none and she saying is man what supposed to bring the money and feed her and clothe her and put ring on she finger. And is when he going marry she after so many years living home, cleaning and cooking for he rass, and giving he she patacake and she bubbie them and she life, Eh! Eh! When is the time he going put diamond and gold ring on she left hand finger so she can call herself Mrs. Soto; and when he going have enough money so they can add another room to the house in case baby come?

This is when he make the mistake and tell she that no baby coming cause maybe she barren. How she go make baby all of a sudden when they together for five years and he giving she he seed three-four time a week and still no baby; how nuh, tell me? She start one crying and right away he realise he gone too far; right away he vex with himself for hurting she. She cry and cry the rest of the night, even when she put food in front he on the table. He feel so sorry he say what he say that he reach out and try pull she on his lap to hug she up nice and tender and say he sorry and other nice words, but she just knock way he hand and run outside and he hear her crying still as she unhook clothes from the line, lock up the chicken coop, tie up the cow calf and bolt the downstairs kitchen door. He sit there and he can't eat the cook-up rice with fry fish she make. So, he pour a glass of rum and go out in the veranda and sit and take toops. She come upstairs and see the food not eaten, and start cry harder, saying how he don't even want eat the food she cook, and he run in the house quick and pick up the food and start eating, pushing rice and fish in his big mouth like dog self until all finish. She take away the plate to the kitchen and don't say nothing. He go back to the veranda and sit and look out on the road and drink high wine, until she poke she head outside and ask if is forget he forget that he have bed to sleep in. So, he go inside and climb in beside Myra. She back turn away to him. He throw his hand over she waist and pull her close and go to sleep like that.

Now in the foreday morning, he just looking at her while him dress. Then he take up his cutlass and bag and go out the yard, careful so the gate don't slam and wake her. He walk on the dam to the Main Road, crappo jumping away as he walk. He thinking about Myra and saying to himself how much he love she, and he vex with himself for calling she barren when is probably he that can't make children because he semen not strong. He know this because, before Myra, he live with another woman who didn't make baby with he, but after they split up, she take up with another man and start making baby. He didn't have to guess who the problem was.

He walk down the road telling heself he going make it up to Myra. He going buy she a new dress with the money he get today, working on Ramphal trawler. He going admit to she is he what can't make baby. He going confess it when he come back home, God spare life. He should have done the business long time now.

How he supposed to know that he going never come back home, that this was the last time he see Myra? How was he to know that a big man go sit down heavy on his chest while he sleeping and squeeze the life out of he? And when he dead, with eye wide open, this same big man will cut he belly open like he is double-belly basha fish or like pig hanging from tree in Boo Leggae yard, and pack he belly up with big rockstone and throw he off *The Amassagana* into the deep deep sea? How he to know this, eh? How he to know that five days later his stinking, bloat-up body going float up like sea sponge on a beach many miles from where the man murder he? Soto don't know any of this. Like any living man he sure that he going return to where he leave. But is not so it work. Nuh suh things stand.

24. LOCUSTS

Derek's house is a big broad bungalow that has five bedrooms inside. Is the second biggest house in the village but with the biggest yard. It's painted blue and has plenty of louvres to let cool air in on hot days. Inside, the house set up nice with fans in the roof and nice chair and table from Foreign and Away, and a big recorder player to blast reggae and calypso when you want. When blackout comes, Mr. Reynolds, Derek's father, has a big generator so he still gets electricity. He build a room in the back part of his bottom house where he keep chicken feed and plenty machine tools and old things. In the front part, he park his red Lada VAZ-2101. Mr. Reynolds was the only Black man who have a Lada car, and in the afternoon, on Sundays, he uses to drive his little family, Derek and his wife, MeLady, to the Anglican church in Georgetown.

The house was big for a family so small. Was only Mr. Reynolds and MeLady, who really name Susan, and their one-grain son, little Derek Donnard. But they not a family anymore. Mr. Reynolds and MeLady gone to America over a year now and leave Derek in the big house. People say is because Mr. Reynolds thief three million dollars of ricemill money. Other people say he gone and study at a big American university.

Mr. Reynolds use to be in charge of the whole rice mill, manager over everything. I don't think he gone and study in no foreign snow-country, I think he did thief the money because, after he gone, some government people come and ask round about his habits. They stay for days, going from house to house and one time they come to the sluice and ask Bhoje plenty question because Bhoje and Mr. Reynolds were tight. I ask Bhoje bout this and he only smile his secret smile and say, "Reynolds have it up here, boy," and point to his head. Bhoje has it up there too, because I think he getting rich off ban goods. Truth is that Bhoje was the only man Reynolds lime with.

Mr. Reynolds and MeLady didn't mix with village people. The two of them was town people from Kitty with big education and thing. MeLady was too proper with her fine self and Mr. Reynolds have too much education. Is only Derek we know. I only see inside the house when Derek's mother and father leave for America. They leave quick without saying bye-bye and don't tell skunt about where they going. People cruel bad. Derek in the big house on his lonesome with plenty of rooms and fancy furniture ever since. This start over a year ago.

Derek stay inside for three weeks and he don't bathe and he don't want to eat. He just lay down reading plenty book. *A Quality of Violence* by Andrew Salkey, *The Hills of Hebron* by Sylvia Wynter, *Minty Alley* by C.L.R. James, and *The Kaywana Trilogy* by Edgar Mittelholzer and plenty more book. Is me had to get all the books. I stop doing it so we can get Derek soft self out the place so he can start to act regular. He stubborn bad and don't even listen to Hari who good at making people do what he wants. After a time, we have to take things in our own hands. Teacher Clive says Derek in depression. What is depression but mad state skunt, and what is the solution but talking to people, getting them involved in life? I tell Mamai this plenty of time, but she don't listen when depression takes over her head and body.

Me and Hari and Lamuta Dave have to go there and bathe Derek like a small child and feed him with a spoon like a baby and dress him and brush his dutty mouth. When school start, we even iron he pants them until he catches himself. That takes about three months. He only change when he gets a letter from America. He ain't tell us what in the letter, but we guess his mother and father sending for him soon. Is so he start to get involve with life again.

Derek is soft like rice-pap and moves in a girly style. As boys, we careful how we move to make sure no softness gets seen in our actions. We do man things like we father, if we have one. But Derek can't help himself. He was born with woman ways. His voice soft and his hip move too much when he walks, like he wining, and his waist narrow like a girl's. I try to teach him how to walk like a man, but he didn't take to it.

Derek don't like the way he is. He goes to the Methodist

church and prays to God to change his womanlike ways. But God says no, he should stay the way he get create, in the perfection of His image. Derek starts liking man the way woman like a man. He falls in love with Carl and Carl don't tell him to stop – as if Carl support soft behaviour in Derek. I don't understand Carl. How this thing happen? How come Derek don't follow pattern? Who we have round here like he? Nobody.

I tell myself maybe Derek stay so because he is born so. If it is so, then God make a big mistake, but how God can make a mistake? Is God self what destroy Sodom and Gomorrah where man and man lay down and put tolo in wrong hole and woman and woman kiss up and rub up patacake with one another. Things strange eh! One time I hear a preacher give sermon against sodomite behaviour when me and Carl go to the Adventist Church, where Carl have an eye on a nice girl name Long Toenail, who really named Sarita James. This preacherman only talking about sodomite and man laying down with man, going on and on like he in trance. But we don't know any man like this. Me and Carl just leave in the middle of the sermon. Next time we see Long Toenail, she says we disrespect God and we don't reverence his sanctuary and we going dead soon. Carl get vex and cuss up she skunt good and proper on the road.

I am thinking about this as I walk down the dam to go see Derek. Carl there on the back step of Mr. Reynolds's house with a big bucket of locust tangle up with one another. He pulling off the locust leg and wing, one by one, and throwing them to fowl what scratching the yard. He looks up at me when I come in the yard and don't say anything. I sit down next to him and take my book out my back pocket – *Christopher* by Geoffrey Drayton, about a white boy.

Carl enjoying tearing off locust wing and leg. He smiling to himself and wetting his big lip with his pink tongue. When the bucket empty, he walking toward the back gate near the duck pond. He stop, turn round and say, "He upstairs," and walk out the back gate into the open pasture beyond.

I hurry upstairs and see Derek laying down on a big chair in the living room. He wearing just a singlet, not even underwear. He little black beetee expose in the naked air. He lay down on his belly, moaning soft, making cooing sounds like rookery pigeon. I stoop down beside him and call his name.

"It hurt," he says. "It hurt bad bad bad."

"Alright," I say.

He beetee bleeding and I stand him up so that he hanging on my shoulder and walk down the step, with him groaning and moaning, to the downstairs bathroom. I go to the standpipe and fetch water and bring it back and wash off my friend, wash the blood from his leg and beetee and take him back upstairs to lie down in the big bed. I run quick to Poopaloops shop and buy a pain tablet and ointment. When I come back, Carl on the step with another bucket of locusts, pulling off wing and leg like a mad-cuirass man.

"He ask for it," he says.

I don't say anything to the skunt. I go upstairs and Derek sleeping. I wake him and feed him two aspirin tablets and put ointment in his beetee crease and pull a sheet over his bony chest what like starvation child chest. It comes to me sudden that I never see Derek eat proper food. The boy always saying he just eat, or he's not hungry. Maybe Derek wants to dead.

"The pain going stop soon," I say, but he don't hear me; he shuts his eye tight and turns on his side toward the wall and goes asleep, snoring like little baby.

Carl still sitting on the step when I go outside. I sit on the step above him and look out at the pasture where cow grazing. A cool breeze blowing from the sea, smelling like crab. I hear the sea strain through the mangrove with a hushing sound. Sky blue like bird egg and a big lemon sun in the east.

"He ask for it," Carl say.

I don't know what to say to Carl. What I know is pain not pleasure, pleasure not pain. Is good to know the difference. I am thinking is wrong to use man like he is woman.

Carl stand up in the yard looking at me. I can feel his eye on me, but I don't look down. I look out to the pasture and the empty cricket pitch and two boys under a tree passing a spliff. Carl walk out through the back gate to the basmati where he catching locust with his bare hand and putting them in the bucket, like we do in we small boy days. That time gone now. Fucking is big people business. Once you do it, you is big man with big man worries. You can't be a boy again once you do man thing. Mamai say when boy start doing man thing, he lose his innocence. I ain't know if this a true-true story. I think is plenty boy in big man. I don't know what it mean to lose innocence. Could be that Mamai mean we grow out of ourselves and become different. I don't know.

Carl come back with another bucket of locust, but this time he don't pull off wings and leg. He take a long pinta from a yard broom and bore them locust through the belly one after the other, until he have a long pinta of locust wriggling and suffering with pinta through their belly. This upset me bad-bad and make me want to vomit up. It remind me of another bad thing I see last year when me and Hari coming from Central in Sookuru car.

Sookuru driving careful like he always does. We pass Green Farm estate and Huntley and Airy Hall and Dundee. When we get to Novar, we see a mother duck crossing the road with five-six ducklings behind her. Sookuru pulls up and wait for the ducks to cross, but a man behind us blowing his car horn hard. When Sookuru doesn't move, he drives round at a rate and drives over all the ducklings and mother, mash-up wings and smash legs and head and scatter small feathers floating in the air. I feel to vomit and start crying in Sookuru car. Sookuru just silent, leaning on the car wheel.

"Why he do that?" Hari say, but we can't answer, because is no reason on earth for what happened.

Is so with the locust Carl bore through, wriggling on a pinta. And Carl just smiling and looking at them as if he enjoying how they die. I don't understand, because death not a thing man must like. But Carl smiling like he in love with death.

Just then I hear the gate open and Hari comes in with a fine girl what belly big with a baby. This girl dark with long, shiny Coolie hair tie-up ponytail style. She is tall and thin like a conga pomp tree. She smiles at me and her smile is pretty as she face. My spirit take to her right away in a brother-sister style. Maybe is because she so fine that I feel protective right away. Maybe because her smile so nice and she favour Anita a little.

"Where Derek?" Hari asks. "I want ask he to live in he house with me new wife. She name Dulpattee, but we never call her that. She Lil Girl, because that name fit her fine-self more. Lil Girl, says howdee to Carl and Bubbie, who really name Kip. Kip, where we auntie-man friend?"

"Hi," Lil Girl say.

"Carl bugger he and bust he beetee," I say.

"He get what he ask for," Carl say. "He is a auntie-man skunt."

"But is who bugger who?" Hari says. "Derek bugger you, Carl? So who the auntie-man?"

"Yeah," I say, "who the auntie-man?"

Carl runs up the stairs and cuff me two times in my head before Hari pulls him off. He holds Carl by his hand and leads him toward the gate and they stand there talking a long time. Then Carl goes up the dam toward Main Road.

Hari comes back and looks at me strong-strong.

"Hear this now, Kip," he says. "We never talking about this thing after today. Never, never, you hear me? We know Derek and Carl, and me can't say who wrong or who right. Let we go upstairs and take care of Derek. Lil Girl can't go back home because me big she belly and she father have cutlass looking for me. And I can't take she home to my mother house. So, we staying with Derek. He have plenty room."

"He alone live here?" says Lil Girl.

"He father and mother gone to America over a year and don't come back. This house plenty big inside, you go see," Hari says.

I check in on Derek again and he still asleep. Hari and Lil Girl in the next room talking soft.

He says, "You want to?"

She says, "If you want to."

Hari says, "I want to if you want to."

"Aright," Lil Girl says, "but you have to kiss it first."

"Eh! Eh! You like that eh?" Hari says.

My face hurting where Carl cuffed me two times. I take ice from the fridge and hold it to my face and slip out of the house and go home.

25. LICKS

Rain falling hard, making small rivers in the road corner, and knocking drum on the zinc roof. We in Dado rum shop taking shelter, me, Derek, Carl and Hari. Bhoje drinking rum with Sookuru and a man name Crappo Cassie at a table in one corner; another man name Rookumbine Canal sleeping in another, snoring like horse. Hak Deonandan talking to Curry Cuirass. Dado fixing rum bottle on the shelf behind the bar wire mesh, and singing a Raj Kapoor song in Hindi. You have to watch Dado close like a chicken hawk. Sometimes he does water the rum the same way he does water the milk he sells.

The jukebox break so we can't play the new Yellowman and Fathead song. Dado has a record player but all he playing is Coolie song in Hindi. None of us understand Hindi. Dado says if we don't like his music, we should take we rass out his shop. Where to go now in all this rain? We drinking soft drinks and eating stale buns Dado wife, Two Panty, make four days ago with rancid cheese. He don't care if we die from eating spoil food. Dado is a man you can tolerate, but you can't like. He is not like Bhoje or Sookuru. He heart is bad and the thing about a bad heart man is he not going change. How Dado comes to be with bad heart, nobody can say. Maybe he just born so. Every time he gets chance, he robs you, even if it is just a cent. He takes your money for paying for something and says you didn't pay. He don't care if you are family or friend. The man has plenty money but still his wife only has two frocks. One she wears when she cleaning up, and one she goes out with. The woman so fine is like she doesn't eat proper. But Dado fat like a beast and hairy all over, like ogre in a fairytale book.

Everywhere he goes is pure fart coming out he big bamzee. He always sweating through his shirt and smelling high of perspiration. Dado's wife name Rookmin, but we call her Two Panty because she only has two panties the same way she has two frocks. When you see two panties hang out on clothesline, that means she don't have any on. Two Panty doesn't like her false name and does quarrel with we on the road when we call her so. Dado has a daughter, Shanti, who run away with a Blackman. Dado says she dead to him. Shanti old like Lamuta Dave, eighteen or nineteen, and live in Airy Hall with her man.

Hari standing at the front door looking out like spy self, with part he body out and part in.

"The man only playing Coolie music, buddy, like if we in India," he say. "I can't listen to one more song of a squealing pig."

"This man torturing we," Carl say.

"Dado," Hari yell, "we want Yellowman and Fathead. Put some on your record player, nuh man."

"Or Big Youth or Jacob 'the Killer' Miller skunt," Carl say.

Dado don't say anything, he just opening and pouring rum from one bottle to the next like chemistry teacher.

"U-Roy or Gregory Isaacs," Hari shout.

"Boy, I don't have small boy music," Dado says. He have a voice like sandpaper rubbing up with concrete.

"Turn on Action Radio," I say.

Hari kick the table hard. "We want Fathead and Yellowman."

Dado open the bar and come out and box Hari across his head with his fat jiggly hand what slack with flesh like walrus.

Hari falls down on the floor and standup quick with his nose bleeding ready to pashway with fat skunt Dado. Bhoje walks over slow and get between Hari and Dado. He looking Dado straight in his eye, man to man.

"Dado," Bhoje says, "I don't allow nobody to knock these boys, you know that. What is your complaint?"

"Cuff he," Hari says, wiping his nose on the back of he hand.

"Sit down. And keep you mouth shut," Bhoje say. "I asking this man a question. What is your complaint?"

"I is big man," Dado say. "This is me shop and I ain't allowing no dutty-skin small boy to get out of order."

"I respect that," Bhoje say. "Boys must know they place, but hear this now, if you put hand on this boy again, me and you go tangle, fat man. That is all I going say to you."

Hari looks at Dado and smile with blood on his teeth. Dado vex bad but don't do anything. He just goes back to the cage.

"We watching see if you going water the rum," Hari says. "We watching you close, fat man."

Carl falls asleep on his hand resting on the table. Dribble coming out he mouth like long slime. Derek just looking at him strong-strong with love-look.

We hear a scream and look out in the road and see Satie, naked as the day she born, with soap sud on her shoulder and legs, like she just bathing. She bubbie going up and down as she runs, long hair swinging behind her head. She mother, Dhara, chasing her with coconut broom. Satie runs in the mandir yard next to Dado rum shop, with Dhara running after her. We never see a fat woman run so fast. Satie has a good lead on the woman until she stumbles and falls. Dhara catches her and start peel lash on Satie, saying, "Tell me, tell me, tell me, who big you whoring belly."

We up against the paling stave fence, watching the show. Satie curls up in nutgrass like shrimp, covering her head with her hands, giving we plenty fat-eye of she hairy patacake and bubbies them.

"Who, who, who, who, who the father is?" Dhara says, as she rains down plenty lash on Sati, who doesn't fight back. She just silent like a nice respectful child and take licks like she is stone. Is because she doesn't fight back that this thing so cruel, the way Dhara gone mad with vexation. Is a sorry thing to see. I look away and want to cry. But I don't cry. I bear me chafe like a big man.

"Whore! Whore! Whore!" Dhara says after each lash. Coconut broom break up, so Dhara using her fat foot and kicking up Satie in she belly good and proper.

That's when Bhoje put stop to the whole rigmarole. He goes out in the rain and pulls Dhara away from her daughter.

Bhoje says, "You going kill the girl in broad daylight in front everybody. You think she doesn't feel, make you beat her so like a dog. Go home now and calm down you damn self."

Dhara huffing and puffing with plenty of rage and vexation. She turns and goes back to her house across the road. She shoulder drop and she start to cry. Bhoje lifts up Satie and brings her into Dado rum shop. She has plenty swell marks on she body, with bruise and bungee on her forehead. Her lip split open and bleeding. She making soft noise. Two Panty comes down with a sheet and wrap up Satie and take her upstairs.

Carl busts big laugh and come over and hugs me hard round my neck and says, "It looks like you going be a father."

"I never put it inside," I say quick-quick. "I only suck she bubbie."

"He just joking with you," Hari says. "We know is who, though."

Carl looks at Hari and their eyes make four. Then they go in a corner and start whispering like thief man, same as just before Blue Ganesh disappear.

I try finishing my mauby and bun and cheese, but it tastes like vomit. So, I just sit at the table and write a story in my mind. Is a thing I do when I don't want to be where I am. I write a story about a pandit who like to sex-up girl children. The story has plenty of cruelty in it. The story ends when them girls the pandit rape get together and kill him and cook him and eat him.

Just as I going to leave, Lamuta Dave comes in.

"Big news," he say. "Yankee Bai picked up at sea. He still alive but in a coma in hospital. *The Chronicle* say the doctor them don't know if he go live. They say he floating in the sea for six days."

Bhoje say the man is a survivor, but who could live that long in the sea? Maybe because the rain been falling for days, some water fall in he mouth. Otherwise he sure to dead. Derek say he hope Yankee Bai survive. He's a man with style.

"Must be Crabfoot the one who dead before. I like Yankee Bai," I say.

"Everybody do. The scamp tell me he trying to turn over new leaf. Is why he work on *The Amassagana* instead of living off woman or thieving from people house or planting ganja."

"Fishing?"

"In a way, but not just for fish. This boat used to take fish to Paramaribo but come back with ban goods, mostly flour and split peas and powder milk, things like that."

Then Lamuta Dave tell us he just get retrench from a job shying padi. He sad and saying how soon he going to Ekereko to dive for gold and be a big man like Aaron Smart in Jan Carew's *Black Midas*.

The rain doesn't stop, so I decide to run home and get wet up. The pasture flood and cross-trench overflowing. The latrine hole run over and coonsie floating around on the road and stick in the baima grass. I have to watch where I step. The dam to Mamai house, too, is deep in floating shit. So, I walk up the road two houses over to Anita's house to see her. She not in the yard so I plan to go up to the veranda. All I hearing is rain knocking cumfa drum on galvanise roof and sound of wind and tree muttering. I call Anita and when she don't answer, I go up the back step quiet like mouse so that drunk skunt Mr. Ramsammy don't come out he room and catch me. Anita bedroom in the back of the house near the kitchen. Just as I tiptoe inside the house, the door to her bedroom opens.

Mr. Ramsammy standing there and he tolo hard and shiny and sticking out like sword ready to stab me. He has a little smile on his face, but is not really a smile, is the look of a man who suddenly feels pain. But already my mind pass him and I'm looking at Anita lying in the bed trying to cover she patacake and little bubbies with her hand. She looks at me a second then looks away and close her eye tight. I don't say anything. I turn and walk out of the house and go down into the rain. I don't know what to say or do. I feel like a helpless child. My heart mash-up and smash-up and break-up good and proper. I start to cry like a baby all the way to Mamai house.

26. THE END OF THE AFFAIR

Suck bubbie days done. Satie set to marry a koonoomoonoo old man from Essequibo call Souse Mouth, really Ramjit Ramkissoon, a sixty-something-year-old chamar. I sitting on the back step of Mamai house cleaning fish, Derek peeling cassava and eddoe for a metagee we planning, when Satie waltz in the yard with her new shoe, a mauve one with high heel, and wearing a new lemon dress with small blue flower on it, and a fine belt round she waist. She face paint up good and proper with red and brown blush and blue eye-shadow business and she wearing lipstick what on her front teeth. She look older than she is.

Satie sit down on the step below me saying is not she who want marry old man, but she mother making her because she belly big with child and how she love another man who put the baby in she belly and who does give she plenty pleasure with his lips and hand and fat tolo, and if it wasn't for she fat skunt mother, Dhara, she would runway long time now and live with she man in Wismar, but if I want marry she and take she baby as my own-own child, she not going marry Souse Mouth old skunt, no, and if she become my wife with she new Blackman name, Satbama Plass, I can do plenty more than suck she bubbie. She tell us how last night, when she bathing sheself from hard work feeding pig and digging copra and milking goat and fetching water and washing plenty-plenty clothes, when she washing sweat and dust and dirt from she tired-body self, that old skunt Souse Mouth, with his bruk-up self, try to feel she up by the gutter cistern. Souse Mouth not for she and she not for Souse Mouth. That old koonoomoonoo make she skin crawl and give she junjuh. She tell us how she get vex and cuss rass till he leave so she can bathe in peace. But this morning, he bring present of fancy watch name Citizen, what is gold-plated with diamond stone in it, and take she to Central and buy she the new dress what she get on and new mauve shoe and lipstick and face powder. The man have a big roll of plenty paisa what full she eye and she think it could be nice to own she own house away from Mamee rass, who treating she cruel since she belly big, and Dadee too. If she marry Souse Mouth, she can cook what she want to cook and dress in a short mini skirt to show she nice leg and when Ramjit dead and gone, she go marry she child father and live happily ever after.

I tell Satie I am too young to marry and she starts cry and say she going to marry Ramjit, but if I want suck she bubbie one last time is alright. So we go upstairs and sit down on Mamai big chair and I suck bubbie till I fall asleep sitting on the chair like a little baby self in Mamai's house.

When we wake up and go downstairs, Anita sitting on the step eating metagee from a calabash bowl. Derek looking up at me with a wicked smile. Anita don't say anything but she not smiling at all.

Satie starts again the story about how she getting married.

Anita perks up and say, "So you getting marry and go way to Essequibo?"

"Yes girl," Satie says. "I going marry the old rass."

I sit down next to Anita and try hold her hand, but she gets vex with jealousness and pull way strong and gives me a bad look. But I don't let her pull away too far. I just hold her hand and kiss she face by her neck, which she likes, and she starts one giggling and she relax and twine up she fingers with my fingers and listen to Satie tell she lang-wata story. Derek just standing around eating a piece of cuirass like a bird.

Satie sit down and eat the metagee and bust big laugh. Anita lay down and put her head in my lap and look up at me with her big-big eyes and I smooth back she hair and comb it with my finger and feel tender inside with unmanly softness. Then we silent and is like I hear my mother walking upstairs, but is only a ghost of Mamai. Is just what use to be. Sometimes, too, I think I hear Mamai talking or singing church song, and this too is not Mamai, is just memory of Mamai. Is like a dream what never comes true.

27. THE WEDDING PARTY

Satie invites us to her wedding, but we don't go to her Ganesh puja cause Pandit P says we are wutlisss boys and not fit to stand in the presence of sacred rite. Me and Hari take a trip with Lil Gal to thief she clothes out her mother and father's house in Dundee while they in rice field working. I have to climb up a genep tree, then onto a limb to get in through a window. I scrape-up my belly on a rusty nail what on the windowsill.

The second night we don't go to Satie's wedding neither, cause is sheer Coolie woman business there, painting themselves with abeer and doing woman thing. Anita bring back food for me wrap-up in a leaf, which me and she bashes with we bare hand sitting on Mamai veranda. This was after me and Carl come back from a film show in Central where we see a picture name *One-Armed Swordsman Vs. Nine Killers*, starring the baddest of bad Chinese karate actor, Wang Yu.

On the third night of Satie's wedding, we go and eat up Coolie wedding food, but when we try to get we hand on hard rum, Pandit P standing over the daru with a beating cane, like he is headmaster. Pandit P lash Hari hand and start talk rigmarole about how we young and wutliss. And when Hari starts cuss up Pandit P skunt with bad-word, Curry Cuirass, who really name Vladimir Goveia, pick up me and Hari by we neck-back and throw we in the cross-trench. The trench is full of hyacinth and plenty eel and snake, alligator and biting yarrou and hoori fish. The water stink with fish spawn and mud and dead sheriga, and it stain up my going-out clothes, a nice green chambray shirt Mr. Plass bring from Foreign, and a khaki pants Mamai sew with her own-own hand. Hari's new dashiki get tear up on trench bramble, and he pants – a nice three-pleat blue gabardine – turns black with mud what looks like shit. I coughing bad because water goes down my throat and I spitting up pieces of root and stick and moss. Curry Cuirass on the dam busting big laugh, holding he belly like a pregnant woman. Then he turns and goes back into the wedding where Satie and the old man sitting under a big umbrella thing and getting feed sweetmeat and parsad. Me and Hari have to stand outside on the road, soak and dirty with mud, and look in to see the action because we stink to high heaven of trench water.

Satie dress up in red Coolie sari dress and have thousand gold bangle on she arm them and shiny choker round she neck (that Anita tell me call hasuli), and a gold chain what runs from ear to nose. She smiling a shy girl smile at people who giving she money present and gifts of cloth. I think how I never going suck Satie bubbie again, and I remember how nipple feels in my mouth – hard and soft and slippery.

Pandit P doing his preacher business. I watch him close and see how he talking to Satie, cause Carl says is *he* big she belly. But Pandit P acts the way he always acts, like he is the king of the whole place, with his chin raise-up high like brygah. He staring us straight in our faces, telling us with his eyes to behave ourselves. He looks at me so strong I get uncomfortable and want to run. The old skunt.

Pandit P not no real pandit like Reepu Daman Persaud what study panditry in India with long hair, long-beard Coolie man. Pandit P is a fake skunt pandit what has no education. He didn't go to India but studied pure banditry right here in Guyana. Is he what kill Tantie Pinky. Hear how the thing happen. Tantie Pinky wake up one morning and see she have a small sore near her foot-back. The sore not something to bother about. She was bout a hundred and three years old at the time, but strong. People say she still climbing coconut trees because all her life she was a big copra woman and sell coconut oil and thing. Eh, eh, the sore still there three days later, but it grows like plant grow in rich soil, quick-quick. And it hurting poor old Tantie good and proper and it look like the purple mouth of a terrible beast. Tantie clean the thing with bay rum and methylated spirit and daub some Limacol on it and tie off the business with a clean strip of white cloth. But the thing don't heal and Tantie's foot stinking up the house. So she calls Pandit P because Tantie don't believe in quack doctor who always feels up her dry bubbie them, like she is fruit at market, and press-press her legs and listen to her breathing with a cold thing he put in his ears. Chupidness and Whiteman science obeah. Tantie believes in bush medicine and pandit.

So, when Bhoje come to see she one day, to drop off her Sunday soup, because the woman stopped cooking for herself, she tell Bhoje to fetch Pandit P, who is then the new pandit who replace Pandit Lemon, whose real name was Balwant Balkansingh, who sit down in latrine to coonsie one day and dead right there. Pandit Lemon was an old-old man with a terrible bend-back disease what make him curve like grassknife sickle, so he always looking down at his feet when he walks. Tantie Pinky was close-close with Lemon, but she didn't have any dealing with this new fellow until the day Bhoje bring the skunt to cure her leg.

Even before he go in the woman's house, Pandit P asking her what she going pay. "Two dozen fowl egg," Tantie say. This was the price she used to pay Pandit Lemon for his healing, but Pandit P is a different man; he *steups* and turns to go away. Bhoje stops him and say he will pay Pandit P in real-real money. Pandit P looks at Tantie leg and say he going make a poultice. He does that with ricefield mud and neem leaf and nutmeg and one part thyme and two-part pear leaf and he wraps Tantie leg and collects his money from Bhoje. Two days later, the woman limping down the Main Road and faint away *brap*. Sookuru drive her to Georgetown Hospital and a doctor had to cut off the woman's leg because of something call gangrene and necrosis of the flesh. Everybody blames Pandit P, calling he a fake pundit and saying the man have a bad mind. Is because he playing around with small girls. Satie is not the only girl he take for a plaything. And he not kind to his wife, a mousy, sickly-looking woman name Shanti, who talks so soft you can hardly hear her. Her children, Sita and Ram, they soft and sickly too, and afraid to talk.

Pandit P is a beater. He terrorise his whole house, though when he start cut tail, nobody knows because his wife and children cry so quiet and soft nobody hears. But you can tell Ram and Sita are not regular. They are so sad-sad and quiet. What also makes we plenty vex is the way Pandit P acts like a know-it-all. He too proud and stern. You can't make joke round he, you can't talk too loud and he always chastising you with proper English, even when you not doing anything bad, though when he angry he talk just like we.

Simone self tells me that one time when she went to see Pandit P daughter, Sita, he tackle her against a wall and tries to touch up she patacake. She hollers out and says she going tell her father, Lickamore Chops, what spent time in Mazaruni jail. But she doesn't tell. That is what Pandit P counting on; he shame the girls so they don't tell big people.

Is so it start with Satie. She use to fetch water from a standpipe in Pandit P yard, and he use to call her under the house and kiss her up and let her touch his big man tolo. She tell me all this one time while I sucking she bubbie. Then one day, he takes her behind the mandir and fucks her. She tells me that she like it. It was a nice sweetness and after a time she want it herself, his hand on her patacake and his tongue in her mouth. She was never tired of it. "We do it everywhere," she say. Then she start trying out other men, not caring who, where or when. Is so she turn village slut and had to marry Souse Mouth skunt. She don't know for sure if is Pandit P baby in her belly. I ain't know how she feel about what he did to her. Satie is a pap-brain girl, just a person who feels things, a little girl who doesn't think hard about her life.

Mamai tell me plenty of time that people who don't think is blind like a bat; they get eyes, but they don't see. For them, life go have plenty pain and bitterness. I don't know how the Hindu gods feel about Pandit P's bad behaviour. I ain't know what it says in the Hindu bible about how man must behave. The Black people in this village are Methodist or Adventist or Anglican, but with the same god, and we know that the bad road leads to hell, and it is a hot place and terrible with hurt. Maybe Hindu bible doesn't have a hot hell place for bad people? I don't know, I never read the book. And if Hindi god not going punish Pandit P for beating up his wife and children and fucking little girls, who he have to frighten of? Maybe man. I don't know. But he going to get what's coming to his skunt.

When me and Hari go home early from Satie's wedding, Hari grunting that he is planning a panchayat of pain for that mother-skunt Curry Cuirass and a bad-bad thing too for Pandit P skunt.

28. THE PANCHAYAT OF THE DOOLAMS

Hari call a panchayat the day after Curry Cuirass throws me and him in the trench at Satie's wedding. Was he and his father, Hari Doolam, who known as Godee Blue, and Hari mother, Sitira, and he small brother, Roti Curry, who really name Shawn, a mannish boy what always in mischief for thieving or peeping girl in latrine. Everybody know Roti Curry bound for early grave or big jail in Mazaruni. And there was me, too.

The five of us sitting in the house round a table while Hari rant and rave about how Curry Cuirass have no right to maltreat he, and make him tear up his nice clothes and get dutty water in his mouth what make him shit like if he take castor oil. Is not the first time Curry Cuirass take advantage, he tells them. One time, he sitting by the koker, this same skunt come sit next to he and push he down and take over his seat, and when he, Hari, get vex and start tell the man a thing or two about his bad manner and his wutliss ways, the same skunt take out he big hand, and right there, before plenty people standing round gaffing, cuff Hari two times in his mouth and call he a Coolie skunt, and when he fall down in the grass, this same asshole give he a hard kick in his seed that make him faint way right there and blackout. He don't remember what happen next, but people tell he that this same Curry Cuirass take out he tolo and piss up all over him. Since then, every time he see the man, he feel shame like small child, and the man always laughing *kehkehkeh* laugh and making other people laugh at he. He say that now he is big man with baby to come, and living home with common-law wife, he not standing for no more abuse, and he want revenge skunt, right now.

Sitira and Godee Blue and Curry Roti listen careful all the time Hari working up a sweat and getting vex while he talk. They don't say nothing till he stop and take control of heself. Godee Blue is first to talk.

"Bai, me way is to deal rough with rough and soft with soft," Godee Blue say. "You say Goveia knock you and tear up you clothes. Well, this is a soft thing and require a soft response."

"Burn down he house," Curry Roti say. "Kill all he chicken and duck."

"Boy, let big man talk; when is you turn to talk, we go tell you," Godee Blue say.

"Rape he wife."

"He don't have no wife," Hari say.

"Boy, I say close you mouth when big man talking," Godee Blue say.

"Shawn, listen to Dadee," Hari mother say.

"What I saying, boy," say Godee Blue, "is we have to go soft. And beside, you have this business in Magistrate Court concerning thieving the Blue Ganesh. We must walk soft and walk proper. Let we discuss."

"Chop off he hand," Shawn say.

"That is too rough," says Godee.

"Cut out he tongue."

"This boy ain't have no manners. Shut you stink mouth before I shut it for you."

"Listen to Dadee," says Sitira.

"What you should to do is go ask the man to pay you money for tearing the clothes. What them things cost?"

"One pants length cost twenty-five and I pay Fat Bai twenty-five to sew it in a nice style. The dashiki I buy for twenty dollars."

"The man get seventy dollar for you then. Go and see he and let he pay you back for damaging up the clothes. If he don't, then we go get rough with he skunt."

"We go fuck up he skunt," says Shawn.

"Boy, I tell you plenty time not to use bad word in this house."

"We go mash up he rass."

"Yes," say Sitira in she man voice. "We go teach he good lesson."

Hari don't see Curry Cuirass for a week. People say the man gone away and visit family. A boy call Leak, who really name James Rollins, staying in a room under Curry Cuirass house. This Leak is real skunt, what like talk and play bad. Ask him a question and he have a thousand things to say before he answer with his stink self. Hari don't like him too much.

Leak feeding Curry Cuirass pig them the first time Hari go and see the man.

"Where Curry?" he ask Leak.

"Who want know?"

"I want know."

"Who is you to know the where and whereabouts of big man?" say Leak.

"I have something for him."

"The man ain't interested in you beetee hole," say Leak.

"Cause he have you beetee hole?"

Leak get vex and try lash Hari with a slop bucket. Hari bob and weave like Patrick Ford or Lennox Blackmore and kick Leak in his seed like David Chiang in *Boxer from Shantung* co-starring Chen Kuan-tai. Hari run and leave Leak holding he balls and trying to breath soft.

Second time, Hari go to Curry house, same thing. Leak standing guard over the man's place. The man not home.

Godee Blue tell Hari he must address the man, not he servant.

"Chop off he skunt head," says Shawn.

"This boy out a hand," says Godee Blue. "Sitira girl, what kind of son me and you raising."

"Is you seed make he."

"Plenty girl like play with me seed," says Shawn.

"This boy wutliss too bad with he mannish self."

"Boy, listen to yuh Dadee," says Sitira.

"And when they play with me seed…"

"Bai, take you rass out me eye-sight," says Goodee Blue.

29. HOW MAD IS MAD?

In a dream, Mamai and me riding a TATA bus eastbound for Rosignol. Sun out in a blue-blue sky over the trees. Is green all the way, the road running before us, little pools of rain in road-holes, and dead dog and crab dog and crappo and manicou run over in the night. I watching trees go by quick and cow in the pasture and the long laterite dams separating the villages. Plenty house facing one another at the sides of the road, hiding behind trees and sharp paling fence. Behind the houses is dry pasture where cows graze and the long canal race the road. Sometimes, you see no village at all, just rice fields in gold and brown, lying down like man bowing and standing up in the wind, or big estate of coconut trees and wild bush thick under them.

In the dream, we travelling to buy ban flour in Bush Lot from a Coolie man there, Mr. Ramsingh. Mamai sits nervous by me in a pink frock. She says nothing, only looks in front her and blink she eye and play with a handkerchief in her lap. We travel for a long time, just me and she and the back of a conductor who never turns round and come to punch we ticket. He tall and thin and have the ticket machine on a belt over his shoulder. Then we stop sudden. I look out and see a sign say Weldaad. A policeman comes on the bus and takes us off. He is a short man, dark like night, and he smile when he sees us and put his finger them in his belt like cowboy ready to parlay or bust shot with six-shooter, like John Wayne in *The Sons of Katie Elder* or Clint Eastwood in *Two Mules for Sister Sara*. He has on a police uniform and a police hat. He asks Mamai if she carrying any ban goods. She say no. He asks if she carrying ban foreign currency. She say no. He says he has to search her body. "The boy too," he says. We stand on the corner where the land dips down into a trench below.

Mamai stands there quiet and the police put his hand and feel she bubbie. She closes her eyes tight and makes a long sigh. He stoops down and put his hand on she foot-back and touch it and move he hand up up up under her skirt and she jumps like grasshopper, like she get electric shock. The policeman smile and stand up and say, "No contraband." We get back on the bus and the driver start drive again. But I don't look out the window because Mamai crying. She cries all the way to Bush Lot where we going to buy ban flour from Mr. Ramsingh.

I wake in the empty house. Is dark inside and outside. I don't get out of bed, just lie there looking up at the roof beam where marabunta building a nest. A gangasaka walking upside down on the beam eating fly with its long-long tongue. Beetle going round and round the dim yellow bulb. Since Mamai left, I can't sleep without the lights on.

Is too dark to go running, but I can't go back to sleep. I just lie there thinking. I think about the dream, not sure if it is a dream. Plenty of times before, I go with Mamai to buy ban goods and two-three times we get stopped and search. But is only in the dream that I remember a face. In the dream, I remember the man's face and how Mamai jump when he touch her. I was maybe eleven years old when this happen. I remember how Mamai cried and cried and cried. I cried too because she cried, and she let me put my head in her lap. I remember this and the conductor coming to talk to Mamai when we reach Bush Lot. We get off and stand in the corner of the road. He climbs down from the bus and comes over and stands in front Mamai and tries to say something. He opens his mouth and closes it and opens it again, but nothing comes out. Then he just shakes his head and turns away. He only talks when he reaches the bus door.

"Everybody is thief and scamp now," he says. "We all dishonest and corrupt now." Then the bus drives away.

Bhoje says the ban is nothing but "politricks". He doesn't explain what that means. All I know is that things that use to be is no more. We start pounding rice into flour and using more ground provisions. We stop getting milk in can and nut crush from school. We have less of everything and only more of things you can plant in a kitchen garden and a big farm. The rice turns bad; it full of weevils and stink. Politricks become a word to explain everything wrong with the whole country.

I get up and go out to the veranda and sit down in the dark, but not for long. Mosquito too plenty. I go back inside and crawl under the mosquito net and finish read another book I borrow from Uncle Percy. It name *A Man Come Home* by Roy A.K. Heath, who is a real-real Guyanese writer. Is a really good book and I have to slow down so I don't finish the thing too fast and cut short the pleasure.

At the first sign of sunrise, I get up and go running. I take the long way to the beach. I run west toward Bary and cross the road and run north towards the sluice. Dew falling heavy and the dam wet in places and my foot slip in a cow-hoof mark. I run slow and sure like the great marathoneer Clement Fields, moving my hand and foot in time with a rhythm in my head. I can hear the sound of the sea coming through the mangrove, the waves repeating themselves, saying the same thing over and over, until that becomes the rhythm of my footfall.

When I get to the sluice, I sit with Uncle Percy on the sluice house step and drink bush tea make out of congo pump leaf.

Uncle Percy spends all his money buying book. When anybody goes to Foreign and Away, he asks them to send back books from America and England where people print books. I wonder what Uncle Percy doing with all he knows from books.

Today, he reading a book by Andrew Salkey. Last year I read a book by the same man called *Hurricane*. I like that book bad and go to the library, and Ms. Ursula, the Potagee librarian, give me three more books by this man Salkey: *Riot*, *Drought* and *Earthquake*. I like them books, too.

"Another dead man come last night," Uncle Percy says, looking up from the book. "I hope is the last."

"A drown man?" I ask.

"With the belly cut open like them other ones. It must be Crabfoot. I couldn't tell. Things was done to the body. The man have no face. He didn't have much left over. Things eat him – eel and such, crab, rockfish.

"All them other drown man work on the same boat?"

"I don't know that. I don't know if all them drown man was on the boat. The police trying to find out. They bring down a big investigator from Georgetown. They take the body and gone not long ago. The body get tie up in Clement seine near Big Reef, so Clem put the man on fish ice and continue fishing. You know he don't like waste time. The investigator man ask plenty questions. I never see so many drown man in me born days. Is a frightening thing, cause they not just drown; somebody or something tear away their belly. Is a frightening thing when you stop and think about it. It take a bad mind to do this to another man, a hard mind of stone and iron. Is a great evil."

"Pokey Lotan says is so them man can sink easy in the sea, when them belly cut."

"So I hear. That can't have happened to Yankee Bai. He must of escaped. They say he still in a coma and they don't know if he will come round. So the last dead man must be the man they call Crabfoot. He was a quiet churchman what use to talk to himself sometimes. You never know what he think. He didn't drink. I remember a time he gets into a quarrel with Curry Cuirass, who always drunk and talking too much. Well, he and this Crabfoot have words and things get out of hand. And Curry grabs Crabby and break he hand. But that is not why I remember this story. The reason is because of the way this Crabby didn't fight back, how he calm while getting beat, how silent he was taking blows and when it done, he get up and dust heself off and walk way without throwing a punch. Next day he come back with plastercast on his hand ready for work. Is a strange man that. Now the man dead. And it turn out we don't know he at all – the thing newspaper say he do with children. Man is just brilliant disguise when you think about it, just mask and mamaguise. If he dead now, that is good. May he die many more deaths."

"Why you say that about this Crabfoot man?"

"The papers say he is raper of children all over the country. He did go from place to place doing his dutty business. It even say he kill some little girl up the coast. This same man what go lightly on the street and go to church every Sunday was nothing but killer of children and raper of innocence."

"Things not what you think they is," I say.

"We learning new things now, boy. Things what not in books. Whatever devils out in the white countries and foreign come here now. They living in the midst of us. Now we have right here them dead fisherman. You ever see so much dead fisherman?"

"No, I see the first dead man on Deodat boat, when they come in," I say. "Deodat put him in the grass."

"Yes. I remember. That was the first one?"

"Yes, a dark coolie man. We didn't know he but Bhoje say is a man name Husain what is from somewhere in Dundee side."

"Well, that is that. You going run to the beach?"

I look at the sky, big cloud rolling over one another like smoke, lightning flashing and thunder start pop. The rain coming in from far away. I could smell it on the wind.

"Storm coming," I say.

"Better run home," Uncle Percy say.

I get up and go down the stairs, but I don't run. I walk slow down Canal Dam and think. I think about Mamai in mad house. I wonder if she getting help to get better, or people just keeping mad people away from sane people. I don't even know if Mamai deserve to be in mad house. How she in mad house and Kangalang Harry Arnold walking around scot-free? Is true I always know something not regular with Mamai. She have times of strangeness and times of silence and sometimes talk to sheself, but she never violent or bother people. How mad is mad?

30. FISHERMAN 4

The first time Crabfoot sees the little girl, she dipping water from the canal in two paint can and fetching it to a little fence-up garden near line-top, where trains used to run. The train doesn't run anymore but the train line still there, and the high dam what it was set on. The train line cover over with crabgrass and the bush grows tall all around. Black sage, bellyache herb grow there, and Crabfoot, when he was big huntman, use to go there for labba, accouri and iguana, and catch plenty. That was a sweet time when he first come from Wismar to Cottage Hall with his friend, Mirai. He move into Mirai's small house and the two of them live good. Then Mirai goes to Eteringbang goldfield and catch malaria and come home dead. Crabfoot stays on in Mirai house with Mirai's grave under the mango tree in the backyard. Four years now.

He ain't tight with the people in the village because he is a stranger. The girls act like they scorn him. One-one time he catch a desperate woman, who husband away, for a little nastiness, else he have to make do and beat meat or turn rapist and take the pokie where he see it.

The little girl come and go, come and go, and Crabwood never see her come with any big people. Plenty days he watching the little girl go down the laterite dam from the road corner house she live in with an old lady. The girl about ten and he hear the old lady call her Shatrisha or Sharita. The girl call the old lady "Granny", but Crabfoot see plain that the old woman so old she more like great-great granny. The old lady up in her nineties, can hardly walk, is small and thin and wrinkle up like dry fruit, with no teeth in her head, and always sitting in the veranda of she little logie, fanning sheself and waving she fine hand slow in old people way when people pass and call she. People call she Tantie Dhata and the villagers respect her because she interpret dreams. People always stopping by to make sure the old girl have food and bathe proper and not sick in bed. Mostly they stop by to comb she long-long Rapunzel hair what white like cotton. Plenty schoolgirl come by and spend many hours combing the old woman hair and plaiting it neat, and oiling it with coconut oil, nice and proper.

Was Mirai what tell Crabfoot that the old woman is an interpreter of dream. People go see she and she tell what dream mean, like Bible Joseph or Daniel. "Is a powerful thing," Mirai say. He tell Crabfoot he go see the woman two time and what she say about his dream come true. Obeah skunt is what Crabfoot tell Mirai – evil, black art business, magic what come from Africa with plantation slave. He is Methodist and don't go in for that kind of thing when he have God on his side. Is God self what shepherding he through the valley of the shadow of darkness, and God what in charge of his going out and coming in. He safe in the Lord, in his blessed assurance and his mercy and grace, and if God protecting you, what can harm you? Nobody. Nothing. He don't care for the old woman powerful magic. Mirai tell him he can believe what he want.

The little girl pretty and have hair like the old woman, though not yet so long, part in two plait on each side of her fine face. This girl not too clean, he notice; she wear the same tear-up frock every day, a mauve frock what too big for she, and she walk barefoot, kicking up the dust as she go down the dam. Just one or two time the old lady come with the little girl to the farm, walking slow like turtle self. But mostly is the girl alone, going to water plant and pull out weed and pick greens. Sometimes she singing song. Crabfoot hear she bust tune one day, singing how *Sanko lick he lova pon de dam and de gal ah halla murda, Bupbap police ah come and de gal ah halla murda*.

Another time he hear she singing a Fathead and Yellowman song he don't care for name "Pooping Temper Contest". One line go, "We going on a pooping contest/to see which one fart the best." Crabfoot don't think farting is a worthy subject for song. But he also hear she singing love song by Pamela Maynard who he like. Give he Bob Marley anytime, or Big Youth, Jacob Miller and Gregory Isaac, the cool ruler. Yellowman and Fathead is pure skunt.

It come that he seeing the girl so much he can predict when she coming and when she staying away. She don't come when it rain. She come when sun shining hot, which is most time, and she always come round five o'clock afternoon when the day start cool down and shadow get longer. He like this time of day. He like to go out on the road and stand with the boys and drink a beer or eat a bun with mauby, or gamble dollar pool rap rummy cardgame under Ella cakeshop zinc roof.

The first time Crabfoot chat with the girl he sitting by the canal pretending he fishing for cuirass. He have a rod in the water with a hook on but no bait.

"You ain't catch anything yet?" the girl ask.

He tell she no. The girl get the water and go back up to the farm. Crabfoot get up and follow her. He watch she water callaloo and then shallot and celery. She singing all the time, a queh-queh song Crabfoot use to sing when he was she age and living in Wismar. Is a vulgar song like most queh-queh song. It go:

Oh mama me ketch wan buck oman
All am carry am a lang dam go nack am.
All am carry am… …go nack am.

Crabfoot like that part. He know what it mean. He think that he must "knack am" the little girl, and then his thoughts move quick-quick from knack am to murder am. What he go do is wait one day till she finish watering the plant and heading home and the place a little dark. He hide heself behind a tree and when she passing, he come out quick and hit she with a big rockstone cross she small head and haul am, carry am behind a tree to knack am.

He do nastiness while she dead and do it three more time. Then he leave her and start walk home. But when he look back, the little girl coming, walking like drunk girl. Crabfoot think maybe is a jumbie. He go back and he looking at the little girl with blood dripping out a hole in she head, when she open she mouth and say in she sing-songy voice, "I want Granny, Mister Man," in that polite way children have.

Is a marvel this, he think, a talking dead girl. Well, he don't have no granny to give her. Is no people here, just the new dark of the night. What he have is big rockstone at his feet and talking evidence of his crime standup in-front he, saying how she want she granny. So he pick up big rockstone and knock she five, six, seven, eight, nine ten time more on her long-hair small head until it smash-up and mash-up good and proper. Then he lift she – she was light like baby self – and throw she skunt in the canal to land *plu-shung plash*, and sink down in mud at canal bottom, where snake can bite she, cuirass chum she, eel suck she, alligator rip rip she off from the map of the world. No more Shatrisha or Sharita; no more Yellowman and Fathead song from she small mouth; no more watering plant or picking greens. No more evidence. All that done done done forever.

Crabfoot get sand and throw it where he see blood, and bathe himself in the canal and go home and rest he tired body, because nastiness make man weak to rass. He fall asleep quick and dream a dream of loveliness and peace.

They don't find the girl for a week. The tide drag she away two village upriver and dump she in the tall arrow reeds where a small girl find the body after crab take piece of she belly, eel worm inside she stomach and tear out piece of she inside part, and hard dutty shell and shrimp-like thing make room in her mouth and ear and eye socket. The police come and ask question and then they go away. Crabfoot continue living in Mirai house like nothing happen. Then one day, while he walking the road, the old woman, Tantie Dhata, call he. She have a strong voice for an old woman.

"Come help me with something," she say.

Crabfoot go in the yard and go upstairs to the veranda where Tantie Dhata sitting with sheet over she fine leg, with she skin wrinkle-up like elephant skin and shiny with coconut oil. The woman rocking in she chair, back and forth, back and forth like small child getting enjoyment.

"What you want me do for you, old woman?" Crabfoot ask.

"Sit down," she tell he. "Is no hurry. Is you them call Crabfoot?"

"Yes."

"Crabby."

"Yes."

"Is why you kill little Sharita? I see you in me dream. Why you do this bad-bad thing?"

After the shockwave go away, is deny he do anything. "Is not me, old woman," he tell her. The old woman just shake she head sad-sad and look at he strong with she black-black eye them, what favour massacuraman eye. Crabfoot get up and start walking out the house. But the old lady say something what keep he there like tree what root gone down deep in hard earth and stone. What she saying? He only see she lip moving but nothing coming out. Then sudden, everything clear up and sound come back in his ear.

"I put curse on you," the old lady say. "I put pain on you and suffering. And nothing go be more painful than when you dying. It go hurt and hurt and hurt. She go haunt you and put terror in you soul and vex your days. You going get no peace in the day or the night. Your life go be vexation and sufferation and aggravation forever."

Crabfoot move to Bary after that year. He rent Boo Leggae bottom house room and start going to sea on trawler with anyone what take he, until he get steady work on *The Amassagana*, Mr. Ramphal boat.

It was on this boat that he wake up one night and feel something being pulled out of he and the pain bad bad bad to rass and he scream, but is not a hard scream is a soft one, because he didn't have strength for hard scream. Then a face appear over him and smile. The man say, "Eh, eh, Crabby man, you mean you ain't dead yet," and jook he two time in his chest with a sharp knife, then three-four-five more time, but he ain't know about six time. The pain too much and the man pulling out something from his belly, ripping away something inside he. Then water baptize he. It cold cold cold and get inside him and bring bright pain. He sinking down deep deep away from the light to the crabby sea floor with wild trees of kelp waving goodbye, in a ghost world of dead thing and skeletons of drown man. Sea toss he and fish tear he and he was no longer himself when he wash up in the mangrove.

31. A LITTLE NASTINESS IN THE NIGHT

Anita come over one night and she acting strange. She acting hungry bad for tolo. Just she come inside Mamai house, she start kiss-up my mouth with tongue in the French way and feeling-up my tolo good and proper, rubbing it hard and hurting it lovely. I try hold her hard against me to calm she down. But she railaway and slap my face hard with she bony hand. After that I just let her do what she want. We lie down on the floor. She take off my clothes, *wap-wap* quick and then she own. Anita bubbie small and she stomach flat and the hair between she leg dark and long. She have a smell that is very nice, like wet land or rain beneath bush and I love her bad. But Anita magga like wet rat. When I hold her close, I feel the bone of her rib and her little breast against my chest.

Then she stand over me naked, saying, "I want you to take me, I want you to take me." But is she who taking me. She the one in charge of man-raping me. She take my tolo in hand and lower she self down down down till I feel the warmness of being inside patacake. Is a slippery sensation. Is when she start moving she hip with wine and grind that I know it sweet with plenty loveliness. It don't take long for me to break. We do it two more time. Anita whispering, "I want you remember me, Kip", over and over again like parrot bird. Then she go home and murder sheself in latrine with insecticide poison name malathion and dead. But I never know this till almost two days later.

That night, after we do sweet nastiness, I watch she walk home and duck under Mr. Ramsammy cowpen fence and go up the back stair. I go back inside and lay down in bed under the mosquito net and feel lovely inside with warm feeling of love and happiness, going over in my mind how Anita rub up my tolo and how she patacake feel and the sounds of pleasure. Then I start think about how me and Anita meet in school yard. I remembering how, after I kiss she in the school yard, Teacher Clive take me to see the headmaster to get licks, but the headmaster not there, so I just sitting outside he office waiting.

I sitting there over half hour when Anita poke her small head through the door and frighten me. I don't mean I frighten of her, but I frighten Anita get catch and get licks like me. I not afraid for myself. She give me something wrap in a piece of paper. She didn't say anything. I open the paper and is a bara with mango sour.

"You eat it," I say, and give it she back. She just look at me and start eat like small rat. "I like you," I tell her. She stop eat the bara and look at me with a small smile on she pretty face.

"I like you bad," I say.

She don't say nothing. She just look at me in she brazen way, but harder, trying to see something in my face, to read it like obeah woman self. I look back and give her a wink. She wink back. The tender feeling raise up in me again like balloon in the air, make me feel lithe like spore flower.

She say nothing.

"You want be my girlfriend?"

"Yeah, if you want," she say, and start eating the bara again. She looking away from me at them girls playing rounders across the yard.

"Go back in class before headmaster come and find you."

"I want stay."

"You will miss class and get licks."

"I want stay with you."

"I will see you after school."

But she stay there without moving, like Everstick fasten she in one spot. She look rough and dutty in her old dress and she barefoot cake up with mud. I hold she hand what thin and feel small like baby hand. She make up her face like she going cry.

"You going cry?" I say.

"No."

"We will go to the shop after and have cake and sweet drink. We can talk. Don't miss class. You going get licks for skulking. I will come for you, aright?"

"Aright."

Headmaster come two hour later with rum on his breath. He don't talk long. He just say, "Five strokes," and take me in the office and let me hold out me hand them for lashes. My hand burn like fire when he done. I get my book and go downstairs in the yard. School done over, but I see Anita waiting. She just run up to me and put she hand in my hand.

"You get licks?"

"Yes, but is alright."

"Kiss me again," she say.

I pull her behind a tree and kiss her again long and long. From then on me and she is girlfriend and boyfriend. People calling us all kind of names but me and she thick like guava cheese; we inseparable, stick-up on one another with the Everstick of love.

Then sudden she stop coming in school. Nobody know where she go. It was hard for me. I can't even explain my own feeling to myself.

A month later, I see she going in Mr. Ramsammy yard. She and Ms. Sabita come out Sookuru car with some bag and go up the stairs. Me and Carl and Lamuta Dave sitting across the road under the *genep* tree taking shade. I never feel so happy. Is so we come closer than close, which lead to touching and kissing with tongue in the French way to pure nice and lovely nastiness.

32. DAYLIGHT RAVERS

Next morning, Bhoje come and wake me. Dew falling plenty. I bathe from the barrel under the gutter. The water cold bad. Bhoje up on the veranda smoking and waiting to drive me to Fort Canje so we can get Mamai out of Berbice Mad House. I put on my Sunday clothes, so Mamai doesn't get vex with me. Mamai always like me to look clean and tidy, not like starvation child and *rangatang*. I put on a nice yellow shirt and a blue long pants and my new Converse shoe. Bhoje standing in the yard when I come out of the house. Rain drizzling a little. We walk out to the road and get in Bhoje old Lada Riva, and drive west with the road still dark and manicou and labba running cross the road and big crappo and crappo children popping under Bhoje car wheel like a bomb going off.

Bhoje turns on the radio and a song by Pamela Maynard comes on. Pamela singing *One day at a time, sweet Jesus, that's all I am asking of you oooh*. Pamela Maynard is a real-real singer with a nice voice. One time me and Carl go with Bhoje all the way to a hotel in Georgetown to hear Pamela sing song after song with Sid and the Slickers band. Now Bhoje turns up the radio and we sing along, duet with Pamela and her nice voice self. I think I can help Ms. Pamela Maynard from being lonely and lost with my tolo. I tell Bhoje this as we drive. But he laughs and says no, Pamela Maynard is a big woman and doesn't mess with a small boy. Bhoje says only he big enough to make Pamela Maynard not be lost, lonely, and helpless with his big man tolo. We laugh and laugh as we drive.

It takes a long time to reach New Amsterdam, cause Bhoje stopping all the time to do this and that business. One time in Kingelly, Bhoje stop at a big house and we go up the stairs. He opens the house with his own key and we go in. A woman comes out of a bedroom naked and when she sees me, she runs back in quick like a scamp. Bhoje bust big laugh and go in after the woman and for an hour they do nastiness, the woman groaning hard and saying, "Yes, yes!" and shouting, "Fuck me, Fuck me!" All this time the bedspring screaming and the headboard racking and banging in a ruckus of noise and moan.

I sit on the front veranda watching the village come awake, watching the fires come on at the milking post. A man goes by on a donkey cart. A girl with shoes in her hand, wearing a lemon party frock, comes out a yard and runs quick to a house across the road. A fat woman stands on the road corner waiting for a bus. Two men stand up bare-chest under the street light smoking and gaffing and slapping mosquito. A baby starts to cry in a house.

Bhoje woman, a nice Coolie thing with long-down bubbie and black hair down to her waist, come out and go in another room and come out again with a baby sucking her long bubbie. I go in the upstairs bathroom to take a pee. Bhoje in there washing he long tolo with water from a bathroom basin. I go outside and stand up in the kitchen. Bhoje comes down, tucking his shirttail in his pants. He kisses the baby and the woman and goes out the door. I go into the bathroom and pee quick and follow him to the car.

"That is Indira, she is one of my children mother."

We stop again in Onderneeming to see Bhoje next children-mother, a pretty Indian thing, about twenty. When we drive up to the place, Bhoje goes to the car trunk and bring out a bag of ban flour and sardine and a tin of biscuit. Bhoje uses his key and we go in. The girl standing over the scullery fire blowing flame under a kettle. Bhoje put down the bag of ban goods and start to feel up the woman. I go out to the veranda and watch the road. Bhoje in the bedroom sexing-up the girl, making her say he name over and over and over like puja prayer.

My mind full of thinking about Anita, how she was sad, and happy at the same time. How after we did the nastiness a third time, she just put her head on my shoulder and cry and cry and cry plenty of eye-water. I just lay there holding she close and rocking her so she sleep. When she wakes, she just stand up in the bedroom in the moonlight coming in from the window, just looking down at me strong-strong. I feel a tenderness in me to make me cry. I get up and hug her tight and we stand together for a long time. Then I hold her little red panty so she can put her fine leg in and pull it up for her and kiss her bellybutton. She like that. She giggles like somebody tickling her armpit or foot-bottom. Then I pull her frock over her long hair and put her fine hand them through the sleeve and zip her up in the back.

Anita just stands there while I dress her like a small child. Then she starts the crying business again, so I just rock her back and forth as if we fine-wining in dance hall party to soft Eric Donaldson song. Then she let go and run out of the house. I didn't see her after that because it is dark.

Bhoje second woman baby is bigger than the first one, about four or five years. He comes out of a room next to where Bhoje sexing the woman and walks out to the veranda with his thumb in his mouth. He looks up at me and says, "You is who?"

"Kip," I say, and reach down and try to pick he up, but the small boy screams loud and says, "Leggo me, skunt black man," like big man self.

I think maybe is a bacoo child and get ready to run. But the mother come out the room and pick up the boy and take he back in the room. Soon I hear her singing soft lullaby.

"That is Nalda," Bhoje says when we get back on the road.

I tell him how the little child cuss.

"That boy is devil self," and he bust out he big-big laugh, leaning back his head and showing plenty teeth.

The road bright again, and all along the way Bhoje meeting and greeting people. He selling ban goods from the trunk of the Lada. He has American onions and split peas and sardine in red sauce, and real wheat flour and marmite and nut butter and sausage in cans and corned beef and plenty other things from Foreign and Away that government ban long time now.

In Inverness, Bhoje pulls over the car next to a tall fine girl standing on the road corner with a baby on her hip. This girl black until she purple and pretty with eye slant like Chinese eye and long Coolie-type hair and straight nose; a mixed woman with plenty races inside she: Coolie, Chinese, Black. Is a strange-looking woman and very beautiful. The child on her hip looks like she, but clear-skin with strange blue eyes. Bhoje gets out of the car and immediately the woman starts to quarrel with him.

Bhoje takes the baby from her and starts to kiss up the child making him laugh and giggle. The woman steups her teeth and goes to the trunk and take out a heavy bag of goods.

"Let Kip help you," Bhoje says.

The woman looks in the car and sees me.

"Well, come out nuh," she says.

I come out and take the heavy bag and follow them into a yard full of croton plant and fern all over the place. We go to the house. Bhoje hands me the child and he and the woman go in the kitchen and start a fight. The woman throwing pot and pan and thing.

Bhoje saying, "Woman, don't let me make you taste my hand."

The woman saying, "Do it nuh, do it if you is man."

Bhoje comes out the kitchen vex to rass, with two glass of lemonade and give me one. The child reaches for it and I let him sip from the glass.

The woman in the kitchen shouting, "You must think me is you whore or something."

Bhoje says, "Truli, I warning you, you know. I warning you."

"I is you pickney to warn?" Truli says. "Warn you other woman them. I not your child."

"You ready, Kip?" Bhoje says. "Let me leave this place before things get out of hand."

I put the child down and move with Bhoje toward the door. Truli runs out the kitchen and blocks the door, spread out her fine hand and foot jumping-jack style across the doorway.

"You not going anywhere," she says.

"Is like licks you looking for today-today," Bhoje says. "You want test me eh! Move from the door, I say."

"I not no dog to come and go when you call. I is woman skunt person, you better learn," Truli says.

"Girl, you making me mad, you know," Bhoje says, going up to the fine girl like he going give she some slaps, *whatap*, *whap*, cross her fine face, to discipline her proper with heavy manners, big man style.

I standing there looking on, thinking this fine girl brave bad to get in front big giant man like Bhoje. Maybe she mad.

"Try it and see what you get," the girl says.

"Alright," Bhoje say and he pick up Truli like a wet rag. She railing and struggling, hand going this way and that, fine legs whipping out in crazy karate-style kicks. Bhoje holding her hard against his big body, trying to kiss her mouth, trying to lick her neck.

"Leggo me skunt," she says. "I is not you whore."

She starts to cry then with plenty of passion and rage in her small body. But she not fighting now. She just full of passion. Bhoje put her against the wall and start kissing up her mouth. She crying all this time. Bhoje licking away her eye-water with his tongue like a dog while he holding her up against the wall, then he pushes open the bedroom door with one foot and take her inside and slams it shut.

I hear Truli say, "I is not you own to take any time you want."

"Anytime and anyplace," I hear Bhoje say.

"No," she says.

"Yes," Bhoje says.

"Never," she says again and sighs softly.

"Yes," Bhoje says.

"No," she says softer now.

"Yes," Bhoje says, almost shouting.

"Yes," Truli says, "yes, yes, yes."

The woman starts to cry and moan at the same time, crying and moaning and crying and moaning.

I take the little boy child and go out onto the veranda.

Bhoje comes out of the room an hour later with his neck and shoulder scratch with fingernail marks. We go out into the car. Truli in the veranda with the child on her hip, waving goodbye.

I look at Bhoje.

"She not always like that," he says; "she vex with me. When she mad is like hurricane self. The woman is storm, I tell you, storm self. I love she bad though, man."

On the road again, Bhoje silent like he remembering something. I looking out the window trying to remember every village we pass through, saying the names to myself.

We have to wait for the boat when we reach New Amsterdam. Bhoje takes me to a place for tea, a little shop near the river. The woman cooking float bake in big canary over a coal-pot behind the counter. Salt fish stewing in oil and seasoning and smelling nice on a one-burner kerosene stove.

"Serve yourself," Bhoje tell me. "Let me and Melba do business. He pulls the woman behind the curtain in a little room.

The woman saying jokey-like, "Eh eh, but is who going fry the bake?"

"Kip can fry bake," Bhoje says.

The woman is Black and smells fresh like lime juice or cool breeze with the scent of flowers. While the two of them in the back room talking, Bhoje tells her how much the ban flour cost, the ghee, the split peas, the nut butter, the cheese. I fry bake. I even serve customers – two drunk men what come in the place cursing and carrying on. One saying how he like Dr. Rodney and the things he saying. "The man talking truth to the people." The other one says, "Dr. Rodney have a big mouth, he better watch he self and don't get the fat man vex."

"Who is this Dr. Rodney?" I ask Bhoje while we fetching the last of the ban goods into the woman's back room.

"Is a man what trying to start trouble for the government," Bhoje says. "The man has plenty of education and saying truthful things to people. I see trouble down the line, though."

The boat doesn't come when it supposed to. We waiting for three hours. Me and Bhoje sitting in the car with the window down to let in cool fresh air off the river. The sky is cloudy with big black clouds. Bhoje taking toops from a half of XM Gold rum and chasing with coconut water he brings from the woman.

"Man Bhoje, you have plenty woman!" I say.

"Boy," he turns to me and say, "I don't have women; them woman have me. But that is big man business, eh."

"I like Ms. Jenny," I say. "Where you meet she?"

"I meet she right there in that house. Is she father house. This is long time now. Possible you didn't born yet. Let me tell you the story so you don't ask plenty question and irritate me with working up you big mouth."

"I don't mean to vex you, man Bhoje man," I say.

"Never mind that. We get time. I best tell you the thing anyway. Hear this now."

33. THE HAYNES WOMAN

Bhoje knew her as the Haynes girl, a bright pretty child name Jennifer, who people call Jenny for short. He don't remember talking to her though. In them days people were always talking about the high marks little Jenny get in school tests and how she nice, has manners and doesn't stay away from people who poor. But she make Bhoje feel less than heself, that he small and unimportant. Is not like she acts like she more than he. She does this thing just by being herself. He remembers she was a very quiet girl with nice skin, she hair pull back and tie behind her head. She uses to wear glasses and he remembers her green-green, white people's eyes, what they use to call cat-eye. She was not his friend; he was younger by a year, and then he stop going to school and gone in the rice field to shy padi to make ends meet.

He hear she gone away to the university in town. He not going anywhere. People he grow up with gone outside or to other islands and come back talking Yankee or palawala talk. He hardly leave Mahaicony. Then he hear she gone to Russia to study big book and mystery mathematics. Then she goes to New York for more studies. When she come back again, he on the sea, working trawl for Mr. Ramphal. His mother sick-sick with diabetes skunt and anaemia what makes her weak and fall down all over the place. He and his father, Rass Mouth, always have to watch her. They keep her in bed most time, but two-three times a day, he lifts her and brings her in the veranda to sun, like clothes on a clothesline, until she gets better on the medicine they buy from a doctor in Georgetown. Medicine cost plenty of money and this keeps him and Rass Mouth working like slave in rice field, in cane field, in coconut estate, in big garden, on fishing trawls.

Next time Bhoje sees the Haynes woman, he sitting on the koker selling shallots to people waiting for the TATA bus to Berbice. She's very beautiful, hair in Afro like Angela Davis, short and curly. She has a scar that looks like a sickle on her forehead. Her frock has flowers on it, her slim body erect and proud, leather sandals on her foot, toenail paint red like buck bead. He notices how she calm and collected, lithe on her feet like her mind is free of worry and vexation. The woman calm like hightide water and though she not laughing *kehkehkeh* like hyena dog, she smiling and saying nice things to people when she goes down the road.

She has come back with her husband, a tall Black man who spends many mornings running up and down the place like Clement Fields. They living with her father, Mr. Haynes. They have two fine-face girls, strange, quiet children, huggers, affectionate, who cry easily. Plenty times Bhoje sees them playing their strange foreign games from Away in the big yard, kicking a ball, and talking Yankee talk. The oldest girl about seven or eight.

One time, he gets a job weeding the yard. The husband speechifies with a thick accent Bhoje doesn't recognise. He sound like Blackman villain in Tarzan filmshow starring Johnny Weissmuller.

"Olusegun," the man says one morning when Bhoje sitting in the yard sharpening he weeding cutlass. The man holding out his hand to shake. So Bhoje takes it and shakes.

"What is Olusegun?" Bhoje asks.

"My name," the man says. "What is your name?"

"Ramesh Bhojedath."

"Ramesh," the man say, "you're not afraid of snakes in the tall grass?"

Bhoje find himself talking carefully when he answers the question. He says no, he not afraid of snakes but of marabunta. He explains how when he was a child, he get bite and fall down in a fit, how he swells up like dead crappo, and how the pain was terrible.

"You are telling the truth," the man says in his filmshow villain voice. Bhoje praying silently that the man go away, but the man sticks around so Bhoje has to drag on his long boots quick and attack the thick grass near the septic tank. This Olusegun standing there looking at him like foreman or slave driver skunt, his dark face a mask of concentration. Bhoje thinks that the man trying to work some obeah on he with his eye. Bhoje stays away from him after that.

Sometimes he sees the Haynes woman holding hands with the man in the village and laughing private laugh and showing she white-white teeth them. Then the two of them disappear. People say they gone to Georgetown to teach at the university.

Bhoje leaves round that time and goes to the goldfields in Eteringbang to find big gold and become a rich man. He finds mosquito instead and catch bad malaria. He comes back to the village, bruk-up, and bellyaching, shitting and pissing on heself like small baby. Ten years ago that was.

When he sees her again, he's selling bora on the market; she's coming his way with a basket in her hand, saying, "How much is this?" picking up bora, turning it over this way, that way. She smell nice. She voice like a song self. Their eye makes four.

He says, "It hurt you?" – wondering immediately why he asked the question, maybe to hurt her? He doesn't know.

The Haynes woman give him a gentle look, a small smile on her face.

"Yes," she says, "very much."

"But you living through?" he says, surprising heself again.

"Yes," she says, and pays him for the bora.

Bhoje read about the killing in a newspaper after he comes back from the goldfield. How the Haynes woman husband, Olusegun, shoot them two small girl child and shoot himself. Why he does this thing nobody can say.

The Haynes woman comes back to the village to live with her father who too old to take care of himself, though he still running the business. Mr. Hayes around eighty-five then.

One morning, Bhoje passing by Mr. Haynes's house when the woman leans over the veranda and calls out to him.

"Come," she says, "come quick."

Bhoje runs in the yard and up the back step to the landing. The Haynes woman opens the door and pulls him inside.

When the two of them in the room, the woman says, "Help me get him off the floor and back on the bed, please."

Bhoje looks down and sees Mr. Haynes dead on the floor. The old man fall from the high big bed and lay down lalaff, eye wide open and unblinking. Bhoje bends down and sees if the man breathing. No. The man gone from the world. Bhoje shakes his head. The dead man's stiff tolo, a big one, points up to the ceiling.

"I need help to dress him," the Haynes woman say. "The people from the mortuary will be here soon."

The two of them get the old man dress after lifting him and turning him and straining against his dead weight. Bhoje does the heavy work. Was a big problem pulling the man's pant zip over he tolo, what still not going down. Bhoje feels strange and unmanly when he has to take hold of the man tolo and bend it back and pull the pants over it quick and zip it up quick-quick like hummingbird wing. The Haynes woman turn away she face, giggling in her hand.

They arrange the old man nice in clean clothes and stretch out like king of the bedroom. Bhoje put two coins over Mr. Haynes's eye and try to close the man's mouth, but it still open, like he getting ready to say something.

Bhoje thinking that the dead man is the woman's last connection to this village and country. She will go soon, he thinks, and never come back.

"What are you thinking?" the Haynes woman asks.

"This is a final thing," he says. "The last change."

"Yes," she says, "there's nothing else. Grief and memory is for the living." She point to the old man. "He's beyond everything."

The mortuary men them come, three of them in dark suits like carrion crows. They work quick, knowing their business. They stretch the old man on a cooling board, making his foot straight and strap he down and lift him out, as one would a bag of padi, to the waiting hearse in the road.

The Haynes woman goes down into the yard and stands with one of the mortuary men talking soft. She signs some paper and gives it back to the man, who gives a small bow and goes out to the road. From the veranda, Bhoje watches her. She looks calm and collect. Bhoje wonders if she did the same thing for her daughters them and her husband. She looks up at him and smiles.

She comes through the house and sits on the veranda next to him. She gives him a glass of red liquid and he takes and sets it down on the low tea table between them. They sit in silence for a long time, darkness descending around them.

That night he sleeps in the house and in the morning she was in bed with him. He looks down at the top of her head and feel himself blown apart into space because of this new thing she was doing, a thing beyond just touching and holding and squeezing; it was a real intimate thing and real nice.

Bhoje start live in the woman's house and starts run Mr. Haynes's business, though the Haynes woman controlling the money. She still teaching at university and sometimes they don't see one another for months. Sometimes she goes away to America or England or some other snow country. The woman lives in Georgetown and him in the village. They have a kind of love Bhoje can't describe. Is like a business thing but it more than that; is like she and he married in an unmarried way, but it feels good and proper and so they stay together, going on ten years.

"Everything I just tell you is between me and you, Kippy," Bhoje says after he finishes telling the story.

We in the car on the early steamer crossing to the other side, almost nine, ten o'clock, rain falling, but the sun bright and hot already. Bhoje drives off the steamer when we get to the other side and pick up the highway again and we drive the rest of the way to Fort Canje without saying another word.

34. THE BAD MAD IN CANJE

The only thing I know about Fort Canje is what in history books. Is a haunted place from dunno-when and full-up with plenty ghost: Dutchman jumbie and spirit of slave buried alive under trees in the pedocal, with no stone to mark their passing. The whole place is a graveyard, the tall bush nourished by their flesh. Fat tree roots dive fathoms down to drink their blood and crush their bones to splinters.

Was first a barracks for British soldiers, then it turns into slave plantation where whiteman work Blacks till they died from too much digging and cutting. This was two hundred years gone. In those days Canje was just swampland with trees growing where house build now. Slaves used to live in the niggeryard logie, close to the field. After slaves get free, the white man them bring over Coolie to cut and grind cane and squeeze cane juice into Demerara sugar for tea and coffee cup in skuntian England.

Things different now. All this history turns into nothing more than talk and word on a page in a textbook. The land becomes a place where you build a madhouse. Is a wide pasture of low, khaki-colour grass, and here and there some twist-up cedar trees. The place has three buildings that like barracks. They not old, exactly. They just look used up, the zinc on the roof rusty, and the windows have old boards that open like eyelash and wood ants trail on them. The buildings them flat and not on stilts. The whole place fence round with a high chain-link fence with barbwire on top. It has a big gate with a watchman in a small house, checking who coming in and going out. He leans out of a small window and talks to the car driver or bus driver or man walking on foot. The place has a tarmac patch beyond the fence and plenty of cars parked there.

Bhoje drives up in the Lada and tells the man he here to see Paulette Plass. She doesn't have any false names. The man checks in a book for a few minutes. Bhoje signs his name in another book and the man presses a button and the big gate slides open. Bhoje park on the tarmac near an old truck.

"When we go in," Bhoje says, "let me do the talking."

The place silent inside and smell like Dettol. An old woman is sitting behind a desk reading *The Daily Chronicle*. She looks up and sucks her teeth. Before we say a word, she tells us to sit down and wait, without taking her eye off the newspaper.

"Wait for what?" Bhoje asks. "We come for Paulette Plass, this boy mother."

"Doctor Beckles ain't come yet," the woman says. "He the one what decides who sees who."

Behind the woman is a long corridor of silence, clean and empty like morning road when no traffic going. Is like people not even in the place.

Me and Bhoje sit down and watch the lady read her paper. We wait for about an hour before the Beckles man come. He tall and black with white-white hair and spectacles on the tip of his nose. He wear a white dashiki and white pants and black shoes.

Me and Bhoje go with Dr. Beckles in an office and sit down in front of a big wood desk with plenty of paper pile up on it. Bhoje tells him we come for Mamai.

"Ms. Plass is very sick," Beckles say. "She must get better before she can leave." Then he tell us how Mamai try to kill herself and how the tablet she taking helping her but not enough; how this and how that, and the schizophrenia coupled with the depression cause a trip in the psyche which results in catatonia; how her lucid moments are characterised by suicidal ideation. I listen good, but this man talking pure stupid nonsense like *he* is the mad man. I don't understand half the thing he saying. What is schizophrenia skunt? What are catatonia and suicidal ideation? Bhoje shaking his head like he understands this quack. When the doctor finished talking, Bhoje says in a soft voice, "When we can see her?"

"Now," the doctor says, and me and Bhoje follow him down the long hallway pass plenty close-up door right and left.

Mamai in a small white room with soft walls and no window and no chair. A small bed in one corner make-up neat with a white sheet. Mamai sitting on the bed looking like a madwoman. I run to her quick and hug her up, but she pushes me away and bites my ear. It hurt and I move away. I feel my ear and see blood on my finger. Mamai sitting on the bed, barking like she is a dog, baring her teeth what look yellow and not brush in many mornings. Mamai face like devil face self. She hair not comb and she has a pee smell that strong and vexing. She sitting there barking like a little bitch dog. Dr. Beckles kneels in front of she, whispering something. Mamai eyes them red. She doesn't look like Mamai. She looks like a madwoman self, like Kangalang Harry Arnold.

Dr. Beckles talking soft to Mamai, saying she name over and over again, like he reminding her who she is. He talking like he talking to a baby or lamuta-paglee child what don't understand anything in the whole world. But it makes Mamai stop bark. She just fixes her eye on one spot and doesn't blink. When I call her name, she doesn't answer; she doesn't look at me.

Bhoje goes up to her, holds her hand and says, "I bring Kip, your son, Kipling, Kip, Kipling Plass, your son Kip, you know, Kipling Plass."

Bhoje says my name over and over and over again. But Mamai far away. She body sitting on the bed, but she mind gone elsewhere. She like a living dead woman.

I should never have come. It was a bad thing to come. If she gets better, how I can see her as normal again?

After, we sit in Dr. Beckles's office again. Again, he talking with plenty of big words of pure skunt and stupidness.

Bhoje asks him when Mamai can go home.

Dr. Beckles says he doesn't know. She has to get better than she is now before he can sign the paper and let her out the madhouse. He says she wants to kill herself. She try two times.

I never know anything like this before. Is true that I know since I young that Mamai different from other mothers, that she not regular. She cries too much for one thing, and she has long periods of sadness which keeps her in bed for weeks. And Mamai talks to people what not there, ghost people in the open air, and people what dead long time gone. Yes. And Mamai doesn't like people round she plenty. She gets vex.

Mamai not regular and she knows this, and I know this. But the question I always ask is why? Why is it that Mamai is madwoman, not far from walking street like Kangalang Harry Arnold with his long tolo sticking out he tear-up pants? No one can say. Some say it is because Coolie people kill her whole family during riot time that make her run-off. Others say is obeah work put on her, that she has a demon in her body that eating up her mind. I ain't know about such a thing. Demon not a thing I ever see, to know whether they eat mind, and obeah is a thing from Africa, from the old gods that come over with slave. I don't know how it works properly. Ma Tussette knows, but she is a big old lady.

So that day we don't take Mamai home. We say good-bye to Dr. Beckles and drive. We drive for a long time without saying a word. I just crying and crying all the way, plenty tears. We drive and drive and catch the steamer before it crosses the river. Still, we don't talk. When we reach New Amsterdam, Bhoje takes me to a place to eat. Like before, the owner is a woman he knows.

While Bhoje in the backroom loving up the woman, I sit and eat curry and roti and drink I-Cee Cola and think about Mamai. What cures madness? Dr. Beckles says he gives her tablet so she can be regular again. How does it work? Why Mamai try and bite off a piece of my ear? The thing that hurts me most is that Mamai didn't recognise me, how she eyes them dull and bright at the same time, how she look right through me and see nothing there. I am nothing to her, me, her one-grain son on earth. How can this happen? Is too much question in my brain. They sour up the food in my mouth and make it hard to swallow; make me feel like vomiting. So, I just sit there and look at the river and try not to think.

But things keep coming in my brain. Mostly I remember how Mamai used to be lost away in her mind, how plenty time she runs out she head and do strange thing. But that is still Mamai. What not Mamai is when the skunt depression thing inside her head, titivating with her brain connections them.

I use to come home from school in the afternoon, take one look at Mamai, and want to go somewhere else. I couldn't stand the silence between us. Sometimes I try and make a joke, talk to her, hug her up, bust big laugh at nothing at all so she can laugh too. Nothing.

When she talk at all, she sends me away. "Go to the butcher, get some greens from the road corner stall, and buy some bread." I stay away for hours and she says not one word when I walk in. Nothing, not, "Where the greens, the beef, the bread?"

"Why you want bread, Mamai?" I use to say. "We have plenty of bread what you bake in the box."

"We need more," she says.

"Is two of we; we don't want all this bread. It going to get mouldy and spoil."

Silence. Mamai staring out the window, playing with the hem of her dress.

"And why more greens when we get plenty in the garden."

"You getting mannish with Mamai?"

"I just asking. We don't need more things. Is just you and me."

"Do what I say. Go do homework."

"I don't have homework."

"Go and sweep the yard."

"You sick, Mamai?"

"I ain't feel like talking. Leave me. Come when I call."

What it all mean? I would stand in the yard with the pinta broom in my hand. Dust flying round. Chicken scratch where I sweep, making design in the dust. My dog, Rascal, curl like a C near the chicken coop. Behind the back fence, cows graze in the wide pasture. The cricket pitch bare. Too hot to play. I go and sit with Uncle Percy on the sluice house step. Try and read one of the man's big book. Bored, I go out to the koker on the Burma River, sit with the limers and talk skunt. Watch the girls pass on the road. Watch water flow through the koker. Lime. Drink sweet drink and eat buns. Play domino and card in the bruk-down shed on the dam. Think about Mamai sitting quiet looking out into space.

We set off again after Bhoje done with the woman. When we arrive back in Central we get out the car and go in a bar where Bhoje has another woman friend. I sit down while he talks to her in the back room. I hear somebody call my name. Hak Deonandan comes up to me and tells me Anita dead. Hak is a cruel-face man, in a secret way. He has a face that always look *like* it smiling, not a happy smile, but a smile like a bad man in a filmshow. He doesn't talk much and he always look like he planning something against you. He smiling as he gives me the bad news. Is why I don't believe him at first. I believe him when he says it again, cause Hak is not a talk man. He talks only when he has to.

"She drink poison," he says. "Her father find her in the latrine."

That is when I faint away. Is the last thing I remember. I wake up in the backroom of the bar, Bhoje and the woman standing over me.

"What happen?" I say.

"You faint away," Bhoje says. "Hak says he tell you about the little girl."

"It not true," I tell Bhoje.

"It is true," he says, and sadly shake his head. "He tell me it happen yesterday."

The woman wipes my face with a towel that smells like methylated spirits and looks at Bhoje.

"She is he girlfriend," Bhoje says.

"Oh my god, oh my god," the woman says. "And with his mother in madhouse, too. He having a very rough time."

She wipes my face with the towel again and says, "There, there, dear," like me is lil pickney. But is true, I feel like small child and start crying plenty eye-water and my heart mash up good and proper.

"What you going do with he?" the woman asks Bhoje.

"I taking he back home," Bhoje says.

"The poor, poor boy," the woman says. "Me feel sorry for he."

All the way home I cry and cry and cry without stopping. Bhoje drives in silence, his big hairy hands holding the steering wheel tight.

35. THE WAYS OF THE DEAD

After we leave Lyken Funeral Home, I go with Anita's mother to Demico restaurant. We sit there together in quietness, the smell of death still in my nose; it's a chemical smell with soap and perfume together and a rankness like the sea or something spoil. That smell is always going to be associated with the funeral home and Anita's naked body and what I was thinking as I watch Ms. Sabita bathe the body and prepare her for fire in the ghat. For a time, watching this brings me calm. There's nothing to be done, nothing. All you can do is accept and go on living life and loving whoever, go on fucking and kissing and eating and sitting and talking and sleeping.

Now Ms. Sabita eating an ice-cream cone and licking it with her long tongue in a sexy way. I look at her and she smiles. Then I know she realises what I also know. Is no time for grief.

"What can you do, boy?" she says, "What can be done?"

"You carry on living and try and forget," I say.

"Yes," she says, "and you stay alive as long as you can."

I look out the window at cars moving on the road, horns beeping loud and long.

Anita never come to town until now. She live all her days in village places. She in town now but can't see it. She is in a fridge like meat, ready to burn, Coolie-cremation style. I will never see her again and when I think about the last time I see her, I will remember it was in a funeral parlour and she wasn't aware I was there with her, watching her mother clean her body.

She lay down naked on the cooling board, smaller than I remember and too thin. I go close and look and touch her hand. It cold. I look in her face and she doesn't wink and she doesn't smile and no breath comes like a sigh from her nose-hole. I say her name in a silent way and she doesn't react.

I watch Ms. Sabita take the bowl of water and wipe Anita's dead body down. She washes her face and behind her ears and under her chin. She doesn't cry, but a mask of sadness on she face.

Now, watching Ms. Sabita eat ice cream, I feel a lightness and calm. I start to eat my ice cream thinking I better finish it before it melts.

Ms. Sabita leave me and gone back to Lyken Funeral Home to make arrangements. Is she what riding in the hearse with Anita body to take it back to the village for burning. I stay and eat my ice cream. After, I walk around Georgetown. I walk to the seawall and watch the sea for a long time and feed the brazen dogs that loiter around the place, then I walk some more into town. I buy a new pair of pants and shoes at the market for the funeral, a white shirt, and black pants. Then I take the Rosignol bus home and bathe and dress in Mamai house and wait, looking out from the veranda for the hearse to pass with the burning party. When it comes, I go out to the road and walk quiet with the rest of the mourners.

36. GHAT AND THE BURNING GIRL

I think how when you dead, bird can come and pick at you, hungry-belly dog can tear you guts out, fly can crawl in you nose and mouth and lay egg and shit, worm can eat you and fire burn you, but Anita don't care. She lay down on a pile of wood and allow tall tongue of fire to burn away she flesh and turn she to black ash. She don't move; she don't holler or cry out, "Come, take me off this skuntian firewood what burning up my beetee and back!" She take she self out the world with a toops of poison and leave me in it and missing she bad-bad – missing she voice, she soft skin, she patacake and bubbie, she mouth, she teeth, she hand and leg and finger and toe and her hair what smell sweet of coconut oil and all she was and can't be again. I vex with Anita. I vex with her and vex with the whole world. I wake up vex and sleep vex and everything is vex in my eyesight. Is like I don't know how to *be* anymore since Anita drink malathion and dead in the latrine.

Anita white wrap burn off and black smoke raise up and drift away. Anita face turn black like tar and burn. She hair burn and she eye burn and she finger them and toe burn.

People stand-up in a circle, crying and bawling. Ms. Sabita leaning on a tall man who holding she up. Pandit P swinging a little thing on a chain what people call thurifer, with smoke what smell like burn black-sage bush and agarbathi and sandalwood. Mr. Ramsammy standing by himself with his hand fold cross his chest and he head looking down at his foot them. He not crying. Two Panty standing with Dado crying dry-eye tears. Marcel crying and Simone and Derek and Lil Girl crying. But I can't cry. Is like my eye don't have eye-water. I just standing and looking.

I remembering how the next day after I see she father fucking her, I come out the house and she leaning on the cowpen fence waiting for me. I plan in my mind not to say a word to her skunt ever again, to see her and not talk to her, to ignore she rass. But that morning, when I passing, she call my name in a soft way that give me a terrible longing, and I go over to her. Is like I love her more bad than before. I climb over the fence and hold she close with her head on my shoulder and she cry and cry and cry. And we sit down in the cowpen yard quiet, and we never talk again about what I see she father doing to her. I never shame her and call she bad vulgar name; I never tell what I see to anybody. And me and she come closer than close and nearer than near. I ain't think of she in any wrong way.

"Is alright," I tell she, "is aright, girl."

"I never never never letting it happen again," she cry. "I rather dead, Kippy, I rather dead."

We talk about many things but never again about what she father do. She use to talk like if she don't have a future; she don't talk about going to college or going away. She use to talk about Skylab and how she waiting for it to fall and destroy the whole world, so only me and she can survive in the hole she dig in the ground.

Now she is ash in a bed of wood. She gone, turn ghost and fly away in the sky. People say she spirit leave she body on the burning ground and go to Coolie heaven of plenty where things peaceful and without pain, a heaven, where she don't have to eat anymore rice-flour cake and cassava bread and rice pap in the morning and drink rice mar tea. I imagine her talking to the Coolie god version of Jesus Christ. Brahma, maybe, but more like Vishnu who Pandit P say is preserver and protector of mankind, who saying all the time, "You are forgiven, go and sin no more, turn your life round and be good, don't fornicate and thief other man things and restrain from nastiness with other man wife." Is a nice God, this Vishnu, who is like a Jesus in Coolie heaven in the sky.

I imagine she and this Vishnu leaning out a wide window in high heaven, looking down on earth and she pointing a accusing finger at Mr. Ramsammy house and telling the Coolie Jesus to send down thunderbolt on she father skunt, destroy he with lightning and brimstone fire and smite he with wrath that he may know incest is a great and terrible crime. Yes. And she tell the

Coolie Jesus to brukup he land and lay waste to his cattle and property so he suffer many degradations and loss, like Job. And don't leave she mother alone, Anita tell the Coolie Jesus. Punish she whoring mother, but not so much, cause she mother love she just a small eenie-weenie bit. She tell the Coolie Jesus to help me cause I is a fatherless, orphan incest child, never mind I suck Satie bubbie them and make she vex too bad. I is she precious love. She tell Coolie Jesus to help me take Mamai out the mad house in Fort Canje and give me a freck of money so I can live good and proper in the world of hard-hard rockstone and rice flour.

Is so I imagine Anita in Bhuva Loka. But in the real-real world she is burning with fire in her hair and bones burnt black as coal, and she not speaking a word of love or parting. Now ash and dust is all she is and will be from now on until the end of forever.

After the cremation, I go with Carl, Lamuta Dave, Derek and Hari to the cowpasture. It dry and brown with the water gone low from the coulees, so you can see eel and crappo cassie moving like snake in the shallows, and fat plovers with tall legs gobbling up small fry and black dutty polliwogs in pools of shadow. These things alive and moving. Anita is not moving. Anita burn up and gone and nobody can tell what is she from the embers.

We sit under a courida tree and drink rum from the neck of a bottle Carl thief from Poopaloops shop. We take big toops of hard stuff like big man. Is like swallowing fire. Just the cow on the pasture around to see we, just dove in the low grass to hear we gaff and cuss and carry-on.

"Why she kill she self?" Derek say.

"People don't need any reason," Carl say. "They decide and then they do it. And when they dead, is the living people what ask question. But I never know why they ask question. Dead people can't answer question from alive people."

"She was Kip thing," Lamuta Dave say. "She only talk to him."

"That girl love Kip bad," Carl say. "Remember when she use to live in Creek and come to school barefoot. Is only Kip she talk to. Then, after that she just go away. Where she go, Kippy?"

"Corentyne."

"Yes. And Kippy sick all that time pining away for the Coolie thing. She go away a whole month and Kippy mother get so worried she take he to see Ma Tussette, cause she think somebody work obeah on she one-grain son. But Ma tell she nothing wrong with the boy. Kippy mother ask me how Kippy sick so and don't want play with us. I ain't tell she, though; I ain't say the Coolie thing have Kip basodee over love. Then one day, me and Kip sitting at Poopaloops shop playing draughts and Sookuru car stop and out jump the Coolie thing with she whoring mother, and they go down in Mr. Ramsammy yard. Is so I learn that man is little Anita father. And now is only two fence yard between Kip and the thing, and right away the two of them start back with the lovey-dovey business. She and Kippy like married man and wife. If Kippy been older, he would marry she by now for true, not so Kip boy?"

I nod and take a big drink from the rum.

"Kippy drunk," Derek say. "Look how he face wrinkle up like he taste sour milk."

"No more rum for you, Kip," Hari say. "Kip too small to drink plenty liquor. But I going let he take one more toops cause Kippy mother in mad house and he sweetheart drink poison and dead. The thing I don't understand about Coolie people is when booleggae brace them, quick time they drink poison and dead."

"But youself is Coolie," Carl say.

"But I learn to bear me chafe like Black man," Hari say, "and take pain after pain and go through pain and come out of pain."

"Let we watch Kippy, though; maybe he have more Coolie in he than Black naigger man; you can't tell with people nowadays. You have Coolie in you, Kip boy?" Derek say.

"My mother say she father father father was a Coolie from a far place in India, a man name Balgobin," I say.

"You see what I saying," Derek say. "Kip is part coolie. How you feel about drinking poison and killing youself, Kip boy?"

"Will it help me be near Anita?"

"No, it don't help you, you half-coolie skunt," Carl say and snatch away the rum from my hand. "It only make you dead. No more rum for Kippy. He drunk already."

"Tonight, we taking Kippy to the big house," Derek say. "I don't like how he answer that question. Maybe Kippy do a suicide when we not looking."

"Kippy mother have malathion; she does use it in she kitchen garden. I see it plenty time. If Kip go back to Ms. Paulette house, maybe he take a toops and dead like Anita skunt," Carl say.

"Yeah," Hari say, "Kippy can't stay in he own house alone. Let we take he to the big house. Lil Girl will mind he proper. The two of them close and he always listen to her."

That night I went to stay with Derek and Lil Girl and Hari in Big House.

37. DARK NIGHT INTO DAY

I tell Carl and Hari and Derek that I need to be by myself and I promise them not to do myself any harm. Even so, they take the malathion away. I want to remember everything about Anita and the time I had with her. We were just children at school, but after Mamai gone away, we play more than children's dolly-house. We sleep together in one bed like husband and wife, me and Anita, but only in the daytime. We sleep snoring and dribbling on the pillow and when Anita go, she leave me she nice hot smell. One time she dance for me naked, a ragged Coolie dance named Bharatanatyam we see in a film show with Amitabh Bachchan. She makes a bird with her fingers and with her head movements, like a bird on a wire, this way and that, like if it get pulled by some invisible string. Then she fine hip move up and down and she turns on the heel of one foot in a pirouette. Is a dance what say she in the mood for the sweetness of nastiness. She smiles at me, oh it was a lovely smile, she white-white teeth showing clean when she lip pulled back, and she eyes narrow, winking an invitation at me. Come kiss me it says, and I do. She let me take her standing against the wall, trying to hold on before we fall. I remember these plenty nice times and cannot wash my sheet with she smell on them. I lay down in bed with eyes wide open so I don't miss the return of her jumbie to tell me what it's like to be dead and in a place of peace. But this is just wish, I know; hope for things unseen. Mayhap she in a dark place, with no light leading her back to me, no crumbs left on the track, like for Hansel and Gretel, to trace the winding way home to Mahaicony. She's lost in a dark forest. I beg the Hindu Christian Muslim Greek gods of above and below to send Anita back to me, but know she's in a far country with no passage back home. I cannot read or write my book. I just want to lay down all the time and rest. But always something disturb my peace. There is lowing cattle, birds cawing and the bawling of a child getting beat, and people coming to comfort me and lambast me to get me skunt up and rigmarole up and down the village.

Mary comes. I hear her hawking her fruits down the dams before she come into the house. She sits down on the bed beside me. She says she can be my new girlfriend if I want. I want her to be Anita, but she is Mary. She rubs my face with Limacol and methylated spirit, then she leaves. I watch a gangasaka walk upside down in the roofbeam. The nail holes in the galvanise roof wink like stars. Cobwebs hold the trapped flies and beetles. I watch the roof for days. The wood-ant's trail drops fine dust on the ground. At night, the beetles bang their carapaces against the naked bulb and fall to the floor. They land upside down, on their backs, and all through the night pedal their little legs like bicycle racers until they tire and dead. In the morning, a train of kurubeti ants come and lift them away. Is a whole world of creatures in my room. Outside, I hear Mary singing out the names of her fruit loud and then quieter as she moves further away. Carl and Hari come and make threats, saying if I don't get my skunt out the house by tomorrow morning, they go strip me naked and throw me out. But is just talk. When morning comes, I bolt the doors and windows and lock them out. I tell them to go away when they call and pelt rockstone at the Berbice window. Sleep is all I do; is like I can't get enough. I sleep but do not dream. When I wake I think of Anita.

We shared love, we shared spit, and one time, just after Mamai disappear, in the silence of the house, we shared the music of the heart. But now I cannot sing it because one man cannot sing a two-people song. But me and Anita sing a true song, and I remember where and when and how we two make the music for true.

Just after Mamai disappear, on an afternoon of rain soft like mist, I sitting on the veranda reading *The Games Were Coming* by Michael Anthony. Is a good book, true to the business of sports. The whole thing is about a boy name Leon who preparing for a big bicycle race in Trinidad. This Leon don't care about no wining and grinding of carnival; all he thinks about is bicycle race skunt and keeping in shape and keeping he body prime and proper for race day. The man even stops doing nastiness with he little girlfriend, a girl who remind me of Satie, who know good how to get man to give she what she wants. The girl plotting to get Leon to give she he tolo in the regular style. He refuse because he is true athlete and keeping he strength for the big bike race. I was reading the exciting part where the girl playing a big bad trick on Leon to turn he into her koonoomoonoo and pokey lotan, when Anita come through the gate dress nice and pretty in white dress and sandal shoes, she hair combed just so, she skin shiny with coconut oil. She have a bunch of wild flowers in she hand. She stand on the landing looking at me in a lovey-dovey way. She smell like new rain water.

"Go in the house, man Kip man," she say.

"You look pretty," I say.

"Yes man," she say. "I dress up just for you. Is we special day. Go in the house nuh, man."

I get up and go in the house and sit down in the Berbice chair. Anita stand up in front me like statue with the flowers in she hand. She looking down at me with a nice smile on she face. This smile pull some string inside what make me tremble and shake. Is knowing Anita loves me and is mine, like I love she and am hers to do what with and where. The feeling make me want cry right there and then.

"What is this special day about?" I ask. "What make you dress up in Sunday-best clothes and nice sandals? Is not your birthday, is not my birthday."

"We getting married," she say. "Like man and wife in real real style."

I want bust big laugh but I know not to. She won't like that. I know she good. When she vex for true, she won't talk to me for days, until I have to beg.

"Where the preacher?" I say.

"We don't need no damn preacher."

"Where the bridesmaid them and bridegroom?"

"You is all and me is all. Go put on you nice clothes."

My nice clothes is a bright lemon chambury shirt and a green gabardine pants. I put on my argyle socks and black church shoe from BATA shoe store. She out there waiting, sitting quiet like yard fowl in a cherry tree in the nighttime. When I come out the room, ready for the kanya daan, ready for the marriage business, she look me up and down.

"The bridegroom come," she say. "Beep beep beep," and laugh she fine laugh, a happy laugh, and sometimes a surprise, because Anita don't laugh plenty; mostly she face still and serious. To hear this laugh is a gift. Plenty times I ask myself why Anita didn't laugh more often. Is a strange thing, because a person would have to try hard not to laugh, cause laughing come easy and don't need strength to do it. So, it was special to hear Anita laugh with her head thrown back and her mouth open so you could see the white arc of her top teeth.

"You is the bride *and* the car what bring the bridegroom to the church?"

"Yes," she say, "and you is the pandit what say the nice words and ask the questions."

And so I did. We said, "I do", and we sit down in the Berbice chair and hug up nice. Outside, rain start falling down in the yard and sputtering into the barrels under the gutter. A darkness come sudden like night and the house quiet and the world quiet, so quiet I think I can hear my heartbeat and the blood running through my veins, and I can hear Anita's heart and it beats to the same rhythm as my heart. She looks at me puzzled because she hears it too.

"Listen, listen," she say. "Listen."

"I listening," I say.

And she hums along with our heartbeats, and I join her in singing the song and is the song only me and she sing. But the song cut now. Some skunt pull the needle off the record player and scratch the LP. Is Mr. Ramsammy what do it and ruin the song and skuntify we tune.

I know I should get up and go out and meet the day. But is too much. I should stay in the dark of my room and dead. I feel like I falling and know I must grab onto something, but is nothing to hold on to, so I set sail into a deep sleep. I think I am turning into my mother when she sleeps with her eyes wide open and wakes and stares at walls and says nothing. Now I am weak and turn into my mother, laying down in bed in a room that smell like piss. I do not know night from day, watching the wooden walls of my room. I am frighten of what I'm becoming. Is like I see a future where this single room become the world, and darkness and light makes no difference to me, and people and places all count for nothing. I must get up, I tell myself, but I don't. I turn into a mad skunt boy, and I forget myself, not giving a skunt what is the name of day. Pure skunt is my state and I drift between the satisfaction of nothing, the ease of nothing, the nothing of nothing, and it feel good and it is proper. But sometimes the drift of my mad thoughts catch on a snag and I remember who I am and say my name and feel ashamed of myself in this state of skunt. This frighten me into getting up. I throw off the bed sheets and get up quick, pulling them out of the room and over the clothesline to air when the sun comes up. It's early in the morning and dark and silent except for the sounds of cricket and crappo, nighttime jumbie bird, and the sea quarrelling with itself, repeating the many things it has done wrong, the plenty slave people it drown, and the fisherman them it drown, orphaning their children and widowing their wives. The sea repenting, "Sorry, sorry, sorry, sorry, sorry, sorry, sorry, sorry," its lamentations breaking on the rocks. I get sorry for forgetting myself and abandoning myself in time. I sit down on the step and cry like a soft boy. The language of the sea is only for itself. I need to hear my own thoughts and see my way clear, and to make my way out of grief back to myself. I think of the fishermen who drown and know I'm glad to be alive.

The morning air cool on my skin. I stand near the gutter barrel and strip naked and throw my clothes away from me like dutty things. I dip the calabash and sluice myself. Water cold and good. I wash my tolo; it feel like a foreign thing in my hand. Is like I forget it was there. I wash my beettee crease; I soap and scrub my skin clean with nenwah. I go back upstairs and wipe my skin and dress in clean clothes what smell of the naphthalene balls Mamai put in my clothes basket. Is a fresh smell. It seems like a long time since I think about Mamai, long time. Is like a man can forget the world even while he inside it; he can forget to be.

Sun coming up now, yellowing the window of my room, reflecting off the glass. I open the window; see the green pastures coming out of the shadow of the dawn, and the houses, and the pointed steeple of the Methodist church. Now birds are on the wing, wheeling west, a flock of curlew. I pick up *The Games Were Coming* to read it again, and meet the sun spilling light from the blazing yoke of itself. I sit down in Mamai veranda and turn the pages and read, and read on and on through dayclean. I think about writing more of the story I start.

When Bhoje, Hari and Carl come later that morning with axe and hatchet, mattock and crowbar to tear out Mamai door and drag me out the house, I sitting on the veranda to greet them proper with, "Good morning," and "Howdee do."

Bhoje say, "What's this I hear? You turn mad-cuirass boy and lock youself in the house like prisoner-man?"

"I see the light," I tell he.

"You see the light eh," Carl say. "Where is the light?"

"There," I say and point to the sun.

Bhoje sit down on the step and light a Bristol and take a long draw and blow smoke out he big nose hole. Carl sit down next to him and try to bum a cigarette off him without success. Bhoje tell he that he not contributing to the wayward behaviour of minors. Hari don't say anything. He standing in the yard looking up at me, making a study of my person like a head doctor. I smile at he but he don't smile back. He just staring me down, like he making a calculation.

"I have my eye on you," he say finally. "You come from mad people and you is also a incest boy, and that make plenty people mad. I go make sure you don't run out your head for true and turn like mad skunt Kangalang Harry Arnold. Don't think you fool me with you tricky ways."

"I recover, Hari boy," I say; "I see the light."

He don't say nothing to that. He squeeze between Bhoje and Carl and come up the step and sit down next to me on the veranda. We say nothing at all for a long long time.

38. MASQUERADE

One afternoon, for an out-of-season bangarang, we meet by the river on the koker. Is me and Carl and Hari and Derek and the toaster Willard Mack, who win Junior Calypsonian at Mash last year. This Willard Mack is a small-size boy with big lip who like to read book like me, but mostly poetry. Willard dress up like lion with his whole head cover over by the lion head so he can see through the sharp bars of the lion teeth.

I dress up like Tar Baby scarecrow what catch Br'er Rabbit in a story I read as a child. I is the treasurer of the fete and the sharer-outer of the dunzai what people throw as we pass. Sun shining but the day cloudy with big black cloud threatening rain. We in a hurry to get the business over before rain start fall. Is not a good day for a masquerade, and is not even masquerade time, not Christmas when the masquerade take to the road with more dancers in the band, playing long lady and donkey boy, moongazer and jumbie. Christmas far away, though. This masquerade is for the president and his party.

Is they who say come play Mash out of season, come wine and rigmarole in the village road; is they what paying the piper paisa to perform. The party men in the Land Rover moving slowly up the road like a wedding procession, talking through megaphone, telling the people to vote PNC. The Land Rover have a big banner on top with the president picture, Mr. L.F.S. Burnham, paste up on it; he smiling and showing his little puppy teeth. He have a face what round like tawa, with a little goatee and his eyes them bulging out slightly like crappo eye. But he don't *look* like the real dog my mother say he is. He look like a man who might buy shave ice from a vendor on the village road. He look like we, dark and with a little Afro, wearing a smile.

This August bangarang is not Mashramani when we have float and calypso singing and girls dress up in costume to show plenty flesh, and you can wine up on them good and proper. Mash is for fun. We doing this for pay. Today, we beating drum and toasting to bring out the people so the party men can tell us how to vote and what nice things the party doing for us, like free education and rice flour they make themselves and such-like skunt, so they can talk loud about the terrible badness of the Coolie opposition party.

The band strike up and we start move. Uncle Charlie on bass, Mr. Derek on snare, Uncle Charlie son, Pashway, who really name Charles Junior on tenor, Hari knocking cowbell and Derek on triangle. The party Land Rover in front and the man with the megaphone hollering out *Vote for PNC* and how soon, very soon, the party will make the country into a paradise with no blackout and no ban on Tip-Top cheese and sardine in red sauce and new exercise book and fancy Converse shoe. The world will see we is the breadbasket of the Caribbean. Produce not perish… and skunt and skunt and skunt and much more skunt as we start up the road.

Willard Mack is toasting as we go, saying:

Boomboom me bass
Tingting me steel
While the heroes was in the field
The heroes blood I do maintain
Suck bubbie is Kippy bad name.

And people laugh and throw money on the ground as we go and I pick it up and put it in my little purse. Willard start another rhyme saying:

She is into me or she is out
She get nuff pleasure from me mout'
She pumpum sweet is what I talking bout,
Pussy galore.

She don't know how to cook curry or cook-up rice
With salt-pork meat and hot pepper spice
But she salt-fish sweet and that is nice,
Pussy galore.

Is a cat on the mat when evening come
Curled snuggly in her eiderdown
Is Mahaicony me get um from,
Pussy galore.

And when is morning, she fix the tea,
Gimme she lips for breakfast, she breasts, she pussy
Curl up warm on the floor, she honey,
Pussy galore.

Lunch hour she call me in the house for more.
She have a dainty platter spread out on the floor.
She say, eat man, sip from my store,
Pussy galore.

And in between, when I raw and sore,
Staggering out she broad back door,
She pull me back say, "Is where you goin, I want more."
Pussy Galore.

Is a thing I see plenty time before,
Strong man like Samson beat until he not sure
Which way is up, down, out, in, cause of hardcore
Pussy… Galore.

Carl is the long lady and he dance the long lady dance in front of the masquerade band and the people come out of their yards and throw coins at his feet and Carl dance the coin dance and pick up the coin and hand them to me. Willard Mack, in front the band like drum major, put up he hand and stop the band playing so he can toast another rhyme saying:

Flour gone, rice gone, sardine gone,
Cheese gone but politician on the lawn
Making long-water speech
Saying nut-butter not gone it only out of reach.
Rice still around but is not enough
Is only hardship self, life tough.

Tomorrow come, you will see
Once you get use to rice flour and no chickpea,
A better, a bigger best and beautiful future,
But is who will feed me hungry belly, sir?
Who go give me soup to sip
Instead of cuff, kicks and the whip?
Who go build my big house of imagination
When there is more vain hope than ambition
More skunt than skunt and more rass than rass…?

"That is enough, Will," Uncle Charlie say.

The band strike up again and we march on. Carl, tall above us in his long dress and on his stilts, knock a rhythm on the macadam as he move to the beat of the snare and the boom bass and the tingling triangle. Children follow us, dancing behind the band, dark thin boys and girls. They waving small party flag what the party men hand out. The party Land Rover move slowly before us. A big party man in a dashiki sit shotgun and holler VOTE PNC, VOTE PNC over and over again, like mantra at morning puja. A few people on their verandas cheer and clap.

The government man tell Uncle Charlie that we getting paid when we get to Airy Hall. Uncle Charlie is the man what own the drums and part up the money for me to distribute. He is the negotiator. The government man say band men getting one hundred each. The dancers getting fifty.

Carl say he don't see why he shouldn't get the same money as the band men.

"I is the long lady," he say. "I is what people want see."

Uncle Charlie tell Carl to get off the stilts and take off the dress. "Put them down on road corner and get you ass out of here, boy," he tell Carl. Carl calm down.

"The world is what it is," says Mr. Derek, because that is what he always say, about small things and big thing. It is all he have to say.

"That boy going end up bad," Uncle Charlie say. "He going end up in big jail."

When we get to Airy Hall, rain start fall but it don't last. We end up in a rum shop and the party man start buy rum. Teacher Clive and Bhoje in the place making sure we don't drink. The party man order rum for so and beer and Guinness stout. But me, Derek and Carl only drinking soft drink and eating stale salara. Teacher Clive and Bhoje and some big man talking to the party man about politics. The party man talking about how great Comrade Burnham is. Bhoje and Teacher Clive just nodding their heads but not saying anything. Uncle Charlie sucking he teeth steady but he not saying anything either.

"And what we will do," the party man say, "is ensure that the youth them have something to do to occupy themselves and persevere. Produce or perish. We must remember that."

"That is skunt," Carl say.

Everybody stop talk and an uncomfortable silence fall over the place. Is like when somebody curse loud in church or shout in the library. I look at Derek and he shake he head at me and mouth with his lip for me to say something. But what I suppose to say? How I suppose to correct this thing? Is not like I didn't agree with what Carl say; the party man was talking pure skunt and everybody know this; everybody know we suffering under the government rule; every day is pure blackout blackout blackout; and not enough in the shops to buy and not enough money in your pocket, unless you is a dishonest man, scallywag and scoundrel politician.

The streetlight what stop work five years ago still not working, and plenty youthman don't have no job or even ambition, even them with college education. The rice mill bruk-down and fall apart, and because of this, when the skunt of the government what have only words to give we and slogan like *Better must come one day* and *Produce or perish*, the smart people leaving and gone to this island and that island and big snow city in Foreign and Away. Is mostly from them we getting any money, from we relatives in Away and friends in Elsewhere. Is how people keep body and soul seam together with barrel coming regular with food and clothes inside. And if you not getting any small piece from Foreign and Away, cat eat your dinner. Everybody know this; everybody see this. So how can you talk against the truth?

I look at Derek and he look at me and I keep my mouth close tight as beetee hole. Is Teacher Clive what break the silence.

"Comrade," he say, "the boy don't understand deep politics."

"I understand when I ain't eating proper," Carl say, "and when I hear skunt with my own-own ears."

Teacher Clive give Carl the hard look he use with pupil when he want them to behave, but Carl not even looking at he. He looking at the party man with his neat Afro and trim goatee beard, dress up in nice dashiki suit and shiny leather shoe, polish just so.

Bhoje get up and come near Carl and hold his hand and bend down and whisper in Carl ear some threat. But Carl pull away his hand and move closer to the party man.

"All I hear from all-you is talk and talk and talk. If talk was food, I never go hungry in this place. But I go hungry plenty time. To feed myself I have to climb tree and pick fruit or feel in trench for fish like everybody round here. That is the way we living, and how we living have nothing to do with what you give we. You is a useless skunt and come round only when is election time and tell we what go happen if Coolie get back in power and stir up badness between we. But I can get food from any Coolie people in this place, but I can't get none from you. You is a skunt and the party is skunt and politics is skunt. I say so."

The party man jump up like crappo and raise he hand to cuff Carl, but Uncle Charlie hold the man hand and turn he round so the party man facing away from Carl. The party man and Uncle Charlie eyes make four and they staring one another down.

"Me can't allow that," Uncle Charlie say. "Me can't sit here and tolerate no maltreatment of this boy. We go manners he weself, cause he is one of we, we own-own son, born and grow here. Tell me what your complaint is?"

The party man pull away he hand. He look at Uncle Charlie like he don't understand the situation.

"Tell we the complaint, comrade," Teacher Clive say.

"We want the complaint," Hari say.

"The complaint?" the party man say.

"Yes, the complaint," Bhoje say. "You can't discipline the boy without a complaint."

"Very true," Mr. Derek say, "very very true."

"This boy have no manners. He talk too rash to big man," the party man say.

"Yes," Uncle Charlie say, "we go discipline he good and proper for that today-today. You can put you mind at ease on that Mr. Party Man. Now pay we."

When them party man leave an hour later, Carl in the corner putting the long lady costume in a polythene bag. Uncle Charlie and the rest of the village men sitting close round a table like in some panchayat.

I hear Bhoje say, "Carl need a holiday."

"Very soon," Uncle Charlie say.

"I will talk to his mother," Teacher Clive say. "He have people in Essequibo."

"And you, Will," Uncle Charlie say to Willard, "I don't like this political business in your toast. Cut it out."

"Is my new style," Will say. "I going into politics. I write a calypso already call *Fat Man and the Devil*. Is about the Prime Minister. Hear how it go:

In the time of shortage and pay to play
Of Produce or Perish and Walter Rodney
Vincent Teekah and Shirley Fields Ridley
Me have a little sadness to make you happy
I talking rice flour daal and cocobey
What the PM wearing on his face
And if you look close, you can trace
In his eye-corner wrinkle when he mouth out of place
The first distinction of a lie…

"Enough!" Teacher Clive say. "Boy, you never singing that song."

"Never," Bhoje say.

"Never," Uncle Charlie say.

"Say it," Teacher Clive say.

"Never," Will say.

"Again," Bhoje say.

"Never," Will say.

"Politics is dangerous business, boy," Uncle Charlie say.

Two days later, I liming on the koker with the boys talking cricket. Carl ride up on a bicycle and say he going to Essequibo soon for a holiday. He don't say when but he sound excited.

"I need a change in my life," he say. "Different faces to see."

Willard Mack sitting with me, writing calypso songs in a little exercise book with the president on the cover. He look up at us and say, "I just finish me new calypso; you want hear it?" He don't wait for we to answer, just start up and beat with his mouth and launch into the song called, "The Dead Will Rise".

39. BUTCHER BOYS

Bhoje say we too idle and take us to work for Boo Leggae who real name is Jacques Crawford. Boo have a butcher shop on Mill Road. We find him outside the shop cutting a cow tongue out of a cow head. Cow tongue long for so. He clothes full of blood and little piece of meat and slime what get hard in the sun. Is me and Hari and Carl. Hari saying how he can find he own work heself. Bhoje not hearing that. He say if Hari have to pay lawyer for thieving the Blue Ganesh, not one red cent coming out he pocket; no, cause if boy want play man, boy must learn responsibility of man and do man work and earn man pay. He spend plenty days making sure we stay on the straight and narrow; he tired and vex with we and we is not he children; he not taking on no more responsibility. If we don't take this work with Boo Leggae, he wash he hand of we right now, today skunt.

Hari suck his teeth hard, so Bhoje give him a cuff and knock him down on cow shit grass. Hari get up ready to fight Bhoje, but Bhoje give he a strong look and he calm down and say Bhoje ain't get no right to knock he, cause he is big man what make baby what coming any day now. Bhoje look at him strong and say he sorry, but he ask Hari how he going feed Lil Girl and the child if he don't work. Hari ain't have no answer for that.

Boo Leggae take a small axe and split the cow head in two so that the cow brain, what look like sponge self, come out slow on the table. Boo Leggae pick it up with ladylike softness and put it in a bowl. We can see cow teeth in the cow head with grass still in it.

Is so we start working for Boo Leggae, slaughtering cow and sheep and pig and goat. We turn real butcher boys, wearing cow blood on we skin like Boo and cutting up meat with a small axe and sawing through big soup bone with a sharp-teeth saw and washing out shit from cow intestine and making sure cow blood don't clot up when it bleed in the bucket.

Boo Leggae is true kill artist. He serious when he cutting cow throat. He don't like playing round. He don't talk either. Is like he saving all he concentration for butchering animal. The butcher shop only open three days a week. We kill the other days. The way Boo do it is art self. He take a big sledge hammer and swing back with his big muscle self, like Clive Lloyd about to hit six over fence at deep mid-on at Bourda, and he bring the sledge round centre on the cow head what tie to a milking post. Quick time he drop the hammer and pull out two sharp knife from his waist and cut the cow throat. Me and Carl and Hari job is to pull on a rope what over a limb of the plum tree, so the cow hang down by its foot and bleed into a bucket with salt in it, so blood don't clot. After the cow hang up like that, Boo tie it on the limb and start skinning, moving quick-quick with sharp knife.

Carl like the butcher job badly. He tell Boo he want do the killing part. And Boo let him. Carl good with the knife and Boo say yes, he is the best apprentice he ever see, yes, and if Carl want, he can learn from he. Carl like this very much. But Carl not like Boo. He like the killing part too much. He don't do business like Boo, quick and clean; he like to watch animal tremble and wiggle round, hurting on the killing floor; he like too much how light go out in cow eye. For Boo, killing sheep or goat or pig is business, but to Carl is a pleasure.

Me and Derek don't like the killing part.

"The cow don't get to fight back," Derek tell me. "Is like killing a helpless thing. Like killing a baby."

Carl say animal is not people, is food. It don't matter how cow dead. But when killing start, Derek turn away he head from the bloody scene. I watch and get a new understanding. Man can get his throat cut like cow and skin like cow and cut up in pieces like cow. Because man is just meat like cow.

The good thing about the whole killing business is that we get pay. Boo pay we fifty dollars a week, plenty money. We like that. Another thing, we eat good at the butcher shop. Boo is a bad-bad cookman. When cow kill, we always have liver stew and rice. If is goat or sheep, we eat curry. Boo cook on an outside stove behind the butcher shop. He take his time when he cooking. He have to wash out meat fifty times and soak it down in fresh seasoning for two hour and make sure no dirty wares around when he start, and that the fire catch proper and the rice pot clean and the rice not stinky and the water not rusty from the standpipe; he careful bad.

Only when these things done, Boo put pot afire. But this just for a start. After he wash the rice five time, he don't throw it in the boiling water just so. He take a pot spoon and throw it in one spoon at a time. He have little spoon things he measure everything with; this take a while. When is time to eat, he have rule concerning that, too. He make we sit at the table while he serve. He make we chew we food twelve times before we swallow. We can't drink fruit juice before we finish food. He don't say nothing when we break the rule. He just give we a look what make us shame and say, sorry Boo.

Boo Leggae have plenty auntie-man ways what not proper and regular in a man. And he strange in other ways, too. We notice the bathing business. He bathe eight, nine times a day; he wash he hand a hundred time. The worst thing is he don't like people disturb things he set up; everything in order in the shop and he have systems for doing everything. He have system how to hold knife, how to cut cow throat, how to skin cow, how to cut meat, how to hang cow tongue on a hook in butcher shop. Is a hard business working for Boo. I try and imagine how it would be to live with him. He would always be saying how often I should bathe; how many times I should brush my teeth; how to cut bora; how to wash your beetee crease. He'd be saying, if I tell you once I tell you a thousand time, this is the way you scale fish; this is the way you wash shit stain from your buckta; this is how you cook curry. When you go to latrine, don't perch like bird in tree; sit down over the hole so you don't strain and get pile. Pure skunt.

That is why he still bachelor. Woman never live long with him. Two-three days and they gone. The woman he live with last, Doudou Darlin, really Orta Gibbs, leave he and gone because Boo always trying to get her to dress regular. Doudou is big mannish woman you never see in frock and skirt. She climb coconut tree and throw castnet like man self and she don't go in for gossip business over paling stave fence with neighbours. She is like Mamai in this way. We like she bad, because she kind and sweet and call every child *doudou darlin,* and *pumpkin*, and *sweet-*

heart and *honey love*. She was a fine man-woman. Was Boo what drive she away with his strange self. We didn't like he after Doudou left, but you can't stay vex with he long. He the man with the meat and he don't hurt nobody. He just strange. In some country, Boo Leggae would be up in a madhouse daubing shit on a white wall. Here in Guyana, he just walking round normal, bathing every half hour and washing he hand every five minutes.

40. THE DEVIL IN THE INTERIOR

We liming on the koker, me, Derek, Carl and Hari, who waiting on Sookuru car so he can take Lil Girl to Central to see a baby doctor, when Simone run come say thousand people dead in big massacre in bush village name Jonestown. I thinking that is a terrible number of Amerindian people to dead at one time. How come? Maybe them get together to dance round fire and drink paiwarri from calabash and the paiwarri get poison. I read about Warrau and Akewayo and Patamona tribe in history book last year. But Simone say is Americans what dead.

Well, I think to myself that maybe Simone pretty like flower, but she is a stupidy skunt. Whoever see Americans in Guyana? Is we Guyanese what go to America; American don't come here; they too busy making Charles Bronson flick in Hollywood and eating whatever food they want in restaurant and drinking special Coca Cola and walking under skyscraper tall as the Tower of Babel, a million storey high, above the street. Americans not in Guyana. No. They in restaurant eating hamburger and hot dog and beef steak and they going to funfair park – mother and father and children – riding on merry-go-round and Ferris wheel what go round and round and give you bad high-turn. Or they busy sitting in nice room, the whole family watching TV and laughing with wide smile and good teeth, like the pictures you see in *Ebony* and *Jet* magazine. Or they standing next to big Cadillac car, washing it nice to shine in the summer sun. Simone is a skunt. She don't know American stay in America. But deep in my mind I know Simone not stupidy; she bright and get plenty good marks in class test, yeah man, and sometime does top she class them. So, I listen to her talk with her nice voice about how children and woman dead in this massacre, and how they drink poison Kool Aid – a drink I like.

"It in the paper me father reading. It sad sad, Kippy boy," she tell me, and start one big boohoohoo crying what make she face turn ugly like regular girl. She sit down next to me on the koker, make me have to hug she up and say to her, "There there there," like old woman.

Carl get up and say he going to Poopaloops shop and get newspaper because he ain't up to hearing no nancy story, and he gone to get the real-real truth, because everybody know what in newspapers is true.

We hear big rattle on the road and see Sookuru car moving slow and dragging some iron thing, what look like a piece of its exhaust, underneath it. Hari suck he teeth and get up and go back to Big House to get Lil Girl. Sookuru pull off the road and park the car on the koker dam; get out and stand there looking at it and shaking he head sad-sad, like pity-po-boy. Simone get up with she brazen self and go over and tell Sookuru to turn on the car radio. She don't ask him, she tell him. Simone brazen bad. Sookuru do what she say. Most man do what Simone say. Is because she so pretty and fresh with sheself.

But Sookuru radio don't work. What skunt is this now? Just then Carl run come back with *The Chronicle,* the government paper. He put it down in the grass and we all gather round to see the pictures of dead people lying round on the ground, plenty people dead, looking like filmshow pretend dead people, only this is real, but still it hard to believe the ground full with people laying down close together like they sleeping – children and mother and father, all different kind of people. A big massacre, too much for the pages of the newspaper even. You turn the page and more dead people lying round who not in the photograph on the front page, what is too small to fit all. Death is all you see; people on the ground, all face down, no one looking up at heaven. They hand hug-up one another in clump like polliwog in drain water. All this in the bush village of Jonestown, in Guyana.

I see a baby, not the whole baby but the baby foot-bottom, peeking out between a lady and a man what hug up round the baby in like a love-hug. The baby barefoot and it foot bottom clean and white, and it dead like the big people. The more I look at the picture them, I see plenty more baby like this one. I read the words under the pictures and words in the columns. I read, but my mind not with the words; my eye is the leading sense.

Questions raise up. What kind of man can kill baby? A man with no heart, a man of stone and steel, without feeling and pity, without fear of God. But is there a living man like this? Then I think of the dead fishermen and Crabfoot. And I was frighten just then, frighten like a little boy of two years, alone in a room, frighten of sudden darkness. I tremble like the last leaf on a naked tree and struggle to compose myself. My heart start race quick-quick, and is like I getting high-turn. Ning-ning moving up and down my neck-back like crab foot. I turn from the paper and vomit over the trench, because something in me break like salt biscuit, though I can't say true what it is. Maybe is knowing that a man is capable of so much death and that people with brain allow it to happen. How this possible? How this can be? But I don't have answer. I get up and run home. Carl calling me but I don't stop.

I take the short way across the pasture and see Mary tying a goat under a tree. She call and I run to her and hold her hard against me, hold her tight. She say nothing. She hold me back tight, and we stay that way a long time, holding one another, saying nothing at all.

That night I can't sleep proper. I keep seeing dead people picture. Dead people laying down on the ground like piece of wood or stone, face turn away from life. I can't stop seeing them pictures and it keep me up. I go out and sit on the veranda and try to think of something else. The village quiet. Even the birds stop sing, donkey stop bray, and dogs stop bark. The whole place silent like a cemetery. I ask myself how this thing could happen here. And a small voice in me answer the question. "It already here. The evil already come in the village. It murdering small child and killing fisherman and cutting open their belly on *The Amassagana*."

41. THE FAREWELL PARTY

Lamuta Dave tell me he going to Eteringbang goldmining place in the bush, where it have camudi snake and labaria what like the taste of man. He say he have to go and make his fortune like Aron Smart in Jan Carew's book, *Black Midas*. He say he going come back and build big house and marry Marcel. We have a party for him in the dance hall on Saturday night. Carl get drunk and try and fight with Choke-um Charlie, who really name Desmond Van Cliff Charles (what kind of skunt name is that?). Desmond is a real ignorant badjohn. Is two three time now he get sent to jail for bad behaviour and disturbing the peace. Desmond tall and strapping like tree. He other name is Tar Baby, but people don't call he so to he face. Choke-um look at Carl and walk away.

"I ain't getting into trouble for no small boy," he say.

Later, Carl fall down in the grass and vomit up on heself.

Jukebox playing Yellowman and Fathead. Marcel and Lamuta Dave brace up against the wall wining slow. I standing by the bar with Derek and Simone. Simone wearing a pretty lemon dress with white polka-dot and sandals on her nice foot, toenails paint cherry red. She refusing to dance with any other boy and standing close to me, like me and she is boyfriend and girlfriend. Every minute she asking if I feel alright, if I want anything. I tell her I don't want anything. I don't say I want my mother, I don't say I want Anita sitting on the step between my leg while I comb she hair, and smell her and feel she warm-warm skin touching my skin.

One time, somebody tell Anita how I sucking Satie bubbie all over the place. So she come to Mamai house and ask if is true. And because she didn't lie to me, I feel I shouldn't lie to her. I tell she yes, I suck Satie bubbie two-three, four-five, six-seven times.

She say, "What is wrong with my bubbie. I have bubbie you can suck."

So, she take off her clothes and I suck she small bubbie. It was different than with Satie. But that was all I wanted to do with Satie, suck she bubbie. I didn't want to do anything else. With Anita I want to do everything. I wanted to touch and taste and feel. I tell her this.

She say, "Take off your clothes, Kip boy; I want see you tolo please."

I stand-up in my room naked and my tolo hard and sticking out. She show me she patacake. It make me hot inside meself.

"Touch it," she say. And I did, around and inside, and underneath and she touch me too with gentle care.

I still want to be left alone, but in this world people don't leave you alone, they want you involve in their life. I suppose is a good thing that people don't leave you to starve, or go without love. This is what I thinking as I fine-wine with Simone and smell the nice smell of her sweet shampoo hair and feel she softness against me. Is a good feeling and we dance another song name "(If Loving You is Wrong) I Don't Want to be Right." Simone look up at me and say, "I like you bad, man Kippy man." I kiss she nose and she put she head on my shoulder and we dance slow and long to the cool ruler, Mister Gregory Isaacs, singing "Sad to Know (You're Leaving)" and "Objection Overruled".

We in the dance hall until bright foreday morning when the church people come to clean up the place for service. The music not even done and they come and kick us out. A woman we call Dutty Rice, who really name Charlotte Hall, cursing we out the place, saying how we is drunk and good for nothing, how is His Sunday Sabbath, the penitential morning of the most high God, what look down and see wickedness, who, praise Him, see we dutty ways and will spank the wicked with many stripes of lash, that we may know God is God. And she push past us with a mop and bucket and start cleaning up the floor so it smell like Dettol. This same Dutty Rice use to be a bush whore, Aunt Esther tell me, who did sell she pokie to Tom, Dick and Harry in British colonial time when Guyana *was* British Guiana.

We leave Charlotte Hall dutty rass and go home. Lamuta Dave and Marcel hug up and gone home so he can pack for gold mine in Eteringbang. Carl staggering in the road with his drunk self. I go to the big house with Hari and Derek and Lil Girl with she big belly self. Lil Girl belly bigger than she whole body. Simone gone long time – her ignorant father, Lickamore Chops, rush in the place and pull her out.

42. A CHILD IS BORN

Lil Girl screaming how she patacake too small for baby head to pass out. She crying and screaming hard. By the time Hari come with Sookuru to take she to hospital in Central, she pee up herself. Is not regular pee but a big gush of dutty water what come out she patacake and wet up the chair she lay down on. I lift her and walk her out to the road with Carl following with she little bag of woman things. She have she hand on my shoulder, holding on tight.

When we get to Main Road, Sookuru come with Hari and we put Lil Girl in the back, breathing with puffing sound, she leg open on the car seat. Hari riding shotgun with Carl; he shaking like child what see jumbie.

Sookuru car slower than slow; it take almost fifteen minutes to reach Airy Hall.

"Is the carburettor," Sookuru say.

When we get into Huntley, Lil Girl start screaming hard. When I look down, I see big thing coming out she patacake. I look close and see is baby head.

"The baby coming out," I tell Hari, but he just staring outside at tree and house and cow grazing on the road corner. Then Hari fall over on Carl lap and faint way. Sookuru press down on the gas and we go a little faster, but the car making plenty noise, banging and clanging and backfiring.

Lil Girl jaw lock, she teeth grinding like if she sitting on latrine seat after eating plenty green guava. I put my hand under she skirt because the blue baby almost half out. Is an ugly baby this, cover up with a grey nasty liquid thing. He head big and he wrinkle up more than Ma Tussette. Lil Girl screaming. I put my hand close and hold the child coming out she patacake. Then *foop*, the whole baby come out in my hand with a gush of more dutty water and a worm thing hanging from its belly. I hold the baby with his slimy self and think it is so I come into the world, smelling like seawater and blood.

I take the baby from under Lil Girl skirt and hold he close. Then sudden the baby start bawl loud like bacoo mama self and moving he big head and small foot like he trying to kick me. What the skunt is this? This must be bacoo child what already want to use violence on mankind. Something tell me throw the dutty baby out Sookuru car window. Lil Girl laying down quiet and breathing soft. She looking at me strong and she smile big smile of relief and joy.

"Give me Ganesh Burilal," she say, and stretch out her hand.

Sookuru pull in the hospital yard and two nurse come with a wheelchair and take Lil Girl and the child in the maternity place. Hari go with her, shaky and weak like paglee man. Carl take me to a standpipe near the hospital fence to wash slime and blood off my hand them. Then we go to Gonsalves shop what near the Mahaicony River, not far from the police station. We buy Pepsi and cassava pone and sit down and eat, not saying anything. We stay so for a long time. Then Carl say he don't know how big baby head like Ganesh Burilal can come out of small patacake hole. I tell him what I see. I tell him that patacake skin stretch open wide like elastic, so baby can come out. He say, well if is so, then patacake can take man big donkey tolo.

We decide to walk home because we spend out we money. When we get to Dundee, we see Sookuru car burning up with big fire of tall flame, black smoke raising up high in the sky and smelling like burn rubber. Sookuru standing across the street holding his head in his hand and bawling *boohoohoo* tears like is funeral he seeing.

Carl try and say nice thing to Sookuru, but the man only have tears for he burn up Morris Oxford. Sookuru like old car too bad. We walk on, Carl saying he going to Essequibo for holiday.

"I going to England," I lie.

"You not going to no England," Carl say.

"You go see," I say.

Carl laugh loud and slap my back hard. "You ain't never going anywhere," he say. "You go spend all your days here in Guyana, selling pastry like you mother, or maybe you turn mad skunt like she, and spend your days in mad house throwing coonsie at the wall in a white room."

I had no reply to that. We walk the rest of the way in silence.

Three days later I go with Bhoje and Carl to Parika so Carl can take the boat to Essequibo for a holiday. We don't tell nobody. I think was them big man plan to get Carl away from the village. On the way back home, me and Bhoje stop at a Chinese restaurant in Tuschen. The daughter of the owner of the place, Mr. Lee, come sit down on Bhoje lap while we eat.

She have a mix baby on she own lap what look like Bhoje. The baby pulling Bhoje hair and saying Chinee word while the woman rubbing up Bhoje neck-back, massage style. Then they go upstairs and leave me with the baby. Mr. Lee come out the restaurant and sit down with us. He ask me if I is Bhoje son. I tell he no, I is a fatherless incest child, orphan of this world. He start laugh but get serious again, quick. It make me think about the mystery of how some who don't want child, and some who can't support child have them, and others who want child don't get them. I think again how Big Willie Soto and his woman Myra trying for a child and that now they will never have one.

43. THE INTERROGATOR

Sunday morning and the sky full of rain. I standup near the standpipe in Mamai yard and bathe; wash my beetee crease and my tolo skin and my armpit and behind my ears. Mr. Ramsammy on the back veranda digging his seed and looking at me strong, threatening me with his eyes. Every time I turn, he looking at me like he want do me something. Since Anita dead, I don't say nothing to he drunken skunt, not even good morning self, which Mamai would say was disrespectful, but there is nothing in the man I respect. I know his secret, that is he what make Anita kill sheself. She whoring mother know this, too. I don't know which of them, the mother or the father, I hate more. Until Anita dead, I didn't know the word hate. It was a filmshow word that actor say and I never think what it mean to hate another human person in a real way. I didn't even hate Mr. Ramsammy when I catch him fucking Anita, because my mind wasn't on him. Is she I was thinking about all the time. And I decide on the spot not to tell anybody, because if I tell on him, I tell on Anita. I didn't want to shame she and have people wash their dutty mouth with she nice name and make up a story what have she worse than the father. I know when is a time to speak and when is a time to stay silent. Anita never ask me not to tell people, but I know is what she want, because I know her. So, I keep it to myself. At first I did think was only me who know the dutty business, but one morning, after I finish running and walking the road, I see Ms. Sabita sitting in Dado shop yard with Two Panty. Was early, near seven and bright with sun. Anita mother come out Dado yard when she see me and stand on the road corner and, as I passing, she call me. She didn't say Kip or Kippy like my friends and Bhoje do, she call me, like Ms. Jenny do, by my real-real name, Kipling. She cross the road and stand up in front me and look me up and down like I is thing under microscope. She have pretty eye like Anita and a red-red whore mouth. She smell nice too, like a whole bunch of flower.

"How you doing, boy?" she say. "You holding up good?"

I tell she yes and the woman grab me and pull me close so my head resting between she big bubbie them. She start cry, boohooing and mehmehing as she drag me across the road into Dado shop. We sit down at a table and Two Panty run come quick with tea and float bake.

While I eating, Ms. Sabita asking questions. She want know how Anita get along with she father and how she behave sheself. I eating and thinking how this woman so barefaced; she don't even know she own daughter. Then she ask me if I ever see Mr. Ramsammy do anything to Anita.

Rumour going round that she taking skunt Ramsammy to court for divorce; she asking for land and cow and what not.

"Anything?" I say, like I is idiot boy.

"You ever see he touch she, feel she up?"

I tell she no.

She say that she see he trouble Anita one time, and he beat she so bad she end up in hospital. She go with Anita to Corentyne, but the man she live with don't want Anita, so she take Anita back to Creek to her Dadee, but Mr. Ramsammy with his ignorant ways go there and thief the child from she father, so that she have to come back and live with he. Then he beat she up badly again and she run and leave Anita and gone.

I listen and don't say anything, but my heart sick inside and hurting. I want vomit up right there, because is pure sadness this woman bringing down on my head. I don't want hear she skunt anymore. I don't want to think how Anita suffer bad. I get up soft and just walk out. I don't start cry until I get near the mandir where I see Pandit P in the yard supervising weeders. He have on a white kurta and it shiny in the sunlight like angel frock in Sunday school book, but he is no angel. He hollering at the weeders and moving his hand this way and that way with plenty gesticulations, like politician giving speech.

When I get home, Bhoje sitting on Mamai step smoking a Bristol. I turn me back and wipe away eye-water and put on tough-boy face, because Bhoje not a man to stomach softness in man. No, he say to us plenty times, man must behave like man and not like woman. He say plenty time that tolo not for no man beetee hole, but if man like that kind of thing, let tolo be for woman beetee hole if the woman like it that way. Man don't touch man tolo and hug up man and kiss up man. Is wrong, Bhoje say, and not regular. He say, too, that crying is woman style and man must bare he chafe and go through plenty pain and bitterness without boohooing like woman and girl. So Bhoje don't think much of Derek, because he say Derek lack iron in his vein, and he not regular. He don't say this to Derek, though. He just tolerate Derek girlishness and try to treat us all the same. He say that the world have space for all kinds.

Bhoje long hairy leg, what look like werewolf leg, stretch out on the step. He blowing cigarette smoke in the air. When he see me he pinch out the fag with two thick finger and throw it in the grass. He wearing short pants and singlet and no shoe. Bhoje don't care for shoe. He go around barefoot everywhere, and he foot bottom hard like road self.

"You come from running?"

I sit down on the step and take off my track shoe.

"I see a big piece of *The Amassagana* on the beach," I say. "It not far from the *Hans Bahlin*, but more up under them crabwood tree."

"How you know is *The Amassagana*?"

"It have writing on it."

"Well, them police coming back today. They going find it."

"Is the same boat what the drown fisherman come from?"

"Yeah!" Bhoje say. "But I not here to talk about fisherman. I come see how you doing, living here by youself."

"I aright, Bhoje."

"You eating proper?"

"People bring food and sometimes I cook."

"School starting back soon. You prepare for that."

"Yeah Bhoje, I ready. I buy pants length and take it to tailor already. I have new shirt and Converse shoe Mamai buy."

"Well, good then. I been and see you mother last week when I was up there."

"How she doing, Bhoje?"

"She the same like when me and you see her last time. The

Doctor tell me she have pain in she bubbie and they taking she to see regular body doctor. Don't make it twist up you mind, though. It not going help you or her. The reason I come here, though, is I want you to take Derek to Georgetown tomorrow. Is Sunday, I know, and you might want go to church, but do me a favour. In the morning, Wookum Paradooks will take you and Derek to Georgetown. Sleep in the big house tonight. Derek going explain heself if he want. He know what to do."

"Aright, Bhoje," I say. "That is all you want me to do?"

"That is all for now, but if you not too weary, me and Hari going to pick up Ramsammy cow them, the goat too; we have to tie them up before things get worse. That man don't care rass what happen to them. You can make it?"

I thinking how things falling apart for Ramsammy since Anita dead. Guilt killing he skunt. The man don't even leave he yard. I don't know if he even eating. He certainly not caring for his animals them. The cow gone mad and break down the corral fence and run away; and the sheep and goat so hungry they eat their way through wood and wire and bust out. They eat all the garden vegetable and even clothes hanging on the line, and still the man don't come out the house and pen them. The cow get in the rice field and get impounded and end up in the police station yard; two get hit down on the road by big padi truck and people butcher them and share the meat. Still the man don't budge. People complaining and cursing, but Ramsammy doing nothing. Is like he don't care. Morning come and I see he standing on the back landing scratching he balls and hawking and spitting down on the septic tank. He looking at me with dangerous eye because he know I know he secret. But he don't say nothing to me. He just drink rum and lay down lalaff in the house and let everything go to shit.

"Aright, Bhoje, I coming."

"Meet we at Dado shop bout a hour from now."

Bhoje get up and leave and I go upstairs to eat rice porridge for breakfast. When I go in the house, a big box on the table. I open it and take out sardine and corn beef and flour, cornmeal, marmite, cheese and a bar of chocolate. All thing what ban. I run out to the veranda and holler thanks to Bhoje, but he just wave he hand and gone.

I sit down in the veranda and think about going to Georgetown, wondering why I have to go with Derek. But I excited to go somewhere else, especially when is a freeco and no money coming out my pocket.

Ramsammy come out on the back landing with his hand deep in his trunks. He look at me and spit down on the septic tank and go back inside. The chocolate nice bad and I eat slowly so I can keep the taste long in my mouth. I hear Mary singing she wares two house down: "Banana here, soursop, sugar-apple, pear and pomegranate, come and get it." When Mary come in the yard and sit down on my step, I help her get the basket of fruit off her head and give her piece of the chocolate. "Eat it slow," I say.

"This thing taste sweet, man Kippy man," she say.

Mary is a small girl what suffering from a wasting-away disease name sicklecell anaemia what always inside her blood. It making her weak and fine and inside hospital now and then.

She is suppose to be family of the Abnas who live near Half Dam, down by sluice side, but is really they servant. Royston Abna is a mousy man what don't say more than three sentences a day. He works in the coconut estate doing things with numbers and writing in a big ledger book. His wife Sepulcrita stay home and do nothing at all.

This Sepulcrita always calling me inside the yard when I pass that way, whispering in my ear what she will like to do to me. A nasty woman, and if you near her, early or late, you get the fumes of rum in your face. Mary is she slave, what always working like dog, fetching water, washing clothes, cooking food, sweeping yard, feeding pig, milking cow, baking bread, plucking chicken, planting garden and selling fruit all through the village with big basket on her small head in the blasted hot sun. And sometimes, this drunken skunt Sepulcrita does beat Mary too bad, saying how she lazy and good-for-nothing. I never see this Sepulcrita raise hand to do any work, except to bring rum glass to her big lips and talk plenty skunt.

Some woman bring Mary when she was a baby and leave her with the Abnas, sixteen years ago. Mary never go to school but she learn to read on her own with help from village people. From since she small is work work work and no play. Sometimes she does faint away and have to get treatment for the wasting-away disease. Two-three time she nearly dead from this thing. One time, bell even toll, say Mary take-in and dead in Central Hospital, but God say no, not yet, and she rally and come back to her regular self. This Sepulcrita spread rumour that Mary was only pretending. Hateful bitch woman. May lightning bolt burn she skunt.

Mary only small but she older than me. She in love with me too bad, always giving me fruit for free and holding my hand and letting me cop a feel and a kiss from time to time. I like her. Sometimes she comes by with big basket of fruit and take a rest sitting with me on Mamai veranda and we gaff some and bust big laugh because Mary is a funny girl what like to tell jokes. She know plenty things from going up and down in the village. She tell us how Pandit P does beat up his wife; she say Poopaloops always crying over his wife sickness; she say a man what name Rookumbine Canal, what live by himself, bachelor style, near train tracks, does fuck his heifers when he think people not looking. She see he do this nastiness three times. She say one time when she selling banana, Carl pull her in his yard and feel up her small bubbies in a rough style and make them hurt. She say he squeeze too hard. She only like when I feel up her bubbies because I do it gentle and soft like them is a precious thing.

44. AEROPLANES

It dark when we leave Abary. Wookum Paradooks, who really name Lal Singh, pick us up in Bhoje Lada just before dayclean. Derek dress up in his church clothes. We walk down the dam under Lil Girl old umbrella to the road, rain falling slant-way, and the wind dancing the trees. Derek have a small bag in his hand with papers but nothing more. He know where he going and Bhoje know where he going but I don't. I just doing what Bhoje say I must do. No moon in the sky, just a faint light behind thick black cloud. The air full of bats and flying thing. Dog barking, cock crowing, insect buzzing – the morning noise in the village.

"Where we going, Wook?" I say.

But he just *steups* and say, "Where Bhoje say I go. Get in the car, man." This Wookum is a man of few words and plenty attitude. His favourite word is no. When he work for Bhoje on the trawler *Mengelde*, they say he was hard man to deal with. He didn't like to explain heself much, only telling them fellows *No, never, no way* to every question, or else he don't answer them at all. Them other fisherman threaten to drown he if things don't change. Bhoje take him off the trawler and put him to drive tractor in rice field. Same thing there. He make the fellows angry and one try to run he over with the tractor. Bhoje take he out the rice field, put him to weed trench. He didn't last there. He just no-ing and never-ing them boys to vexation. Now he work in Bhoje shop with Bhoje small half-sister, Peep, and she mother, Nora Darlin, who don't ask question or even talk. Sometimes Wookum drives people around in Bhoje Lada on special fare to airport and other far places.

Derek already in the car, sitting shotgun. I get in the back and Wookum start drive. I looking at the back of Derek long head, with a bump in the back and ears a little too big for it; they stick out like handle on a amphora. It look like he soon asleep. Last night, when I ask Derek where we going, he say is secret and don't say more. Then he tell me I must go with him and see Carl. I tell he no, never, no way, sounding like Wookum. What Carl have to do with anything?

We sitting in Big House dining room – me, Hari and Lil Girl who rocking Ganesh Burilal on she lap and kissing he up saying, "Mamee Lovie docee love dove," and such, and squeezing up the ugly child, smiling up she fine self.

This Ganesh Burilal is something else. All he do is eat and shit and cry. Plenty times when I sleep in Big House, he bawling all night so Lil Girl have to wake up and feed he rass. Hari don't get up. He say is woman business. Lil Girl tired all the time. Sometimes I have to hold this Ganesh Burilal while she wash he shit from napkins and hang them white on the clothesline, and cook food and scrub floor and sweep yard. Ganesh Burilal don't cry when I hold him. Is like he like me or something.

"Is because you deliver he," Lil Girl say. "You face is the first face he see."

But this not so true. When he come out Lil Girl small patacake, Ganesh Burilal eye close tight like beetee muscle so he couldn't see fart. I don't tell her this though. Lil Girl with she nice self like me too bad. I like her too. She is like real-real sister to me.

Last night, though, when Lil Girl get up to dish out we food, is Derek who hold Ganesh Burilal, rocking him same way Lil Girl do and singing lullaby song to the child, itsy-bitsy spider song and making spider movement with his fingers. After that he sing lullaby song about three little black birds sitting on a wall, and one black bird accidentally fall and bruk-up he skunt on the road below and dead. Derek singing the song sweet and just so, from out the blue, he start cry plenty eye-water. Me and Hari sitting there sucking our teeth. But Derek don't stop. When Lil Girl come from the kitchen with the hassa curry and daal and rice, Derek don't want eat. He say he want go see Carl. Me and Hari look at one other. We don't say nothing. But Derek getting on like woman self, saying how he can't depend on he friend and how he always helping we and we not helping he. He going on like this for a time like real skunt, while me and Hari *nyaming* hassa curry and daal and rice and Lil Girl rocking Ganesh Burilal. Then Derek just storm out the house.

"Hari," Lil Girl say, "you and Kippy go and get back Derek before Carl hurt he. I ain't know what get into he tonight."

"He forget how he beetee bust," Hari say and start big laugh.

I laugh too but Lil Girl don't laugh. She stand up and look at me hard and take Ganesh Burilal in the bedroom and close the door.

"She vex," I say.

"Yeah, she vex," Hari say. "She does get quiet when she vex. She can stay so for days. I ain't have no control over it. But if I do what she want, things go be alright. Let we eat out this food and go fetch that skunt after."

"He don't know Carl gone to Essequibo?" I say.

"That is good," Hari say; "no beetee busting tonight."

We find Derek an hour later on Carl mother step. He just sitting there.

"Ms. Malo say Carl gone to Essequibo and he ain't coming back till next month."

"Good then," Hari say. "Come home and we can listen to cricket on the radio."

"You knew Carl gone to Essequibo?" Derek asks me.

"Me not Carl shadow," I lie. "Carl can do what he want."

Now in the car Derek snoring like lion. Wookum silent at the wheel. When we reach Mahaica, he stop and run in a yard and come out and put a basket of something in the trunk. Derek don't even wake up. I try and sleep, but I can't. I just think about Mamai and Anita. Then I think about the drown men. These days all I think bout is sadness. Though, yesterday, when I read newspapers, it say Yankee Bai come out of his coma but is still in hospital. I feel happy that at least one person not dead from *The Amassagana* crew. Also, I like Yankee Bai who live near Canal Dam with his mother and the white girl Tulette, who walks around the village collecting sand and stone and rock. *Chupidness*.

Newspapers say Yankee Bai don't remember a thing but that he getting better and the police hope to talk to he soon bout what happen on the trawler. Who kill who and how and when and where, no one can say. I think that whoever murder them fisherman will be hoping that Yankee Bai don't get he memory back. I hope the police are protecting he.

In the car, Derek still snoring like goat. I looking out the window, wondering where we going. I ask Wookum again and he say I going see when we get there. It is somewhere far cause we keep driving, racing fields of bush for a time, then no bush, then villages, then just empty space and bare land, then village again for many miles and then the seawall on the right of the Rupert Craig Highway we travelling on. Then we are in the city and passing through a place what smell like rum and cane sugar, then through small villages, each with their own smells. One smell like cow, another like pig, yet another like fruit. We speeding now, going round bends at a rate.

In Soesdyke, Derek wake up sudden, dribble all round his mouth. He looks ugly to me with his eye wide open like jumbie self and he small teeth bared like Count Dracula, like he about to bite Wookum neck like Christopher Lee. The ugly face Derek have on is one I see before, a long time ago in primary school, when we was in standard two. That time Hari come up behind him and pull down he pants in the school yard. Derek get vex bad and run after Hari with his teeth bared and hand swinging like demon child. We laugh and laugh to see him running round after Hari with his pants down and showing he lil totee. We laugh because we happy to see little Derek not heself. He always come to school dress prim and proper, with pants pleat just so, and hair cut just so, and he shirt white and clean with his Spiderman lunch box and matching book bag with five slate in it and two ruler and ten pencil in a case. And while we was eating rice pap and rice cake and cassava bread for lunch, Derek eat nut-butter sandwich cut just so, and drink orange juice from a small can and Tip Top cheese. Sometimes he father come and drive he home, or MeLady come, prim and proper, and call out in she Englishman voice for Derek Donnard (she always use his middle name) and she hugging him up tight-tight and kissing him in a spoil-boy way that is not regular, and to we boys girlish and soft. Is only when Derek Donnard start bring we thing like cricket ball and bat, and toy truck and car, and buy we thing like polori and mitai and fudge that he become friend. Is so, little by little, he come to buy us without us noticing; is so we become slave to his wily ways.

He wearing the ugly face now as he turn round in the seat looking at me. I smile at him.

"Is what you smiling at, Kippy?" he say.

"I remembering something, Derek Donnard."

"You not call me that for a long time. What time is it?"

"I ain't have no watch. Is you what get one on."

He look at it and look up at me with his fine face what normal now. Is a girl face, very beautiful and soft with smooth skin and pouty lip, and he teeth white and sharp like dog teeth. Is a face of kindness and gentleness. I think just then it would be better if it have a scar on it to give it character and sign of danger. But is a girl face, a beautiful pretty face, a face that will never frighten no man.

"We a little early," he say to Wookum. "Stop, so we can eat something."

"Alright," Wookum say.

We drive a little more and pull off the highway and stop near a shop. Me and Derek get out and go and pee near a lantern post. Wookum gets out and lean on the car and smoke a Bristol and scratch his seed.

A trench running along the road. We go and sit near the trench looking out on the water and don't say anything for a long time.

"I going to America," Derek say. "Mommy and Daddy send for me. We going to the airport now. Only Bhoje know."

"Where in America?" I ask.

"Is a place name Boston. Daddy get a job teaching there."

"Try and see New York. Everybody going there and say it nice. I wish I could go there."

"You is a good friend, Kippy. I want to tell you that."

"You must write me when you get to America, and send me something."

"What you want?" he says, getting up and dusting off his pants seat.

"Books," I say, "by Caribbean writers."

When we get back to the car, Wookum snoring big like a donkey. We go back in and *blam* the door. Wookum wakes up and starts the car quick. The rest of the ride short and we get to Timehri Airport in no time. Is the first time I ever come there. Two big aeroplane on the runway. One says British West Indian

Airways and the other say PAN AM. Derek says he travelling on PAN AM. After he goes out through a gate, I don't see him again, but a constable says I can go up to a top place and see when the plane leaves. I do that.

Is plenty of people up there crying and carrying on like is funeral or something. I sit and wait till I see Derek climb in the plane. When he reach near the door, he turn and look back and wave before going in the plane. I feel jealous. Why is it not me going on the plane to America? The answer come quick like lightning. I don't have a father and my mother in the madhouse at Fort Canje. Strangely, thinking this brings a calm feeling and I smile and raise my hand and wave back, but my friend has already gone. I sit down again and wait for the plane to take off. And while I waiting, knowing that nobody going to rescue me from this place, I think about my future. What is it I must do? Turn fisherman, teacher, work in the rice field as padi shyer, get married to Simone and make plenty of babies I can't feed or clothe, go home drunk nighttime, and beat Simone for no reason at all? How must I raise myself good and proper to get away from futures like those? How can I, without father and proper mother, succeed and get a chance to go to America and have good work, build a house and marry a loving wife, and live in peace with people and with peace of mind? Maybe I should take chance and go to the goldfield in Eteringbang like Lamuta Dave. Maybe I find a big fat gold stone and get rich? Maybe I get malaria and dead or drown in a big river or get eaten by a big fat camudi snake? I have questions but no answers.

When the plane take off, I wonder how a heavy thing like a plane can stay up in the air. That start plenty more question. I am thinking, and thinking hard. But is like I in a big forest and can't find my way out. Question hunting me down left and right and centre. I full of worry and vexation of spirit, and just so I start to cry silently at first, then hard. Wookum put out his hand and touch my shoulder and say, "Is alright, is alright, I know you miss your friend." But I ain't thinking about Derek. I thinking about me.

45. CUTLASS

Rass Mouth take his small daughter, Peep, who really name Sarita Bhojedath, to see Pandit P. The girl have a spirit in her belly. Is this same Peep what drink pesticide poison when she turn eleven years and say is bacoo tell she to dead. This child not regular. But she so pretty and smart you can't even look at her for long or you head start turn basodee. All kind thing come in your mind when you see she face. One time, sometime back, I walking behind Rass Mouth house-back fence, which go out in the savanna, and Peep, who is Bhoje little sister by a different mother, come out the gate and stand in my way and make me stop.

She say, "Kippy man, me head hurting me too bad, boy; is plenty pain I feeling, you know."

When I look at Peep pretty-face self and she shiny Coolie hair and she small mouth and white teeth is like the whole world stop. I want to do everything I can for her and don't know why. I just staring like mad man and feel tender and want to cry cause Peep face so appealing.

"I going run to Poopaloops and get you pain tablet," I say.

"And Chico gum," she say, "and tennis roll and Tip-Top cheese and Demico ice cream."

When I come back, Peep still standing in the same spot with the same look on her face. The look is like when you not looking, when you thinking hard and you lost way in your mind-world and nothing in the real world affect you. Is like Peep was in trance what cumfa dancers catch when spirit take over their body during the dance. I had to touch Peep so she come back to me.

"Kippy, you is the nicest nice boy," she tell me.

She take the tablet, put two in her mouth and start chew. Then she gobble down the tennis roll and cheese in two big bite like craven girl and chase it down with the ice cream and finish off the food *boodoom bam*. All this time she looking at me straight in my eye and moving she head slightly this way and that like parrot. Is like Peep is some naked bulb in veranda roof and I is scarab beetle or mosquito, circling round she light. Just then Rass Mouth come out his back gate and call Peep away. Then was just he and me standing in the savanna. He slapping a cutlass flat against his hairy leg.

He says, "Kippy, is like you is a rass big man now; is like you want get married. If you rass think you is man and you smell your rass sweat, then make we pashway right now, skunt."

"We just talking, uncle," I say.

"Who give you skunt permission to talk in secret fashion with me daughter? Pass you rass home before I get vex and dig chops cross you rass head."

This happen the same year Peep stop school because she getting children to do dangerous thing with she mind. Was she what get Rita Wendells to push Teacher Clive down the stair so he break he foot, and it was Peep who tell Jasmattie to take off she clothes and run naked in schoolyard during rain so we could see she naked patacake and bubbie out in bright daylight.

Peep use she mind power on me plenty time. Always I have to buy polori and sugar cane, and bara and mitai and daal poori with sour and chicken toe for her. All she have to do is give me a look with she obeah self. Headmaster make Rass Mouth take Peep out of school. Peep stay in the house and cook and clean and scrub floor and wash wares and pound geera masala and bathe she two small brother Ramesh and Suresh by standpipe in the front yard. And sometimes this same Peep, with she don't-care self, bathe naked at the standpipe in bright daylight. The girl not regular. When she turn teenager, she start work in Bhoje dry goods shop with she mother, Nora Darlin, selling and measuring and counting.

Nobody know the real reason why Rass Mouth take Peep to see Pandit P. Some people say is cause Peep have two spirit in she skunt and turn mad-cuirass girl; others say is three spirit Peep get in she belly, what make her fly out Rass Mouth house at nighttime to suck small children blood.

We know that Rass Mouth *did* take Peep to see Pandit P to fix the girl, but whether it was to take the strangeness out of Peep belly, or to stop her controlling Rass Mouth and she mother with she mind-reading power, or because coolie demon from deep in Hindu hell make home in Peep, we can only guess. We suppose that Rass Mouth trust Pandit P with her, because the pandit say he can administer spiritual cure, but we suspect Pandit P take advantage and do dutty business with Peep. We know Pandit P history with small girls.

What *I* know is that one day I was sitting in Dado shop with a boy call Raggamuffin Love, who really name Egbert Blair. Fat skunt Dado and Two Panty was there and Pandit P standing by the bar talking with Dado. He is the loudest in the place, talking in proper English style. He saying something about Somerset Maugham, a white man writer he like, and how the Hindu tradition is exemplified by the characters in *The Razor's Edge*. Dado nodding he head, yes yes yes, but saying, "Man, I don't know what the skunt you talking about." And he let go a big fart like exclamation point to what he just say. Pandit P go on talking, though, about how *The Moon and Sixpence* was the subjective realisation of the individual man.

Mr. Ramphal sitting far away from everybody at a table with his driver, Mohun Maharaj, what use to drive rice mill TATA bus till he run over a small schoolboy in Litchfield and get terminate from the rice work. Next to Mr. Ramphal is he foreman, Mahendra Narine, one of his son-in-law. Mr. Ramphal other son-in-law, Tit, at the counter ordering rum. The three of them talking soft, with head lean forward close together like village men at a panchayat.

Mr. Ramphal is rich man like Mr. Haynes was, but he secretive and silent. He not a talk man, but when he talk, he voice scary like Vincent Price voice in *The Abominable Dr. Phibes.* Plenty people work for Mr. Ramphal in he rice field and on he trawlers and coconut estate and mind he cow them and serve in his dry goods store. Ramphal tall and fine with bumpy face and eye what look inside you like moongazer skunt. He and Mohun and Mahendra whispering like snakes. Ma Tussette say I must never take anything from Mr. Ramphal. She say I must never ask him for anything or even talk to him. When I ask she why not, she wring my ear so it hurt. "You do what I say," and she pinch my ear again, so I learn what she say from pain.

Raggamuffin Love telling me he read in *The Chronicle* that

Yankee Bai had left the hospital and the police don't know where he go. He hear people say that *The Amassagana* not no fishing trawl for true. Like Bhoje trawler it bring ban goods from Suriname – flour, sardine in red sauce, nice cheese, foreign white sugar, butter, and big tinin of lard, corn beef, even thing like stove and fridge and radio. That doesn't surprise me.

"Is pirate what kill them fisherman," he tell me.

I tell the stupidy skunt that pirate only in film show like *Sinbad the Sailor* or *Captain Blood*. Raggamufin Love say no, is real-real pirate he talking about. He tell me he read it in the newspapers.

"Well, if it in newspapers, it must be true," I say. But still I doubting.

"The newspaper man write about them fisherman what was on the trawler," Ragga say. "I read about Husain, what the paper say was the first fisherman found."

"What they say about the man?"

Ragamuffin telling me a long-wata story about the man, so I interrupt the skunt and ask what paper the story in so I can read it for myself.

"*The Chronicle* man, *The Chronicle*," he say in a vexed voice.

I still thinking that boy talking pure rigmarole but I let he go on, and he say how the boat didn't have no ban goods on it when it go down.

"But it have something better," he say.

"Trunks of treasure and precious gem?" I ask. "Gold and diamonds like in *Aladdin and the Forty Thieves?*"

Raggamuffin Love whisper, "Nah, buddy. *The Amassagana* must have plenty money on it what the captain hold for buying all them ban goods."

"A hundred million thousand dollars," I say.

"The paper say it could be fifty thousand."

This Ragga just like telling a story like he father, who good at telling true lies, like Aunt Esther.

He asking me if I know who own *The Amassagana*, when Rass Mouth walk in Dado rum shop calm and collect with cutlass in his hand.

The first chop he give Pandit P was cross his shoulder. The second chop take off three of Pandit P's fingers cause he put up he hand to block the blow. When he fall down, Rass Mouth give him three more chop, *whistle-pestle*, one near his waist and a next one cross he head what cut off Pandit P's left ear and piece of jaw bone. The next chop slice-way a piece of Pandit P leg so blood spurt out all over the place.

"Take that and that and that, that," Ras Mouth say before he turn and walk out the place, calm like he come in.

Two Panty, who sweeping the yard, start holler, "Murder, murder, muuuuuurderrrrrrr!"

Pandit P on the floor bleeding like butcher pig and moaning soft. He eye turn up in his head so we just see white. Then he faint way. Blood leaking out on the floor like red river, slow and sluggish.

Mr. Ramphal and Tit run come and kneel down next to Pandit P. I hear Tit say, "That Rass Mouth good with cutlass. You want me put he in the car and take he to hospital?"

Mr. Ramphal kneel down next to Pandit P, watching he full in the face like if he want to see light go out the man's eye. Then he stand up and dust off his pant and go out to his car.

"Left he right there," Mr. Ramphal say; "he is a disgrace and a dog."

I run quick and get Bhoje who come with his Lada car. He bandage up Pandit P and put he in the car and drive away quick-quick to take the man to the hospital in Central, with me riding shotgun.

We pick up Rass Mouth on the way. Rass say he going and turn heself in at Central police station. He turn round one time and look over his shoulder at Pandit P bleeding all over Bhoje car seat, and ask Bhoje if Pandit P going dead.

Bhoje get vex with his father and say, "But Dadee, why you chop the man?"

"That is me business, Bhoje," Ras Mouth say. "I should have kill the mother skunt."

Pandit P in the hospital many weeks, fighting for his life, but when he fix up proper, with big scar cross he head, with half his face gone and walking hop and drop style like paglee man, he go away and leave he wife and children and never come back.

Peep walking round with she big belly self, but she don't have no magic any more. Joke go round say Pandit P use he tolo to dig out spirit from Peep belly so he can plant he own devil seed. People laugh *kehkehkeh*, but they don't laugh hard.

46. A STORY AND A DEATH

One morning, I come out on Mamai veranda with my running shoes in my hand, ready to run. I sit down on the step and lace them up. It still dark but the east sky yellow. A moon curve like a sickle over the tall trees of the estate. A flock of ibis like a big V pointing to the marsh near the seashore. Mr. Ramsammy on his veranda looking at me in his threatening way, scratching his dutty seed and smelling his hand. He spends most of the time in the house like a hermit, drinking and playing music, and sometimes hollering a raga in a hoarse drunken voice. He never cooks and he never eats. His hair grows long and the smell of rum and piss on him is strong to make man vomit. May he die a thousand deaths and go to hell.

Then he does a nasty un-big man thing. He pulls down he buckta and turns round and skin he nasty hairy beetee on me and go back inside. Is a thing that boys do, but not big grey-hair man like Ramsammy.

That morning, I don't run far. I go out on Main Road stretching my muscle and getting ready to run when Ma Tussette comes out on her veranda and calls me. It is a voice you listen to.

I go down in the front yard what full of croton and fern and other kinds of plant Ma use for when you sick from nara and white-mouth and cracra, and plants what make a man shit for days, and plant that make a man not shit, so that coonsie turn rock in his stomach and poison he good and proper. People say is Ma who make Skunt Hole dead. This man, real name Carlton Smith, uses to beat his wife, Darla Rao, a sweet Coolie girl, with his belt like she was a small child skunt. Two times Ma warned him about his bad behaviour. But he cusses her old grey hair. Two weeks later Skunt sick. His coonsie turn concrete in his stomach and bust open his belly so big concrete block of shit fall out. Ma is not any koonoomoonoo to play small-boy games with.

It was Ma mother, Tantie Dalis, who been a hundred and five

when she fall and dead from a coconut tree, who teach Ma the many uses of bitterness and pain – like them potion Ma make what bitter on the tongue but is a good cure. But that is not how Ma put it. She says pain and bitterness is a teacher and we must learn to use them to make ourselves better. She says pain teaches us more than love and bitterness teaches us more than honey.

"Today is my anniversary," Ma say. "Fifty years since Edgar dead and gone. Go in the coop and kill two fowl, the big cock, and the red, ring-neck yellow. Leave them on the back veranda and come up and talk to Ma nuh. Is a long time since me and you gaff proper gaff and laugh out loud."

I go behind the house and do what Ma says. I climb the stairs and go up in the house.

Inside dark and smell like old things. Ma have two rooms. One she sleeps in and the other where she keeps her dead babies in glass bottles on the shelves. This is the obeah room. I walk past it fast and don't look close. I don't like to see the dead babies nor any of them other obeah things Ma have there. She has plenty dry animals suspend on wires from the roof, and different bushes in baskets, and animal skins and lizard tail and eye of crappo and alligator teeth and brown tinctures in medicine bottles. There's a little altar in one corner with small African statues on a table, with a picture of her long-dead husband, Edgar Minister, gone long before even Mamai born. He buried in Ma backyard under the big neem tree. A smelly black candle always burning near his pictures. Sometimes Ma says a little prayer.

I don't like the obeah room at all. Nothing scarier than the dead babies line off on the shelves in their bottles of murky water from the first one to the last, twelve in all. The last baby is full size while others are tiny. If I look too long, them dead babies will talk to me. They will say, "We drowning, let us out." No, the dead babies don't talk. They are there though, line up along the shelf in the same order Ma give birth to them. I hurry out to the veranda.

Ma in the kitchen. I smelling float bake and fish; I smell bush tea, conga pomp tea, *teasum,* or tulsi. I ain't sure. What I know is that it not going to taste good. I prepare myself for that. Is time for bitters, anyway. I ain't take none since Mamai gone in the madhouse. She used to give me bitters steady, so I don't get bilious and turn yellow like porknocker what catch malaria in the jungle.

"Sit down on the veranda," Ma say. "I coming with breakfast."

I sit down and watch the road until Ma comes with the bitters.

"Drink this," she says and goes back in the kitchen and comes back with float bake and saltfish.

"It bitter and burning up my mouth," I say.

"They get plenty use for bitterness and pain in this world," Ma say. "You know that?"

"No."

"Life go teach you yet. Drink the rest quick before it get cold."

I do what she asks. Then Ma put the bake and saltfish in front of me. She say she think me old enough to hear her story, and how bitterness and pain school she. She tell me about her life with Edgar, saying how in 1916 she was an old maid living with she mother, with no hope of having a house of her own or knowing pleasure and release in the arms of a man. When she meet nineteen and not one man coming round to say, *Girl, me like you bad, let me and you go in backdam bush and lay down beneath tree and hug up close,* she begin to think that is either they don't see her or seeing her they get repulse by what they see. Is she a dutty woman? No. She dress clean, even when she working copra with she old mother, Tantie Dalis, in the yard. Is true that she tar black and tall like man, but so what, plenty woman who black like she hug-up on Main Road with man and marry and bear children and have they own house. She never let colour dictate how she feel about herself. So, is what about she that man don't come round? What is it about she that man, what sit on koker after work, don't turn and sweet-talk she and hold she hand, while she pretend she want to escape?

The first man that look at she in a barefaced way was Edgar Minister, an Amerindian man who was raised by the Ramphals, she schoolmate many years back. Edgar have curly hair and he face square like kankawa kite and he of the Patamona, Warrau or Wai-wai tribe – she never can remember which – in the far bush interior. She did meet he at the cross-trench, the two of them dipping water. He look at she and smile a white-teeth smile. She did suck she teeth to think that this man barefaced enough to want black meat, a big thick woman like she, taller than he. But she like he smile and she like he hair what dark and curly, like he wearing helmet on his head. She like how strong he look. He not tall but he muscular with powerful leg and broad shoulder. He have a body like quarry men what knock stone with big hammer and fetch stone all day long. Soon she going to cross-trench not to fetch water but to see Edgar. She like the way he say she name. "Good morning, Tussi." Soon they having conversation, sitting near on the trench bank, close enough to touch, and he touch she right under she chin-chin, turn she head toward him and let her taste his tongue. His tongue taste like guava and she suck it and feel nice.

Edgar say they must marry before things go too far. She go home and tell she mother. Tantie Dalis say, "Me never think that buckman had it in he." Ma Tussette tell her that Edgar is just a man, like most men. He not a Black man, Tantie Dalis say, but he will do for a husband. You can make him your slave. Ma Tussette didn't want no slave for a husband. She say so to Tantie Dalis, who say, "Yes girl, slavery hard. When me mother was a slave on Plantation Farm, plenty white man uses to take advantage. One of them did drag she behind a latrine and rape she." This was a man from England or Scotland, a snow country place of white people. Tantie Dalis ma put obeah on he skunt and make he swallow he tongue.

Edgar and she marry and go away to Hakama, a far bush place among his people in the interior. Ma learn more things there; learn the piaiman medicine and bush cures for snakebite and marabunta bite and such. Then Tantie Dalis dead and they come back to the village. Edgar start plant big farm and earn plenty shilling selling greens, but year after year Ma Tussette giving birth to dead babies.

And is so she live with she dead foetus children in jars, day after day seeing them there on the shelf, knowing the pain they cost, the strain when she pushed them out into the world, but they make no cry, not even when midwife slap them, blap-blap, on they small bottom. How, after the third, she used to close she eyes them and not look, but just listen for sound of the slap and then hear no sound of baby crying. It seem her womb was a death chamber. And how this could be was a question that full up she heart with plenty rage and vexedness, with confusion mostly, for how could she, a healthy woman in her twenties, bring forth dead children? Must be something somebody do to she; must be obeah skunt in her womb.

Yes, must be cocobey put in she food in some house of an enemy where she did eat cuirass curry and pepper-pot stew, with wickedness stirred into the deliciousness, yes. She try and think back to when the first pickney born. Who she quarrel with? Who get vex with she? Who she did curse out on road-corner or over paling fence? No one. She think and think. She could find nobody she offend, nobody what get bad-mind enough to do wickedness on she womb to make it barren like dry well and empty calabash.

She had Edgar to comfort her; he always there, and when she recover quick, she take he in again, whether is in the garden when she and he plucking weed, or under the house digging copra or sitting quiet on an evening on the veranda. She take he like man take woman. She throw he down in the dirt, on the floor, on pile of banga, in the bed, and take out he long tolo, and ready she self with moistness, and climb on and ease he inside, sweet and lovely, and ride till he spill he seed inside she womb to make, she hope, a living child. She wonder what cruel god would not give her this thing she crave for most, a child of she own to suck she bubbies and call she Ma, and run around the yard and provoke she to her last nerve. What cruel god could there be – Indian and African and most high God of Christian church – to prevent she in this way of natural motherhood? She did appeal to all, make supplications and promises to the statues in the mandir yard, pray in the mosque, in the makeshift Shango shrine, in church after church of plenty denominations. No cry come after the slap; no breath.

A madness take she skunt. She get basodee. She blame Edgar; he seed weak she tell he; he long-long tolo what curve at the middle don't get to the right place in she womb; he have cocobey and junjuh. Is what woman he did go with behind she back to bring cross and misery in she life? Everyday, she cursing he; tell he don't set foot in she bedroom long as he keeping secret from she. Take you rass from me sight.

Edgar sleeping in the downstairs room; he don't protest no more. He spending more time in backdam side on the farm; he going by Ma brother Percy, sleeping there, coming home in the morning with eyes red like blood.

Percy come and he vex with she, asking how she could treat her husband so appallingly, using big book word on she, reminding she of "for better and for worst", and she "nuptial vows", and how "the sanctity of marriage not to be taken lightly", saying how "love should not alter when it alteration find or bend with the remover to remove", and other such skunt.

She tell he a thing or two about when she used to clean he shit when he was baby-pickney, and he get vex and go way and don't come back for years. And Edgar on the farm, sleeping in the bush, getting strange with grief. But she not having he back; she want the name of the whore what do she nasty with obeah. But there is nothing to tell, and Edgar getting magga and soft.

She take another man. Big strong Cooliemam what work in coconut estate, tall and black with dark hair all over his body, a badjohn in the rum shop and brawler in broad daylight, one of them rough-tough Coolie what quick with cutlass. This one, all six feet of him, handsome like starboy, who, people say, make pickney with this woman and that woman all over the place. She watch he and say to herself, Yes, yes, yes, let me do the nastiness with him and spill his seed inside me womb. She know is two-three Black woman he play round with. She know he like dark jamoon with the juice.

When he walking by one day, she call he, saying, "How you does never stop and sit-down and gaff, Baboolal? Is frighten I frighten you?"

He say, "Woman, is nothing I frighten of in this world. Is woman *me* does frighten, especially when I clap them with my thing, make them bawl out me name."

Soon Babu live up in Edgar house with Ma Tussette, practising on a daily basis to make live baby.

Somebody tell Edgar and he come out the bush to the house. He stand on the road, sad sad, shaking he head. He say, "Tussi girl, is this you do me? Take other man and turn me into pokey lotan of shame? Is this you do to me, girl?" She don't answer; she just look down and look away. Is Babu what do all the talking. He tell Edgar to carry he skunt back to backdam; nothing ain't here for him. Edgar in the road like man lost in dream skunt. He don't know what to say; he stand there a long time making up he mind what words to use. He trying not to cry or stammer or stutter; he trying but he not succeeding. He could not speak so he left them on the veranda with a little crowd of villagers standing in the road watching. He tuck tail between his legs and go back to his farm, and when, two-three month later, he hear that Ma Tussette belly big with child for Babu, he climb tall jamoon tree, throw three splice of hempen noose round he neck, tie one end to a tree and jump. He swing there one day, two day, until small boys climb into his farm to thief mango and find Edgar Minister deader than stone skunt.

The dead baby come at the end of that year and another a year later and another after that. Same like with Edgar, same with Babu. Time take toll. She body rounding out like market woman; grey hair spouting here and there; she drying up. She hear Babu making baby with a Coolie girl in Dundee. Old woman, he tell her when she ask, I is a man who like to share my seed, who like to plant it in fertile ground, not among stone where my seeds wither up and go to waste. Ma have to think about these harsh words after she tamp down her anger and rage. These words familiar; is the words she use to Edgar, a terrible realisation that make she sick in bed plenty days. She whipping sheself into wheals and lashes; castigating she self, flaying sheself.

People in the village worried. Two-three women go and see her, go and spoon cow-foot soup in she dry-lip mouth; go and sweep roach wing, dust moths and dander from her floor; go rub limacol and methylated spirit on she black body after she bathe; go cheer she up with old time gaff and peals of white-teeth laughter; go read to her from holy book the wise words of Jesus Christ. These women nurse she out her darkness. Slowly-slowly, like kreketeh snail crossing road, Ma pick up the drooping end of her life and straighten out.

Babu in the house still. She and he like strangers in the place. She lust for he touch, for the sweetness only he can satisfy. She tell him one morning he better help out round the house. He say to her, "Help skunt, me know what you want." He grab she right there in the kitchen, turn she round, bend she over the fireside and do his business. Then he rush out the house and gone to that whore girl in Dundee. Ma thinking how she must disappear Babu before he turn her into a thing what don't have a mind of her own.

The last baby make way in her womb until it was dragged by

the rushing tide of womb water into the bright light. This boy, blue like sky and with big calabash head. He turn he head away and dead. Ma scream for five days until doctor and five men dress in mad-house white come, and they gag her, put she in a straight-jacket and haul she skunt off to mad house in Canje.

She not there long enough to get real mad. She brother, Uncle Percy, come and take she home and nurse she back to health. She stay by herself, she reading more. Big people what did remember Tantie Dalis had no doubt that Ma was picking up the obeah wand of her departed mother and practicing spells and laying down curses.

Ten people say Babu was walking down the dam at Novar when he disappear. The man just been there and suddenly he not there. Nobody ever see Babu again, anywhere on the earth.

Ma say she never take other man after that. She spend the rest of her life practising bush medicine. When she drift off into silence, I know is time to go.

When I leaving the yard, she lean down over the veranda and say, "Don't worry bout he."

"Who?"

"Mister Man. I going fix he rass good and proper. Go on you own way now. Ma go take care of everything."

That morning I run only three miles, thinking about what Ma say. When I reach the sluice, I sit down on the step with Uncle Percy. He gives me a cup of tea and I just sit there while he turns pages in a book name *The Suffrage of Elvira* by this Coolie man, V.S. Naipaul, a Trini, who also write, *Miguel Street*, a funny book with people in it what favour people I know right here in the village. We don't say anything. I drink tea and Uncle Percy read his book, sometimes busting big laugh to himself like a madman, and slapping his leg like he killing a mosquito.

"What's is the meaning of suffrage?" I ask.

"Is for me to know and you to find out," Uncle Percy says, and he throw a big fat dictionary in my lap what crush my seed and make me want to vomit.

"When you feel better," he say, "look up that word. Is only so you going learn."

Uncle Percy is a real skunt sometimes. That day I too vex with him and don't look up the word.

"So, you find the meaning of suffrage?" he ask. He doesn't even look up from the book.

I get up quick and get the big dictionary before he throws it at me again. I find the word, read it, and close the dictionary.

"Is like the right to vote in an election."

"An election," he says. "Though as we know, here, sometimes an election not an election. Go on home now. I have to concentrate."

I left without saying another word.

When I reach Main Road, I see a small crowd standing up near Mr. Ramsammy's house. Mr. Ramsammy stretched out on the grass at the road corner with a white sheet over his body, with he face looking up at the sun. A woman bend down low, fanning him with a piece of cardboard. He making a soft moaning sound. Curry sitting there holding Mr. Ramsammy's hand. I ask Norah Darlin, Peep mother, what happen.

"Is pure tragedy what happen, Kip boy," she says. "The man fall off he back landing and knock he head on the septic tank. I think he neck break or something. Look how lebey he is. Hari gone and fetch ambulance."

"He drunk?"

"He just done drink he breakfast of rum when the thing happen."

"He a glutton for rum," a lady say who I never see before. "Me husband was same way. Then one night after he drink up the daru, he ride in the trench and drown. He left me with nine children to feed, make me have to pick fare and sell me pokie. Man is weak and pure skunt."

"Aright Nalo," Curry Cuirass say, "we know your story."

"You don't know the half, Curry Cuirass," this Nalo say. "Rum had me husband so he can't even get a tolo stand and I lying in bed with me leg wide open, ready and willing, saying come and take what belong to you by marriage-right as husband. You think he come take what I offering? He can't even walk to the bed when the rum get he. Was pure shame and bitterness and pain. This skunt Ramsammy go dead same way if he don't dead today. This fall not go stop he from drinking daru, and one day he go drown or get knock down on road like cow or sheep or dog, or he fall and bust he drunk head on hard road and dead. Wait and see. The world full of useless man what only give woman plenty aggravation and sufferation in life. God don't give we more than we can bear, but I bearing too much, too much."

The woman start cry with vexation and passion. I look down at Mr. Ramsammy and he eye close now and he face turn grey like the first dead man we see at sluice what come off *The Amassagana*.

We hear the ambulance coming before it come. Two nurse man jump out and check Mr. Ramsammy and lift he inside and gone. I stand in the road and close my eye hard and hope that the skunt dead.

Ma Tussette leaning over the banister on the veranda. She see me and wave me come close.

"It look like Mister Man fall off he back veranda," she say. "I never know drunk people to be careful. All kind of thing can happen to them, all kind of thing."

"Drunk people don't even know what they doing most the time," I say.

"That is right," she say, "that is very right."

Later that day, when I hear church bell toll, I didn't have to ask who dead. I go out on Main Road and stand-up with the other villagers. Ma Tussette on her veranda, Uncle Percy next to her reading newspaper.

"Mister Man done gone," Ma say to me.

"Yes," I say.

"Everybody goes," Uncle Percy say, without looking up from his newspaper.

"Yes, me brother," Ma say. "I just thinking so how Edgar gone over fifty years now."

Ma shake she head and silence fall between we three. Is like Ma in she head now, remembering things from long time. Uncle Percy turn the page of the paper and say something under his breath that I can't hear. Ma head bow and water fall out her eye. Is first time I ever see her cry. I turn away and walk back home.

47. SIMONE

Sunday, after church, I take Simone to Tantie Lane cake shop for buns and mauby, but she don't eat buns cause coconut make she vomit. She dress up in a pretty lace dress and wearing new white shoe from America what she auntie send. Is a high heel shoe what make her tall almost like me. She tell me is a special shoe and show me where the shoemaker stamp his mark on the inside. It say Florsheim. This Florsheim man, Simone say, is the best shoemaker in the whole world and make shoe for Queen of England self and Shirley Field-Ridley, Pamela Maynard and Shakira Baksh, who marry Michael Caine. She say she see prime minister wife, Viola Burnham, wearing a shoe just like her own. Simone is big fashion girl. She too stylish with her pretty self.

Me and she thick these days. I surprise by it, me an orphan incest child of a mad mother, turn boyfriend of a pretty girl. How come? Cupid shooting arrow what intend for someone else and it jook me.

Last week, when we come out of church and stand up in churchyard under the bell tower, Simone run come hold my hand and lace up we finger like boyfriend and girlfriend. When I try pull away, because I frighten bad of she ignorant father, she don't let go. She hold on more tight and look at me with her big eye self and smile. When we walk out to the road, the girl still hold onto my hand strong, like tick in dog ear. I say to myself, *This girl want me dead?* And what this girl go and do? She tiptoe and kiss me mouth in bright daylight so people see and go tell she skunt father – this same father what chop up a man call Two by Four for whistling at he wife. So, I pull away me lip from Simone lip and tell she leggo me skunt. But hear what Simone say now.

"Kippy, you is me man."

"Never," I tell her and I pull away from she and start walk up the dam to the big house to help Lil Girl take care of Ganesh Burilal.

The girl start making a big cry scene right there on road corner. I go back vex bad and take she hand and pull her hard after me down Cross Dam towards big house, my heart racing.

Lil Girl in Big House yard washing clothes. Ganesh Burilal laying down in a big basket bawling for bubbie milk. Simone pick him up and start rocking he in she arms them and talking baby talk. "How is manny gannee Ganesh, baby waybee Burilal boy?"

Ganesh Burilal start smiling baby smile and making happy baby sound. Simone sit down on the back step with him and start sing lullaby.

I take a big basket of clothes Lil Girl wash to the clothesline, so she can hang them out.

"Where Hari?"

"Dayclean, he get up and gone to sea with Bhoje."

"On a Sunday?"

"He say is a special work."

"Derek uncle come and say anything about the house?"

"He moving in next week. Me and Hari moving in with Marcel in Lamuta Dave old house. Hari buy zinc to fix the roof and board for the floor."

"That's good," I say.

"For now," she say.

Me and Simone leave and walk near Waterside Canal so people don't see we. We stop couple time and kiss up in the French way. Simone is a good kisser and like to suck tongue. I let she rub my tolo two time, but when I try and touch she patacake through she lace dress, she back-back like Ms. Pam in Mighty Sparrow calypso song and say is not touching patacake time because of her monthly business. We stand and kiss more in the French way.

I don't walk her all the way home. When I reach Short Dam, I turn back and go home and sleep. I am sitting on the veranda two hours later when I see Simone father coming down Long Dam past Mr. Ramsammy house. I run inside and bolt the door and go in Mamai bedroom and lock that too. I hear he come up the stairs soft like cat self and knock on the door like he is regular man. I don't answer the skunt when he call my name.

"Come out and talk, boy," he say. "I not here to knock you. Let we talk."

I stay in the bedroom and don't say a word. After half hour I hear he gone. I come out and peep through the window blind and see him walking toward Bary, but I don't go out. I stay inside and clean Mamai house and cook dry fish choka and daal and rice. I in the kitchen eating when I hear rap on the door again. I get up and get ready to run back in Mamai room when I hear Bhoje voice.

"Come out! Let we talk about this thing, Kip," he say. "I have the girl father with me. Nothing going happen to you."

"Is she what kiss me first, Bhoje," I say. "I didn't do nothing."

"Let we talk about who do what and who don't do what outside in bright daylight, like man and man."

"I coming, Bhoje," I say. But I don't go out right away. My mind racing with plenty thing. Maybe Simone father want me to marry she like Mr. Gidharee want Shell to marry Rosalie in *Green Days by the River* by Michael Anthony. Maybe Lickamore Chops playing Mrs. Tulsi and I suppose to be lamuta skunt boy Mohun Biswas who have to marry Shama because he pass her a note, or maybe I is Tiger from *A Brighter Sun.* I don't mind being Tiger though, who is a Coolie boy what resemble Hari good and proper. Lil Girl even favour Tiger wife Urmilla in some ways. Strange how real life can turn fiction *bradap bap*.

"You coming, boy?" Bhoje say.

"I coming, Bhoje," I say. "I just fixing you a plate of food."

"Bring another one for you father-in-law." Bhoje bust big laugh.

"This is not fucking jokey business, Bhojedath," I hear Simone father say in he ignorant voice.

Mr. Edmonds sitting on the low step and Bhoje sitting on the veranda when I come out with the food. I give Bhoje both plates and he pass one down to Lickamore Chops who look up at me with rough face and squinty eye of vexation. Then he take the food from Bhoje and start eat.

"The man say you troubling his daughter," Bhoje say with his mouth full of food. "People see you kiss up the girl on Main Road in bright daylight."

"Is she what kiss me," I say.

"You saying big people lie on you?"

I don't answer Bhoje because every child know big people don't lie and is only disrespectful to say otherwise.

"I don't want this fatherless, incest child orphan, who mother in mad house, playing round me daughter," Lickamore say. "Heads go roll."

"Let we be reasonable," Bhoje say. "You daughter and the boy go to the same school; they use the same road and live in same small village. What you mean when you say he not to see you daughter? You want the boy dig out his eye. What if you daughter want see he?"

Mr. Edmonds take another spoonful of food and chew and stay quiet. Then he lick he finger.

"Maybe he can walk she home sometime from church. But no kissing on the road," Bhoje say.

"No kissing at all," Mr. Edmonds say and stand up and put the empty plate down and start walk out Mamai yard. When he reach close to the gate he say, "I going talk this thing over with the girl mother, but make sure this boy stay away from me daughter till decision make bout this thing, or pot put afire and somebody go dead, Bhojedath." Then Mr. Edmonds walk fast to Main Road.

"You hear the man?" Bhoje say.

"I hear him, Bhoje."

"Now do what he say."

"Yes, Bhoje."

"Where you learn to cook so?"

"Mamai teach me."

"Well, I think I going home and take rest. My belly full."

"Where Hari?" I say.

"How me to know?"

"Lil Girl tell me he get up this morning early and left saying he going fishing with you."

"I don't go to sea on Sunday, Kippy. If that boy thiefing cow again I go fuck he up good and proper."

"Hari don't thief cow anymore, Bhoje," I say.

"Where he gone then?"

"Maybe he have sweet woman."

"When you see he, tell he come and see me right away. I have work for he so he don't get into mischief not doing anything. And maybe I need to keep you out of mischief, too. You come with me on the next fishing trip. You big enough, now."

"Sure Bhoje," I say.

"Remember what Lickamore say."

Two days later Bhoje come and say he talk to Mr. Edmonds who talk to his wife. They make decision and say I can walk Simone home after church and maybe take she out for ice cream weekend time. There must be no kissing in the French style.

Since then, me and she liming round the place. Holding hand even on Main Road so plenty people can see. Two-three times she let me suck she bubbie in secret bush place behind primary school, and one time in the dark of the bus shed.

One time we walk up Cross Dam, hand in hand, sheltering from sun under Simone umbrella. Near the brickwork, she pull me under a calabash tree and start kiss me up like hungry girl. She suck up my tongue good and proper. When I feel up she patacake down she skirt, she don't say anything, but when I try slip a finger in to touch the inside part, she push me away and laugh big laugh and say, "You is too much, Kippy boy, you is too too much." I want tell she that I never too much for any girl I know. Girl is always too much for me. Is they who always in control. I is just plaything, like any man. I don't say this though.

48. THE NIGHT IS DIWALIAN DARK

The night is Diwalian dark. A blind sky over we heads, with no moon or stars. But the sea is calm, wind is whistling softly and the waves slapping the side of the trawler as we drift out far into the sea. Bhoje cut the big motor on *The Mengelde*, and wind full the belly of the mizzen sail. It darker at sea than on land, darkness so dark you can hardly see your own hand in front your face. Bhoje stands by the rudder and we move across the wave slow and steady, heading west. Where we going, I don't know. Bhoje never say. Hari sit down on the aft-thwart knotting a monkey fist. Me and Carl, who just back from Essequibo, lay down on a high pile of seines in the bottom of the trawler, heads resting on corkwood buoys. The seines stink with fish smell and rank of the sea. In the dark, Carl voice sound like a sound what come from everywhere, first loud, then low low until it go away and gone.

"Why Bhoje don't light the damn cresset?" Carl say. "And where the skunt he taking we?"

"Ask he nuh," I say.

Carl shake he shoulder and say nothing. I get up and stagger over to Bhoje, as *The Mengelde* rock and roll across the wavebacks. Bhoje looking out into the dark like owl listening for a meal of rat, or like a man thinking deep thoughts, probably about woman and patacake and money, what big man and boys like me always get in their minds. I wonder if girl and big woman think same way about man: tolo and money. Bhoje's head raise to the sky where the cloud break and a slim and sickle moon strain to shine. Clouds thick, big and dark. Rain on the way.

"Is a grass-knife moon," Bhoje say, "cutting the head off clouds."

"Let we light a lamp, nuh, man Bhoje man," I say.

"What stopping you?" he say. "Bring that one over there, and wakeup Hari and Raggamuffin Love." Bhoje recruit Raggamuffin after Lamuta Dave go porkknocking up Eteringbang.

"Come closer, boys, I have Anansi story I want to tell."

"Me like Anansi story," Raggamuffin Love say. "Nansi is a big cochore and thiefman."

"We is all Anansi now," Bhoje say. "Thiefman on land, thiefman at sea, thiefman flying big plane full of ban flour and ban butter in the sky."

"Thiefman in the church, thiefing the tithes and the offering," Hari say, coming nearer Bhoje and me.

"Thiefman in the school," Carl say.

"Thiefman in the government, making big lang-water speech with plenty nice words of skuntifications so little school children can sing the slogans in the schoolyard," Bhoje say.

"Produce or perish," I say.

"Self-sufficiency is self-determination," Carl say.

"Who say so?" Bhoje say.

"Ptolemy fucking Reid." Carl say. "It in the newspapers."

"Guyanese not starving. This is not Bangladesh."

"Who say so?"

"Hamilton fucking Green," I say.

"And Shirley fucking Field-Ridley, and Vincent fucking Teekah, and Desmond fucking Hoyte and Arthur fucking Chung, and the big man heself, LFS Kabaka Bee fucking Burnham. The whole party say the same thing, spread the same lie. Meantime the shelves empty to rass. No more sardine in red pepper sauce, no lard, no flour for parsad and roti, no daal, no channa. Them things gone. What left is plenty political talk and plenty fuckery. Produce or perish, my tolo, that is pure skuntery. They get nothing to say. They say nothing at all when they open their stink mouth and skuntificate."

Is the first time I ever hear Bhoje talk so much about politics. He voice loud like he shouting, and it full of scorn, and he serious-serious like he never been before. Is probably because we out at sea and not in the rum shop where other people can object to what he saying or report he to the PNC. Bhoje used to be a PPP party man but now he is WPA.

"But I never understand this saying, though, produce or perish," I say. "What happen when you can't produce, when you too old or weak, or too young?"

"Cat eat your dinner then," Bhoje say. "That is how they separate the chaff from the wheat, boy. That is how the mango fall."

"That is how the tolo drop," Carl say.

We turned to look at the skunt. His black face lost in the dark. Is only white-white teeth showing. The lamplight shine on the orbs of his watery eyes.

"What the skunt you talking?" Hari say and bust a big laugh what echoing out into the darkness.

"You know," Carl say, "when tolo soft and just hang there in your nest of tolo hair."

"Flaccid," I say.

"Yes," Carl say. "Flaccid, that is a nice word; tell we what the skunt it mean, Kippy boy."

"Drooping, hanging loosely, inelastic. I read it in a dictionary."

"In we own-own language, man Kip boy, tell we," Raggamuffin Love say.

"Lebey," I say. "Lalaff, hang down low, good-fuh-nothin."

"Yeah," say Raggamuffin, "I understand you good and proper now."

"This ban thing quick like lightning self, Bhoje man," I say. "Before you know it, flour gone, lard gone, no split peas or yellow cheese in a tinin. Is just pure long lines we seeing at the market stalls; foreign goods just disappear; no powder milk for school breakfast tea, no saltine crackers or Ovaltine tea. How things turn bad so?"

"It didn't come so quick as that," Bhoje say. "It take a little time. You ever see the trains what use to take people all up the coast? No, you too young. But there was trains and train stations and iron rails for the trains to wheel on and spark and whistle, and rumble into the station. But is just silence now. Trains gone. That was the start of the disappearance of things. Then them white man up and gone with all the pound sterling money and the US dollars money from America and the Canada dollar from Canada, leaving we high and dry. Everything crash down *bladam bam* like glass on a concrete floor and break skunt into plenty pieces. And no-man-Jack can put Humpty Dumpty back together again. Then come the government excuses and the lies. Then come the skuntification and fuckery. Then come this taking food out of we mouth. Now is sufferation and the holding of head and pulling out of hair. People bawling like in Bible, crying woe is me, woe is the world, lord help me feed the children, help me pay the rent, help we get a pittance of cash money from family in Foreign and Away. Is the way now. It vexing to hear. So things stand, so things go stay. But I get another way. Life is what it is, but we go work with it. We go take this cross we have to bear and chop it up and sell it for firewood to cook we pot of food. I going teach you boys. What we want is more boats upon the sea to do a little more fishing, not for fish, we not fishing on the sea for fish, we fishing for flour, we fishing for sardine in red pepper sauce, we fishing for split peas and onions. We transgressing – is that the right word, Kip?"

"Yes Bhoje," I say. "It mean to go against the law."

"Yes, as you say," Bhoje say, "we going to transgress all over their skuntian law."

"I hope them food things come back soon," Raggamuffin Love say. "I like sardine fish in red pepper sauce and regular flour roti."

"Hope is wish," Carl say, "and wish is skunt, like trying to turn straw into gold. Is faery tale skuntery."

"What you think about what Carl just say, Kip?" Bhoje say.

"Nothing I ever wish for come through," I say.

"Me neither," say Raggamuffin Love.

"We go work with what we get and make what we want," Bhoje say, "an what we get is nothing. We must take this nothing and make something. Them party man give we this nothing. They give we words; they give we lies. They say the reason foreign things ban is because they want we to plant we own thing, grow we own field of this and that and be self-sufficient. That is big word. But hear me now, boys, is only lies they spreading; is falsehood, is fibs. Foreign thing ban because we don't have money to buy them. The government broke. We pocket empty. The party take over all the company and kick out the whiteman them; they take over everything and nationalise things and skuntalise things. We can't even buy parts for factory machine when they break down, not even proper medicine, because them things cost plenty money and you buy them in US dollars and pound sterling money. We don't have them kind of paisa, we have Guyana dollar what not worth fart in the world of commerce. Is a thousand Guyana dollar to one US dollar. We money is useless. That is bad. And because of this, plenty man turn thiefman, plenty man turn choke-and-robber. Everybody fight everybody; we is all crab in a crab barrel, and who get get and who no get want. That is why I does deal in a little contraband, that is why we going where we going, to make a little freck, to put little paisa in we pocket. Is survival of the fittest and death to the frail and the weak. Hard times come now, and every man must pull his own weight. Tonight, I teaching you boys to transgress. But we far from where we going. You boys get some sleep."

Me, Hari and Carl go lay down to on the pile of seines. Raggamuffin Love stay with Bhoje asking plenty questions.

"Nothing wrong with planting a little field of sinsemilla," I hear Bhoje say, "because that is honest work, but I against cow thieving and I against choke-and-robbing."

"Nothing wrong with making a small piece," Carl say.

"Nothing wrong," Hari say, "with contrabanding."

"We is big pirates now," Ragamuffin Love say, "like in *Treasure Island* and *Scaramouche*."

Hari suck his teeth. "You read too much book, Ragga. You like Kippy. Book go turn you into a soft-soft boy, and make you run out your head like Kangalang Harry Arnold mad-cuirass skunt."

"I writing a book," I say. "Reading book help me write better."

"Write your book, print your book," Carl say, "and when you done, I will take your book skunt to the latrine and wipe my beetee with pages of your nice book."

"Don't worry about Carl," Hari say. "He not bright and clever like me and you. Is only after I read your nice print book I go use it as latrine paper and wipe my coonsie beetee on it."

The two of them bust big *kekeke* laugh showing their white teeth skin-up like roast dog, until Bhoje make them stop.

"I tell all-you to get some sleep," Bhoje say.

"I can't sleep on this seine," Carl say, "it too hard and bumpy."

But we did sleep even with the boat rocking and the bumpy seines and cordwood buoys for pillows, and even with the damp of the sea-spray the wind whip on us, we snore and dream. How long we sleep for I don't know. After a time, we get shaken awake by Raggamuffin Love screaming in we ears, "Get up, get up, get up!" pelting we with something. We get up and grab for anything we can hold on to as *The Mengelde* rise up extraordinarily high and then fall fast. We left our feet and crash down hard, *bradap brap*, against the trawler bottom. Rain falling hard and the wind whipping the pennants from side to side. The sea pelting we with high billows of water over the boat side. We scramble to hold on but can't. We three crash against the inside of the boat and then roll to the side, one on top of the other, Hari on top of me and Carl on top of Hari. But Carl too close to the edge and go smooth and soft over the side into the deep and skuntian sea. I hear myself scream and see Bhoje shadow as it pass over me and over the side quick quick, as he plunge after Carl. I stand up, holding on tight to the life ring inside the boat and peep over the side, but don't see nothing. Hari and Raggamuffin Love grab quick the life rings and tie-on rope and throw them over board. Then we see Bhoje raise up sudden with Carl under his arm like rag doll. He grab on to the life ring as we drift away. But Hari hold on to the rope and we pull and pull with plenty straining and suffering until we get Carl and Bhoje into the trawler what twisting and turning so we can't set feet proper to get a grip. Bhoje stagger to the tiller and grab it to set the trawler aright. Carl huffing and puffing and vomiting up salt water out his mouth and nose, and Bhoje just shaking and shaking his big broad shoulders them. We looking at him with new love, not like he is man, but like he is new Coolie saviour of the drowned and the doomed. If before he was just father of we wayward boys, a man what show we respect, he was now much more. He was a man who get between death and we; a true man and like a saviour, a God in we eyes. O worship him with gifts of offerings, with plenty dollar money, with loyalty and respect, Ramesh Sunil Jagabir Bhojedat skunt, saviour of we friend from the maw of the skuntifying sea, praise him! May Bhoje live forever. All kinds of things running a rat race through my mind to tell Bhoje, but I just stare at he like he is the true redeemer what lives.

We sitting there, admiring Bhoje and happy that Carl not drowned in the sea to be fishfood or watamumma lover. The rain falling hard on us, but now wind slow down and the sea not so rough. Carl bent over and Hari beating his back and rubbing it, while Carl hawk and spit and splatter vomit all over the trawler deck. Bhoje get up, start the engine and we go on.

It brighter now, the sun rising slowly out of the sea. The east brightening lemon and red and grey. The breeze light and smells like sweaty armpits. Bhoje cut the engine and throw a rusted Danforth overboard to anchor we in the water. To the south I can see trees and a flock of birds winging westward, but the place unfamiliar. Not long after, two boats come alongside *The Mengelde* and Bhoje talk to the man them in Dutch. Was about eight men, and most get on soldier-type clothes like the GDF. They wearing gun, too, in sockets around their waist, worn low in a cowboy style. There was much joking and palaver, Bhoje smiling and carrying on with the Surinamese Black man them. Then they start loading the boat with ban goods, split peas, salmon in can, corn beef, flour, corn meal, potatoes, onions, salt-beef in big buckets, and other foodstuff, even a big stove and a fridge. Me and Ragamuffin Love help pack them things away. One of the soldier boy gave me a chocolate bar and I started lambasting it like hungry-belly-dog, taking big bites before Bhoje make me share the thing. Then we say goodbye and turn back home.

The ride home was sweet, the sea smooth and settled like water in a glass. We don't talk much. Carl lay down on the seine with Hari. Ragamuffin Love looking out into the distance where now three trawlers appear out of the darkness with flocks of seagulls flapping behind as the fishermen haul in the seines. Bhoje have the outboard motor going and I watch the churning trail the propeller leave behind, like a cut in the ruffled cloth of the sea.

We never went again together with Bhoje for ban goods, not together as we was that night. Three times after that I went with Bhoje alone and other time with he and Hari. We had to make something out of nothing and put paisa in we pocket. And it was good to transgress the skuntian laws, and as Bhoje say, give the middle finger to the party and its ministers of no one and nothing.

49. BUTTERFLIES

First time I see Alton Fisk, he in Poopaloops' shop yard. He standing looking at a butterfly what land on a croton leaf like he never see butterfly before. The butterfly stay on the leaf like it like being admire. Alton put his hand out and the butterfly walk on and stay there, and he bring the butterfly hand close to his face and start talk to the thing. I ain't hear what he say, but he talk to the butterfly a minute or so before it fly away. I see right away that this boy not regular and that he not from here.

He have on nice clothes, short pants with a belt and a white jersey tuck inside the pants waist. His hair cut nice and close to his head and he wearing fancy sneakers I never see before. It have a tiger jumping in the air. But is he skin what tell me he is not from here. It too smooth and don't have any scratch mark from cane stalk or bramble bush or razor grass; it don't show where sore or mosquito bite heal or where cuirass spur you or plimpla jook you or marabunta sting you or crab bite you or chigger lay egg inside you. He skin smooth and unblemished like baby skin. Right away I know this boy must be from from Foreign and Away.

I looking at him strong when he turn to me and say in a Yankee voice, "I am an amateur lepidopterist."

I had to ask him, "What is lepidopterist?"

"A person who studies butterflies," he say.

"Why?" This stupidy skunt suddenly sounding like white girl Tulette when she get on and on about sand and rock and tree.

"To understand them," he say.

"To understand them? Butterfly is butterfly."

"They can teach us a lot about all kind of things."

"If you say so."

"I do say so," he say, and smile a smile full of white teeth and pink gum. "By the way, my name is Alton Fisk," and he put out he hand so I can shake.

"Kipling Plass," I say. "You is from outside or something?"

"I live in New York," he says. "I am on vacation."

"Like a holiday."

"If you say so."

"I do say so."

The stupid Yankee boy bust big laugh. "What do people call you, Kipling? I notice that nobody get called by their right name. Why do you call Uncle Edgar, Poopaloops?"

"People call me Kip or Kippy," I say. "I don't know why they call Poopaloops Poopaloops."

I hungry and want to go home but he trying to make me stay and talk. He run inside the shop quick and bring out a cube thing with many colours and say is a game. I look at the thing and give it back to him.

"You have to put all the same colours together," he say. "It's called a Rubik cube."

When I don't pay too much mind to the cube thing, he start talk fast about some writer man name Robert Cormier and another man name Kurt Vonnegut. He talking about these writers like they is king of the world. I tell him I never hear skunt about this Vonnegut or Cormier. I tell he about books I read. I tell him about Earl Lovelace and Austin Clarke and Ismith Khan. I ask him if he ever read *The Jumbie Bird.*

"No," he say, "I've never heard of it."

"*In the Castle of My Skin* by George Lamming?"

"No."

"*A House for Mr. Biswas* by V.S. Naipaul?"

"No."

"*The Year in San Fernando*, by Michael Anthony?"

"No."

"*Sixty-Five* skunt by V.S. Reid."

"No."

"*Crick Crack Monkey* by Merle Hodge."

"No."

"Zee Edgell."

"No."

"John Hearne."

"No."

"Frank Hercules?"

"No."

"The palawalla man, Derek Walcott?"

"No."

"Edward Kamau Braithwaite?"

"No."

"Paule Marshall?"

He hear bout she, he say.

"Ian McDonald?"

"No."

"Edgar Mittelholzer."

No. He don't know any of these writers. He never heard their names. What kind of book they write? He read Hemingway skunt, James Baldwin, fucking Faulkner, Styron, Truman Capote, Ralph Ellison, John Steinbeck rass, Richard Wright, LeRoi Jones, John Gunther skunt, William Golding, Ursula K. LeGuin. He asking if I ever read *The Lathe of Heaven*.

Lathe of Heaven! What the skunt is a Lathe? This boy don't know nothing about real-real writer so I leave he skunt in Poopaloops yard and mystic home to eat fry egg and saltine biscuit crackers with strong *teasum* tea. How, I wonder, in this world, a boy his age never read *Sixty-Five.* And who the skunt is this Ursula K. Le Guin?

50. SOMETHING WICKED

On Monday morning I go with Lil Girl to the mandir to see the new Pandit, Karl Singh, to arrange the *Namakaran* for Ganesh Burilal who getting big from sucking up Lil Girl small bubbie them six-seven times a day. The man sitting under a tree in the mandir yard reading a book and eating a mango with juice running down he finger and hand. Is a big man, around fifty, a tall, clear-skin man with hair cut close to his head like karate star-boy monk in *The 36th Chamber of Shaolin*. I think he look more like white man than Coolie.

After we say good afternoon, I ask what he reading.

"Carl Marks," I think he say.

"Carl?"

"Yes, Karl with a K and Marx with an X at the end. Karl Marx."

"Who is he?" I ask.

"A philosopher and writer like Tagore."

"This Tagore, he is…"

"Another philosopher and writer," Karl Singh say.

"We want to make arrangement to name the baby," say Lil Girl.

I take Ganesh Burilal from Lil Girl and go in the shade next to Pandit Singh.

"How old is the baby?" he ask.

"He almost a month," I say. "We want a 101-day *namakaran*."

"You is the baby father?"

"No, my friend Hari is the father. I is the godfather."

"Bring the father when you come next time. Now let we set the date."

When we leave the mandir, I take Lil Girl and Ganesh Burilal next door to Dado shop for buns and mauby. Two Panty in the place wiping down table and singing Hindi raga. She come over to see Lil Girl and take Ganesh Burilal from her and start kiss up the baby with her dry-lip self. Dado behind the bar with his back turn.

"Two soft drinks," I say.

Dado spin round, look at me and flip up the freezer door so cold air rush up. He reach down inside and bring out two cream soda and open them and give them to me.

I give him a twenty-dollar bill.

"Boy, how you mother doing?" he ask. "She still in mad house or what?"

I don't answer the skunt. I open the soft drink and take one to Lil Girl. She talking to Two Panty in the low voice they use when they talk man name. I leave them and walk out to lean on the gate and watch traffic go by, one car every half hour or so.

Peep Bhojedath come out Rass Mouth yard and walk across the road and stand by the gate with she big belly and Pandit P child growing inside. She smiling at me like stupidy child.

"This baby kicking and kicking up me belly, man Kippy man," she say. "Feel it."

She grab my hand and put it on she belly where a bump raise up near she navel; the bump move across she belly and gone. The thing feel too strange.

"What Ma Tussette say the baby going be?"

"She say is a boy child."

"That's good."

"You want to be the father, Kippy?"

"I don't know how," I say. "I can't even take care of me. Come in the shop out the sun. You want a cold drink?"

"And salara cake," she say.

I ask for another soft drink and a salara cake for Peep. Dado bring it and look down his nose at Peep like he scorn she.

"Bring my change," I say.

He go over and press two-three button on the old iron thing and pull out a drawer and take out money. He give me six dollar. I count the money.

"You missing ten dollar," I say. "I give you twenty."

"You give me ten."

"I give you twenty," I say, vex. "I only had a twenty-dollar bill."

"Boy, I don't have time to bother with small child. I say you give me ten. That is all I go say."

"I want my ten dollar," I say.

He don't answer me. I feeling hot inside and vex so bad is like I can't see. Everything white and red. My heart beating fast like wing of bee.

"You go regret this," I say. "You cheating fat skunt."

"Nuh worry with he, Kippy," Peep say. "Is because his mind bad that he always robbing up people. He is unhappy and suffering inside. Is how he always is. He think he getting revenge on people what have more than he. But he wrong. He just make people hate him more. Now he just a fat man what people don't like. Pay he no mind."

Dado stand up near the cash machine, not saying a thing. He head bow down and he pouring rum or water from one bottle to another.

I get Ganesh Burilal and Lil Girl and go out the shop. My heart beating fast-fast with vexation. After I take them back to Marcel and Lamuta Dave house I go home and try and have a midday sleep, but all I keep thinking is how that man cheat me right infront my face like I is stupidy person what can't add and subtract. And the more I think about it, the more I get vex.

That night I do a foolish and cruel thing. I go in Mamai kitchen and pour some kerosene in a can and get some match. I wait till round midnight and go in Dado yard and burn up his coop with all he fowl inside. Then I go home and sleep good and proper.

Next morning I make breakfast and sit on the veranda and eat. All the time I expect to see Bhoje or Teacher Clive or Ma Tussette coming to accuse me of murdering fowl. But none of them come, only Simone. She come up the stairs and sit down in a chair near me in Mamai veranda.

"Dadee want see you, Kippy."

"Why?"

"To have man talk. How me to know? I is woman of the weaker sex."

"He vex or something?"

"Maybe somebody tell he how you does feel up me patacake and kiss me lip them in the French style with tongue."

"I have to take Bhoje."

"You frighten Dadee go massacre you with chop from his cutlass?"

"No. You want tea?"

"What is it, Kippy darling?"

"Liver and bread and Milo tea. Come inside."

"Let we sit here and take breeze man, Kippy man, and talk a bit."

"Aright. You want piece cheese?"

"Is where you get them ban thing from?"

I don't answer her. I go in and dish out the liver on a plate and cut a penny loaf bread in two piece and pour a big cup of Milo tea.

After Simone bash out the food, we sit there and talk for an hour. When we done talk, I don't remember anything important she say, and I make a note in my head to make talk more meaningful in the future.

Simone say I can feel up she patacake now. So, we go in Mamai house, but when I try to touch she softness, she say no, what she really want is me to suck up she bubbie hard. So I do that, but she say "Harder, harder, and harder." But no matter how hard I sucking, she not please. After time, she push away my head and say, "You not doing it right," in a vex voice. She button up she dress and walk out the door and gone. I go back on Mamai veranda and sit down in state of confusion. Then I ask myself, but is who she comparing me to? Who is this person what doing it right if I doing it wrong?

This thing bother me a little bit, until I see Bhoje coming down the dam and know he coming to talk to me about burning up Dado fowl. Quick time I let my mind make up a big black lie and prepare a facemask of seriousness.

51. CONFESSION TIME

I go with Pandit Karl Singh to Dundee to meet a man about some cassava sticks. He say I must come with him to fetch them back to the mandir. But when we get on the road and I stand to flag down a car, Pandit say no, we walking. Is a good long way to Dundee and the sun blazing hot; already I sweating like pig and smelling like one, too. No breeze blowing and the air dry and hard to breathe. All the trees still and a thick trembling pane of heat shimmer in the distance up the road. Main Road quiet; almost nobody out. Is nearly twelve noon. I take off my jersey and wipe perspiration from my armpit and tuck it in my pants waist and let it hang down low, like badman in a filmshow.

Pundit Singh wearing his white kurta and his cricket cap, but his feet bare on the burning road, his foot them clapping loud on the asphalt. Even when he go to Georgetown, he say, he foot bare like day he born. It let his toes them breathe. He say is so he stay all his life.

He is from Tunapuna in Trinidad, but you can't tell from hearing he talk. He talk like Guyanese, not in the sing-songy style of Trini people. Is because he come to Guyana a long-long time ago. Then he go to India and study this pandit business and come back here. He live bachelor style in the house behind the mandir. He tell me and Carl that long time ago he had a wife but had to put she aside. His exact words were, "I had to put she aside for certain reasons I cannot mention." Pundit Singh sometimes talk like book writing, in a proper dignify style, but then switch between talking proper and talking Creole. Sometimes he talk Hindi or Urdu styles, which he say is the Coolie language of the real India Indians, in places like Bombay and Delhi. Pundit Singh know the Hindi language and can read the books of the man Tagore and Harivansh Rai Bachchan. Sometimes he try to teach me a few of the words them, but I don't take on the thing too hard.

When he see that he say, "Eh, eh, look like this thing not for you, Kip," and give me a R.K. Narayan book name *The Vendor of Sweets*, written in English.

Pandit Singh is the very opposite of Pandit P, who live to sex up little girls and talk plenty of hifalutin words. He always calm and plain and direct. The only thing about the man I don't care for is that he always telling truth, even if it hurt. He don't spare you. He get people vex when he start with the truth-telling business, and looking you straight in the face with his bright-bright eyes, pointing out your dutty ways. He make people uncomfortable. He favour Ma Tussette in this way. I know that truth is not always what is needed when a good lie will do just fine. You have to chose when to lie and when to tell truth; that is what I know.

Today he carrying a rice bag under one arm and a small book in the other. He turn the pages with his thumb and move his lip, reading as we walk. He walk straight and don't go off the shoulder of the road, like he seeing with another set of eyes. In Goodfaith, we stop and go in a small shop and he buy two cream soda and we sit at a small table under the zinc in the yard. No one in the place except a man called Everytime I Let You Have Your Way Marie. The man nickname is a whole sentence and I never understand how he come by it; what I know for sure is that nobody call he anything else, and there is no shortcut to the name and I never know his right name. The man is a copra seller and does make coconut oil and sell in Mahaicony market. He sitting at a table by heself, moving chess pieces across the board and then studying the moves.

Pandit Singh say, "Good afternoon, Every Time I Let You Have Your Way Marie, things alright?"

"Things is so and things is such," the man say, "but we must make do, must we not?"

"Yes," say the pandit, "we must."

We sit at a small shaky table with two chairs against the concrete wall. I drinking my drink and Pandit Singh looking at me in a keen way, like he trying to read my mind with he bright-bright eyes and tar-black pupils. Something not right about the way he looking at me. It is a disapproving look, I think. I smile at he but he don't smile back. He just stare at me hard and don't blink.

"Man is violent and cruel," he say, "but he don't have to be."

Is not something I disagree with, but I wonder why he bringing up this idea right now.

"Yeah, man cruel bad," I say, "and he don't have to be."

"I was on my back veranda the other night," he say, "looking out into the nighttime. The night was dark, but I have good eyes. I always had good eyes, Kippy, so good I can see through the most tenebrous night. You know the word?"

I nodded, yes.

"And what I see in the dark, Kip, I go tell. I see a dark-skin boy with red hair moving between the trees. Is not jumbie or bacoo or any other evil spirit. I look close and see is a boy with a bottle of kerosene in he hand. I see when he jump the fence and go into Dado yard. I watch he good and proper, and shake my head cause I think he going to thief mango or even a fowlcock. But not long after, the boy jump back over the fence and leave a big fire behind he. The boy wearing a blue shirt and khaki short pant. The boy wicked, Kip. What can be done with this cruel boy who burning up turkey and chicken and guinea fowl? Is a vicious thing that and I want to understand this boy. I must know if he heart black as he face. I want to know this. I want to know, also, if the act of fowl murder is an inkling of what this nasty dutty boy will do in the future? Look me in the eye and tell me."

All this time Pandit Singh talking, I thinking of them chicken and turkey and guinea fowl in the coop, flapping around with fire in their feather, with flame burning them and nowhere to run, no trench to jump into and no sand to bury their burning heads. I think of the pain they can't explain with their fowl-talk and their cock-a-doodle-doo. I imagine them fluttering in panic in the coop, and the flames burning them all. Then I imagine being trapped in a burning house. I run to get out, but fire in the way around the door, and the heat hotter than the sun, and the smoke choking me; it snakes in through my nose when I breathe; it cork up my nose-holes and go in my lung and I can't breathe. I only cough and now fire is inside me, burning a way out, and now I am the fire, and I blaze like the sun itself.

I start to cry right there.

"Yes," he say, "you crying. This mean something. You recognise you do something wrong. Is good to see. Your heart can't be same way as the colour of your face."

I look at him, not sure what he mean, trying to read meaning in his eyes.

"You want to understand what I mean?"

"Yes," I say.

"You want to understand the blackness of the blackness? You want me to explain how darkness different from blackness? You want to know my meaning?"

I nod my head like dasheen leaf in the rain.

"Kip, you so black I can barely see you in the dark, and with your red whiteman hair and cat-eye, everybody can tell you is not regular, and them know you is a incest child and devil boy. Truth is, you is like a clown boy in a flimshow. I ain't making insult or tantalising you. I just saying we must live with what we get. We must make do, you and me, with who we are. Everybody have their own cross to bear and some more heavy than others but is either you bear up or buckle skunt and fall. Every man have to bear he chafe, and is fall apart or stay whole. So don't cry plenty eye-water for me. What we need is a scheme to get we out this place; we need to make a way from no way. We not born with no silver spoon in we mouth; we family is not in no position to help we when we brace hard against a wall. What we have to sell? Nothing but weself, we body, and is nothing much. We not worth much, Kippy; we not precious like gold or shiny and bright like diamond. We poor and dark and nothing can erase this. We can't start over in the womb of a rich woman and come out bawling with pride and vanity, knowing the privilege we have since we born. We come from a poor womb into the world, silent and shameface and hungry. We always hungry, not for food, boy, no, we starving for something we can't see and don't know. Is lack we lacking, something deep inside. And so how to proceed is the question; where to put we feet when we walk is the consideration; what word to say and act to do is the challenge. We not confident. I think poor people not confident because they always doubt what they know for sure, doubting what is true. In the face of rich and powerful people we lose weself and become silent and useless. Our feet are moved by them here and there like pawn in a chess game. We live a vexed life, so we prove we power by burning chicken, drowning dogs, beating children and abusing women. Is no justice in that, is just cruelty. What you did is not justice, Kip. Is a dark thing, darker than your face; it cannot be the colour of your heart. Is nothing wrong with blackness. I just as black as you, and that is why we must be careful. You see me, Kip?"

"I see you, Pandit," I say.

"Now drink up and come. We get things to do today."

52. KILLER, KILLER

Pandit P devil child in Peep belly tell she to take a walk to Bary Bridge and, when people not looking, traipse on one of the narrow gables up on high, far up top of the bridge, the highest point, and throw sheself off into the skuntian dark waters below at high tide and drown sheself good and proper with the demon child tuck safe inside.

"Like the child self don't want born," Peep say.

Is nighttime mostly when Peep hear the voice of the child, when everybody gone to sleep and she hearing Rass Mouth and she mother snoring loud and she small brother Suresh talking to himself in a dream. She wide awake, staring up at the roof in darkness and can't go back to sleep. All she can do is listen and hear the demon child voice. The child talking in a fine voice what sound like it inside she head, whispering in a secret voice, telling she do this, do that. He tell her which different people keep malathion insecticide in their bottom house and where to find it.

The baby tell Peep how much she must drink so that she can dead quick and stay dead forever. Peep don't know if is she saying the bad things to sheself or is the demon child. What she know for sure is she listening and thinking about what the voice say.

While she telling me all this, I weighing she words. The more she talk, the more she make me understand that I have a part to play in the business. She talking like I have to be her saviour or rescuer.

"Kip boy," she says, "is like I going mad in my own body."

Well, I don't have cure for no demon child. I start think quick about exorcist filmshow starring Linda Blair. Maybe Peep need a priest man with cross and holy water to pray over her and sprinkle the water so it burn out the demon skunt. Or maybe she need Jesus to cast out the devil child from her belly. Maybe she need big obeah woman like Ma Tussette to give she special potion to make her vomit up the child.

"Go and see Ma," I say.

Peep don't say anything. She just look out in the road and shake her head. Me and she sitting by Dado gate, sitting with we back against the paling fence with the hibiscus vine overhead full of buzzing bees sucking up the flowers, and full of marabunta and fine kurubethi ants. Dado say I can't come inside his yard anymore because I is the fowl killer what set fire to his coop them and burn up his fowl. He don't know this is the truth, though. He just guessing.

Sun out in the blue sky and we sheltering under Peep umbrella. Next door in the mandir yard, Pandit Singh sitting down under the mango tree, half naked, eating mango and reading a book. Road empty. A man we call Jumbie Draws throwing castnet in Long Dam trench for tilapia. Hari brother, the wutliss Roti Curry, who really name Shawn Doolam, climb up a genep tree near the dam, singing a vulgar Mighty Sparrow calypso name "Congo Man", singing how he never eat white meat yet.

Peep take my hand and put it on her big belly. "Feel it," she say. "Feel how the devil child worming up heself in my stomach, Kippy man. He trying to tear out himself."

A big bump appear in Peep belly, then it move across to another place in she lower belly. Peep move my hand there. I feel her and she is hot there, like fire self. I pull my hand away.

"I not getting no sleep, Kippy boy," she say.

"Ma Tussette have medicine to make you sleep," I say. "When she say the baby coming?"

"The devil child never coming out, Kippy boy," Peep say. "He tell me so in a dream, say he want stay in my stomach for all time to make me vex, day and night. Sometimes I want take knife and cut he skunt out myself."

"Let we talk to Pandit Singh," I say. "If is demon baby you getting, Pandit will know what to do."

Peep shake her head, no. "You talk to him," she say.

"Alright."

Since Pandit P take advantage of Peep and big she belly, she don't go back to the mandir. She go to Methodist Church, which vex her father Rass Mouth bad. But Peep is big woman now, with baby in her belly.

When I get up to go, she hold onto me strong.

"I feel like eating ice cream and special salara cake, man Kippy," she say.

"I have to go to Arka cake shop," I say. "Dado say I can't come in his yard."

"I go wait," she say.

It take me ten minutes. When I come back, Peep still sitting in the same position. She gobble down the salara quick like glutton child and eat the ice cream slow with the small wood spoon, making sounds of satisfaction with every mouthful.

"I going and see Pandit now," I tell Peep. "Maybe he have cure for the devil child what inside you stomach."

Peep don't say nothing. She eye close and the ice cream spoon inside her mouth. The taste of ice cream get the girl basodee bad.

I walk up the road and cross the trench and go in the mandir yard. Pandit Singh look up at me and smile with yellow mango flesh between his teeth. I break off a branch of black sage bush from a tree and give it to him. He take it and clean his teeth. Next to him on the tree root is a book name *Beyond a Boundary* by this man, C.L.R. James, a Trini who write *Minty Alley,* which I read long time now.

I just start tell Pandit Singh about Peep and the demon child when big rigmarole start. Two Black Marias pull up in front Dado shop and out jump about ten police with baton, making plenty noise and frightening Peep, who start scream crazy woman scream, like horror flick actress. Me and the pandit run out the mandir yard same time police rush into Dado rum-shop. I hear shouting, then see Hak Deonandan run past them and jump the paling fence into the mandir yard like Olympic jumper, but get he pant hook-up on a nail. He rip away heself from the fence before them police hold he skunt. He fall down on the other side of the fence and get up and start run. He run past me and Pandit Singh, heading toward backdam side. Two police man run on the road and run after him, while another two get in a Black Maria and go up the road and turn on Cross-Trench Dam toward backdam. I grab Peep hand and me and she run after the police through the mandir yard. We can't see Hak and the police man them. The place thick with money bush and bellyache bush and carrion crow bush whipping up and lashing us in the face and the foot.

When we reach near Line, where trains use to run long time ago near rice field, we see them policeman standing up, looking and laughing. We get close and see what they looking at. Hak twist up in a barbwire fence. Them two police man take out baton from their belts.

One of them say, "But look, what is this thing get catch in trap?"

"Is a iguana?" the other policeman say.

"No is not a iguana."

"Is a salipenter?"

"No."

"Is an accouri?"

"No man, is not no accouri."

"What is it then, man?"

All this time them policeman talking, they giggling like shy girl and swinging their baton at tall bellyache bush.

"Is Br'er Rabbit skunt get catch on scarecrow tar-baby?"

"Is it a *watrash* bush pig with he neck in a noose?"

All this time Hak wriggling on the barbwire trying to loose-way heself. But the more he wriggle, the more them barbwire hold on to him skunt and jook his flesh, like thorn crown of Jesus Christ.

"Is a fucking murderer of men," the first policeman say.

"And we don't tolerable people killing people. No, we don't stand for no murdering of fisherman," say the second.

And just so they start rain down baton blows on Hak skunt. All you hearing is *budup bop*, *watap bap, bladam bam*, *crack wack, brack, boom*, as baton licks fall down on Hak head and back and shoulder and foot. One lash take Hak in he mouth and I hear teeth break and flesh bust. Hak screaming like pig self. This go on a long-long time. Policeman lashing and smashing and crashing and mashing up Hak skunt with blows. Peep start cry and bury she face in my chest, but that don't stop them policeman; they gone devil on Hak skunt. Bones break, flesh bust open, blood spill out on the leaves of the black sage bush. When them policeman tired and breathing hard, then they stop and drag Hak out from the barbwire fence. He scream like bacoo mama, hollering like starboy in Tarzan film show.

"Oh God, ah torn up," he scream, "I torn up."

"So tear," say one policeman.

"So rip, you murdering skunt," say the other.

Barbwire hook up in Hak foot and he side and back, but them police don't care. They put handcuff on Hak skunt and throw he in the Black Maria. He bleeding all over the place, piece flesh from his leg-back hanging down; an eyeball bulging out; bottom lip tear in two, blood, blood, blood dripping down his swell-up face.

Me and Peep walk back to the road where Bhoje standing talking to one of the policeman. Hak in the Black Maria, his hands behind his back like tie-up iguana. He huffing and puffing. Big snot coming out he bloody mouth. He crying soft-soft with tears of despair. He look pitiful. I look at Hak and my heart almost burst with anger and rage. How come this man crying, I ask myself, this man what kill plenty man and take sharp skuntian knife and slice open they belly and throw them into the sea. He make orphan of their children and widow of their wives, he make mother childless and sister's brotherless. Hak do this terrible thing for money skunt. Why he cry long-water tears now? Fuck he mother skunt. May he name never fall from any tongue. I wish he all this because Hak, like Jim Jones, massacre truth in the village and all our ease. I look at him and he look at me with blood dripping from he mouth, and I bring up a big hawking spit and fling it in he face and walk away.

Plenty people standing round asking question after question. What Hak do? Why them policeman have to maltreat he so? Where he friend Curry Cuirass? No one can say. Curry nowhere to be seen. He mystic long time now, in the wind.

Dado standing on road corner asking who going pay for the furniture them police bruk-up.

Two Panty standing round crying like a child.

I hold Peep tight next to me. She trembling too bad.

Bhoje finish talk to them policeman and tell the crowd is Hak what murder them fisherman on *The Amassagana*; is he what cut open them man belly and throw them overboard so fish can eat them, watamumma suck them down, and sand polish their bones white like beach wood.

Bhoje say Yankee Bai get his memory back and go to the police and tell them policeman what he know. True, he was a suspect for a time when the police think he was the only survivor. But the hospital people confirm that Yankee Bai had been hit on the head and until he tell his story, no-one know that Hak was on the trawler. When people hear this, big row start. They trying to attack the Black Maria to hang Hak like posse in *The Ox-bow Incident*. The police run quick and lock the Black Maria. Some boys knocking on it, trying to get inside; some trying to lift up the thing and throw it down. The police them jump in the vehicle and drive away fast.

People on the road talking about going to the police station and burning it down with Hak skunt inside. Some boys say is an easy thing to do. But Bhoje talk in his stern voice, saying vengeance is mine sayeth the lord, quoting from bible, and soon the crowd quiet and Bhoje tell them go home and let the police take care of Hak skunt cause he know police go spank Hak with many stripes of bull-whip lash and bruk-up Hak bones good and proper.

I sit down with Peep, brace up against Dado paling fence. She crying and crying and make me have to take her home. She father Rass Mouth sitting on the veranda when we come inside the yard.

"Eh, eh, Kippy boy," he say, "is like you rass want be my son-in-law, eh! You think you rass ready to be father of child? Is like you rass like Coolie thing. Leggo she hand, skunt, before me and you *pashway*."

"Thank you, boy Kippy," Peep say.

She go in the house and I turn and start back on the road.

"Kip boy, I don't mean nothing by big talk. I is an old rass man," Rass Mouth say to my back. I didn't look back at the skunt.

53. YANKEE BAI

Newspapers say Hak Deonandan murder them fisherman on the trawler *Amassagana* and thief big set of money that on the ship that belong to Mr. Ramphal. Hak cut open them man belly and pack stone in them and throw them in the sea. Hak makes a big hole in the *Amassagana* so it sinks. He jumps in rowboat and row to the shore. He sinks the corial near Accouri Island what at the mouth of the Bary River and buries the money somewhere. Then the skunt come back into the village like nothing wrong.

Newspapers say how Hak gets to murder so many men is he poison the rum they drink, then he knocks them man head with a big hammer and cut them man throat like he slaughtering pigs. He kill Husain first. Then he kills Teach, who was not no fisherman. Then there was Big Willie Soto, then Crabfoot, who have a room under Boo Leggae's house and the police say kill a little girl. Plenty of times when I go in the yard I hear he talking to himself. One time I hear he say, "I do for you and done with it. Now you come back looking for more." Another time when me and Carl putting meat in Boo Leggae's big fridge, we hear a big moaning sound coming from Crabfoot's room. We look through a crease between the boards and see Crabfoot lay down on the bed beating meat. He has he big fat tolo in one hand and stroking it gently and talking to himself saying, "Don't move, don't move, stay right there. Oh yes, Oh yes." Then he hollers out and breaks and spills his seed. Crabfoot was a big Methodist churchgoer, but when he talks to people, which not often, he always talking obeah talk, saying how some old crone woman put spell on him and how a ghost girl haunting he for no reason at all. This is how we come to call him Ghost as well as Crabfoot. He was the fourth fisherman who get washed up from the sea.

The mistake Hak make is not killing Yankee Bai, who have a long history of scamp survival. He was a choke and robber and spent time in Camp Street jail. After he gets out of jail, he stowaway in a shipping container to Trinidad until they deport him three years later. Is then he try to reform. He starts going to the Adventist church across the road and meet Shari and marry her quick, *bladamblam*. But the marriage only lasts a few months cause, as Yankee Bai tell us, all the woman talk about is god, and this Adventist business has too much rule, and the woman doesn't want to give up she pokie to him in bed, and tells him, no, he can't play Mighty Sparrow on the record player on Saturday, nor buy a soft drink at Poopaloops shop. What blasted skunt is this, he say to us; this woman thinks she is ruler of me or what? He say he tell her he wants wife, not no angel to save his soul, and the woman gone back to she mother, but not until he big she belly. Then he lives in town and comes back with a white girl who talks like a bird and use to sun herself naked in Yankee Bai's backyard. She name Tulette, but we just call her White Girl. She's the first white girl I ever see close to chat with. I ask her one time if she likes Richard Roundtree from *Shaft*. She says in her sing-songy way that she don't watch flicks. From then on, we start calling film shows flicks. We find out, too, that this Tulette not even from England, like real white people. She from froggy France. She tells us she is an anthropologist and geologist who researching stone and dutty soil and Black people in the Caribbean.

Was soon after he come back with Tulette that Yankee Bai take work on *The Amassagana*, because Mr. Ramphal only hire rough character and big badjohn men, thiefman, choke and robber, rapists and such. Yankee Bai, with his gold teeth and gold ring on every finger, and he dark glasses what he wear even at night, get the job easy. He on the job three months when Hak attack.

The paper report how Yankee Bai say he didn't drink rum that night, so he didn't fall asleep, that he was taking a piss when Hak bust him head open with a big wood. He fall over the side into the water but he don't drown. Instead, he fall on thick floating grass and drift for six days till he get rescue.

He tell police he don't know why Hak kill them man and that he don't know anything about bringing ban goods from Suriname. He don't know nothing about that, or about any money Hak thief from *The Amassagana*. He is just a fisherman.

When he back in the village, he tell Mr. Ramphal the same thing, even though Tit had his balls in his hand, squeezing them to make him almost faint away.

Two days later, newspapers report Hak Deonandan kill heself in prison cell. Hang himself with bedsheet and dead. But people say is not so the thing went down. Was no bedsheet involved. They say one of we village boys, a constable at the Central Jail, a man call Roti Daal, who really name Cecil Kallicharan, walk by Hak jail cell and throw in four fathoms of hempen rope and say to Hak, *Do some justice, you murdering skunt.* Hak take up the rope like lifeline and kill he self on it.

Hak do what the judge was going do to him for sure. But what Hak do with the money, people asking. People say he have a partner. Other people say no, is just Hak do the murder and take Mr. Ramphal money.

Meantime, Yankee Bai planning how he can get to America, to New York.

54. FISHERMAN 5

Yankee Bai just drift on water, float and look up at stars winking down at he and a mocking moon like a shiny coin in the sky. Like the man in the moon laughing at he and making joke. Where was he? He drift so long in the water he can't feel he own skin and can't think clear. Darkness at sea darker than Diwali night and plenty more frightening because you can't see through it. He just drifting on something what floating in the sea, thick bush or seaweed like bird nest. Is he a dead man?

If he dead is cause Hak kill he while he arcing a piss over starboard and shaking the last drops from his tolo. He was thinking that later, if things go as plan, he going take his new girlfriend to a nice hotel in Georgetown and give she sweetness, and while he thinking this, Hak come up behind and kill he. As he floats, he wonders how a dead man can think about fucking a live woman. He is a mad man to think so, a stupidy skunt.

Sun burn he, and rain come down and wet he, and he drink some. He is baby self in the cradle of the sea. How long he in the sea he don't know; how far away from land, he can't tell. Night come and then day come and then day again and night. But he never move; he just sleep and wake and think and remember. He remember Hak coming up behind he, and he puzzle to see the man, cause Hak not part of the crew. How Hak get on *The Amassagana*? He can't say, but the man stand there in the dark with something like a big cricket bat in he hand, but shiny, like it make of steel or something. And what is this now? Why Hak raising the bat thing with two hand like cricketer getting ready to lash a six over Bourda fence. Hak bring the thing down crossways and lash his head. He fall back and say "Oh fuck... what the skunt," thinking, *Oh Christ! Is murder that man trying to murder me*. And he duck too late. Hak lash again for another six; Yankee Bai stumble and try hold onto the boat, but his hand miss and his weight take him over the side as the trawler come down off a wave swell, and he fall far down down down into the sea and land in the birdnest thing what floating on top of the sea. His head explode and white light come and then darkness. Then he wake in the dark. How long after he don't know. He head hurting real bad and he just sleep and dream a long dream of the white girl, Tulette, how the two of them meet up.

He was in the Demico restaurant waiting for his dealer, Rampertab, when this slim white girl walk in the place, looking like tourist never see-come-to-see, and stand up in the middle of the floor, looking round like lost child. The girl about twenty-five with she blonde hair tie behind she head in ponytail. The girl dress up simple in a white frock with a tiny brown belt round her waist. She pale foot brown from sun in leather sandals, her toenails paint pink like she lip.

Yankee Bai get a feeling in his stomach and tolo. This feeling tell he that the thing standing there just waiting for he. So, he get up quick and walk over and introduce heself, smile he gold teeth smile and flash gold ring on every finger.

"Come and sit with me at my table," he say.

"Are you the concierge?" the white thing say, in an accent he don't recognise; is not American or British.

Yankee Bai don't know skunt what the word concierge mean. Why every time he say a nice word to a thing, white or black, they start using big word? But he ignore that because, as a man schooled in the art of picking up girl, he know that soon they going get past big word and get down to what matter most, the thing you can't see between man and woman, the thing what is like, as far as he can tell, pure obeah. He think that any man can get any woman if this natural obeah working. He never meet woman who can ignore the thing. And he never meet woman – white, Coolie, Black – who can resist he because obeah strong in his person.

"No," he say, "I is a customer."

The white girl smile and hold out she fine pale hand like actress playing queen in a film show flick. Yankee Bai take she hand in his and walk her over to his table, which is against the wall where he can see Rampertab when he come through the door with his ganja. He pull out the chair and the white girl sit down, brushing the frock over her fine beetee as she do so. He sit down on the other side of the table so he can look her in the eye, man to woman. He see the love obeah strong in the white thing. She mouth moving and she telling he she name, "Tulette", and now she telling he some skunt about rock and stone and tree and all kind of boring business of this thing she call geology, an how she studying to become doctor of dust. He just nod his head and say, "Yeah, yeah, and yeah." Then he take she back to his place in Kitty and fuck her to trembling fits of joy.

The memory last a long time, cause when Yankee Bai wake up, he still riding the rolling monster up and down, up and down. Plenty stars in the sky winking. So he wink back. The stars and he play the winking game till he eye close and he can't open them anymore, no matter how hard he try. Behind he eyelids he can see the darkness and the darkness is dark.

55. THE MARATHON

Bhoje takes me to run a half-marathon race in Berbice. When we get there, looks like a thousand man and woman standing round in running clothes and running shoe, talking, stretching, flexing and warming up. Some sitting on the grass lalaff, others tense, impatiently waiting; some standing on the road corner gaffing, others jumping on the spot; some drinking and eating, others lining up next to tables to sign their name. I get on short trunks and singlet with my number on the back what say 23; I get on my old Converse shoes. I tie a kerchief around my head to keep sweat out my face. Is the biggest crowd I ever see. I never run with anybody before and I not good feeling enough to be here in this big crowd. When I tell Bhoje this, he laughs he big broad laugh.

"Everybody feel same way," he says. "Get out in front and leave everybody behind and you don't have to worry. You go be by you own self in front, just like if you running alone."

This is a good plan it looks to me.

Bhoje takes me to a table and I give the woman my name.

"Kipling Plass?" she says. "Spell it."

I spell it.

"You related to them Plass what live over the river."

"What river?"

"The Demerara, boy. Them Plass what live in Wismar."

"I not related to anyone except Mamai."

"Well," she says, "maybe you don't know. You look like them, though."

Bhoje pays a small fee so I can enter the race.

"Is Clement Fields in the race?" I ask.

"No," she says; "he sick this time."

Bhoje sees a woman he knows and starts talking to her while I do my warm-up, stretch my legs and do breathing exercise. Bhoje whispering in the woman's ear. The woman, a dougla thing with thick fat legs in tight pants, giggling like little girlchild. I see Bhoje holding her hand, then he disappears with the thing. I didn't see him again until race end thirteen miles later.

For ten miles I lead the race, running faster than I ever did. Three miles before the finish line, eleven runners pass me. I come in twelth place. I feel so bad I sit down on the road corner vex with myself. Then people come over and start to congratulate me. I don't know why. Some fat man from the radio come and say I come in first. I tell the fat skunt, no I come in twelve, eleven runners pass me on mile ten. Other people come round and say I win. I ask how this can be.

One of the officials explain. I come in first for people age thirteen to seventeen. They give me a big trophy and one hundred dollars. A man with a fancy camera come and take my picture, me holding the big jackass trophy and smiling bright. The next day I in the newspapers. Underneath the picture it says, Junior champion Kipling Plass with his first-place trophy. I go home and sleep for a long time but decide I can't make living off running. Too low pay.

I go and see Teacher Clive about what I should do for the future. He sitting on his veranda taking toops of rum with Fat Bai, who name Derek Wu, a half Chinese man. This Derek not fat at all, so I don't know why people call him Fat Bai. He owns a chicken farm and sells plenty of chicken. He marry a dougla woman that always use to order plenty cakes from Mamai. His big son Dennis use to be in class with me in primary school before he get knocked down on the road by white man car and died.

Derek Wu coming down the stairs as I go up. He gives me a hundred dollars.

"That was great running," he says. "Keep it up."

I tell him thanks as Teacher Clive wife, Teacher Dora, let me in the place. This woman too serious with herself. She squeezes my ear when I take too long to say good afternoon.

"You mean manners don't come to you lips as quick as the cuss words I hear people say you using?"

I don't answer her.

Teacher Clive sitting in the veranda reading *Paradiso* by this man, José Lezama Lima, a Cuban. He has two more books under his chair, one call *The Ripening* by Edouard Glissant, from Martinique, and a small book name *The Fire Next Time*, by James Baldwin, an American Black man. He has *The Daily Chronicle* fold in half. I pick up the book and read the cover.

"You can read them when I am done," Teacher Clive says. "But what brings you here, Kip?"

I sit down in the veranda next to him. Teacher Dora brings a glass of guava juice and I say thanks quick before she gets hold of my ears.

The woman smiles a secret smile and says, "You learn fast."

She leaves and goes back into the house and start rattle pan and pot in the kitchen.

"I read how you win big race," Teacher Clive says. "What was your strategy?"

"To run in front away from the crowd when race starts till it ends."

"Why?"

"Because when I run in the morning, I run by myself. I not use to no crowd of man getting in the way."

"You did well."

"Eleven men pass me at mile ten," I say. "That is not good at all. If it was Clement Fields, he would win."

"You know Clement Fields?"

"I see the man one time and talk to he and he wife. She very nice."

"Maybe you will do better next time?"

"I can't do it for a living," I say.

"People do make a living running," Teacher Clive says.

"Not here, though."

"Why did you come and see me, Kipling? Something happened? How is your mother?"

"She still in madhouse. I come cause we about to start the last year for me at school and my mind full of things and worry. I don't want end up like porkknocker or fetching padi bag in rice mill."

"A nurse then."

"That is woman thing. Bhoje says only woman is nurse or soft man, auntie-man style man."

"That man has too much influence over you boys, but never mind that. How about a teacher?"

"It looks like too much worry all the time bout other people's children."

"What do you like doing?"

"I like reading books."

"I know that. Maybe you can be a writer. But not all writers write books. Some write for the newspapers and magazine."

"I writing a book right now."

"You think it easy?"

"It not harder than running thirteen miles."

"Bring it when you finish it."

When I getting up, ready to go, Teacher Dora comes back in the veranda and gives me a glass with a small spoon.

"Eat that," she says, "is custard."

I say, "Thanks," quick and sit down again in the chair. I eat slowly so I can savour her nice custard. I pick up Teacher Clive paper and look at the cover that has a picture of the president on it. I read how he getting ready to sell more rice to the Caribbean islands at a higher price. I don't finish the piece. I just glance over till I come to a familiar face, Hak Deonandan face, but younger than he is now, he hair longer and his eye bright like a madman. KILLER COMMITS SUICIDE it says above the picture.

56. THE RETURN

When Carl come back from Essequibo a month or so ago, he come with a girly Coolie boy name Rakesh. One morning, after I finish running, I go by his mother's place to see him. She is sweeping the yard with pinta broom what makes a nice design in the sand. Ms. Malo is a pretty woman, tall and thin. I always think she belong somewhere else. She talks like she from England, and walk bout the place with she back straight and always dress-up nice in African dress and she head tie-up African style. She has a superior attitude, Mamai used to say. Is like she saying, *Don't talk to me, I am more than you.* I hear big people say she has pizzazz. I ain't know what that means. What I know is woman hate her and man want do nastiness with she.

Ms. Malo looks like she too young to have a son like Carl, but she does, and she has another son too, a boy we call Lebbay Lip but who name Dustan Holiday. He have a different father than Carl. This Lebbay younger than Carl by two years – he's fifteen or sixteen. He doesn't live with Ms. Malo anymore. He in Essequibo with his grandmother, where Carl went. Years back, Carl's father just disappear and people don't know where he is till one day we read in the paper he chop up a woman into pieces.

Ms. Malo stops sweeping when she see me and smile she nice smile, showing she white teeth them.

"How is your mother, boy?" she says in her English voice.

"Mamai in madhouse, Ms. Malo," I say.

"We all have a cross to bear. You come to see Carl? He is upstairs." She calls out to him, "Carl, Carl, Kippy here to see you."

Carl poke he head out the window and look down at me.

"I coming down, Kip," he says and pulls his head in the house. Then he appears on the step, pulling a white singlet over his head and his muscular chest.

"You hear any more from Derrick in America," Carl ask.

"Yes," I say. "He send another letter saying how things nice. He living in a place name Boston now and going to high school. He likes it bad."

"I sure he likes it," Carl say. "Is plenty auntie man in that place I hear."

"He didn't say."

I ask Carl if he thought any more about school because it starting soon.

"Me and school done, buddy," he says. "I am seventeen now and big man."

"You tell Teacher Clive?"

"Why I must tell that skunt anything, Kippy? I tell you I is big man. Teacher Clive not my father. He never big me mother belly."

Carl says he moving to Essequibo soon to live there for good. He has a job at a rice mill there and is renting a house.

When I get up to leave, the Coolie boy name Rakesh comes down the step and goes straight and sit down on Carl's lap and hug him like a girlfriend. Carl looks at me and pushes Rakesh off his lap so the boy falls in the sand. Rakesh runs upstairs. Carl looks at me strong-strong like he getting ready to kill me. He stands up with his hand balled into a fist. Then he relaxes and smiles.

"See you again, Carl," I say.

I hold out my hand for a shake and he takes it and shake, and I leave.

Ms. Malo in the back yard, still sweeping. She singing "Saviour, saviour hear my humble cry, while on others thou art calling, do not pass me by", in a mournful heartache way that makes me want to cry. Instead, I just run and I keep running for a long time. When I stop running I see that I am in Champlain, seven miles away from home.

57. THIEFMAN

I have a dream of Simone. We in a big pasture, she on one side where no tree stands and I in the green of trees, and we run toward one another, going fast like wind self, eating up the distance. I hear she holler my name, Kippy, Kippy, Kip, Kipling, and she runs towards me like lovers in a flick, with hand stretch out in front to hug up when we meet and waltz round and round. Sunlight on the grass, a bird in the air and butterfly landing on bellyache and carrion crow bush with new flowers of bright lemon. Somebody singing soft, like Eric Donaldson or Boris Gardener, not far away. Simone in she polka-dot frock running towards me, but she never gets there; we never reach to hug like in filmshow. Is like we just running in place, and the distance between me and she stays wide.

I wake up and it is still night. It's hot under the mosquito net and I sweat like rain. A big moon shine silvery inside the room, reflecting off the vanity mirror. Mosquito making plenty of noise and beetle banging on the window glass and falling to the bedroom floor. A wind raises the window blinds, comes in and cools me. I can feel sweat drying on my skin and taste old food in my mouth. Something I must remember and it hurts my head to find it. I get up and go to the kitchen for some water. The clock says almost four o'clock. I go outside and sit on Mamai veranda in the moonlight and darkness.

I see three dogs sniffing one another tail. I can hear the sea beating up the shore and wind whistling through trees. Dew plopping on the dasheen leaf near the downstairs bathroom. Is jumbie hour, but where are the ghosts of people dead and gone? Where Anita? I want to see her, even if she is a ghost. I want to see her cause I want to hear she words and smell the coconut oil on her hair. I want to suck up ghost tongue and lay down on the cold floor in the living room of Mamai house and feel she fine hand gently hold my tolo and feel the nice sweetness of going up up inside she patacake like that last night I see she alive before she goes home and drink poison and dead. But I know ghost is a thing of filmshow, or a nightmare of the mind.

Suddenly darkness cross the moon and rain start fall *ratata ratata ratata* on the roof; then a clap of loud thunder crashes down. It feels good to hear the rain, smell its freshness and let it wash away what I was thinking. I want to be in the rain like when I was a small child, running around saying *Rain rain, go away, come back another day*. I stand up and take off my sleeping clothes and go down in Mamai yard and walk around in the rain and feel the shock of the rain like needles jooking my skin. I open my mouth and let the rain full-up my mouth and I swallow it.

When I start to tremble from the cold, I go inside and crawl in my bed under the mosquito net with my wet self and listen to the rain for a long time. When I hear a voice between the sounds of the rain I get up and go to the door.

Hari standing on Mamai veranda with a rice bag over his shoulder and mud covering his whole body.

"Kippy," he says, "take this."

He gives me the rice bag and goes stand under the gutter, what overflowing with rainwater, and wash the mud off his nasty-skin self.

I open the back door and he comes in. I give him a towel to dry off and one of my old pants and a T-shirt that says Jaws on it – it has a shark with plenty sharp teeth with big mouth open ready to bite off a white girl pale nice foot.

"Where you put the bag?" Hari says.

"Is in the kitchen on the floor."

"You look in it?"

"No."

Hari gets up and I follow him into the kitchen. He picks up the bag and puts it on the windowsill where we can see inside by the moonlight. Inside the rice bag is another bag make out of black plastic and it tie-up tight. Hari pull it out and puts it on the floor and opens it. We look inside at plenty of rolls of money fasten with a rubber band.

"Oh gawd, Kippy," Hari says. "Oh lawd, man, oh rass." And he just sits down on Mamai's kitchen floor like he is suddenly tired.

I reach in and take out a roll of twenty-dollar bills and take off the rubber band and start to count.

"How much?" Hari asks.

"Is a hundred twenty-dollar bill," I say, "what makes two thousand dollars."

Harry throws out the rest of the money rolls on Mamai's kitchen floor and we count them quick.

"Seventy-five roll," Hari whisper. "That is a hundred and fifty thousand dollars, Kippy. We is millionaire man."

"You have to have million dollars to be millionaire," I say. "Where you get it from?"

"Is Hak murder money what he thief from *The Amassagana*."

"How you get it?"

"Is a long story, man Kippy man."

"Tell it," I say, standing up and moving away from the money.

"Aright," he says. "Let we put the thing back in the bag and sit down and talk quiet. Look outside and see if anybody round the place. We have to be careful. Is Curry Cuirass who not careful what make me know about this thing."

"What Curry Cuirass have to do with it?"

"Make some tea, then we talk quiet," he says.

We stand in Mamai kitchen while congo pump leaf boils in a pot. When it done, I strain out two cups and add sugar. Hari take out cheese from the icebox and scrape off the mildew and put two big slices in two tennis roll I have. We go in the living room and sit down close together and eat. Then Hari locks all the window and come back and sit down.

"Let me tell you how me and you get rich, Kippy," he says.

Is when he sitting on the koker when out jump Curry Cuirass from Sookuru new old car, a 1959 Morris Oxford, fetching a portmanteau like man what just land down from Foreign and Away. Hari follow. The man walk down the dam and go in his house. Hari tell he self he will wait till the man settle in before he go talk with the man about the seventy dollars.

Hari go in the yard quiet, expecting Leak to come charging at him. But Leak don't come. Dog don't come barking and making big rigmarole neither. Is just he in darkness, the light on upstairs in a room. He hear people talking soft, but is not from upstairs.

Is from the bottom house room where Leak sleep with he stink self. Hari get close under the window and listen. First, he thinking is Leak self with a woman. But then he tell heself no, what woman want hug up and kiss up with stink man like Leak?

So, he listen careful and hear Hak Deonandan say, "I bury it on Accouri Island under a twist-up cedar tree. Somebody paint a word on it in lemon paint. Is easy to see, man. It bury on the back side between two root what raise up."

Then Hari hear Curry Cuirass say, "You want me get involve in a whole lot of murder business for you. Me is you friend but not like that."

"I giving you half," Hak say.

There was silence, like if Curry thinking about the thing.

Then he hear Curry say, "Why you don't do it yourself?"

"Is best I not around in case the police start looking at me. Them go ask Yankee Bai question and I feeling I go be a suspect. Them already ask me question and I don't think I answer them right. But not you. You was away when they question people. And besides, you have a boat. I will have to swim. Water high and rough."

"I ain't saying I not going do the business," Curry say, "but it have to be when things calm down. Maybe a week. I have to think."

"That's when I left," Hari say. "I go straight there and get the money. I take it and hide it in another place. Next day, them police come and arrest Hak. When I hear Hak dead and Curry Cuirass disappear, I get it. I make sure nobody see me. But now I have the thing and see how much it is, I don't know what to do, Kippy man. Every time I try to do big thiefman work, I get catch. I don't want to get catch this time. I hear Ramphal already asking round the place about this money.

We stand in the room and spread the money out on the coffee table, more money than I ever see in my whole life. Already my mind moving to the many ways I can spend the paisa. But I find I don't reach out like I was going to; I don't pull it to me and claim it. I can't look at it like is a thing to admire and adore. I watch it, and the more I watch it, the more I do not see it. Something is in the way of me seeing the money. What I see is the story behind the money, how it came to be here; how it was earned, and who kept it. I look for blood on the bills, the blood of them fishermen what dead. There was no blood. I look for life in the money. Is just paper rolled up and tied with rubber bands. There is value there, but the value of paper is not the value of life. The value of this money cannot buy back life. I am thinking too much, seeing too much. Take it and forget what it means and who and where it from. But I don't reach for it, I only look at it and think and remember. I taking the three minutes to think before I act like Mamai tells me to do and Pandit Singh remind me.

There it was, the gift that curse me and save me. What to do, what not to do, what is right. I could reach out and take my part and convince myself I earn it. That would be easy. I could find a way to live with that. But when I look at the money, a shadow fall across it and darken the table. I look up. Hari looking down at me. He seems just then ten feet tall.

"We not giving it back," he says. "I can hear you thinking, and we can't take it to the police. That go be a lot of explaining and other skunt. And we can't give it away so easy to people; that is a whole bunch of trouble when mouth start fly. We can only keep it and give it to we self."

I nod. Hari pick-up the empty plates and cups and walk to the kitchen. I sit there thinking about my talk with Pandit Karl Singh about the burning fowl and the darkness of evil. I trying to justify keeping the money, but something tells me that if I take the money I will be going down a road of no return. I would become like Hak Deonandan, murdering men for what they have. Is a disgusting, repulsive thought. I shake my head, trying to shake out the sensation, but it was there, the nasty dutty feeling of becoming a man like Hak. Hari right, I know. We can't give it back to a crook like Ramphal. That way is paved with trouble, but what to do? I wondering if keeping the money for myself will change me. Is a perplexing feeling; it makes me pause and ask questions.

The question I asking myself now is do I need the money? The answer comes quick. You don't need the money. You have money what Mamai leaves and you have her Co-op rice money. You have rich English man father who has money and rice field and tractor and such. But the thing I know for sure is that the money will make me feel bad about having it, because it connected to murder, to death, to Hak, a man who have no respect for life, like the white man Jim Jones who murder plenty people for no reason.

Hari come back into the kitchen and sit down next to me and put his hand over my shoulder and rub it.

"When I had it in my hand, bringing it here, I think plenty about the thing," he said. "My mind full of plenty questions and fears. Is a strange thing, man. I wasn't happy about having it; I know where it come from and I know what people do to get it. But it here now in my hand and I know that I can't give it back to the owners. So, you see the problem. This is dangerous money. We can give it to weself only. Any other way is trouble and more trouble."

"I agree," I say. "I giving you my share."

"Me, why?

"For Lil Girl and Ganesh Burilal."

He look at me like he thinking of many things. This goes on for a long time, then he stands up and comb his dark black curly hair with his hands.

"Tell me how this thing going work," he say. "Tell me how I go spend this money without people knowing is me what have the thing."

"I know what to do," I say.

"Tell me."

"Hide it. Tell nobody, not even Lil Girl."

"Then?"

"Then we keep a party like we have for Lamuta Dave. We tell everybody that you going to gold field in the bush to make money to marry. Then you go and come back in six months, rich. You build a house for you and Lil Girl and you open a shop and sell things. It don't have to be here. It can be in another village."

"But I can't go to the bush."

"You not going to the bush," I say. "You go away and spent time with somebody else, a family far from here. Lil Girl and Ganesh Burilal will go live with she mother and father."

"Me mother sister live in Tuschen."

"Go there."

"What you going do, Kippy?"

"Nothing. I go finish school and leave like regular. Is not too much I can do. I might try grade twelve and thirteen and then university."

"You think Lil Girl father go take her back with Ganesh?"

"Yes. But you have to pay he something. I will go and see he today. Make sure everything stay the same; act normal; go to work like normal. Avoid Mr. Ramphal and Tit. Don't even talk to them, especially Stepping Razor."

"You mean JagMohan?"

"Yes."

When Hari leave, I take out a thousand and hide the rest behind God back and go back to sleep with the rain coming down hard. I dream a dream strange and new. In the dream I was an old man near fifty years, dress up like Mr. Burnham and living with a pretty coolie girl near a canal with three children.

When I wake up is near midday. The rain stop but the place flood up. Sun shining bright, though. I have to fold up my pants leg and walk out to the road barefoot. When I get to the Big House, Lil Girl already dress and holding Ganesh Burilal in she lap. She face stain up with tears.

"Everything go be alright," I tell her, and take Ganesh Burilal.

"You mean that, man Kippy man?"

"Trust me," I say.

"Dadee not go be pleased with this."

"Hari gone to work like regular?"

"Yeah, Boo Leggae come and get he. They slaughtering cow today."

"Aright, let's go. I have to come back quick and go to the butcher shop too."

I go with Lil Girl to see her father and mother in Dundee. We take Ganesh Burilal in Sookuru car. We find the father lay down in a hammock in the bottom house, swinging slow with one barefoot on the ground. The mother, who call Aunt Tee, sitting on the step picking rice and throwing the spoil grains down to the chickens scratching in the yard. Is a small house with two bedrooms. Plenty fruit trees in the yard, sugar cane, a tall noni tree and a whole bunch of jhandees on bamboo poles.

Aunt Tee is about forty, but when you see her, you know

something wrong with her, cause she look more like sixty, her head tie up coolie style. She fine and dry-up and hardly have teeth in she mash-mouth. She hardly don't smile or laugh. When she used to sell fruit at the bus terminal, I liked to buy from her. She call me Keepee in she sing-songy way of talking that sound nice to my ears. Her husband not much different. He thin – pure skin and bone – with red ole higue eyes and a voice like sandpaper rubbing up again sandpaper. I don't know him well, although I see he plenty time.

"Bring the baby, let me see he," Aunt Tee say.

Lil Girl take Ganesh Burilal up the stairs. I go over and stand next to her father. He stop rocking in the hammock and turn he head and look at me suspicious.

"You is the Blackman godfather?"

"Kipling Plass."

"You is Edgar Plass son?"

"People call me Kippy."

"I fix you father tractor last year; it get something wrong with the starter. Your people is good people. But why you getting involve in Coolie business?"

"I is the godfather, Hari friend."

"A man come in me house and thief out my daughter, make she big she belly under my roof and call it love. I say is something else. I say the man have no respect at all. That man want dead."

"Hari say he want marry she and build big house."

"I scorn he name. What he going build big house with? He empty hand and empty pocket? He go thief cow? Why he don't come heself and ask me this? I get something I want give he; it sharp and ready for the mother skunt thiefman of me daughter; destroyer of peace and quiet. Tell he me say so."

From the stair, Ganesh Burilal make loud baby noise. Aunt Tee tickling his neck.

"He look just like you, Motilal," she say. "He have you eyes."

"He don't have me eye, woman," Motilal say. "Me eyes red like skunt with liquor what I use to drink too bad."

"He have you nose."

"This must be a ugly baby if he have me eye and me nose. Lil

Girl, bring the baby. Let me investigate this chupidness."

Lil Girl take the baby to her father. He sit up in the hammock and take Ganesh Burilal and look at him and shake he head two-three times.

"This boy favour he thiefman father who name I scorn to say."

"Man Dadee man, stop nuh man," say Lil Girl.

"Take you child from out me hand, Lil Girl. I vex with you too bad right now, but you is me one-grain daughter, and anytime you want come back and live here, I prepare for that. But that daughter-thief husband you have can't set foot in me yard or big pashway go start."

Lil Girl take Ganesh Burilal and go back to sit with Aunt Tee on the step.

"Kip, you say you name is, boy?" Motilal say.

"Hari send something for you."

I hand him the paper bag. He take it and reach inside and take out the money and start count. He blow a big whistle when he finish.

"What this boy want from me?"

I tell him.

"He don't have to pay for that. She is me own daughter."

"He coming tonight to say he sorry."

"Well, let he come. Me go talk with he man-to-man."

"That is all he want," I say, "before he travel to gold field."

That afternoon, we rent Rass Mouth donkey and cart and move all Lil Girl thing from Marcel and Lamuta Dave house back to her mother house in Dundee.

"When we get there, you talk to the man," I tell Hari. "Say you sorry for thiefing he daughter. Bring a present for Aunt Tee. The going-away party is next week."

58. MR. RAMPHAL AND TIT TRY KANGALANG HARRY ARNOLD

Ever since newspapers say Hak hang heself or get hang with a bedsheet in jail cell, Mr. Ramphal drive he car *around* the village. Before that he used to drive straight *through* the village. Now he stopping and talking to people. Sometimes he even get out of the car and talk to one of the villagers, though mostly he just stays inside the car, and people lean in through the window and Mr. Ramphal talks to them in his devil-voice.

Most times, one of Mr. Ramphal's son-in-law, mostly Ramesh Tulsi, who we call Tit, comes out the car and does the questioning. This Tit big like Bhoje and marry Ms. Ramphal big daughter, Sarojini, a fat girl who teaches mathematics in primary school. This is the same Sarojini what was having a baby for a Black man named Kurt Godday what hang himself on a mango tree in the backdam. People say is Mr. Ramphal who kill Kurt, who was also a mathematics teacher. After Sarojini throw-way the baby, she marries Tit, who is no teacher. He just a bad skunt who always vex and never smiles. Sarojini doesn't have any more children and is a sad-type woman who tries two times to kill herself over love, like mad-skunt Juliet in Shakespeare's play.

Tit is a better son to Mr. Ramphal than a husband to Sarojini. He is the muscle of Mr. Ramphal organisation, the soldier boy what quick with violence and, people say, big murder. Tit use to be a policeman in Georgetown and take bribe so the big government Minister retrench he skunt and throw he away. Now he works for Mr. Ramphal doing the rough tough work – he and Mr. Ramphal grandson, the fearsome JagMohan, aka Stepping Razor. Another son-in-law, Cheetram, runs the business. Tit is the one Mr. Ramphal calls when he wants to collect money from people who owe him. He practising to be big gangster like Don Corleone in *Godfather* film.

Mr. Ramphal thinks Hak leave the money with somebody or tell them where he hide it. Now that Hak dead and Curry Cuirass disappear, he asking everybody.

Me and Hari walking to Bary one morning when we see Mr. Ramphal green Lada Riva park by the big mango tree near road corner where Kangalang Harry Arnold sleeps. Tit sitting down under the tree with Kangalang while Mr. Ramphal leaning out the driver seat listening.

We hear Tit say to Kangalang, "You the one Hak give the thing to?"

"Ekereko," Kangalang say.

"Where you put the thing?" Tit says.

"Ekereko," Kangalang say.

"People say you and Hak always sitting in Dado shop talking. Where he say he put the thing?"

"Ekereko."

"Ask he where he see Hak last before police arrest he?" Mr. Ramphal says from inside the car.

"Ekereko," says Kangalang.

"Listen to me, you madhead skunt," says Tit, "I tired of this Ekereko, Ekereko, Ekereko chupidness."

"Ekereko," says Kangalang.

"Answer the man properly," says Tit and he grab Kangalang tear-up dutty shirt to discipline the mad man proper like a gangster in *The Valachi Papers* starring Charles Bronson.

Me and Hari standing near the road corner watching the scene.

Hari looks over at me and whistle. "Is like Tit don't know Kangalang at all."

"No," I say, "but he going learn very soon. Mr. Ramphal knows though. See how he winding up the car window."

What me and Hari and Mr. Ramphal know is you never touch Kangalang Harry Arnold – never, never. People don't know why. But we know what happens. He goes crazy with violence and beat a man like a snake self. Kangalang is against the touching of his person; he doesn't care how light or heavy. Plenty time Kangalang nearly kill a man for touching him.

The last one was the madhouse man who come to try to talk to Kangalang about cleaning himself and wearing proper clothes.

Teacher Clive says the madhouse man is what you call a social worker who try to regulate mad people's behaviour and convert them to exist in the world of cleanness and good manners. Nobody tells the social worker about the touching thing. Ten men have to hold down Kangalang when he starts to beat the man. Kangalang breaks the man hand and knock out he front teeth them and bite off a piece of the man neck, like Dracula.

"Run, boy, run," Mr. Ramphal calls to Tit, who didn't have time to answer because Kangalang already hold onto his hand like a vice.

Tit scream when Kangalang pull him close like he about to kiss him, but he dutty mouth close over Tit long nose instead. Tit scream so high it makes people run out of their house. Still, Kangalang doesn't let go. He bite off Tit nose. All the time he squeezing Tit hand until we hear a crack sound like dry branch break. Tit bawl like lady what giving birth. Then Kangalang lift Tit over his head by his neck-back and foot like a small child and throw Tit skunt into the tall reed and branch and bramble of the cross-trench. Mr. Ramphal drives the car quick to where Tit crawling out the water holding his break hand. Blood pouring down the man's face from the spot where his nose used to be. Tit jump in the car and Mr. Ramphal drives away quick.

Kangalang Harry Arnold spits out Tit nose and wipe the blood from his mouth with the back of his hand and sits down on the mango tree root again and goes to sleep right away, snoring like a horse.

"Now Tit knows about Kangalang Harry Arnold," Hari says. "Every time he looks in the mirror he go remember."

"I worry about Kangalang," I say. "Mr. Ramphal don't forget."

"I know," Hari says. "You know the story about The Forever War?"

"Yes, Ma Tussette tell me. But that war start a hundred years before Mr. Ramphal born."

"But he the one what continuing the thing."

The story Ma Tussette tells me about The Forever War of the Ramphals doesn't make sense. How this thing can last so long without the police getting involve and arresting people? Ma says is a special war with magic. She says people only see what they want to see. I don't even know what to believe. The story strange bad.

59. THE FOREVER WAR OF THE RAMPHALS

Ma Tussette says Mr. Ramphal grandfather come from a poor place in India name Haryana to work cane field for white man skunt in Albion. This was a long time ago, just after Black people free from slavery and say fuck it, let we go and study book learning and leave this back-breaking skunt work of cutting cane, and become lawyer, doctor, priest, pot mender, cow killer, farmer, so that we might eat proper from we own pot and drink daru paid for by we own shilling, and every year make baby what belong to we. Yes, and build a house in the swampland white man sell us.

Because the Black people leave backra fields, white man start look for more slaves in other parts of the world, and find regular Coolies in British India who ain't have nothing. And the white man say, *Come with me, I am the white man of love, like Jesus, and I will make you guests of my cane fields and house you beside my father's mansion where there are many doors closed to you Coolie skunt that you may not enter; and I will provide you lean-to logies near my cane fields of plenty wherein you may toil with the sweat of your brow, morning till night, weeding, burning, cutting, pressing cane into the glittering gold of Demerara sugar that I will sell to white people in Foreign and Away for their afternoon tea with cucumber sandwich without crust. You Coolie people will respect me in all things, and we shall live together in harmony: the hurt yours, the wealth mine; and after five years of slaving, if, perchance, in the way of things you do not die, you shall achieve your heaven of a plot in the swamp, where you may endeavour to persevere among anopheles aegypti. And if, perchance, you and your wife bring forth a daughter of loveliness and beauty, when she comes of age, though perhaps sooner, I might favour her with gold bangle and nosering and ring on every finger and gold teeth, and make her my concubine with whom I shall do nastiness and put seed in her belly to grow, that she might bring forth plenty bastards of blue-eye devils to foreman my fields of cane and sometimes rice and sometimes indigo.*

Plenty Coolie people hear this speech and say, *Sure what we have to lose?* So, in 1838, they start to come to what, in them skuntian days, they call British Guiana or B.G., to fill the field of hurt and despair after the Black man gone.

In 1840, two Blackman brothers name Inniss buy forty rods of land, from sea to muddy back dam and the acres of sky above and fathoms down below to the centre of earth, and all the trees on the land what become the villages of Catherine and Calcutta and Abary and Recess. After this done, Black man relax and study book that white man write and become such and such professional men of education, wearing suit and tie and shiny leather shoe. They leave the fields of endless cane of skuntian green for chamars to plough and pluck, to chop and crop.

Blackman gone and work in government office in city and town with typewriter machine, with paper and pen and stamp and carbon paper as civil servant skunt. Reeling out red-tape of regulations in triplicate, saying such and such is not permitted; looking up from theodolite saying, that lot is not angle correct; legislating in the polished pews of parliament; dotting i's and crossing t's; climbing up on lantern post to hang telegraph wire; more stamping; more red-tape reeling; more regulation and civil engineering.

So, this is the place Mr. Ramphal's great, great grandfather, Baboolal from Haryana, come to with his small brother, Rohit, on the big ship *Hesperus* to work for the white man. The white man tells Rohit and Baboolal they have to work for him for five years and when they finish this business, he going give them a piece of land to work till they dead. Then the white man throws them in the cane field and says, *See if you can manage not to die*. Rohit understand this soon when big labaria snake come out a hole in the ground and bite a man what chopping cane next to he and the man turn blue with poison and dead, and another time when he standing on a cane punt, a chain break and lash off a man head what standing next to him; and another time a small chamar get he hand catch in cane grinder, then he head, then all of the man. Rohit listen to bone break and flesh burst and sprinkle blood in the slurry.

Rohit see that he getting fine, like cross-trench bizzi-bizzi reed, and looking like a starvation child because food not plenty at all. Rohit is a smart man, the brain in the family. He tells his big brother, Baboo, that the way things going, with death so near every day, with disease what make you shit all day and mosquito-bite malaria what makes you burn up with fever, we not going live long enough to collect that plot. Let we bruk-way skunt and run.

"Let we go away to other village and marry Blackman daughter or rich virgin Coolie child and work for she father."

Baboo not too keen on the business. He says, "How we go do this dutty business when we make big promise to Whiteman who pay passage for ahbee to come here? How ahbee go dishonour the name of Ramphal in the mouth of man and woman?"

Rohit tells the skunt he must first honour himself.

"Nah, buddy," Baboo says, "this is not the way of the *Ramayana*; let we be honourable and finish up the work at the end of five years."

Rohit doesn't argue, he just leaves and gone and come to Calcutta village, where he chance to meet up with a man name Balgobin, who buy couple acres from the Inniss brothers and is living good with his two daughters, Sati and Bina, and quick time Rohit doing nastiness with the big girl, Bina. Nighttime, he visits Balgobin, and when he says he going home, he doesn't go home at all, he waits downstairs for Bina, and the two of them go backdam where Rohit *knack am good, knack am prapa* Bina patacake.

But Balgobin knows all this; he is a smart Coolie, like Anansi. He just waiting and watching what Rohit doing. Then *blam*, the girl belly big. Rohit have to marry. Balgobin gives Rohit a piece land and tell he to *Wuk am wuk am plenty and pay big rent*. Baby born and Rohit calls the boy, Sanjay, after some uncle he remember from the old country.

Rohit in a trap he can't see his way out of, so he turns fisherman.

One day, plenty years later, who he see on the road but his own-own brother, Baboo the honourable. The man limping around with a whole bunch of beggarman knocking cup from house to house, begging alms. He dhoti dutty to skunt with pee stain and shit stain and mud of the earth. Rohit can't believe it.

Quick time Rohit rescue he brother and take him home and clean he off. He make Bina set pallet on the floor and cook Baboo some braaf with cuirass fish to strong-up the man regular and put fat on bone to get the blood flowing; boil the man some bitters, give the man plenty custard, milk, dasheen.

Baboolal tells Rohit how he nearly dead from snakebite; how he was sick sick sick for many days and months; how he lay down under road-corner tree ready to dead but couldn't dead, cause something strong keeping he alive in the world. Then, after time, like a miracle, he getting better. White man forget he exist, so he get with the beggars and start begging to keep body and soul seam together. He does this for two years.

Meantime, Rohit been able to buy a trawler of his own and starts fish for himself, getting plenty of shilling regular to buy his own three acres and build his own house with bottom house room for his brother to stay, while snake sore on his skin heal. All Baboo doing when Rohit at sea is lie in a hammock and fuck Bina.

This thing start two months after Baboo move in with Rohit. Because he too weak, the girl has to come and bathe he proper with sponge cloth and basin of soapy water. He lies down on the pallet while she washes his narrow chest and big tolo what the girl likes to play with while he pretend he sleeping. Then one day, he grabs her, turn she round, pulls up she sari, and gives her wood good and proper. The girl likes it and soon he giving her daily, so that *he* turns the husband and Rohit is the outside man. Wickedness and betrayal skunt.

Rohit finds out and takes cutlass and chop Bina plenty chop cross she worthless self, then he drinks poison and dies. Bina not dead though; she recovers. Baboo takes over Rohit boat and his wife Bina, what people start to call Scar, because of big chop marks on her body. Baby born and they name the child Rohan. This boy favour Baboo bad, with the same dark complexion and long nose like hawk beak and same big round owl-eye. Rohit son Sanjay sees this too and so hate born between the two brothers from different father-brothers with the same mother. Hate brings more hate and Bina starts to hate Baboo and she puts him out of the house. He moves with Rohan across the road on the same land Rohit own and builds a big house and the two of them start to live there bachee style in The House of Baboolal, as Baboo calls the place.

When Baboo dies, he leaves all Rohit land to Rohan, except where Sanjay lives. Rohan not satisfy, though. He says Sanjay must leave he land or pay rent. See how things turn? Hate fever become war and war become forever. The Ramphals on both sides of the road multiply like the bible say, only more so, with plenty of children littering the yard and walking around barefoot, chasing the chicken and eating mud.

In 1910, a Ramphal call Dark Horse from the House of Baboolal, but who right name was Rajendra Gopaul Ramphal, lead a party of twelve Ramphals, including the famous warrior, Davindra Ramphal and his brother Bai Ramphal, the magician Kurt Ramphal, Sunil Ramphal, Suresh, Sivani, Sarwan, Son-son the Destroyer, Bachoo Ramphal, and Naveen the Skunt against the House of Sanjay in the first of ten wars fought between 1910 and 1942, at a place name Marai Kola, in what we call The Battle of Mari Kola, where ten Ramphal get dead after the meeting of the cutlass.

Dark Horse leads the House of Baboolal against the Sanjay Ramphals, until he get his head cut-off when he was near seventy in The Battle of Novar, in 1968. Is he what is the father of the present Mr. Ramphal, what people call, The Peacemaker.

Except for a small war in 1975, after Bachoo Ramphal, called Longhead, burned down a school with ten House of Sanjay children inside, the peace last. Mr. Ramphal busy finding ways to increase the family numbers and the family fortune for what everybody knows is the big war to come.

The House of Sanjay leader is a man name Carlos Ramphal, who people call The Builder because he expands the House of Sanjay by many houses and sons and daughters and sons-in-law, and he storing up swords for the war people say coming.

"What I want to know," Hari says, "is why they fight."

"Use to be over a piece of land, Ma Tussette tell me, but now they forget the reason and just war for war sake."

"You think Mr. Ramphal will leave Kangalang alone."

"Yes," I say, "but Tit not going to."

60. RICE MONEY

It is time for the rice money meeting when we share out the profits, decide on the next time to fallow, next time to fertilise, next time to plant and harvest the planting; decide what to do about the rice blast in the north field, and when to spray gandee flies in the south field; report how last year salt water get into the field at Middle Walk and money had to be spent pumping out the whole thing, so the cross-trenches must get dig out and the kolas and meri shore up; when we explain how it is that the members' share is smaller this season than last; when we instruct Bhoje and Burn Cookup Rice, who really name Rooplal Kumar, how they must buy the fertiliser for next year from Samuels Stockfeed and not from Mr. Ramphal; when we declare that something has to be done with cows getting into the rice and damaging the harvest – and something has to be done with the alligators – is too much of them now – and with the kecks and the curlews and the blue sackees them – and the locusts and the tares – and the bad business with the wild basmati.

I standing next to Bhoje in the dance hall, suffering through the whole rigmarole, wondering when they going to get around to giving me Mamai share of the Co-op money, so I can leave and go home and rest my tired body. Bhoje scraping dirt from his dutty fingernails with a penknife and nodding his big head and now and then making a sound from deep in his throat like crappo croak. Is like the whole village in the dance hall today. The place pack to the brim with ladies sitting on the long pews and men standing brace up against the walls. The place smell like sweat and work and burnt coconut husk. Uncle Charlie talk and Poopaloops talk and Ma Tussette talk and say maybe is time the comrades select new young leaders for the village Co-op, because she too old and getting tired of coming to the meetings to hear old men talk their toothless mash-mouth talk and go on and on about plenty of nothing. Teacher Clive knock the gavel and say she out of order; and the old men them agree. "Yes, man Tussette man, you is out of order." And Ma sucks she teeth loud and get up and start walk out the place.

"All-you send me money with Kip," she say. "I done with this long talk."

The talking don't stop though, because the agenda long. Now someone raise the matter about a certain hog plum tree near crasspah, and the need to trim it back to prevent the birds them from getting too close to the rice, and how it most necessary now to buy two-three water pumps for all the rain that does fall out of season, and how, how – "I didn't want to mention it before, comrades," say Boo Leggae, "is time the trench them get weeded to look spick and span and prevent big poisonous labaria snake from raising snake pickney in the tall grass and the arra and bizzi-bizzi."

Inside my mind, I leave the meeting and write a poem. I find, though, that the poem is about rice. In my mind, I see acres and acres of gold, with the meri and kolas crossing the wide expanse between the high dams that hem all in, and the fringes of jamoon trees by the edging trenches, and the fields waving like the sea in the wind, and the ripe rice making a sound like scratching dry skin. I hold these images in my mind and trap the words to put them down on paper as soon as I get home. Is something I like to do when boredom too much.

I almost finish the thing when big bangarang start in the road outside. Then we hear voice and Kangalang Harry Arnold run inside the place followed by three big men in white nurse-style uniforms. Kangalang run all the way up front and stand behind the table where the Co-op officers are sitting at a long table. Bhoje pocket his penknife quick and step in front the man them in white. They look he up and down with a scornful look, but Bhoje stand he ground and Wookum Paradooks and some other men join Bhoje and make a man-wall so the men who chasing Kangalang Harry Arnold have to stop and stay.

"Comrades," Bhoje say.

Teacher Clive bang he gavel three times on the table and the place turn quiet quick, except for Kangalang who breathing loud like bull cow from his big nose holes and repeating, "Ekereko, Ekereko, Ekereko." Everybody turn and look at Teacher Clive.

"Comrades," he say to the three men in white, "this is highly irregular to burst in on a sacred function without a how-dee-do. Explain yourselves, please."

"We here for the madman. We tackle he in the road, but he run in the place," one of them say.

"What you want with Harry Arnold?" Uncle Percy ask. "What he do to you?"

"He mad," say the man. "He belong inside mad house where mad people live."

"Who the rass get to say who mad and who not mad?" Rass Mouth say. "Is you must be mad rass to bust in the place like a child without manners and talk your rude rass talk. Please go away, man, so we can go on with the meeting. You is not no rass member of this Co-op."

"What is the complaint, comrade?" say Teacher Clive.

"We can't have people going round the place biting off people nose and throwing people in trench to drown."

"That is called self-defence," Hari say loudly from across the room. The man was provoke. Me and Kip see the whole thing."

"The man *was* provoke," I say. "Tit wrong to do what he did."

"We get witness," Bhoje say.

"I ain't care about all that," say the leader man. "I just here to do my appointed duty. The man mad and I take mad man and put them in mad house. I don't care about ought else. The man mad because jumbies get hold of he skunt, make the man walk round the place in he raggy-raggy clothes, not bathing he beetee crease, not brushing he stink-mouth teeth, with he long-long tolo hanging out and insect making nest in he tolo hair and he nasty-dutty dreadlocks. Is because precious school pickney can see he nakedness, and smell he dutty stinkness, and hear he repeating all day long "Ekereko, Ekereko, Ekereko", like the mad skunt he is, that we must take he rass and remove he from the sight of polite society and put he away in the madhouse, where we will treat he good and proper, and feed he nice food and, mayhap, if he not as far gone as he look, make he proper again. So now, sirs, I must insist that you do not get in the way of government business and the commencement of we legal duties to take one Harry Montique Eric Arnold, called Kangalang Harry, as it say here on this warrant paper, into we custody according to proper law and warrant signed here by one, Dr. R. Rajkumar Singh, Psychologist – that mean head doctor for mad people – stamped and sealed and duly sworn. Attend to me now, sirs. Do not stand in the way and prevent the work of officers of the law duly sworn and warranted in the name of the law and the Lord heself. I have the paper of proof. Hey, you there, what is you name?" the man say to Bhoje. "Come nearer and read the paper I get here. Tell me your name."

"Bhojedat," Bhoje say.

"Bhojedat, come nearer man, and peruse the thing for your own-own self."

Bhoje reach out and grab the paper and look at it back and front and sideways like is first time he see a piece of paper.

"Read it out loud," the officer say, "so that your crewmattie can hear and understand the way of things."

Bhoje look at the paper some more, his eyes them moving from left to right, he lips moving with the words on the paper. Then he stop and look at the lawman officer and pass the paper to Teacher Clive who read the thing and pass it to Poopaloops who read it and pass it on to Boo Leggae. The lawman officer looking at this and getting vex.

"Why not read the thing so everybody understand what it say."

"Because we is big man and woman and can read for weself," Bhoje say. "But never mind that, we go soon be done. What I want know is, why now? This man mad since 1969, walking round the place behaving as he do now, doing what he do. Why this big thing about putting the man away now?"

"Because he is a menace to society," the officer say.

"Menace, you say," say Teacher Clive. "Is not menace to defend yourself against people who mean you harm."

"Not menace at all," say Boo Leggae.

"Not menace," say big beettee Dado.

"No, not that. Not menace, no," say Uncle Percy. "Nobody get menaced by nobody."

"So, is mean you all mean to tell me that you going to tolerate this man walking around the place mad like cuirass and do nothing about it?"

"We do what we do," Teacher Clive say, "but what we don't do is turn over this man to you. This man is family, this man have people here; he is part of the community. You can go now, sir."

"Go? I don't have what I come here for."

Teacher Clive bang he gavel on the table. Silence fall in the whole place and we turn stern gaze on them three men. They just standing there looking at we looking at them. Then they start back out the door, slow at first, and then, fast like sprinters, they run down the stair and get in a big Land Rover and peal-out skunt like accouri getting chased by hunting dogs.

Kangalang Harry Arnold look up and smile a brown-teeth smile and go out the place, whistling a tune we don't recognise. Teacher Clive bang the gavel and we start the palaver again, how something have to be done with the African bees what nesting in the jamoon trees at Station Line. They already kill five sheep and three goats. Something have to be done about the canal trenches what need deep digging; and something have to be done about the fencing of public land in Bary. I stand next to Bhoje, who now shaving the coarse porcupine hair on his handback with the penknife. Long and long the skuntifying go on with everybody putting in he or she two-cents. I get up and walk out the building into the wet road. It still drizzling, but now the sun out behind the clouds.

Sheep grazing on the road shoulders and children playing by the standpipe in Poopaloops yard. Mr. Ramphal drive up and park across the street. Sitting shotgun beside he is the bad man self, his grandson, Stepping Razor, JagMohan.

"Boy, what happen in there today?" Mr. Ramphal ask in he big ghost voice, "I hear there was some worries."

"No worries," I say. "Three man dress up in white uniform come and try take Kangalang Harry Arnold. But Bhoje and Teacher Clive and them other people prevent them and make them go away."

"Is so it go?"

"Just so," I say.

"Ummm, ummm," say Mr. Ramphal, "is like they protecting the mad man?"

JagMohan take a pack of cigarette from his shirt pocket and light one and blow smoke in my face. I cough and back away. He smile at me with one gold tooth winking in the sun.

"Hear me now, Kip," he say. "Tell that mad skunt that next time me and he come face to face, blood go flow. Tell he that JagMohan is not Tit."

"Tell he your own damn self," I say, and walk across the road to go back into the meeting place. JagMohan suck his teeth loud, and laugh a dry, movie-badman laugh. Then they drive away.

Back in the dancehall, the conversation turn to the donkeys. How these days plenty donkeys walking around the place without owners, sleeping where they want, making more donkey babies, eating clothes off the lines in the yards, shitting, braying, making a whole bunch of fuckery in the village.

"Is Sulieman donkey them," Bhoje say to me, "but Sulieman dead and gone. Them donkeys wild now, don't take a bit or collar, don't heed a word man talking."

The donkey discussion go on for a bit until a decision's made. Sulieman donkey must be roped and impounded.

"So that is that," Bhoje say.

"I want one of them donkey, you know, Bhoje," I say.

He look at me close. "What you go do with donkey?"

"Ride it."

"No," Bhoje say; "donkey not for you."

Soon after, they start sharing Co-op rice money, but I still have to wait until they get to P for Plass. I hope the money don't run out by then. My last name should have been Arnold or Bhojedat. I have no luck in this world.

61. THE PALACE OF LONELINESS AND FEAR

The second time I see Alton Fisk, he running around with the castnet thing on a pole trying to catch butterflies. I was sitting on the dam with a youth from Novar name Narine, who mind cow for Mr. Ramphal. He's telling me a long and rigmarole story about the time he and Hari thief a man cow. I hear a different version from Hari and I'm glad when Alton Fisk's antics attract his attention.

"Look this chupidness, Kip," he say. "The Yankee boy skunt trying to catch the wind with a castnet thing. Look nuh! This boy too paglee and particular."

"He trying to catch butterfly," I say.

"Why?"

"He is a lepidopterist."

"What that mean?"

"He studying butterfly."

"That is pure skunt," Narine says. "The only thing to study is patacake. Not all patacake stay the same, Kippy. Some patacake big with no hair and some patacake small with plenty of hair. Most patacake have cut what go up and down, but I hear Chinee patacake cut crossway. You ever see Chinee girl patacake, Kip man?"

"I see Chinee girl patacake in a blue magazine what Derek father hide in the roofbeam," I say. "Chinee patacake cut the same way as other women."

"It must be buck girl patacake what cut crossway." And then he ask me if I know all the different names for patacake.

I nod but don't reply.

"Kippy, let me tell you something, buddy."

"Tell me."

"You is bright and know plenty of things. And I glad you and me is friends. Is all I want to say. You want me get another coconut?"

I shake my head and tell him I'm going home to take a nap.

Mary comes round in the afternoon and wakes me up with her hollering. Is near four in the afternoon. I get up and go outside in time to lift the big basket full of banana and sapodillas and soursop off her fine head.

"Where the mango?" I say.

"Mango done."

"So why you saying mango?"

"Because if I take out mango from my song, it out of rhythm."

I go inside and bring water with ice in it and a leftover bun with rancid cheese. Mary sits down on the step fanning she self with the big straw hat she always wears. She takes the cheese and bun and water and quick time the girl put away the food like a hungry-belly dog.

"Kippy," she says, wiping her mouth-corner with the back of her hand, "you is the best boy ever."

"You shouldn't sell when sun so hot," I say.

"I know, man Kippy man. One time I faint away near canal and almost fall in. Lucky thing Ma Tussette walking by. Is she what make me wake up quick. I could have drowned my chupidee self. She take me home and give me a potion what bitter too bad. She says bitterness good for people."

"You want some more water."

"I aright, Kippy boy. I wake you up?"

"Is time I get up, though. I feel like eating tilapia and going and catch some just now."

"You like living alone?"

"No. Living with Mamai is better."

When she coming out the mad house?"

"I don't know. Bhoje go and see her, and he say she the same way as last time."

I take the empty glass and saucer inside the house and come back. Mary fanning between her leg with the hem of the dress what too big for her.

"Kippy boy, some time I feel sorry for you too bad."

I didn't tell her that this is the way I feel about her, with she wasting-away disease and all, and being slave for other people, having to fetch water and cook and clean and sell fruit in hot-hot sun. But I don't say this because Mary don't see herself this way. She never complain. Just do what she have to do and move on to the next thing.

"Why you sorry for me?"

"Well, plenty bad thing happen to you, Kippy man. And also because you is an incest child. Something on my mind I want tell you, but another thing saying don't tell you. I don't want you get vex bad with me. Is a secret thing."

"Tell me if you want. I not going get vex."

"I see something today near Cross Path."

"What you see?"

"You know the Yankee boy what staying with Poopaloops?"

"Alton Fisk," I say.

"Well, I see he and Simone kissing and feeling up one another. He had her brace up against courida tree."

"When?"

"Is less than an hour ago. They didn't see me, though. I sorry I tell you this, man Kippy man."

"Is alright," I say. But it wasn't alright. My whole body turn hot like fire self and my mind already worming up scheme of revenge. But then I hear Mamai voice telling me that when I get most vex, I must give myself three minutes to think before I act. I take Mamai three minutes and clear my mind. What is it, I ask myself, I can do about the situation? Nothing. I can do nothing at all because I have no power. If the person I want to hold is slippery like eel, is best to love people who love you. That is all.

"Is alright," I say again.

Mary leaves an hour later, after me and she goes into Mamai house and do a little nastiness. We just kiss up with tongue in the French style and feel up one another. Mary is a virgin and afraid of the big bad final thing. So, she just rubs my tolo and I play with she patacake until she trembles and goes weak.

When she gone, I go inside and get a book to read. I pick one that I try to read before and had to put down because it hard bad and confusing. But I need a hard book, so my mind doesn't start thinking about Simone. I take down *Palace of the Peacock* by this Guyanese man, Wilson Harris, and go out to the veranda and start read.

I read for six, seven hours and still don't finish the book. This was because I would read something and don't understand it and have to read it over again. This happens plenty time. Is a book that takes your whole mind to read. I read and stop and think and start to read again. When I finally get to the end I was still puzzled and start to read again. Is a strange book and not regular.

The book, as far as I understand, is about a bad skunt man name Donne who takes a long journey up a big river with some people. This skunt Donne looking for some Amerindian woman name Mariella, maybe his wife, what runs away from him because he always giving she licks. He also looking for people to work he plantation like slave persons, to pick his crop and sow his seeds of plenty.

What happens then? Them man on the boat start dead one by one. Then we come to the end. But hear this now. Them man on the boat was already dead; they are really ghost men what reenacting how they died the first time. Is just plenty of dead man pretending they alive, talking and walking and eating food and drinking water like alive people. But they are just jumbie man what taking the reader on a trip like a tourist guide, saying, this is where Da Silva dead and this is where Mariella dead, and here is where the whole boat cant over in the big Mazaruni-type Cayuni, Barima-Wainimi River and drown the rest of the skuntian crew.

The book is not regular at all. Is like some kind of puzzle book with a trick inside. This book worse than dream self or nightmare what you only remember in little pieces when you wake up. Is pure vexation of comprehension to put trouble in your mind.

Later, I read the thing a second time, now with an open mind and accept that what on the page is not what I am accustomed to. I realise this Wilson Harris is not Samuel Selvon or Vidia Naipaul. This Wilson Harris man has a strange understanding of how to write a proper book. This book favours no book I read before.

I put the book in my pocket and lock up Mamai house and go out on the road. I plan to go see Teacher Clive so he can explain the meaning of *Palace of the Peacock*, because I vex bad not knowing all I should know and feeling stupid to rass for not understanding. But I never reach Teacher Clive.

Rain cloud open sudden and I run in Poopaloops shop and take shelter. Who is there but Simone's father sitting and talking hush-hush with Poopaloops. Just the two of them and Kangalang Harry Arnold. Kangalang in the back eating curry fish and rice from a half calabash.

I turn quick to run back out in the rain when Poopaloops call me.

"Kip, come here. I want gaff with you."

"Teacher Clive waiting for me," I say.

"You ignoring when big man talk," Lickamore says.

"Is alright, Kip," Poopaloops say. "We only going to take five minutes."

Poopaloops is a half-Amerindian and Chinee naiggerman what come with his father, known as the Angry God, who really name St. James Garner, down from Bartica. The Angry God was a big bushman. He first own the shop and when him dead and gone, Poopaloops take over and marry a Chinee woman name Chien who sickly with a coughing disease name consumption.

I sit down near Poopaloops across the table from Lickamore.

"Boy, I send for you yesterday. You mean you ain't get the message?" he says.

"I tell Simone to tell you I coming with Bhoje."

"Is like this Coolie is you father. Is that so, boy?"

"I don't have a father," I say.

"Kippy, how is your mother?" Poopaloops say.

"She still in madhouse."

"Ummm. Well. I will pray for her."

This Poopaloops like pray bad. He always praying for something. Sometime in the Methodist church he prays prayer so long-long it makes people vex. He prays like he about to cry, with voice shaking with plenty of emotion, like he feels every word he says.

"We want to talk to you about something," Poopaloops says.

"We want set you skunt straight," Lickamore says.

I see where the two of them going. They conniving to get Simone and Alton together and want me out of the picture. But just sudden I don't care at all. I don't care who takes who. My mind full to the brim with aggravation.

"This about Alton and Simone? Simone doesn't like me anymore," I say. "She tells me to leave she alone."

"Is not personal," Lickamore Chops say. "Is not because you is incest fatherless boy of a mad mother what this moment in madhouse. The girl can choose who she want to choose."

"How you feeling?" Poopaloops say.

"Aright."

"I mean how you feeling inside. Love can mash up man heart bad."

"Is alright," I say and get up and leave the shop.

"I don't want you talking to me daughter again," Lickamore calls after me. "Never again."

I don't say another word to the skunt. I walk slowly back home in the rain to Mamai house.

That night, I go to a double feature flick in Central. They showing Charles Bronson in *Chato's Land* and *The Mechanic*. When the film show done, I walking on the road when I see Simone and Alton hug up near Gonsalves shop. Simone sees me and calls me, but I don't answer and continue walking. She calls me again, but I just walk on. She calls a third time with a trembling voice like she going to start cry. I don't turn round.

62. THE FUTURE

When I try and see the future I don't see far. The limit of all I know is the village. There is so little and this little is shared by many. What is there for me? What am I to do? I don't know. Teacher Clive says one time that I must dream myself away from here. I dream and I wake in the same place. I wake up in the greenery of tall trees and long ropes of liana hanging down like snake, and birds in the blue sky, and people shouting and dogs barking. Today repeats itself like yesterday. Nothing change. I feel you can't escape the place, not even in your mind.

People say this is a paradise, with all the pretty flower and big river running, and the sea so close to a man backyard that he sees it every day, but it's not food for mouth or clothes on back, not money in pocket or a broad life of plenty. Paradise is a foreign word used by white men. People who live here have no use for paradise. It has a serpent in it, like any other place, and even me know that once you have serpent, you have things of the devil.

Bhoje says it is not sin what make Adam leave Eden. He says Adam eat the fruit of knowledge of good and evil because he wants God to throw him out of paradise because is a damn boring place. All day Adam just going around the place naming things. Bhoje says that man is not a man if he just wants to live rent-free. Adam is a real man; he wants to go on his own and be king of the whole world or be king of nothing. This, Bhoje says, is a man. Man what live rent-free is nothing but leech and skunt of the world, nothing and no more. I don't say this to Bhoje, but I wonder what Eve got to do with the story. She's the one who persuade Adam to eat the apple.

When I dream, I dream myself away. But I don't go anywhere. The limit of my dream is this village. What is it I must do? How must I make a way from no way? I think plenty of time that I can write books like Edgar Mittelholzer, novel books like *Kaywana*

Blood and *Shadows Move Among Them* with plenty fucking inside, and man chopping up man so that blood flows plenty and white people burying slave alive – thing what people like to read. I'd become famous and get my picture in newspapers and make Mamai proud. But how a man supposed to print books in this place? Sometimes I think too much and can't sleep.

Now that I going in the last compulsory year, I know school days could be almost done. Soon is big man time and big man decisions to make. Less than a year left. The future is nearer than near. What go happen to me? More questions I don't have answers for. The more you grow, the more responsibility fall on your head. I walk the road and try to see myself in people and things, and the road is not a long road, is a short road. I see tall coconut trees over the tombs in the cemetery yard and tall bellyache bush between the tombs. I see the houses where old people sit quiet and fan themselves; I see the long river running up and down, racing the laterite dam; I see men drunk in the rum shop talking loud and slamming domino, and I think about how long I've been practising to be such men, but now that I grow up, things turn. I see that some such men do nothing but drink rum and beat their wives and children, and some don't care skunt about the world.

I see good men, too, having toops of daru and gaffing low and long with other men; I see men in the rice field and cane field. The rice is golden and bends down low like it bowing, and green sugarcane is wave-like when the wind blows. All this is here and now, but I don't see me in the future. Is a paradise, yes, a nice Eden type place, but is a place to leave and go from; is a place of limits and boundaries, is a place to keep you in your place. Is a place what can't give me what I want. I don't think the whole country can give me what I want. I have dreamed myself away from here already.

When I almost near the koker, I hear a song come sudden inside my ear. Is an Eric Donaldson song name "Tumble Down" what Anita use to like bad. I use to sing it to her when me and she alone in Mamai house. I sing the song in her ear like a whisper and she holds me against her tight and she rubs my back and moans. When she breaks, I have to catch her quick before she falls on the ground. But I don't stop singing.

The days before me are strange and vacant.

63. RAIN FALL

On the morning we supposed to go and thief Mamai out of Berbice Mad House, rain fall hard. By the time I leave the house and reach the bus shed near Mill Road to meet up with Carl and Rakesh, my skin soak good and proper. Is one of them hard rain what flood up the place quick and drown the pasture and overflow the latrine. Days from now the water will still be on the land, and when it leaves, the mud will be thick and deep and stink when you walk. But now is just rain falling like Noah Ark rain, and the road is empty, with no car and no people, only a herd of donkeys in the middle of the road standing like statues with rainwater dripping down their coats. No sun, only a lemon glare what say sun somewhere near.

Carl in the bus shed kissing up Rakesh who sitting on his lap. When I come in the place they don't even stop. Carl just looks at me and continues kissing Rakesh. I stamp my feet and Rakesh jumps off Carl's lap and backs up against the bus shed wall like he see jumbie. He gives me a smile. Is the first time I look at Rakesh close. He is a pretty boy, tall and slim with curly coolie hair with big big eye what clear and shiny. Is he lips what is the girliest thing about him; they red and fleshy and always wet; a moistness that troubles me.

Carl stands and turns his back to arrange his cock-stand in his pants. When he turns back and looks at me and smiles, I think it is a shameface smile.

"It don't look like we going anywhere today, Kippy. It raining too hard. Me and Rakesh going home."

Rakesh smile he girly smile at me. Is the most beautiful smile I ever see on the face of a man. Is an exclamatory face, a face what always calling you to its presence, saying look at me. Is a face that doesn't belong on a man; it confuse a man looking at such a face – the lips, the eyes, the colour of the lips what always half-open, about to say something, the white top teeth barely showing, the slow eyes them with long lashes, the hairlessness of the face, not even shadow of hair. To me, Rakesh look like a man-lady, and so he makes me uncomfortable, because a regular man what like woman could see himself with Rakesh in a sex way, in a lovey-dovey style, the way man and woman do. The way Rakesh looks and behaves troubles my understanding and make me wonder hard and long about man-ness and woman-ness.

Carl make me wonder about this, too, not because of how he looks, but how he is. Carl is an auntie-man and not an auntie-man; there's nothing in him soft or girly, but I know he uses Rakesh the way man use woman; we know the two of them doing nastiness. We also know Carl doing nastiness with a girl called Sarita James who he likes bad from way back. Sometimes Carl and this Sarita walking on the village road holding hands like a regular couple. How come? How this thing stay so? Is strange to my understanding. Do nastiness with man and woman both? Strangeness and skuntian confusion it looks like to me.

Other people wondering like me. People talking, but nobody asking Carl because he turns an ignorant skunt and walk around the village like badjohn. Two times since he comes back from Essequibo he let men taste his hand when they call he auntie-man. One man he cuff six-seven times in his face in Dado shop and knock out the man teeth and bust up he face good and proper. Another time Carl beat up a man we call Monkey Stylin, a giant-size man Carl kick in his seed two or three times to make the man faint way. People afraid of Carl and don't say anything to him. Teacher Clive tells me he leaves Carl to God and Bhoje says Carl is a big man now and big man has to take big man licks when licking time come.

Sometimes, he bring Sarita to do nastiness in Mamai house, and me and he gaff while the girl tidying up herself in the room. She always crying when she leaves. I don't know what Carl does to her in the bedroom. He doesn't even look at her afterwards. Is like she doesn't exist. Is like he scorn she. This makes me vex with Carl. But still she stay with him. How come? How things stay so?

I want to warn her about Carl and protect her against hurt and pain. But I don't, because Bhoje says this is unmanly action; a man not on earth to su-su on other men. This is softness and not regular, so I never say anything about Carl to Sarita. Mostly, when Carl and me talk, is about Carl making plans to leave Mahaicony. He like Essequibo and wants to go back quick.

"People talking about your behaviour," I tell him.

"So what?" he says. "I is a big man now."

"They don't like how you behaving with Rakesh."

Fire comes in his eye and he clench and unclench his hand like mad-cuirass skunt and look at me like I is ant or something to mashup underfoot like kreketeh snail.

"Kippy," he says, "if you and me wasn't friends, I would beat you like dog self."

But that day I feel brave. I risk another sentence.

"You better go if you going to Essequibo. People getting vex and not going tolerate this thing for much longer."

"They go have to tolerate," he says.

But he doesn't say it hard, he says it soft, like he sees the truth of it. He looks at me and smiles and pushes away my face with his hard hand and laugh.

"I listening to you, Kippy," he says, "but I want to help you first before I run away from this damn place."

"What you mean, Carl?" I say.

"I promise to help you thief Ms. Paulette out the madhouse, and I go do it. I is a man of my word."

Is so me and Carl start talking about how we going thief Mamai out the madhouse. But because it rains so hard we don't go until a week later. When we get there, the Doctor tells me that Mamai in the hospital in Georgetown because she has cancer in her breasts. She has been in hospital over a month and is in a bad way.

64. FINDING A FATHER

When Mr. Plass tells me that he is my father, he says it in two short sentence. We two were sitting by Mamai sickbed in the hospital. He holding her hand. I was on the other side of the bed holding her other hand. Mamai was in a coma what take her whole self away from her; she was there and not there, gone far inside herself. She breathing, but that is all. She doesn't answer when you talk; she just lay there lalaff, not dead but dead. She get fine-fine and weigh just 75 pounds like a small girl-child because the cancer eat up she muscle them and fat and flesh. She couldn't eat in a regular way. Them nurse feed her with a tube that goes through her nose into her stomach. Her suffering was great and ungodly. I think plenty of time to hold a pillow over her face the way Lamuta Dave does to Ms. Minette, and done with the business. But I don't, because I had false hope of a miracle that she going open her eyes to a new and splendid morning. I pray to Jesus; I pray to Coolie gods like Hanuman, Ram, Ganesh, but my prayer and plenty eye-water do nothing. What is it I must do, I ask myself? My love couldn't make her better. The helplessness was the hurt and disgust in me.

All this time was just me and Mr. Plass sitting together, keeping watch. We did this in the hospital and then in Mr. Plass's house after the doctor tells him to take Mamai home to die. There, the first thing he does after he put her in the big bed in her room is to tell Aunt Esther that her service no longer required. From then on is just me and he and Mamai in the place like a family of strangers. I cooking and cleaning, and he taking care of Mamai like a man nurse.

Is he who bathing she and brushing her teeth and washing her clothes with his own hand, and he what lying down with her in the same bed like man and wife, singing a song in a soft voice and combing out knots in her grey-grey hair. He is tender with her;

he lifts her with care and brings her out to sit in the Berbice chair on the veranda so she can sun herself. For me, it was a new thing to see about the man, a different Mr. Plass.

Then one day, when me and he sitting quiet with Mamai, he opens his mouth and says, with words I have no problem to recall because it was only two sentences, "Boy, I am your father. I want you to know this." And just so, I was more an incest child than ever, because rumour became reality.

That is all Mr. Plass say on the matter at first. And I didn't want to hear more because there was nothing more I wanted to know. I was losing Mamai and gaining Mr. Plass, and in the mathematic of the adding and subtracting I would have one parent still.

But when he does tell me more, I see there was no specialness to my conception. He doesn't talk about this part much, but the story not unlike the one Aunt Esther tell. After the riot, the two of them come close and start living together and make me. I is an incest child. Nothing special. The two of them would have gone on living together except people start talking, and is the talking that makes them feel ashamed, not doing the incest thing; and is the shame what makes them suffer, and having to part and stay apart that make them lonely and mad, wanting one another and not knowing how to come together.

Mamai die on a Tuesday night with a sky full of bright stars. Me and Mr. Plass was with her, holding her hand on either side of the bed. She makes a long sound like she sucking in a breath, then she tremble and stop tremble and lays down quiet-quiet in her bed.

We bury Mamai in Mr. Plass's yard under the mango tree near the rice field. I didn't cry. I wanted to but couldn't. I was done with tears. It seem a waste then, crying so for the dead as I did when she was alive. Nothing good ever comes from man boohooing like a woman with unmanly emotion. But mostly I didn't cry because I could see no point in it and because I feel neither hurt nor grief. That was done as her long-suffering was done. I feel only a litheness and relief.

Sometimes I think is better if I pack my traps and go back to Mamai house in the village, but what use is that? I am different now, changing, changed, and almost new to myself. The house will feel emptier than before, and I admit to myself that I've got used to living with my father. Some things easier even. School closer to Central than Abary. I can walk there. I think, too, that Mamai was renting the land the house stand on, so why pay rent for a house I don't want to live in? I can sell the house and most of its contents, even if it's not for much.

So, on a Thursday, a balmy day with no rain, but no sun either, just clouds in the sky and an insipid light, a grey sad day, they come and get Mamai house. I stand up in Mamai's yard watching the workmen do their work. They take off the front and back step and verandas and jack the house off its stilts and drive a flat tractor-trailer under the house and bring down the jack so the house sits flat on the trailer and start the tractor and drive away with Mamai house down Long Dam to Main Road, leaving the space empty and lonely.

By then was no furniture in the house. I sell it to Lamuta Dave and Marcel. I sell the chicken and the ducks. Hari and Lil Girl come from Tuschen and take all the plates for their new house. I keep only my own clothes and my books and other personal things. Aunt Esther says I have to burn the clothes of the dead, so one night I build a fire in a barrel in Mamai backyard and feed she frocks and shoes and small clothes to the flames.

When the house gone, there was only the latrine still standing up lonely in the pasture. I think that this move will happen again and again, that from now on I will have no stable place to stay, that my life will be the life of a vagabond. I accept this idea because I didn't want to stay in one place anymore. My connection to the village and friends and things of childhood feels broken. This wasn't just because Mamai dead. Is because I feel I grow up and must make a new life and a good future for myself.

65. IN MY FATHER'S HOUSE AND MOVING ON

Since Aunt Esther gone, is me doing the cooking and cleaning the house. Is plenty cleaning because the house big. Every morning before I go to school is cobweb wheels to clean off the window frame and beetles with cracked carapaces turned upside down on the floor to sweep out; moth wings and moth on the sheet, and gangasaka shit stickup on the walls. I turn maid and wife to my father. And, like a wife, I haggle with the fishermen at dawn, beating down their prices for basha and bangamary, catfish and cuirass. Saturday, I go to the market, like a wife, and stand in the road talking skunt to the wives, like a wife, and lamenting the endless work. And they laugh their big Black people laugh and say, "Kip boy, you go make a good husband when you take wife." I think what they saying is that I will make a good wife to my wife when I have one. This is not regular. A husband cannot be a wife. Sometimes, when I talking to women, I hear myself talking, and reflect that I even sound like a wife. I talking like a woman and assuming their womany ways, and have to correct myself and man-up quick.

My father is no cleaner or cook. I don't know what he is. He is a mystery. Days go by without words between we two, and when we talk, we awkward with one another. Conversations short and halting and careful. After Mamai dead, is like we don't know what to say. Still, I feel that he wants to say more, to have bigger, more meaningful conversations. We working up to it I feel. I still call him Mr. Plass. He calls me Kipling. I hardly ever hear my birth name said by anyone aloud, and is a strange thing to hear my father say it. One time he called me "my boy", but he was shy about it, saying it in a way that made it too precious, like a grandmother would say it, with too much feeling and lady-like affection. "My boy," he said; "this is very good." We two sitting out on the veranda eating mutton curry with rice and daal. Then he smiled, a smile not fully there like a real smile; it was like a smile that did not want to be a smile. It flashed and turned away quick into serious. We ate in silence. My father has a hard time being a natural human.

There is too much silence in the house, so I open the windows to let the noise outside come in: birds tweet, donkeys bray, cows low from the pasture, the children talking quick like engine on the village road. On Saturday mornings, hymns from the Adventist church across the road flood the house with song, and on Sundays, matins brings the sound of the angelus struck in the steeple of the Catholic church. Sometimes, too, you hear the muezzin hollering *Allahu Akbar* from the minaret in the early dawn. My father spends most days in the rice field or closed up tight in the library reading books and trying to swallow his tears.

At night, he cries. Sorrow is his state. He cries and cries like some small animal in a cage before it's killed. He whispers, "Why, why, why," but it don't do no good. Not all the whys of the world can be answered. I hear him through my bedroom wall, muffling his cries and trying not to sound like a child. Sometimes he talks to himself, whispering like women talking over a paling fence in a gossipy style. But is the crying he does most, in a manly way, trying not to cry. I do not know how to comfort him. I done with cry a long time now. What is the use of crying except to get the water out? Mamai gone and no torrents of tears can change this, and no secret whispering or prayer can cure this sadness. Is better not to remember, to distract yourself from the dead. Mamai in the ground under the mango tree at the edge of the rice field behind our house. Is the way of all flesh, the preacher say, to end this way, in dust and dirt and decay, waiting for the second coming, when they say the dead shall rise again. Is the going that hurts. The realisation that she will not return I understand – and this calms my nerves and makes me think about other things. It gets so that sometimes I don't think about Mamai for days. Then suddenly she is there while I washing up the dinner wares or sweeping the yard. She stops in for a visit, but not for long, to remind me of something or to comfort me. I am comforted. Then I go on with the business of being and living and learning at school.

My father keeps a strict routine. He goes out early foreday

morning to the rice field, and he tells me he comes home for lunch around two o'clock, then he goes out again at three o'clock and comes home near six. When weekend comes he stays in the house. Hardly anyone comes calling. He has no friends except a white Englishman, Mr. Blair, who tall and thin and red. His skin is always peeling and his blue-blue eyes shine like new coins. Mr. Blair comes sometimes to the house to drop off books and talk to my father. Is he that bring the fancy rum my father drinks as they gaff while sitting on the veranda looking out on Main Road. The two of them always talking about their university days in England. And my father smiles his thin smile and even laughs when the rum soaks in. He asks the tall white man about this body and that body. And they cheer and throw rum "down the hatch". Then Mr. Blair leaves in his Land Rover until next time. The last time the white man came he didn't stay long, but is during that visit I learn that I have a big brother in England, in a place what called Notting Hill.

"William doing just fine," the white man tells my father, "just fine, mate. He getting on well at uni, like father like son."

That night I asked my father about this William. He says yes, he has a son in England, born before he came back to Guyana. Then he goes in his bedroom and comes out with pictures and hands them to me. It was photos of this William at different stages of life: as baby in the arms of a pretty white girl; as a toddler; as a small boy in a white surround of snow; when he was about twelve in a nice school uniform, and then, when he like my age, standing next to a big black car. Is a red-haired boy what looks more white than black. He tall and thin with large round eyes and white, even teeth. He looks like my father. He looks a little like me, a white version of me.

"You must write to him," my father says. "I will give you the address. He knows about you."

I write to this William half-brother of mine. And he writes back quick-quick, saying many nice things about his life and England. He is a big read-man like myself and we discuss books he reads, and he even sends some for me with a freck of money. My father seems pleased with all this. "Family is family," he say.

Meantime, I play the wife. I go to the market once a week and buy rations. At the weekends, sometimes I just sit in the house and read, sometimes go galavanting all over Central. It's months since I moved out of Mamaï's village and I hardly ever go back. The pull of the place slackens. I don't feel I must go there. Hari and Lil Girl gone to Tuschen with Ganesh Burilal. Carl in Essequibo. Derek in Foreign and Away. Anita dead and gone. Lamuta Dave in the gold fields of Ekereko. Apart from Bhoje, all the close ties snapped like electric wire in a storm. The world is moving on. I have made no new friends in Central except the market wives. I start to resemble my father, quiet and closed-off and friendless. I do not mean to be, but it is so.

I run, much more than I used to, and farther and faster. Is one of my only passions. Bhoje comes with his old Lada Riva and takes me to run in all kinds of long-distance races. I run and win most of them. I become popular and famous. Plenty girls want to hold my hand and feel up my tolo. Sometimes I allow them, sometimes not. A girl named Sushila Roopnandan was sweet on me for a lover. She pulls me behind the latrine in the schoolyard and proper suck up my tongue. Her mouth sweet like fruit and she says if I play my cards right, she go let me meet her father, who is, like, an important minister and thief. I ask her if she wants to meet my father.

She said, "You mean the English Black man what walk like auntieman?"

We never talk again. Family is family, after all.

I go out to the Mahaicony Bridge and watch the fishermen come in with the day's catch. The men are mostly strangers to me. I miss the sluice in Bary and Uncle Percy sitting on the steps all day reading his books. I miss the water sound of the north canal where it meets the Abary River, bound north to serve the sea. Is a gurgling sound where the eddies funnel and froth and flatten. I miss running on the beach past the *Hans Bahlin* rotting in the berms. The beach in Central is a forest of deadwood and deep mud. No place to run. I run on the Main Road, then south on the Perth Road into Perth. The fishermen in Central are less friendly. I try to talk to a few of them, but they ignore me and go about their work. I don't get any free fish from them either. They are silent, serious men.

I meet Raggamuffin Love on the wharf one day, and while we sit in Gonsalves shop eating square cakes and mauby, he tells me that Peep Bhojedath dead.

"She throw down sheself off Bhoje landing and bruk she neck." His cousin's friend's brother tell he so two days ago.

I need more reliable information so I ask Simone.

"No, Peep not dead," Simone tell me during lunch in the school yard. "She just lost the baby and is in Cottage Hall Hospital. How you don't know this when I hear you and she closer than close."

"She in the hospital?"

"Yes, and the baby dead inside she belly from when she fall down. Doctor give she operation and take out the dead baby, but Peep sick bad. I sorry bad for she, boy."

"She can't dead," I tell Simone.

"You not God to say so," Simone say. "Only God can say where and when."

That afternoon, after school, I walk up the road to the hospital in Cottage Hall to see Peep.

They put Peep in the baby mother ward. Is a long room like a great big hall with a wide middle walkway and beds to either side. The place almost empty. Only two new mothers there. One of them don't look like a mother at all; she looks like a small child, but she has a baby sucking hungrily on one small breast. I look at her and see that she crying. Is a sad mother and alone. I walk closer and look down at her. She is Amerindian, Wai Wai or Waspishana, like them what live in the Mission on the Mahaicony River bend. She look up at me.

"Is you what come for the baby?" she ask.

"No," I say, "I not here for the baby."

"You want the baby?"

"No, I don't want the baby."

"Well then, I going keep the baby."

"Yes," I say. "You keep the baby."

"I not giving Toucan the baby."

"Don't give Toucan the baby," I say. "You is the mother of the baby. Let Toucan make his own baby."

She smiled at that. I didn't ask who this Toucan person was. I leave the small girl looking down with wet eyes at the baby, as if is a magic baby. Tears coming out of her eyes and falling on the sheet and the baby, but no crying sound coming out her mouth. Is a strange girl and not regular. I leave her and walk down the aisle. Two nurses stand talking near the other mother. She sitting up in bed knitting a baby socks. She looks up at me and smile. She fat and her face shiny and dark. She has a gap between her front teeth. She looks like somebody I know.

"Eh, Kip boy," she say, "you come to see the girl who baby dead? She on the right side near the wall. See Ras Mouth sitting on her bed there."

I go on down pass the woman, still not sure who she is but somehow knowing I should know her. Ras Mouth sitting on the edge of a bed in his dutty farm clothes. He smell of sweat and work, and the rancid odour of copra. On the bed, Peep lie down on her side, facing away from me. She is covered in a white sheet and seems so small under it. The sheet is drawn tight around her and her outline is like mummy in a film show, wrapped round and round with strips of cloth or like a shroud for a Saracen ready for burial.

"Kip boy!" Ras Mouth say, getting up to greet me. His demeanour is unusually happy for a sad occasion. He who has always been so sombre seems joyous to me. He grabs my hand and pumps it a few times, all the while praising my presence there, as if I was Jesus suddenly come back from the dead. I wonder at the reason for his sudden joy.

"She ain't say a word until today," he say. "She just lay down there quiet quiet like rat for a week, then this morning she wake up and say she want water. I so glad."

I go around the side of the bed and sit down on a low chair looking at Peep. Her face is thinner and her eyes closed, but she open them and look at me and start cry, her whole body shaking like a leaf under the sheet. I pull the chair nearer the bed and take her hand.

"Oh Kip," she say, "I is a murderer. I kill the baby."

I look at Rass Mouth on the other side of the bed behind Peep. He shake his head.

"Is not true," he say. "She was walking up the step and when she get on the landing, she get weak and fall down and start bleeding. Ambulance bring she here. The baby dead. Is almost a week now."

"You never come and see me," Peep say softly. "Is months now since you leave the village."

"I here now," I say, squeezing her hand.

One of the nurses comes back and looks at us. She looks familiar too, like the knitting lady.

"You is the boyfriend?" she say.

"No," I say. "I is more like the brother. Kipling Plass."

"You is the runner. I read about you in newspapers. You just win a big race."

I nod.

"Get she to stand up and walk around a bit," she say. "The muscles need exercise near the cut."

"The cut?" I ask.

"Yes," she say gently, "to remove the foetus."

I look down at Peep. Her eyes closed tight, squeezing out a trail of tears. I don't know what to do next. I want to comfort her, to make her feel better, to make her whole again. I have no tools for the job. I sit down and smooth the damp hair from her face.

"Is alright," I say, "you getting better."

Rass Mouth clear his throat.

"Kip boy, I got to go bring in my cows them. You going stay with she a while?"

"Yes."

I watch him leave. The sun winks on the louvres. The sanitised air of the ward, reeking of Detol, tickles my nose. The slow fan in the roof whirls and hums, the only sound in the place. It seems unnatural. There should be music, I think; there should be songs to cheer up Peep and make her laugh, take her troubles away. The silence of the ward don't take your troubles out of your head, like the sea does when I run; it makes you think more about them and makes you sadder. I need to get Peep out of the place.

"The nurse say you must walk a little," I say; "it's good for you."

We walk in slow motion up and down the long walkway between the beds, she leaning heavy on my shoulder, shuffling across the tiles, holding on to me. I was holding the pole on wheels from which her saline drip and other medicines hang down.

It takes three days for her to walk on her own. I read to her and tell her stories. I couldn't crack a joke though. Laughing made her stitches tear and her belly hurt.

Sometimes we walk to the solarium and sit with the other sick people and look out through the glass onto the tarmac below, where the windows of cars wink in the sun. Little was said between us or needed to be said. That was good. The assurance of silence help us to relax. Later, we ventured out of the building into the sun, she in shimmy and soft slippers, into the hospital garden of blazing crotons, a masquerade of shades of green, gold, orange, black and yellow. Among them, bees buzzed and hummingbirds flit and flashed. Butterflies stayed close to us. I watch Peep look at the life around her, studying everything closely. What she thinking, I wonder, but don't ask. The garden smells of fallen five-finger fruit and the river smells of tannin-dark water. I hear the sea, hear it sigh from the mangroves. We sit on a bench among the green, saying nothing with words, sharing only our thoughts, the things we could not say.

Bhoje come a week later with his car and takes her back to Bary. She still quiet, not saying anything, but able to walk on her own like regular. But just a week or two after she go back to Bary, she start come to my father's house real regular, three-four days a week. She in the place, cleaning and cooking like a maid, hardly saying a word. Me and the old man eating various Coolie foods real proper. My father look at me and I look at him. We don't know what to say to her.

"We should pay her," he say one morning.

"We should," I agree.

He gave me some money and I bring it to her while she in the kitchen doing a chunkay for some hassa curry. She tells me to put it on the table, but when she leave that afternoon it stay right there. This go on for a long time. I just put the money in a vase on the table until it half full. She talking, but not much. One time, I come in from school and she talking to my father. She telling he about me and Anita and he sitting at the table nodding his long fine head. I go in my room and listen to them talk, and I cry like my father cry at night, with my hands over my mouth to muffle the sound.

Peep and my father easy with one another. He talk to her more than he talk to me, talking like they know each other long time. I notice, too, that is he she ask what she must cook, not me. With me she play the big sister, always fixing my clothes when I dress for school, talking to me in a way what make me think she is mothering me. My father, too, come out his shell a little. He more relax and always smiling and thanking Peep for doing this or that, in a way that is a little too much.

Not long after she start being mother to me and wife to my father, Peep bring all her things and move into the empty bedroom in the house. She don't ask anyone. She just move in the place and start live there. My father say nothing and I say nothing. We making new ways to accommodate her in the house. We have to reschedule our bathing time. We become shy and different. But we adapt to her sleeping habits, her bathroom habits, and her early waking habits. Panties and brassieres in the place, and the smell of a woman. Peep in the place changing up the bachelor style me and the old man accustomed to. No more silence in the house; she playing Coolie music on a small radio; she hum along and move her small waist to the rhythm of the raga when the tabla thump, *badam bam, boodoop bup*. She listening to *Let the Lion Loose* at nights, and death announcements.

As time pass, and the school year nearing its end, I feel I should be moving on. Though we've become a kind of family, I think that Peep and my father need some space and I feel ready for what should come next.

I didn't get advice from anybody, though Bhoje talk to Miss Jenny about taking me to her house in Georgetown so I can study for senior secondary in the city and be near the university. She agrees, but I tell her no, I want to live by myself. Bhoje comes and talks to Mr. Plass and Bhoje arranges things because Mr. Plass still doesn't know how to manage things, because he is not a man who knows how to talk to people. I think of him as a hermit man, though he lives among people, and not far away in bush and jungle. When he does talk is not for long and his conversation short and sweet and, to me, very precious. But when people try and talk long to him, he just moves away in the middle of a conversation and goes his way. Mr. Plass is not regular.

I know I'm right about moving when Peep's father, Rass Mouth, come and beg she to come back home to Bary.

"I is a big woman," she tells him, "a mother what already lost baby. I is not no small girl. I staying here with the black Englishman... and Kip."

"Edgar," my father say.

"I staying with Edgar and Kip," she say.

Rass Mouth sitting in the house shaking his head. Then he gets up and shakes my father's hand.

"Who no hear go feel," he says, and walks out the door and down the steps into the yard.

Peep run to the veranda and lean over the bannister, looking down on her father.

"Daddy, Daddy," she says, but he don't look back. He goes through the gate muttering to himself and go up the road without turning back.

"He too vex with he self," she say. "He go come back when he calm down."

He never did though. Bhoje came and drink with my father from time to time but Rass Mouth stayed away. Still vex bad I guess.

One morning, when rain falling hard, I went with my father and Peep to see the house Bhoje had arranged for me to stay in at Festival City. The house has three bedrooms and furniture and a veranda that gives onto a narrow street on a cul-de-sac. As we walked through the place, touching this thing and that thing, opening the fridge and closing it, and looking inside the cupboard and under the bed, my father said something in his very British way. I didn't hear, but when I turn and look at him, he said it again.

"I buy the place," he said. "It's yours now."

I had nothing to say. We go out to the veranda, sit down in silence, and look out on the empty road, wet with rain falling in silver straws like a curtain between us.

Peep inside the house, turning on the taps and opening the louvres. She does this quietly and murmurs to herself like an old woman.

"We go need blinds and cleaning things to make the place regular," she says. "I see plenty cobwebs all over the place."

I look at my father. He is looking out on the narrow slip of road that wends by, beyond the fence. I feel there is more we should say to one another on such an occasion. But the moment passes. My father smiles. I do not know how to be a son to my father. But I am practising. Talking to him is less awkward now; there are less silences and less careful regard. Peep has made it easier for our banter. Almost as easy as when we talked with Mamai between us; me on my side of her death bed and he on the other side, holding her hand or feeding her some pap the doctors recommended; or, in a mood of tenderness, whispering sweet things in her ears.

66. YOU RAISE GOOD AND PROPER

Teacher Clive sitting on his veranda reading *No Pain Like This Body* by Harold Sonny Ladoo, a Trini, when I come to say good-bye at the end of the school year. His wife, Teacher Cora, gone out, and he alone in the place drinking brown rum and reading a book. He have reading glasses on the tip of his flat nose and long hair hanging out his nose-hole them. He half-naked so I see his bony chest with grey chest hair. His hand them look too long, and his leg too, and his head is long, and finger long and fine like he has no fat on his whole body.

I come into the veranda and say good afternoon and take a seat. Two donkey grazing on the road corner and Mary, with the big basket on her head, going toward Bary crying *Banana, sapodilla, mango,* over and over again like chachalaca bird. Sun hot and I can feel the sweat drying on my skin with a tingling sensation, like ning-ning. Teacher Clive sips his brown rum and closes the book and puts it on the bannister of the veranda and turns and looks at me and shakes his head two-three times as if he disappointed in me. I'd already told him that I was leaving Central and going to sixth form in Georgetown.

"I feel I should give you some advice, Kippy," he says, "but I am not sure what to say."

"You always know what to say," I reply.

"That is true," he says, "so I will give you some. Stay away from them Georgetown whores. They will ruin you. That is all the advice I have for you. If you never took any of the other advice I give you since you small, then nothing I say now will make a difference. You have been taught; you have been raised well with good manners and compassion; you just need to remember that. When you leaving?"

"Sunday."

"Bhojedath tell me your father get a place for you in the city."

"Yes."

"How you feel about that?"

"Alright."

"You want a drink? You are almost old enough."

"No. I just come to bring you something."

"What?"

"The first chapter of the book I start to write."

I give him an exercise book with Mr. Burnham on the cover. He takes the exercise book, opens it up and reads the title.

"*The Various Uses of Bitterness and Pain*," he says. "That's the title?"

"For now. I was also thinking of calling it "*How to Raise Yourself Good and Proper*", or "*Limers*", cause the whole thing is like one liming after another.

"You want me to read it?"

"Yes."

"Alright, leave the thing and I will read it and give you my opinion."

Teacher Clive takes another sip of his rum and starts to read again. I sit there for a bit, looking at the face of Harold Sonny Ladoo on the book cover. Sonny Ladoo is not a handsome man. His face hard and bumpy and sad like.

When I leave Teacher Clive, I go out into the road and stand there looking around like lost-way boy, wondering whether I will ever go back again.

EPILOGUE

Fisherman's wharf in Central. Rain is falling, the morning still dark. I stand on the old Mahaicony River Bridge. Its planks have weathered and warped and the iron spikes that held them down have unscrewed with time. The steel girders slough off curling rust like bark on scabrous old alders. I look east at the new Amerindian Mission house. When I was young and troubled, I came here to listen to the lapping tide against the banks, a rhythm that hypnotised and calmed me.

Nearer, the trawlers roped on the bollards shillyshally in the ebb tide. On their decks, silhouetted fishermen bend to their tasks of hauling seines, attaching buoys, and performing ritual duties with the marlinspike. A radio is playing Jim Reeves. Sometimes they stand to smoke, drink tea or coffee, and stare down at the tannin-dark river, as if mesmerised by something there.

I hear the river muttering through the stands of mangroves in the estuary. As daylight comes, I see my twin self staring back at me from the water and I know what Narcissus knew – that the only time to love your face is when you are young, supple and self-adoring. Today, I look away.

This morning, after reading my book, I feel a terrible sadness. It reminded me of another sadness years ago when I went to see Bhoje at the hospice in Elmhurst, Queens. He had been there for a while. The illness that brought him there had started two years before. It had been an innocuous start to a tragic end. One morning, climbing off his boat at Bary sluice, he had stubbed his big toe, raking across a nail that fastened into his flesh. The pain had been a momentary shock, but the bleeding continued long after the pain was gone. The flow was steady and would not stop. They took him to a private hospital in Georgetown. There he languored, growing thin. Even in that place of cures, he bled on.

He was given blood and bled that out as well. Something was wrong with his spleen and they snipped that out, but no diagnosis was forthcoming. His wife was away teaching somewhere in the USA. Hari called me and told me the details and asked that I try to locate the professor. I did, after a week or so. She took over then. And by the peculiar magic of the wealthy and well-known, she whisked him out of the wards to New York where, within a week, they diagnosed him with something called multiple myeloma, a cancer of the blood for which there was no cure, only therapies to manage it. Bhoje died three years later in 1998; he was fifty-seven.

For a while it seemed he was getting better. He and his wife lived during those years in a rented place in Queens and twice a year I would visit from Iowa. He had regained some weight and was making plans to return to Guyana. He never did while he was alive. For me, his passing meant more than I could ever have imagined. The sadness stayed with me for years, a nagging persistent ache without a cure.

Reading my book brought back that sadness. Not the nostalgia I expected, but a melancholy, almost a terror that was so disturbing it chased me out of the house into the street for fresh air and open space, to walk the road in the misty rain.

I looked at the fishermen. A few looked back at me and looked away, incurious. On the *Kelly Kraken*, a big trawler I remember from my childhood, someone called me by name. I went down off the bridge, drew nearer and looked down into the boat and saw no one. The trawler was full of piled bunches of seines, sailing tackle, and other accoutrements of the trade.

"Here Kip," the voice said again. "Over here, man. Come down nuh."

I stepped off the stelling onto the boat, still not seeing the source of the voice.

"Is true I small," the voice said, "but I not invisible. Come closer, man, I over here."

He was sitting among the piles of seines with his back braced against the mizzen, deftly using an awl to mend holes in his nets.

"Prakash the Small," I said.

"Same way," he said, "and as you see, nothing change. I didn't grow not even an inch. I think I get shorter. Sit down, man. What you doing up so early? I hear you deh bout."

He was indeed the same; still a dwarf, small and thin and dexterous with his hands. But he was greyer and had the gaunt weathered look of men who work in the sun. The rest of him was covered in plastic, a rain-slick poncho with a cowl too big for his narrow head. I sat down next to him.

"I was reading about you last night," I said. "Where is your father, Mr. Deodat."

"Dead," he said; "drown and gone plenty years now. What you mean you reading about me?"

"Something I wrote when I was young, about murdered fishermen."

"That is a long time ago, man, thirty-forty years."

"Forty," I said.

"Yes," he said, "a long time. When I look back so far behind is only dead people I see. Dead people and a dead world. Things change so much I hardly remember how things used to be. All this time I been going back and forth on the sea. They tell me Carl dead."

"Yes."

"That fucker owe me money. Two years ago, he come to the sluice with one of his girly boyfriends and say, 'Prakash, you dwarf mother-skunt' – you know how he talk – 'I buying out all your fish today.' He take my whole catch and never pay a red cent. Next time I see the scamp he in the newspapers shaking some minister hand, talking politics. I just have to laugh."

"What is it he did for a living?"

"He used to call heself a transgressor. I hear he say this plenty times. That is just a nice way to say that he was a robber and thiefman. He used to get all kinds of thing from the government; is so he get rich with big house and big car."

In the sky, a flock of parrots crossed low enough to be heard. Their caws petered out with the distance. The sun, a faint light behind the greying dawn, rose slowly above the heads of trees.

"You never left this place," I said.

"No reason to," he said. "I is eyesore no matter where I go. You ever been to the country of dwarfs, Kip?"

"No," I said. "There is no such country."

"Well, then there is no place other than here for me. I better stay put with my son."

"You are married?"

"Yes, man, a lonely dwarf don't live long, they tell me. I send for she from Brazil and I marry she quick and put baby in she belly bam-bam, before she up and leave. Twenty-five years ago it was. My boy is regular though, not like she and me – tall like you. I wonder how this can be, that he not a dwarf like we two."

I was tempted to explain but did not. I stood up and stretched.

"You going?" he asked, his small hand making light work of mending the seine.

"Yes."

"Come back tomorrow. Let we gaff some more, take a shot or two of rum. I go have some fish for you. Where your brother, White Boy?"

"William? He's in England."

"He come home more than you, Kip."

"He likes here," I said.

"I hear your father and Peep gone to England, too."

"For a holiday. They will be back in a month."

"Tell that hot-mouth little sister you get that I go have the fish she want this afternoon."

The market women were setting up their stalls on Perth Road. I leaned on the lamppost and watched them. They buzzed like bees around the stalls, setting the greens and fresh fruit out, parcelling fish, and dumping ice into their gutted refrigerators. One of them burst into song, some mournful hymn full of trembling emotions, which brought me to the edge of tears. Two others took up the song, and they sang loudly in chorus of surrendering all to Jesus, in an unselfconscious way, as if no one was around. I walked down Perth Road to the old Methodist Church and stood looking at the place behind the scaffolding, fading whitewashed boards weathered by time. There were high mounds of sand and stone in the yard for repairing the old church. Once or twice I had gone there with Peep, who, disbelieving in the Hindu gods of old, had taken up with ardour the naked and thorny Methodist Christ on his cross. I turned and went back up the road.

The rain had started up again, harder, faster, and now there was thunder in the west, rolling booms accompanied by quick stitches of lightning in the east. I took shelter under the canopy of a rum shop. An old man joined me there, and while I kept my eyes on the rain, bursting its bubbles on the asphalt, I sensed him staring steadily at the side of my face. He stayed in my periphery, unmoving, clad in dirty work clothes and a grime-stained Stetson. A cutlass hung lazily at his side.

"Plass," he said. "I know you."

I looked at him. A vague memory stirred. It caught onto something but doubted.

"Mr. Crawford?"

"Lickamore Chops. I is Simone father. You remember me?"

"I do," I said, staring at the deep furrows in his forehead and the burst capillaries in his rheumy eyes.

"Time do what it do," he said. "Nothing a man can do about that."

Then he laughed – a laugh devoid of mirth, hiding, I thought, some deeper hurt, some unsaid feeling.

"Yes, it does," I said, and waited for the questions I knew would follow. How is so and so? Have you seen so and so? It was always the same for the ones gone and the ones left behind.

"You see my daughter anytime?" he asked. "She don't call or write. What kind of daughter is that?"

"The one you made," I wanted to say, but did not. I looked at him and looked away, watching raindrops dance on the asphalt. There is a saying: If you stay in Queens long enough, the village will come to you. And so it had, year after year. People passed through or stayed forever. One year, Hari came with Lil Girl for a month and stayed with me for a week. I was happy to see that they were still together, not entirely surprising, given the Guyanese penchant for staying together even in the worst circumstances. It was a happy time for me. Lil Girl talked about her children, five in all, successful people, all employees in their string of dry-goods shops. Ganesh Burilal had migrated to Canada years ago to study and had stayed there and married.

"Damn place cold bad," Hari told me. "Is not a place I can live."

Lil Girl thought she could live there and take care of Ganesh Burilal's children.

"He white-lady wife say I can come and stay a year, even more," she said.

"Well go nuh! See if I don't take woman quick and bring she to live home."

Hari and I laughed. She did not.

Derek came up from Boston and stayed two days with us. He was an attorney for a large firm in the city. We sat around drinking rum while Lil Girl cooked Guyanese food in the kitchen. We spoke of Bhoje and Ma Tussette and Anita and Satie, and all the dead piling up behind us.

Lickamore stirred beside me. "Is like you get lost in memory," he said.

Across the road, the market women were sheltering under their wide umbrellas. The rain kept falling, rattling the galvanise on the canopy. The water came down in the grooves and guttered in a rush of rivulets along the roadside. The distance became blurred and hazy. Three mangy mongrels came out of the rain and curled like Cs behind us under the canopy, and went to sleep.

"I asking if you see my daughter in New York. Is the city where she lives. You never run into her?"

"No!" I lied, "I haven't seen her."

"Well, boy, is years me and the mistress don't hear from the girl; not one word in ten-twelve years. No letter and no phone call. Every month the money come and every Christmas the barrels, but she don't come and she don't call. What we do she make she stand so?"

What they had done, Simone told me years later, was to separate her from me so she could take up with Alton Fisk, who they saw as a way to improve their situation. Year after year he came for his holiday, then he did not. They'd imagined he would marry her and take her away to America. Naturally, they would follow. It was the prevailing scheme at the time: get your children out to a snow country so you could get out later. This was not a bad calculation, but none of it worked out for them. Simone got pregnant. Alton Fisk went back to America and never wrote or called. They made her abort the baby. This, too, did not go as planned. Trying to keep her secret, they did not take her to Ma Tussette, but to some quack in the capital. She got an infection, then septicaemia which made her barren. Her recovery was long and hard, full of close calls. Depression and a nagging ache to be dead followed.

When I met her again in New York, she had sworn off men. She was a cold, callous girl with a touch of madness. She hated her parents. We would meet from time to time to talk. I was not comfortable in her company. Her moods were dark and her hurt, always on the surface, sweated out in our conversations. She lacked, I thought, the empathy that made being fully human possible. Her complaints were endless. We lost touch, which I was glad of; it spared me the hate and vitriol she spewed whenever we met. I was not surprised by her abandoning her parents.

"Well, if you see she," Lickamore said, "tell her we still alive and want see her."

Then he walked out into the rain. I stayed with the dogs, watching him walk away slowly, shoulders slumped, disregarding the rain. Then I too left the dogs to their siesta, and walked west on the empty road, home to Audibey.

She sat in the veranda in her nightgown, a cup in her hand. Her head was wrapped round and round with bright yellow cloth. She waved to me. I waved back as I opened the gate.

"Why you walking in the rain, man? Come in and get your tea. I already prepared it."

"Just now," I said.

I walked along the side of the house into the backyard where, under the big Buxton spice mango tree, was my mother's tomb, bright green in the splayed shadows. No one I knew closely had been dead for so long. Mangoes littered the ground beneath the tree; some had just fallen, others rotted in the mud. The air was sweet with their spice. I picked one up and washed it under the standpipe and ate it sitting on my mother's tomb. It was sweet and juicy. I ate the flesh hungrily and sucked the seed. I thought of Mamai and struggled to recall the particulars of her face. This frustrated and alarmed me. In the end, with much concentration, she emerged from the fog of memory – a thin, boney-faced woman with large marsupial eyes. I tried to imagine what she would have looked like now, if she was alive and among us. I could not see her.

She was a person of her time and place. Anita, too, was locked in the past, though perhaps she was in the wind, her ashes whirring with the breezes, now east, now west, north and south. Mamai, though, was closely confined in the shadows of the mango tree behind my father's house.

I got up and walked further back through the yard, into the rice field. The padi was ripe for reaping, the stalks bending, then righting in the wind and rain. I stood there following the land out as far as my eyes could see. It was the land of my people. I could be a farmer, I told myself, like my father. I could work the land. This thought, so easeful and new, suddenly seemed possible. I could stay here I told myself, and live here and write here while I farmed the rice. I could come home and settle down, maybe find a wife, have children, and, when I wanted to, I could go on holidays with my darling and my son to foreign places.

Audibey called from the back veranda and I turned and made my way back through the rain.

"Daddy and Will on the phone," she said. "They want to talk to you."

I washed my feet under the standpipe and mounted the stairs to the veranda where Audibey stood with the phone in her hand.

"Is anything wrong?"

"Nothing is wrong," she said; "they just want to gaff with you."

A NOTE ON LANGUAGE

It is not our practice to provide glossaries at the back of Caribbean novels and it is not our intention to begin now. There are good dictionaries of Caribbean Englishes, such as those for Jamaica (F.G. Cassidy and R.B. Le Page, *Dictionary of Jamaican English* (1967)) and Trinidad (Lise Winer, *Dictionary of the English/ Creole of Trinidad & Tobago* (2009), and even though there is no definitive dictionary of Guyanese English, Richard Allsopp's *Dictionary of Caribbean Usage* (1996) has a fair coverage of Guyanese words – not surprisingly since Allsopp was Guyanese. Daizal R. Samad's and Aswannie Harripersaud's *A Dictionary of Guyanese Words and Expressions* (2024) is a useful, small-scale survey but makes no claims to be comprehensive.

Kipling Plass is a novel and not a linguistic textbook and there is no word or phrase whose meaning cannot be deduced from context. However, a good deal of the language of the villagers of rural Abary recorded in the novel evidently evaded the lexicographers that Allsopp must have relied on, and don't appear in Samad's and Harripersaud's survey. Moreover, the important collection of essays on Guyanese Creole edited by John R. Rickford, *A Festival of Guyanese Words* (1976, 78) has long been out of print. For these reasons and because the creole language of the novel is so rich, particularly in the mix of its diverse sources in, for instance, African, Indian, Amerindian, Dutch, English and Scottish languages, we offer a compromise by offering a link to a glossary on our website so those so minded can explore this richness further.

https://www.peepaltreepress.com/kipling-plass-glossary

ABOUT THE AUTHOR

Berkley Wendell Semple was born in Guyana. He has published four collections of poetry, *Lamplight Teller*, awarded a 2004 Guyana Prize for Poetry, *The Solo Flyer*, *The Central Station*, and *Flight and Other Poems*, awarded the 2023 Guyana Prize for Literature, and has edited a book of student poems. His poetry and fiction have appeared in *Callaloo*, *The Hampden-Sydney Review*, *The Caribbean Writer*, for which he was awarded a Daily News Prize for poetry, and many other publications. He is a veteran of the US armed forces and a graduate of the Naval School of Health Sciences. He holds an MA and MLS degrees from Queens College of the City University of New York (CUNY) and an MPhil from Long Island University (LIU) where he is a current Ph.D. candidate. From 2010 to 2022 he wrote audiobook reviews for *Sound Commentary Journal*. He is on the Editorial Board of *The Caribbean Writer*, and an editor and book reviewer for *Caribbean Voice*. He is a librarian and currently works for the Queens Public Library system in New York City.

family. At the level of the gentry, a manor would pass to the eldest son when his father died, meaning that his younger brothers had a choice of taking service with him or finding themselves a position that moved them to a different household.

The new lord would normally continue to house any sisters, whose fates were a simple binary choice of marrying and moving to their husband's household, or remaining at home, unwed, as a lowly home help. Incidentally, nowadays we use the word 'spinster' to denote an unmarried woman, and this can sometimes have negative connotations, but in the 1220s a spinster was a self-employed woman (normally unmarried, hence the later usage of the word) making her own money via her skill at spinning. The girls who work for Alys would be proud of their independence and earning potential.

Noble families, meanwhile, were conscious of their blood relationships but could be widely geographically scattered and might not even know each other very well. With boys being sent away in childhood to be pages and squires, and girls sometimes being brought up in the households of their intended husbands rather than those of their fathers, it was entirely possible that older siblings might have left home before the younger ones were born. However, all were expected to act for the good of the family, and particularly its head, wherever they were. Sir Martin's exemplary conduct in the earl's household, over the years, reflected as much on Sir Richard as it did on himself.

Edwin's 'blended' family might seem modern, but in an age where more than half of children had lost either one or both parents by the time they were ten, it was common for step-relations to live together. As the head of his family, he has responsibilities towards his sister, just as he has towards his own children. Finally, the concept of family also encompassed those who were related by marriage, so Alys's family are also Edwin's, along with any trouble they might cause in the future.

Further Reading

Bennett, H.S., *Life on the English Manor* (Cambridge: Cambridge University Press, 1938).

The Charter of the Forest of King Henry III (image of original document plus full English translation), online at http://info.sjc.ox.ac.uk/forests/Carta.htm

Homans, George C., *English Villagers of the Thirteenth Century* (New York: W.W. Norton, 1975).

Sabapathy, John, *Officers and Accountability in Medieval England, 1170–1300* (Oxford: Oxford University Press, 2014).

Young, Charles R., *The Royal Forests of Medieval England* (Philadelphia: University of Pennsylvania Press, 1979).